BUFFALO IS THE NEW BUFFALO

BUFFALO
IS THE
NEW
BUFFALO

STORIES

CHELSEA VOWEL

ARSENAL PULP PRESS
VANCOUVER

ARSENAL PULP PRESS
Suite 202 – 211 East Georgia St.
Vancouver, BC V6A 1Z6
Canada
arsenalpulp.com

The publisher gratefully acknowledges the support of the Canada Council for the Arts
and the British Columbia Arts Council for its publishing program, and the Government
of Canada, and the Government of British Columbia (through the Book Publishing Tax
Credit Program), for its publishing activities.

Arsenal Pulp Press acknowledges the xʷməθkʷəy̓əm (Musqueam), Sḵwx̱wú7mesh (Squamish),
and səl̓ilwətaʔɬ (Tsleil-Waututh) Nations, custodians of the traditional, ancestral, and unceded
territories where our office is located. We pay respect to their histories, traditions, and continuous
living cultures and commit to accountability, respectful relations, and friendship.

Previously published:
"âniskôhôcikan," as "nanitohtamok nanites," *Beside Journals, Green Screen*, Issue 1
"Dirty Wings," *On Spec*, Issue 107 (28.4)
"A Lodge within Her Mind," *Center for the Arts in Society* at
Carnegie Mellon University (online), April 24, 2020

Cover and text design by Jazmin Welch
Cover art by Christi Belcourt, *Offerings to Save the World*, 2017, 72″ × 55.25″, acrylic on canvas
Edited by Catharine Chen
Sensitivity read by Molly Swain
Proofread by Alison Strobel

Printed and bound in Canada

Library and Archives Canada Cataloguing in Publication:
Title: Buffalo is the new buffalo : stories / Chelsea Vowel.
Names: Vowel, Chelsea, author.
Identifiers: Canadiana (print) 20210387009 | Canadiana (ebook) 20210387122 |
ISBN 9781551528793 (softcover) | ISBN 9781551528809 (HTML)
Classification: LCC PS8643.O94 B84 2022 | DDC C813/.6—dc23

For nikihci-âniskotâpânak,
my ancestors and my descendants.

Contents

LOCATING MYSELF

Many Indigenous peoples share a basic protocol that requires people to identify where they come from and who their relations are. This allows people to figure out what kinds of relationships they may have with one another, and what their reciprocal obligations are to one another as kin, hosts, guests, and so on. It is a form of accountability, and it clarifies one's positionality.

It's important to point out that because of the history of colonization and chattel slavery, not all Indigenous people can easily answer these questions, and that this, too, is a legitimate positionality shared by many Indigenous people.

I am a white-looking, cis, queer, neurodivergent, intermittently able-bodied otipêyimisow-iyiniw (Métis person) from the historic Métis community of manitow-sâkihikan (Lac Ste. Anne). My mother is an otipêyimisow-iskwêw (Métis woman), and my father is a môniyâw-nâpew (white man) of Ukrainian and Irish background. nikotwâsik nitawâsimisin, I have six children. I am a first-generation post-secondary graduate with a BED, an LLB, and an MA in Native Studies, and no matter what other work I do, I always come back to teaching. Despite coming from a Métis community that was once multilingual, the only Indigenous language I have been able to reclaim to date is nêhiyawêwin (Plains Cree, Y dialect), and I am nowhere near as fluent as I'd like to be yet.

It is also important to understand that I come from Métis who have been dispossessed from their land, for outside of the eight Métis settlements in northern Alberta, Métis do not have communally held lands equivalent to reserves. I had access to our territory growing up only because my parents own a quarter section of land there, held in fee simple. To address this kind of lack of access so many Indigenous people experience, particularly urban Indigenous people, I cofounded the Métis in Space Land Trust with Molly Swain, and we successfully fundraised enough to purchase 160 acres in Lac Ste. Anne county. Forming a land trust ensures that this land will be held in common, for the purposes of conservation, cultural education, and research. Does it rankle to have to "buy back" land in my own territory that was stolen? You'd better believe it does, but our youth need it, and it can be held in common until such time as we no longer have to endure underlying Crown title.

Like a huge number of Alberta Métis and nêhiyawak (Cree), my great-great-great-great-grandparents were Louis Kwarakwante Callihoo and Marie Patenaude (his second wife). One of their sons, Michel, became headman of Michel's Band and signed a Treaty 6 adhesion in 1878. Their daughter, Angelique "Angele" Callihoo, was my great-great-great-grandmother, and she married Louis Divertissant Loyer, son of Louis Bonhomme Loyer and Louise Genevieve Jasper.

Angelique and Louis had a son in 1867, Samuel Loyer. Samuel married Isabelle Gladu, daughter of Oskinikiw Joseph Gladu, headman of Michel's Band, and Marie "Emma" Amable Belcourt. Samuel and Isabelle had my great grandmother, Katherine Loyer, who married Alonzo Bryant Teague, the first outmarriage to a non-Métis. My grandfather, Kenneth Teague, was their son.

I provide this brief genealogy to find cuzzins! It also locates me within a constellation of relations, of Mohawk, nêhiyawak, and Métis ancestors, some who took treaty, some who took scrip, and who span many different communities throughout the northwest—as well as Irish, Scottish, and Ukrainian ancestors I know much less about. These are the "kinscapes" that inform all of my stories.

Kinscapes, as defined by Métis scholar Brenda Macdougall, are "a network of family relationships knit together in a certain place and time" (Oosthoek 2017, Macdougall 2010). Kinscapes are governed and constituted by wâhkôhtowin, a complex series of relationships not only between humans, but also with nonhuman kin and all of creation.

When I refer to Métis, I mean Métis as People, not métis as mixed, although drawing these lines is neither clean nor easy (Andersen 2014; Innes 2013). At the same time, I want to push back against the nationalist rhetoric of the Métis as being a "distinct People." Yes, we have a specific history and culture; we are "distinct" in that sense. However, the colonial-administrative effort to atomize Indigenous Peoples into clearcut, separate groups encourages us to work at odds with one another, and as Robert Innes maps out beautifully, it also negates the reality of the shared history, territories, and kinscapes we continue to occupy (2013). Where I am from, Métis and nêhiyawak are linked through familial, cultural, and political relations, through a shared history, and through territory.

As Tasha Beeds points out, where she is from, Métis and nêhiyawak have "fluid kinship lines and [a] shared worldview" and this is also true of where I am from (2014, 70, note 1). While she chooses to use the term "nêhiyawi-itâpisiniwin," which means a Cree worldview that Métis share, I have opted for "otipêyimisow-itâpisiniwin" to specifically centre Métis peoples. Where I am from, most Métis will have an otipêyimisow-itâpisiniwin that is fairly similar to nêhiyaw-itâpisiniwin, but this is not true in all areas throughout the Métis homeland, and I wish to keep space open for these differences within the Métis experience. My own work foregrounds my community's nêhiyaw-itâpisiniwin as one possible approach within the plurality of otipêyimisow-itâpisiniwina (Métis worldviews).[1]

Until I moved away from home at seventeen, I was raised on a quarter section of land between three lakes: Lake Isle, wâpamon sâkahikan (Wabamun Lake), and manitow-sâkahikan (Lac Ste. Anne). Lake Isle

---

1 I am using a standard written nêhiyawêwin throughout, and my spelling of certain words may not be the same as sources I cite.

is fed from the southwest by the Sturgeon River and from the north-west by Dussault Lake and Round Lake. Lake Isle then drains back into the Sturgeon River at its eastern end, feeding into Lac Ste. Anne. Lac Ste. Anne, which is also fed by Birch Lake to the northwest, drains east into Matchayaw Lake and Big Lake before flowing into the North Saskatchewan River. Wabamun Lake is fed by Beaver Creek and Jack-pine Creek and also drains east through Wabamun Creek into the North Saskatchewan River.

I locate myself geographically between these lakes and note their interconnections to creeks and rivers because these boundaries make much more natural sense than range and township roads, highways, and hamlets that have only existed for a hundred years or less. These lakes provided sustenance to Métis and First Nations in the area, particularly after the settler colonial genocide of the buffalo was almost complete. These days, the lakes are sites of ongoing cottage colonialism, where the needs and desires of non-Indigenous, mostly white people are given primacy over the ongoing relationships to land, water, and nonhuman kin that Indigenous peoples continue to maintain. Despite all of this, Lac Ste. Anne remains a powerful gathering place for Indigenous peoples every summer, as it has been for generations.

All of my stories are located within or informed by the kinscapes and land/waterscapes of Lac Ste. Anne. And just as watersheds and drainage basins are larger than any single body of water, these kinscapes land/waterscapes expand beyond Lac Ste. Anne itself to encompass all the spaces where my ancestors made relations. I clarify this to explain that while my characters are mainly rooted in and around Lac Ste. Anne, these stories are happening within a much wider time and space that, nonetheless, do not represent all Métis.

Kinscapes and land/waterscapes are also a unifying metaphor for the way that none of my work occurs in isolation, even when I am feeling isolated.

PREFACE

I have written eight short stories that explore Métis existence and resistance through a lens of *being* Métis, or, more specifically, being Métis from manitow-sâkihikan (Lac Ste. Anne).[2] Through the creation of these stories, I ask questions about Métis presence in the past, the present, and the future, in ways that invite the reader to coconstitute potentialities with me. You don't have to be Métis to get it! Our past was full of relationships with non-Métis, as is our present, and who knows how much more that web of relationality will expand into the future?

Each story is followed by an exploration explaining the purpose of the story and the many sources of inspiration that helped me write it, as well as some of the history and literary allusions the reader may be unfamiliar with. These explorations expand this work beyond creative writing; I am "imagining otherwise" in order find a way to "act otherwise" (Justice 2018, Voth 2018).

Stories are an inherently collaborative experience, and all stories have a purpose. Among Métis and nêhiyawak, as with other Indigenous peoples, there are âcimowina (everyday stories), kwayask-âcimowina (non-fiction), kîyâskiwâcimowina (false or fictional stories), âtayôhkêwina (sacred stories), mamâhtâwâcimowina (miraculous stories), pawâmêwâcimowina (spiritual dreaming stories), kiskinwahamâcimowina (teaching stories), kakêskihkêmowina (counselling stories), wawiyatâcimowina (funny stories), stories that map out terrain and resources, kayâs-âcimowina (stories

---

2 Métis people have been referred to and refer to ourselves in numerous ways, including Métis, Half-Breeds, Bois-Brûlés, otipêyimisow, âpihtawikosisân, Michif, and so on.

that pass on history), miyo-âcimowina (good stories), and mac-âcimowina (evil or malicious stories).

These genres within Métis/nêhiyaw (Cree) literary tradition have their own forms and literary conventions, some of which I use in my stories. I blend these with whitestream genre writing without necessarily making the Métis/nêhiyaw allusions and conventions legible to non-Métis/nêhiyawak, such as in "Dirty Wings," where I use seasonal rounds, allude to specific âtayôhkêwina (sacred stories), and reference Elders' counselling discourse patterns, which "work rhetorically to effect learn-ing in the reader" (MacKay 2014, 357). In this way I am making space to respond to mainstream speculative fiction either by Métis-fying it (add-ing Métis literary conventions and allusions/history/cultural aspects) or subverting it by switching observer-subject roles.

It is important to understand that within otipêyimisow-itâpisiniwina, stories, like all language, have power. Language is not merely a tool of communication, but also a place where reality can be shaped. *Language is transformational*; "our breath has the power to kwêskîmot, change the form of the future for the next generation" (Beeds 2014, 69). My writing seeks to engage in that transformation, making space for Métis to exist across time, refusing our annihilation as envisioned by the process of ongoing colonialism, and questioning the ways we are thought to have existed in the past.

Through stories like these, I wish to extend Métis existence beyond official narratives, beyond current constraints, and imagine what living in a "Métis way" could look like in spaces and times we haven't (yet) been. This challenges the divide between fact and fiction, as Métis people assert a reality that is perceived as impossible in mainstream thinking. If Métis people say a thing is possible, who gets to determine that that thing is fictional?

Grace Dillon first coined the term "Indigenous futurisms" in 2003, seeking to describe a movement of art, literature, games, and other forms of media which express Indigenous perspectives on the future, present, and past (Dillon 2020). More specifically, she argues that all forms of Indigenous futurisms "involve discovering how personally one is affected by colonization, discarding the emotional and psychological baggage carried from its impact, and recovering ancestral traditions in order to adapt in our post–Native Apocalypse world" (2012, 10).

Indigenous futurisms are not merely synonymous with science fiction and fantasy, despite how they may be viewed as such within the mainstream. Indigenous futurists express their ontologies in various forms, and as Grace Dillon puts it, "our ideas of body, mind, and spirit are true stories, not forms of fantasy" (2019). For example, Tsilhqot'in filmmaker Helen Haig-Brown's short film *The Cave* is listed on IMDb as being science fiction, but it depicts a traditional Tsilhqot'in story told to her by her great-uncle, Henry Solomon (2009). Indigenous futurisms offer an alternative genre to Indigenous creators that allow us to foreground our worldviews and realities.

Although Indigenous futurism has only in the past decade taken root as a named and self-reflective movement, it does so with inspiration from—and is indeed indebted to—the path-breaking work of Afrofuturists such as Sun Ra, Octavia Butler, Janelle Monáe, Samuel R. Delany, Nalo Hopkinson, and so many others.

Afrofuturisms—so named in 1994 by Mark Dery, but referring to works beginning in the late 1950s and arguably much earlier—explore the intersection between the African diaspora and technology (1994, 179–222). Afrofuturism centres Afrodiasporic experiences and cosmologies across a vast range of themes, offering alternatives to Western views of Africa and of the African diaspora (Esteve 2016).

Dillon points out that science fiction as a genre "emerged in the mid-nineteenth-century context of evolutionary theory and anthropology profoundly intertwined with colonial ideology" (2012, 2). These themes are exhaustively explored in whitestream science fiction, exposing particular settler colonial anxieties and aspirations that tend to erase or completely ignore the experiences and perspectives of Black, Indigenous, and People of Colour (BIPOC). In (re)imagining history, whitestream speculative fiction is particularly adept at repressing the violent histories of colonialism from the public imaginary (Gaertner 2015). This does not mean that the topic of colonization is absent from science fiction—far from it (Rieder 2008). We find constant dichotomous reframing of settler colonials as agents of space-faring Manifest Destiny or the inevitable subjects of colonization at the hands (tentacles, squishy pseudopods, or furry appendages) of aliens (Justice 2018, 149–152). Whitestream science fiction insists that colonialism is inevitable. It's "us or them," and it had better be "us."

Increasingly, BIPOC are becoming content creators, operating from within worldviews that exist beyond the whitestream. Much of this work involves switching observer-subject roles, so that instead of BIPOC being under the external gaze of the white anthropologist/colonizer (the subject), we are viewing the outsider through our own cultural lenses (the observer). This is not merely a pushback against the colonizing narrative of whitestream speculative fiction; it can also be a form of social justice organizing. As Walidah Imarisha puts it, "whenever we try to envision a world without war, without violence, without prisons, without capitalism, we are engaging in speculative fiction. All organizing is science fiction" (2015, 3). Dillon takes the transformative potential of the work even further, stating that "this process is often called 'decolonization' and as Linda Tuhiwai Smith (Maori) explains, it requires *changing* rather than *imitating* Eurowestern concepts" (2012, 10).

Before I get into explaining what I mean by "Métis futurisms," I want to acknowledge what Lou Cornum rightfully points out: that the term "Indigenous" is often used in a way that implicitly excludes Black people from its definition, either denying the Indigeneity of Black people or avoiding the question altogether (2015, 3–5). Speaking of the "space

Indian" as a diasporic figure, Cornum suggests that Indigenous futurists can "participate in complicating our notions of home, Indigenous identity, and shifting relationships to land and belonging" in ways that "evoke similarities with other diasporic figures … specifically … the Black diasporic figure" (2015, 3).

I refuse to exclude the potential and real Indigeneity of Black people, either implicitly or through omission. I take seriously the assertion that "the coupled structure of settler colonialism and slavery calls for new understandings of Indigeneity that can account for diaspora of Indigenous peoples and alternative forms of belonging not dependent on sovereignty over an ancestral territory" (Cornum 2015, 4). While the stories contained in this collection do not all directly address Blackness and Indigeneity, these complexities are part of the theoretical framework I am working from; they are foundational aspects of the world building that I do here and will continue to do.

The futures I envision include expansive notions of Indigeneity, according to the principles of wâhkôhtowin (expanded kinship, including with nonhuman kin), miyo-wicêhtowin (the principle of getting along with others), miyo-pimâtisisiwin (the good life), and wîtaskiwin (living together on the land) (Ahenakew and Wolfhart 1998b; Wolfhart and Ahenakew 2000; Cardinal and Hildebrandt 2000; Belcourt 2006; Macdougall 2010; Ghostkeeper 1995). When I speak of Indigenous peoples, I am not limiting myself to First Nations, Métis, and Inuit of North America, but rather to Indigenous peoples globally, recognizing that these definitions are fraught, contested, and, like all definitions of what it means to be human, often rooted in anti-Blackness (Walcott 2015, 93–95).

Octavia Butler's work expanded my understanding of what is possible in terms of speaking back to mainstream (and mostly white) visions of the past and future.³ Butler's work never elides or pretends to solve racism, misogyny and misogynoir, ableism, homophobia, classism, or any other system of oppression.⁴ Neither do these structures forbid Black possibility; they exist as they do now, as constraints that must be contended with and resisted.

This approach differs from that of popular mainstream science fiction, in particular, *Star Trek the Original Series* and *Star Trek: The Next Generation*, in which it is imagined that in the twenty-third and twenty-fourth centuries, humans have somehow solved all of these structural oppressions. *Star Trek* "is so invested in its liberal humanist multicultural utopian vision, that it can't reckon with the ways in which it replicates fundamentally oppressive and hierarchical power imbalances, especially through its promotion of Starfleet as a militaristic, interventionist (in spite of the Prime Directive) organization" (Swain 2019). Unsurprisingly, this vision of the future mirrors contemporary refusals to acknowledge structural oppression or to understand the intergenerational impacts of settler colonialism and the transatlantic slave trade.

This kind of future imagining requires a form of forgetting that Black scholars like Christina Sharpe (2016), Robyn Maynard (2017), Sarah-Jane Mathieu (2010), and Rinaldo Walcott (1997) all work to resist. Uncovering Black/Indigenous presence in the past, then asserting our existence in the present and into the future can be a way of seeing into, or even making, better futures. To me this is a major component of Indigenous futurisms.

As the term "Indigenous" is fraught, and its boundaries expand or constrict according to who uses it and for what purpose, I have chosen to

---

3   These books include: *Patternmaster* (1976), *Mind of My Mind* (1977), *Survivor* (1978), *Kindred* (1979), *Wild Seed* (1980), *Clay's Ark* (1984), *Dawn* (1987), *Adulthood Rites* (1988), *Imago* (1989), *Parable of the Sower* (1993), *Parable of the Talents* (1998).

4   "Misogynoir" is a term created by Moya Bailey and further developed by Trudy of *Gradient Lair*. It describes misogyny directed toward Black women, thus reflecting race and gender.

call my work "Métis-futurist" instead of simply using and accepting the broad "Indigenous futurist" label.

The term "Indigenous" is incredibly broad, even vague, especially in an international context. It makes little sense for me to identify, individually, as an Indigenous person. I use "Indigenous" to either speak nationally and include First Nations, Métis, and Inuit, or internationally, to include all Indigenous peoples. I cannot be all those people! I am specifically Métis, and even more specifically, Métis from manitow-sâkihikan. That is where my stories come from, and other Métis from manitow-sâkihikan are the people I am most accountable to.

Métis futurism allows me to envision a number of potential futures rooted in my history, community, and worldview—Métis futurism to me is not simply any speculative fiction work done by a Métis person. Imagining potential futures, or alternative worlds in any time, is not merely an exercise of imagining; I assert it as an act of what Scott Lyons calls rhetorical sovereignty, "the inherent right and ability of *peoples* to determine their own communicative needs and desires in this pursuit" (2000, 449).

Accepting Métis cosmology and relationships as true, as science fact, offers alternatives to prescribed colonial roles for Indigenous peoples in the past, the present, and the near and far future. This opens up space and time to set goals for the future that do not privilege the colonial project, without having to provide a step-by-step plan for how to achieve these futures.

I am not interested in being overly specific with genre outside of insisting my work is Métis-futurist. It may include elements of science fiction and fantasy—or not. I wish to, as Grace Dillon puts it, "sometimes intentionally experiment with, sometimes intentionally dislodge, sometimes merely accompany, but invariably change the perimeters" of speculative fiction (2012, 3). Existing whitestream genres are forms I can play along with, subvert, or avoid altogether.

Given the way in which Indigenous peoples are so often forced to reactively hyperfocus on the present and on day-to-day survival, having some space to cast ourselves as far into the future is vital and potentially emancipatory. Setting these stories in contexts that explicitly reject anti-Blackness, heteronormativity, classism, ableism, patriarchy, and white supremacy is one way to think about how to overcome colonial logics. This work can and must be done in a variety of mediums; literature, music, film, art, fashion, video games, and so on.

Métis futurisms offer up world building/prefiguration based in our otipêyimisow-itâpisiniwina, trying to get us to where no Michif has been before and sometimes reimagining where we have already been. It is my hope that these kinds of cultural productions, be they short stories, films, video games, art, or anything else under multiple suns, go beyond merely longing for a difference and a decolonial existence. I operate under the belief that, as Tasha Beeds insists, we can indeed speak/act/imagine to kwêskîmonaw, change our own shapes and forms, as well as "chang[ing] the form of the future for the next generation" (2014, 69).

INTRODUCTION

"Education is the new buffalo" is a metaphor that has been widely used among Indigenous peoples in Canada to signify the importance of education to our survival and ability to support ourselves, as once Plains nations supported ourselves as buffalo peoples. Variations of the phrase have sprung up with increasing frequency, including a particularly vomitous version, "pipelines are the new buffalo." The premise is that many of our pre-Contact ways of living are forever gone, and we must accept this and adapt. The phrase "buffalo is the new buffalo," however, asserts that we can and must do the work to repair our kinscapes, basing our work in wâhkôhtowin (expanded kinship) to restore our reciprocal obligations to our human and nonhuman kin. Instead of accepting that the buffalo and our ancestral ways will never come back, what if we simply ensure that they do?

Buffalo Bird

A work of historical speculative fiction, "Buffalo Bird" is set in the mid- to late nineteenth century, before Canada violently colonized the Plains. Following the life of Angelique Loyer, a Two-Spirit Rougarou (shape-shifter), as she tries to solve a murder in her community and later joins the resistance against Canada, this story imagines that the nêhiyaw-pwat (Iron Confederacy), a political alliance among Cree, Saulteaux, Nakoda, and Métis, successfully stopped Canadian expansion into the West.[5]

....

5   (Hogue 2015; Vrooman 2013). The nêhiyaw-pwat, also known as the Iron Confederacy, or Iron Alliance, was a political and military alliance among Cree, Saulteaux, Nakoda, Métis, and Iroquois (who had moved into the west) during the height of the fur trade. The nêhiyaw-pwat acted as a barrier to US and Canadian expansion until the genocide of the buffalo and decline of the fur trade.

Michif Man

Set in the mid-twentieth century, this is a story about a Métis superhero, Franky Callihoo, who is gored by a radioactive bison and granted super strength. However, he is also plagued by The Distortion, which causes everyone except those related to him by blood to immediately forget about him. Years later, in the twenty-first century, Indigenous scholars push back against the notion that Michif Man was simply a folk myth and present evidence that Franky Callihoo actually existed and served his community in a variety of ways.

Dirty Wings

Informed by Métis metaphysics, "Dirty Wings" occurs in the hazy present and asserts Métis reality in a time when our otipêyimisow-itâpisiniwina (Métis worldviews) are supposed to be fading away. This is a dreaming story that witnesses Métis ontologies bleeding over and superseding settler colonial control.

Maggie Sue

Told in the first person and set in Edmonton, our protagonist literally stumbles into a fox who has taken human form and falls deeply in love. The fox is headed for a showdown with Elder Brother, and the protagonist must make sense of the chaos that ensues.

A Lodge within Her Mind

Pandemic isolation dulls the senses and drains hope. Facing the possibility of having her consciousness uploaded into a digital space where she is the only human being present, a queer Métis woman finds a novel way to escape.

âniskôhôcikan

A work of science fiction set in the near future, "âniskôhôcikan" challenges the notion that Métis are anti-technology, demonstrating how we will continue to innovate without compromising our self-determination. As the Cree language continues to decline, Métis and nêhiyawak (Cree) parents have their unborn children implanted with nanotechnology to ensure they will grow up as mother-tongue speakers.

I, Bison

When Gus returns to her home community for her cousin Angie's wake, she discovers that her cousin's consciousness was nonconsensually uploaded before her death. The community believes Angie cannot pass into the spirit realm while she still exists in digital form. Gus is tasked with freeing Angie.

Unsettled

To solve the global energy crisis, a technique is developed to induce deep hibernation in humans, with small teams rotating to ensure critical infrastructure continues running. A group of Indigenous youth who have volunteered to work one such shift ponder the implications of having the opportunity to rid Turtle Island of settler colonizers. Will settler anxiety be validated? Will the oppressed do unto the colonizer as has been done to them?

BUFFALO BIRD

1854[6]

She found herself on the shore of a vast freshwater lake that seemed to have swallowed up everything before her. The gunmetal sky met quicksilver at the horizon, confusing the eye, blurring boundaries or perhaps merely rejecting them. Instead of sand beneath her feet there was long prairie grass rasping quietly around her naked thighs, colourless and out of place, stretching behind her for an eternity. Thunder rolled above her head, deep and booming, filling her chest but failing to crack her apart. Reflexively she pawed at her side, seeking tobacco to light to bolster the strength of the Thunderers as they battled once again to prevent the world from being destroyed, but her hand found only her own cold flesh.

Mixed with the fetid odour of silt and vegetative rot was the sharp tang of blood, and under it a hint of the unintended intimacy of fluids from deep within the body; it came in waves, carried somehow in the absence of wind, a miasma that filled her nostrils, infusing itself into her skin and hair. Death was coming, and she felt fear bubbling up inside her, weakening her control, coursing in painful jolts through limbs that did not want to obey.

There was a dark spot in that heavy sky. No. She realized it was touching the waters of the lake. A slow fog appeared there, where the water met the sky, rolling forward, towering like a fort wall built to enclose the world, as though it were consuming air and liquid both, blocking out everything but that tiny black figure.

....

6   The scenes in this story do not all unfold chronologically, so to help the reader keep track of the age of the main character during each of the time periods, I am including this guide: 1844 (6), 1852 (13, then 14), 1854 (16), 1870 (32), 1871 (33), 1913 (75). Also, for all the stories, rather than use distracting in-text citations, I am performing hybridity and putting them into these footnotes instead.

The Thunderers continued to make their presence known, a steady reverberation now more felt than heard. Instead of comfort, she felt it was a warning. Perhaps this time they would not be able to protect her People. She realized she could not move, not even to blink, helplessly watching that black figure cross the lake at an impossible speed. There was bile in the back of her throat, and a terrible familiarity. She wanted to turn and run; she wanted to vomit. She felt a terror so complete it seemed to liquefy her insides. As though outside of herself, she could hear her own strangled whimpers. The figure was only a few canoe lengths away now; that wall of mist had eaten the world, leaving only a small semicircle of smooth slate against the shore.

Cowled in thick black wool robes, the being that glided toward her did not quite touch the water; its face and shape were obscured, and it was difficult to gauge its size. It seemed distorted somehow, as though viewed at the bottom of a shallow stream. Inexplicably, she smelled smoke and heard a high-pitched howling.

With a sudden disorienting wrench her perspective flipped: the figure was not coming toward *her*—she was falling toward *it*, cold wind howling past her ears. Spasming in shock, she finally regained control of her muscles, shooting her arms in front of her to protect her head as she fell. At that moment, thunder split the world.

Her eyes flew open in the near-complete darkness, the full-body convulsion that was her rejection of impact with that cowled figure echoing in her muscles. There was something wrong with her hands: the fingers fused together, hardening; the muscles in her arms twisted, pulling away from bone. She struggled against the pain, refusing the change.

Angelique lay on her pallet, worn buffalo hide kicked off during her night terrors, gradually perceiving the cold in her extremities, despite having slept in wool pants and a long linen shirt, and panting while her heart slowed and her limbs relaxed into familiar forms. Her vision adjusted to the faint reddish glow from the dying embers in the clay oven.[7]

A bright flash seared her eyes through the rawhide windows and growing chinks in the clay and buffalo-hair mixture cemented onto the exterior of the logs of her cabin, gone before she'd registered it, but leaving its imprint throbbing at the back of her skull.[8] Thunder again ripped the sky asunder almost simultaneously, and the prairie heavens let loose a torrential downpour that began battering the sod roof.

The door rattled fit to be torn from its rawhide thongs—her heart leaped once again into her throat. With the strange clarity of memories retrieved from the edge of consciousness, she realized that someone had been pounding at her door for some time now. She pulled the buffalo robe up over her head, a ridiculous attempt to pretend absence, like a child hiding during a telling of the Rolling Head story, fear still a shameful tang in her mouth.[9] She bit her own lip in anger at herself. The pain galvanized her to stand, wrapping the hide around herself and groggily feeling her way across the open, packed-earth floor to the door.

She reached the door as it endured another thrashing from whatever was on the other side. The rain so occupied the soundscape that she was barely able to make out muffled shouting. She bit her lip again, the pain

7 (Burley 2000, 30–33). Métis homes before the 1870s often used clay ovens for cooking and heating, with cast iron stoves only becoming commonplace later in the nineteenth century.

8 (Paquin and Young 2003, 4–6). In the 1850s, maisons d'hiver as described in this story were still heavily in use, particularly among communities that participated in the buffalo hunt. They were constructed of saddle-notched logs cemented together with mud and clay mixed with buffalo hair or grass, sod or hay roofs, and bison hide coverings for windows and doors. The floors were usually packed dirt. Unlike settler homes of similar style, Métis homes did not have rooms; rather, they were completely open. As Métis spent the bulk of spring and summer on the hunt, these homes were only inhabited during fall and winter and required annual upkeep (Burley and Horsfall 2009, 23–30). Métis home construction began changing from the 1850s onward to structures that were often one and a half storeys tall and used willow lathe strips and dovetail notches, or tenon-and-groove construction (known as the Red River frame) adopted from Francophone communities. Again, the openness of Métis floor plans is discussed as reflecting Métis views of space.

9 (Ahenakew 1929). This is a particularly terrifying sacred story that Cree and Métis people tell during the winter months.

a goad. It had been a dream—there was no cowled monster waiting for her, though she couldn't imagine what else would be out in this weather. Unwrapping the long rawhide strap that kept the plank door secured, she was knocked back a step as a bulky shadow slammed their fist into the wood and became unbalanced by the lack of resistance, nearly falling across the threshold. Something clattered to the ground, evoking a string of curses from the intruder.

"Cyprien?" Finding her balance, she pushed him aside none too gently and struggled with the door, whipped by wind and rain before managing to force it closed again against the nearly horizontal sheets of rain.

"I dropped my lantern. Don't move, let me find it." His voice was raised so she could hear him over the bedlam outside. She acquiesced and waited for him to bump around, searching for the small metal cage on the floor. The faint glow from her oven did not reach that far, but when he crossed in front of it, blotting out even that tiny illumination, she shivered; the fading stamp of dream fear lingered enough to make the darkness feel cloying.

"What are you doing here?" she finally thought to ask. Realizing he may not have heard her over the din of the storm, she raised her voice. "Wait, did you ride? Is our auntie's horse out there?!"

"No, no, I walked."

A greasy yellow flame flared up, casting huge twisted shadows before quieting into a steady glow. She jumped. Cyprien was all the way across the room, by the oven. He'd fished out a piece of bison tallow wrapped around a braided grass wick from his fire bag and stuck it on the spine meant for fancy wax candles, which they usually didn't have, then lit it with a coal scooped quickly from the hearth. In the dim light she could see what a sorry state he was in, soaked to the bone and shivering. He left the lantern perched on the oven.

"Can you please, Angelique?" he chattered, pointing his lips toward the oven, arms withdrawn from the sleeves of his red blanket coat, hands stuck under his armpits for warmth. The fat wouldn't cast light for much longer.

She nodded sharply and quickly coaxed the coals back to life, building up the fire until the cabin was bathed in soft amber light, and warmth began to radiate from the curved dome of the oven. She set her kettle full of leftover tea to warm and helped Cyprien spread his coat close enough to the fire that it began to steam as it dried.

The intensity of the rain had begun to lessen, and thunder no longer cracked directly overhead. She was fully awake now, the last tendrils of terror fully melted away by the light and a familiar face.

"What are you doing wandering around at night?" She shoved a crude wooden mug full of strong tea into his hands. Cyprien blew on it gratefully before risking a sip, wincing as he burned his tongue anyway.

"Our auntie sent me." He looked at her from underneath a mess of curly brown hair that was still dripping, a worried twist to his mouth. "Angelique—it's bad."

She'd known this wasn't a social call—no one would walk this far along the lakeshore in the middle of the night and rouse her just to chat—but still, his tone chilled her. "Bad? Bad how? Is everyone okay? Is the baby coming?"[10]

"No, no, Marie is fine." Cyprien gingerly sat on one of the two chairs in her home and set his cup on the small wooden table. She suddenly noticed that his knees above his leather wrappings weren't darkened with just water; the grey fabric of his pants was nearly black where he'd clearly been kneeling in mud.

....

10   (Anderson 2011, 40–43). It's important to note that prior to the 1860s, Métis women were using family planning, including contraceptives and abortifacients, as were their Cree and Anishinaabek kin. After the 1860s, Métis families were often larger than settler families. Anderson quotes Nathalie Kermoal on this, noting that the increase in family size coincided with the decline of the buffalo hunt. When we think of Métis families in the 1800s and into the early twentieth century, we often picture very large families, but in the 1850s, there was often a maximum of four children, making my character Angelique's family of two siblings not all that strange. In addition, pregnancies were often planned to coincide with the spring, and this part of the story is happening in late May.

"We're all okay at the house, but …" he paused, seeming uncertain.

"But what? What's going on?" Angelique just barely stopped herself from grabbing the front of his shirt and shaking him until his teeth rattled. He seemed to sense her growing anger.

"Out back, in the pen. The pigs were panicked, so I thought maybe a wolf had gotten in." He stared down at his hands for a moment and continued, "I had to put the three of them down."

She winced at that, pulling the other chair over and sitting next to him.

Cyprien shook his head, closed his eyes for a moment. "That's not why she sent me, Angelique." He opened his eyes again and regarded the stains on his knees. Angelique couldn't help it—her stomach dropped at his tone, and she pulled the buffalo robe around herself even tighter, wishing she could draw it over her head and not hear the rest. She didn't want to see the accusation in his eyes. When he finally looked at her, though, there was nothing there but sadness.

"She needs to know if it was the Rougarou."[11]

It didn't take her long to get more warmly dressed, and by then, Cyprien's jacket had dried enough to be serviceable. The storm had moved on and

11 (Sing 2009, 63–69). This piece compares the Métis stories of Rougarou to the Francophone loup-garou (Cariou 2010, 157–168). Crucial to this story is the different way that Métis relate to Rougarou (Roogaroo, Rigareau, Rigoureau) and, indeed, shape-shifting compared to Francophones. Cariou, who insists his own uncle was known to be a Rigoureau, notes that among the Métis and many First Nations, the power to transform is respected, not feared or treated as evil, the way that the French saw it. In Métis folklore, a Rougarou is not a werewolf, but rather tends to be a black mare or a black dog. Cariou notes that the loup-garou "is also implicitly about race," reflecting European anxiety of hybridity, which the Métis in particular represent. Cariou links the description of Métis as "the one-and-a-half-men," half-white, half-Indian, and half-devil, with the way Métis were seen as inherently evil, untrustworthy, and potentially capable of transforming into savagery. In this story I want to challenge these notions, maintaining respect toward the power of transformation and troubling the notion of savagery as an inherently Métis trait; in fact, I suggest that the savagery lay within the Europeans who so viciously colonized these lands.

the wind had quieted, leaving the sound of waves lapping the shore and the drip drip of water as it rolled over new leaves onto the bushes below. He held his lantern low, sputtering fat casting scant illumination, but it was good enough for the two of them to follow a trail they'd often run blindfolded as children for fun. Not so long ago, really, when this old cabin still lay empty, a place for children to play at being grown. Their breath billowed out before them, the earth not entirely awakened from a winter that had been particularly harsh this year.

Over 150 souls clustered along the shore of manitow-sâkahikan, with Father Thibault's mission, built ten years back, squatting malevolently in the centre, making it seem as though the settlement had grown around him.[12] Uncharitably, Angelique thought that the priest had been entirely too fond of changing the settlement he'd been asked to serve, including the name of the lake. It had been a relief when he'd returned to St. Boniface, but the respite hadn't lasted long. The interim priest, Bourassa, seemed to watch her constantly, she who never wore dresses; she who lived alone when the rest of his flock gathered together, two to four families in a home; she who, so the rumours went, could transform into a black mare.

She hated those rumours.

There was light glowing from within their aunt's house, but Cyprien steered her away from the warmth and welcome. There'd be time enough for tea and bannock. After.

Cyprien stood awkwardly under the sputtering light of a torch meant to provide more illumination than the inadequate lantern had. In that, he'd

12   (Drouin 1975). Lac Ste. Anne, known in Cree as Manito Sakahigan, is spelled manitow-sâkahikan in standardized Cree, which I use here. Father Thibault, originally from St. Boniface, had a mission built at manitow-sâkahikan in 1844, and in September had the lake named Lac Ste. Anne. Joseph Bourassa, a young priest who accompanied Thibault, was twenty-seven.

been successful. Angelique heaved one last time, weakly, and wiped her mouth on the back of her sleeve, glad she'd at least managed to keep the sick from splashing the white wool of her jacket.[13] Cyprien at least knew her well enough to offer no comment while she tried to collect herself.

Where the cousins stood, the earth was unusually muddy and torn up, soft in comparison to the pounded soil throughout the rest of the enclosure. And the smell—it reminded her of her dream. The smell of death.

She took a few steps toward the remaining pigs, huddled together at the far end of the pen, and drew in gulps of clean air before turning back.

"Tell me everything."

1844

The gardens were planted and wind teased the poplar leaves into a dance that the long prairie grass answered, a constant susurration that left her drowsy as they bumped over rough tracks. The large Red River cart wheels squealed on their axles, wood counterparts turning against each other as they made their way southeast. They'd been joined by other Métis and a few Cree and Stoney families along the way, now numbering over a hundred carts.[14]

13 (Adams, Dahl, and Peach 2013, 16–18). In the early 1800s, Thomas Nuttall, a botanist, wrote his observations of "metif" families, by which he meant mixed race. He noted that there "were not necessarily distinctions between 'metif,' meaning 'mixed race,' and other Indian groups." For example, all wore blanket capotes (in this story, a white Hudson's Bay Company (HBC) multicoloured point-blanket jacket popular among Métis and First Nations for centuries), moccasins, etc. One of the things I want to stress in this story is that Métis share more with First Nations than we differ from them, a central premise in Robert Innes's (2013) book, *Elder Brother and the Law of the People*.
14 (Callihoo 1960, 24–25). Victoria Belcourt Callihoo was born in Lac Ste. Anne in 1861 and was part of the last generation from my community to participate in the buffalo hunt. Her mother was a medicine woman who would help set bones of riders flung from their horses during the hunt. Although this portion of the story is set in 1844, I use a number of details from Victoria's description of the hunt.

Sometimes Angelique would lie on top of bundles of supplies with Eunice, staring up at the vast cloudless sky, always watching and listening for the liquid call of the brown-headed birds that heralded bison nearby. Eunice would curl up against her, solid toddler head insistently pushing into her armpit. Attempts to wiggle into a more comfortable position were met with equanimity; Eunice simply shoved herself closer until it felt like Angelique might roll off the cart altogether.

Most times she walked, chatting with Cyprien, or taking turns carrying Eunice on her back. A thick Assomption sash, tied over her shoulders and across her breastbone, helped to support her sister's weight and keep her arms free, just like she saw the older girls do.[15] Eunice would giggle and pretend she was riding a horse, painfully jamming her little moccasins into Angelique's hip bones to stand for a few seconds as though she were a scout.

The wagons were slow, and when they needed to ford streams, as was often the case, the children would sit on the banks stripping seeds from grass while the horses, men, and wagons struggled. Eventually an adult would come and ferry them across to the other side. They'd already made the worst crossing across the kisiskâciwani-sîpiy with minimal loss of supplies and only a few scary dunkings.[16] She'd put tobacco down along with the others, showing her little sister how to press the dry, shredded leaves into the rich river mud.

At night, there was laughter and songs around the firepits, many of the stones laid there generations ago, easy to miss if you didn't know what to look for. Eunice would fall asleep against their father's chest as he told stories of past hunts to an audience of aunts, uncles, and countless

....

15 (Anderson 2011, 70–72). Traditional child-rearing among Métis, Cree, and Anishinaabek peoples involved what Anderson calls a high level of indulgence; whatever the needs of a child were, somebody would take care of them. Older siblings had an important role in the care of younger siblings, often carrying them during travel.

16 The Cree name for the North Saskatchewan River.

cousins, all of whom were entranced, no matter that he'd told these stories a thousand times before.

Cyprien was the same age as she and had not yet decided that he had more important things to do than help her with her chores, unlike their older cousins, who were busy preening like mating grouse, hoping to catch the eye of an unrelated youth from a different settlement. He would help her rub tallow on the wooden axles of her parents' cart, reaching up high where she couldn't, keeping an eye out for wear in the rawhide lashings. Some families took as many as three carts, but her parents had always made do with one.

A day of travel later, and the scouts returned. The wagons fell silent, and the air was full of the mellifluous calls of birds who had abandoned their young in other nests to follow the herds.[17]

Eunice cried big silent tears, but she wasn't allowed to come along with their father, who showed Angelique and Cyprien how to slither along on their bellies as they neared the top of a slight hill.[18] There, stretching in every direction to the ends of the world was a dark mass, hardly distinguishable as being made up of individual bison. The smell was incredible: rich, distinct, familiar.

---

17 (Robinson et al. 1995, 428–460). The brown-headed cowbird, formally known as the buffalo bird, is a parasitic bird that was historically found almost exclusively in the shortgrass prairie west of the Mississippi. Like the cuckoo, they lay their eggs in other birds' nests. This particular article details their historic presence following the bison herds and their subsequent spread with cattle ranching. They had a balanced, symbiotic relationship with the bison, catching insects flushed out by the buffalo and being in most abundance among the bison in May and June. Their activity made things more pleasant for the buffalo by reducing the irritation from insects. However, cowbirds began rapidly spreading east as herds of cattle replaced the bison, yet another example of how long-standing animal relationships have been severely impacted by colonization. If you'd like to hear what these birds sound like, there is a YouTube video here: www.youtube.com/watch?v=gPgFlKa7IDE.

18 (Anderson 2011, 68–69). Anderson details information from various Michif, Cree, and Anishinaabek Elders, as well as ethnologist accounts about the importance of teaching Métis and First Nations children (including babies) to be silent. These practices include gently pinching an infant's lips shut. For the most part, child-rearing among Métis and First Nations communities involved high levels of autonomy for children, with little in the way of physical discipline, but self-control was also taught, and at times the silence of children was a matter of survival. Again, these accounts demonstrate the strong similarities between Métis, Cree, and Anishinaabek (Ojibwe and Saulteaux) peoples.

Angelique gazed out at the herd and imagined she was one of those birds, perched between dark horns, eating insects from the grass. Groups of them startled and rose above the shaggy backs before settling back down. She wondered how their babies found them, how they knew to join their kin.

Watching their strange antics, the way they confidently arranged themselves along the backs of these huge Plains beasts, she suddenly realized she had it wrong. She reached across to Cyprien and squeezed his hand. He looked at her askance.

"They look like birds," she whispered. Cyprien wrinkled his forehead in confusion, and her father scowled at her for making noise before turning back to regard the herd. She shifted closer to Cyprien, her mouth almost touching his ear. She needed him to understand.

"They look like birds, but the buffalo are their real kin."[19]

She pulled away and saw her father staring at her, his dark-lined face unreadable. Without a word, he jerked his head back the way they had come, and they carefully returned to camp.

1854

They perched side by side on the top rail of the paddock, as far away from the ... remnants ... as they could get. The moon, which had been hidden behind towering masses of storm clouds, now hung swollen and low in

---

19   (Goldberg-Hiller and Silva 2015, 1–26). This piece explores the notion of Indigenous people having other-than-human kin, as in this case between Kanaka Mâoli and the ʻulu (breadfruit) plant. Other work of theirs explores similar kinship relationships with pigs on the island. I am keeping in mind the fact that, among Métis and First Nations people, kinship extends beyond the human, and if this is true, then it makes sense that different animal species could be kin with one another.

the sky, an unhealthy pale colour that reminded her of grubs wriggling beneath a disturbed log.[20]

Cyprien pulled out a pipe, packed it from his fire bag, and carefully lit a small twig before handing the torch back for her to extinguish.[21] Cupping his hand around the tiny flame, he held it to the pipe and puffed on it until the tobacco was well lit. Married last summer and already expecting his first child, Cyprien's still youthful profile reminded her of her father.

After a long draw, exhaled in a ghostly stream to the sky, he spoke. "It's Louis, I think. Cecil's brother. The pigs were at him when I came out here." He glanced at her. "That's why I had to—"

She hissed through her teeth, "You were right to put them down." She eyed the remaining sows mistrustfully. "I didn't know Louis was back from Fort Pitt."[22]

Cyprien nodded and handed her his pipe. She took a puff and briefly raised the pipe to the sky before handing it back.

"He'd come with supplies," he explained.

"You mean with the things he'd stolen."

He shrugged.

Louis and Cecil were fraternal twins, following in their father's footsteps as freemen working at times with the Hudson's Bay Company, sometimes working for themselves with what they could pilfer.[23] Equal parts cunning and generous, the two men wintered with their mother's people at Tobacco Weed Plain but had wives and children at Lac Ste.

---

20   (Vincent 2013). This is an accurate depiction of where the moon would have been close to dawn in May in the northern hemisphere.

21   (Duncan 1991, 56–66). A fascinating article about the pre-nineteenth-century origins of the fire bag, and its adoption by Métis.

22   (Ens and Sawchuk 2016, 42–70). Métis involved in the fur trade ranged from Montreal to Fort Pitt and Fort Edmonton on a fairly regular basis, sometimes with the North West Company, sometimes with the Hudson's Bay Company, until the two were integrated in 1821, at which point the HBC was the only game in town.

23   (Devine 2004, 75–110).

Anne.[24] Probably wives and children at Tobacco Weed Plain, too, if she were being realistic. Louis had hired on as a labourer at Fort Pitt last year, while Cecil maintained the summer run to Montréal.[25]

"I don't know how you could possibly tell it's him, though." She shuddered and wrenched her thoughts away from the grotesquerie in the bloody earth just a few lengths away. Cyprien reached into his fire bag and pulled out a small unadorned, stained smoked-hide pouch on the end of a rawhide loop. He passed it to her. She felt an unexpected weight and rolled the hard, flattened object between her fingers through the leather.

"I already looked inside. That's his lucky musket ball."[26]

Angelique knew the story well. In Montréal a number of years ago, during a drunken tavern brawl—probably over a woman—a Canadien had drawn his flintlock and been about to fire into Louis's face point-blank when the Frenchman slipped—probably in a puddle of vomit—and

---

24 (Fromhold 2013). This is a self-published book that does not even have page numbers, but it is an exhaustive chronological history using primary and secondary sources and contains a shocking amount of information on the specific members of certain bands, as well as their whereabouts, so I'm using it for this story! Tobacco Weed Plain, so named for the kinnikinnick that grew in abundance there, is close to Leduc. From the 1830s to about the 1840s, a mixed Cree/Nakoda (nêhiyaw-pwat) band let by Pesew wintered in this area. The sources Fromhold uses in his many self-published books really highlight again the mixed nature of most Indigenous communities within the nêhiyaw-pwat territory; "pure" bands were fabrications by colonial authorities post 1885, and more often contained Nakoda, Saulteaux, Cree, Iroquois, and some Métis people at the same time.

25 (Daschuk 2013, 59–79). In the 1850s, various diseases such as influenza and scarlet fever swept across the plains, but vaccinations at Red River mitigated the losses somewhat. In addition, American and eastern Canadians migrants started a slow trickle that became a flood when gold was found on the Fraser River, and the HBC's hold on Rupert's Land slipped considerably. During this time it's quite likely that men making the summer journey to Montreal were in the habit of pilfering what they could to support their families and communities experiencing the stress of disease and invasion. Smallpox spread like wildfire across the Plains and into BC in the 1860s, but in this story, I imagine that the Iron Alliance was successful at keeping out the settlers who carried this disease and thus was not so severely weakened as is the case in the historical record.

26 (Whisonant 2015, 61–73). Musket balls during this time were made of lead and would often mushroom inside the body, doing maximum-velocity damage to organs and rarely exiting the body. They caused more massive bone and tissue damage than any contemporary bullets, which tend to pass through the body. Anyway, I had to find out what would happen to a musket ball if it were shot into a wood wall, and this chapter made it clear that it would flatten.

the bullet hit the wall directly beside Louis's right ear. The explosion had left Louis partially deaf, but still alive. He'd dug the ball out of the wood to keep in his medicine pouch. The Frenchman supposedly fled in terror, but Cecil had once let it slip that Louis head-butted the man unconscious before ordering another round with the coins from the man's purse.

Louis had embellished and retold that story so many times that he'd have had his audience believing angels themselves had spoiled the Canadien's aim. Every telling had him pulling out the flattened lead slug, while he held it above his head triumphantly to the cheers and jeers of listeners. He never went anywhere without it. Cyprien was right. What was left of Louis lay in a wide circle before them.

She handed the pouch back to him. "What was he doing out here in the middle of the night?"

Her cousin frowned. "I mean, he said he was going to drop by with something for our aunt, but we stopped waiting for him after the sun had set."

"Did he have anything with him?"

He spread his hands and tapped the last of the ashes out of his pipe before returning it to his bag.

She sighed. "Right. Well, I guess we need to talk to Cecil in the morning."

Cyprien hesitated, and she felt her stomach drop. He wouldn't meet her eyes. Reaching back into his fire bag, he held something out for her.

Trembling, she opened her hand, and he gently pushed a tangle of coarse black hair into her palm.

"It was all over the place, Angelique."

She looked down at the horsehair, stomach twisting.

"I haven't *changed* since. You all know that," she stated flatly. Cyprien nodded, but his gaze was still evasive.

"People are going to wonder." He reached out tentatively and squeezed her shoulder. She nodded jerkily. He squeezed again, then let go.

"Come in, our auntie will want to feed you."

· ✦ ·

1852

Cyprien helped her drag the canoe onto the shore, flip it over their heads, and walk it up to her cabin. They'd had a taste for okâwak, the fish that the sullen, baby-faced priest Bourassa called doré, so they'd taken her father's canoe north, out to the hump where the lake rose sharply to just a few spans above a grown man's head.[27] The okâwak loved that spot. They'd caught six between them, enough for Cyprien to take some home and enough for the "fish tithe" her mother would force her to take to Bourassa and Father Thibault. Cyprien had nicknamed Bourassa mahkitôn because he was always gobbling up the food people brought him like a starving man, his overly large mouth rarely closing while he chewed, little flecks of food staining the black wool cassock he always wore.[28]

They lay the canoe down and grinned at each other.

"Say hi to everyone, I'm going to get these to our auntie!" Cyprien slung his sack of okâwak over his shoulder and set off back home.

His mother had died giving birth to a stillborn infant when Cyprien was only a baby, and his father had left the settlement soon afterward, so he lived with her father's sister, his maternal aunt. His other siblings lived with their paternal grandmother on the other side of the mission. Angelique often thought he should come to live with her and Eunice;

---

27   (Waugh 2018). In this piece, a white fisherman refers to the journal of Viscount Milton, who came to Lac Ste. Anne in 1860 as a tourist. The article is a piece of trash, but the Viscount described the Métis settlement and something called the Mission Hump, a real place just north of the old mission, where the lake comes up from about thirty feet to nine feet, and it is a favourite place for walleye (okâwak, doré) to hang out. Angelique is thirteen in this scene.

28   (*Dictionary of Canadian Biography* 1972). I get my physical description of the priest directly from the photo included in this biography.

her mother had wanted more children but been unlucky in that regard, and why not house the cousin who was as close to her as a brother? But whenever she asked, her father would mutter that it wasn't right; Cyprien was her cross-cousin and potential marriage material.[29] She wished she could make her parents understand that she'd never be interested in boys like that.

With this thought fresh in her mind, she started guiltily as she walked through the door to find Father Thibault seated at their long wooden table, in deep conference with her father. There was no horse tethered out front, so he must have walked all the way from his home beside the mission. Her pleasant afternoon fishing with Cyprien melted away, to be replaced with the anxiety she felt around the priests, who seemed to always direct their sermons about modesty and obedience directly at her.

Her father looked up at her entrance, and she saw his lips tighten. She was wearing Cyprien's cast-off brown wool pants, her moosehide moccasins lashed to just below her knees, and a loose linen shirt half tucked in, and her long black hair was scrunched up and shoved haphazardly under a battered, nearly shapeless brimmed felt hat. No different than most afternoons, really. Her father had mostly given up trying to force her into a dress, but Father Thibault insisted that women should wear skirts.

The large priest was clad in worn black robes buttoned up the front to just below a starched white collar. He turned ponderously in his chair to fix her with a disapproving stare, and she noticed a smear of lard in the short, white-flecked beard he wore just under his wide chin. Proof of her mother's hospitality, offered despite the antagonism that lay between Katherine Loyer and the Church. The priest's bushy eyebrows were fixed

....

29 (Macdougall 2010, 51–85). Métis family ties are complex and tend to respect the Cree concept of parallel and cross-cousins, wherein parallel cousins are treated as siblings and cross-cousins can potentially be marriage material. So one's mother's sisters have children that are your siblings, but a mother's brother has children that are your cross-cousins. A father's brother's children are your siblings, but a father's sister's children are your cousins.

in a perpetual scowl, and his short bristly hair was more unkempt than usual. He had a habit of running his thick fingers through it when he was talking, and by the looks of it, he'd been talking to her father for quite some time.

She ducked her head and shot a glance at her mother, who sat, stiff-backed on a stool in the corner with Eunice at her feet, ostensibly fixing nets by an uncovered window to let the tang of lake water and fish escape. Her mother's fingers weren't moving, however, and her expression was stormy. With unease squirming deeper into her, Angelique noticed her mother's nails were thickened, sharp, and long, their colour a disconcertingly flat black. She hoped the priest hadn't seen.

Clearing his throat, Father Thibault pushed his chair back and stood, as did her father. Paying her no more mind, the two men clasped hands.

"I'm sure you'll think on what we discussed," the priest said to her father in Cree.[30] Her father nodded and walked him to the door. Holding her sack of fish and feeling frozen to the spot, Angelique kept her head down as the priest passed her. Her father stood in the doorway for a long while, watching the priest leave before turning back inside.

Her mother let the net drop and bolted upright. She bared sharp teeth, her normally soft brown eyes deepening to black, and waved an emphatic finger.

"I don't care what he thinks. Our daughter is not … she's *not* going to any school run by those, those …" She sputtered, then angrily spat out, "les grises!"[31] Glaring in challenge at her husband, she growled softly, her

---

30 (Kermoal n.d.). The Métis at Lac Ste. Anne were fishers when they were not on the buffalo hunt, and they traded often with Fort Edmonton and the surrounding communities. As well, Father Thibault spoke fluent Cree.

31 (Duval 2001, 65–87). The Grey Nuns, "les grises," arrived in 1844 in the west, opening various missions in Métis communities with a specific focus on ending Métis women's dependence on the hunt by teaching them how to farm and homestead. They opened a school in St. Boniface, which had a high cost attached to it. The Grey Nuns actually came to Lac Ste. Anne in the 1850s, once Father Albert Lacombe took over the mission and invited the Oblates to run it with him. In my story, none of this happens. Father Lacombe never arrives, and, in fact, the church is driven out of the community completely.

lips still peeled back from pointed teeth that did not seem to want to fit into her generous mouth.

Eunice watched their parents, wide eyed. Angelique felt a chill run down her spine. She rarely saw her mother this angry, and it was terrifying. Had they been discussing sending her away? Who were the grey women?

Her father was wary, as he always was when confronted by his wife's temper. He opened empty palms, but made no move to approach her; he cast his eyes downward, staying very still. The growl that had been rising in her mother's throat slowly subsided. Angelique risked a quick peek and saw that her mother's nails were once again short and without colour.

Her father walked, slowly, carefully, over to Angelique and held his hand out for the sack. Peering inside, he pursed his lips in approval.

"Good. Go clean them."

"But, papa!" she protested, feeling that the fish were entirely beside the point.

He made a small warning gesture with his hand and met her eyes. "Then take one to Frère Bourassa. These are his favourite."

"Samuel!" her mother barked, demanding his attention.

"Yes, Katherine, my beloved. One moment." His voice was calm and sincere. He lay a large hand on Angelique's shoulder and gently pushed her toward the door, waving Eunice after her.

Numbly, she let her feet carry her out of the house and down to the shore, where she could clean the fish. Eunice, in her long-sleeved grey dress, shuffled to keep up with her. Behind them, they could hear their mother's raised voice, the growl back in her voice, and the low tones of their father as he tried to placate her.

She knelt down on the fine sand, unhappily dumping her three fish out into a pile in front of her. They slid off one another and settled, sand caught up in their iridescent scales, their cloudy eyes staring sightlessly up at the golden sky as the sun began to set. A chill breeze blew in from the water, and Eunice shivered, sitting next to her sister and leaning into her for warmth.

Taking her knife from her belt, Angelique made the first long slit along the silver-white belly of one of the fish. Warm innards spilled out, steaming slightly in the cooling air, noisome and familiar. She'd offer them to the water when she was done. She tried to clear her mind, focus on her task, be patient like her father had taught her, not jump to conclusions. Still, her mind raced. She scraped the backside of her blade against the scales of the gutted fish, shucking them off into a glittering pile, trying to focus on these sounds, and not the rising voice of her mother.

Eunice made no move to help; she just stared out over the lake with her head resting against Angelique's shoulder. Finally, she said, "The priest wants you to go to St. Boniface. To the Grey Nuns."

Angelique's blood ran cold, and she faltered, the sharp knife nicking the fat part of her thumb. Hissing in pain, she put her mouth against the wound. Eunice mewled softly in sympathy, but the cut was shallow and wouldn't bleed for long. Angelique stared out over the water, her mind racing, telling herself it was impossible, her parents would never send her away. Fear made her stomach clench.

"He said awful things about you." Eunice's voice was soft, with none of their mother's iron in it. "That you're idle, unfit to be a proper wife. That the devil's made you think you're a boy." Her sister regarded her with a troubled expression. "Is it true, Angelique? Is that why you dress like one all the time?"[32]

....

32 (Morgensen 2015, 38–61). This chapter focuses on the ways in which heteropatriarchy and gender norms were both created and imposed upon Indigenous peoples during colonialism, in ways that erased and punished fluid sexual orientations and gender identities that existed pre-Contact. So while Angelique's gender presentation and sexual orientation would not have been a problem among First Nations people pre-Contact, it would have been a sticking point with the Catholic church. Although her father usually didn't care about these things, when the priest made it an issue, it caused problems for Angelique and her family.

The words stung. Angelique's bark of laughter was bitter and mirthless. "No, I don't think I'm a boy, Euny! I just don't behave the way he thinks I should and—and—that mahkitiyêw has always hated me!"

Or, perhaps, the priest's dislike of her mother had just expanded to encompass her. Her mother, whose headstrong nature was legendary, such a contrast to the equanimity and patience of her father. A woman whose glossy black hair sometimes seemed to grow places it shouldn't, whose eyes shifted from gold to brown to black, whose nails at times resembled claws. It ran in families, her father said, but Eunice was fair haired and slender, well liked, and Angelique ... well, Angelique took after her mother's side.

From the house, her mother's voice became even more shrill, almost a howl, and her father was shouting now, something she had rarely ever heard. The sisters stared at each other, both afraid. The noise abruptly ended, and the air was still. After a moment, a large black dog dashed from the doorway of their home. A moment after, they saw their father leaning against the frame, his face unreadable. Eunice pretended she hadn't seen, scattering the tiny mountain of scales, smoothing them over the sand.

"He told papa that Albert Cunningham is travelling next week to St. Boniface to be a witness at his cousin's wedding, and that there was room for you."

The sun was setting quickly now, and with bile in her throat, Angelique laid her knife on the sand. Her tongue had thickened in her mouth, and her heart was beating strangely. She felt flushed and alternately cold and hot; she was dizzy. Staggering to her feet, she swayed for a moment, the drumming of her heart filling her ears, while Eunice stared up at her in terror.

"Angelique, your eyes!"

"You c'n clean 'em," she slurred, nodding jerkily at the fish. Her mind was whirling, crowded with images of stern women with damp grey skin reaching for her, and she shook her head to dislodge the vision. She lurched away toward the trees, breaking into a run before her sister could stop her, hearing her father shout behind her. She crashed headlong into the pine and poplars, letting her feet carry her down a path without really thinking about it.

Her heaving breaths turned into rattling sobs, and tears of anger obscured her vision as she ran. Her blood was surging, pounding, loud in her ears and full of a terrible pressure. Her heart felt like it was going to burst, and for a moment she thought she was going to throw up. She pushed herself forward, needing to get away, needing to be alone.

Suddenly she slammed into a dark shape and was knocked backwards, landing hard on her back so that she gasped for air like a fish in the bottom of a canoe, writhing in pain. In the dim light of dusk, she saw a hazy black figure looming over her. If she had been able to draw breath, she'd have screamed aloud.

There was a terrible wrenching, as though she were being pulled by every limb, in every direction, and for a moment she thought she would black out. She was seized with an intense vertigo, and her eyes didn't seem to work properly. She was wracked with the most intense pain she had ever felt in her life.

The figure that had been looming over her was now directly in front of her, but it seemed somehow to have shrunk; she had to look down at him. It was Father Thibault, and his face was twisted in horror. He lifted a meaty fist as though to strike her. Without thinking, she lashed back in defence. Her hoof struck him on the shoulder and flung him back a number of paces. With difficulty, he picked himself up, his arm clearly broken. Casting one last wild look at her, he staggered off, running as quickly as his long cassock would allow.

She screamed aloud in pain, but all she heard was the panicked whinny of a horse. Confused and disoriented, she crashed into the trees again, trying to get away, branches whipping her eyes and scratching her sides. When she slammed into a branch this time, she sank gratefully into unconsciousness.

She was swaying, being rocked, like when she'd been a baby in the wêwêpisowinis, the swinging cradle. Or when she'd swung her sister in it. Her eyes fluttered open, and she saw her father's face looking down at her, concerned. He murmured something, but she didn't understand. Her mother was there, too—she could feel her concern, a light touch on her brow, as the world continued to swing her though the darkness. She slipped back into nothingness.

Like floating in the warm lake, ears submerged, she could not make out sounds distinctly, but she could tell from the low rumble and the bright brassy hum that her parents were talking. Their voices were pitched too low to hear properly. And just like when one ear rose above the water briefly, she would catch a clear word here or there, in between sounds that made no sense but filled her with a deep sense of safety.

left

Boniface

black mare

stupid priest, he—

Rougarou

Then one clear phrase: "She doesn't know what she is."

As she let herself sink beneath the surface again, she thought she heard her mother's voice breathing into her ear.

"She knows. She knows. She knows."

What did she know, she wondered?

1854

Tears streamed down Cecil's face, and his wife was wailing fit to wake the entire settlement. Their youngest boy looked at his parents in bewilderment before he, too, opened his mouth with its three little teeth to howl his fear and confusion.

"I don't understand what's going on!" Cecil clawed at his hair, the braids messy and nearly undone from the sleep he'd been roused from just an hour ago. He'd be taken to see his brother's remains before men from the community took on the grim task of gathering them together for burial. His eyes were wide and staring, and he trembled intermittently, pacing in front of them with a terrible energy.

Cyprien nodded in sympathy, and Angelique closed her eyes for a moment in annoyance at the role he'd left for her. Taking a deep breath, she opened her eyes again.

"Cecil. Cecil!" she barked. Arrested in his pacing, he stared at her with something between rage and fear. Behind him, his wife was still wailing, the toddler abandoned and the older boys cowering in confusion. With a surge of impatience, Angelique stabbed a finger at them and then at Cyprien, who had the grace to look embarrassed before crossing the room to offer Cecil's wife comfort, scooping the howling baby up in one arm as he went.[33]

Lowering her voice now that she had his attention and the cacophony of grief had subsided somewhat, she gestured for Cecil to follow her outside.

They stepped into the morning chill, and before she knew what was happening, he'd grabbed her by the arm and wrenched her toward him. She was at least a head and a half shorter and nowhere near him in mass.

---

33 (Tsosie 2010, 29–42). Métis women would have held positions of power and leadership, like other Indigenous women, until those roles were deliberately targeted by colonial powers. Métis women began to lose leadership power in the latter part of the nineteenth century with the rise and fall of the buffalo trade. In my story, in this alternate future, that also never happens.

Leaning his face toward her, his sour breath hot on her cheeks, he snarled, "Tell me this wasn't you, Angelique! Tell me this wasn't you or I'll—"

She yanked her arm out of his grasp and shoved him with her other hand, anger giving her strength. He stumbled back, surprised, and a flash of fear crossed his face.

"Oh course it wasn't me, Cecil! iyaw! What the hell's wrong with you?"

He stared at her for a moment, then his face twisted again, and he shook his head and clawed at his hair once more. Not wanting him to start weeping uncontrollably again, she crossed the distance between them and reached up to slap him across the face.

"Stop it!" she hissed, hating herself for her gruffness, but needing him attentive. It worked; he let his hands fall and looked at her helplessly. It might seem a strange scene, a grown man clearly intimidated by a slight girl, but the people here knew there was more to her, just as there had been more to her mother.

She took another steadying breath. "Cecil. We need to know what Louis brought from Fort Pitt. What he was taking to my aunt's house."

Cecil nodded, as though anything made sense in this situation, and scrubbed his face with one hand. "It wasn't much this time," he told her. "He'd left most of it with our mother and our ..." He blinked and coughed uncomfortably. "Our mother, at Tobacco Weed Plain. Just some muskets and a few barrels, whisky, mostly. He thought your aunt could use the buffalo tongues, though."

She furrowed her brow. "Buffalo tongues?"

"Yeah, he knew your aunt would make sure everyone got some." He looked at her sharply. "They were in a big cask. It wasn't there. I thought you'd had it taken inside."

She shook her head. Cecil looked thoughtful for a moment, then shuddered, the grief breaking through again. He put his face in his hands and shook his head.

· ☀ ·

1870

Pîhtokahânapiwiyin and Angelique looked down at the charred remains of Colonel Garnet Wolseley.[34] He lay quite a distance from his troops; he'd almost made it to the river, and it was clear he'd run as soon as he'd seen wall of flame approach. It had been a tricky tactic, setting the prairie grass alight, but the wind had been true, and Wolseley's exhausted troops, laden as they were with supplies and ordered not to abandon their cannon, never stood a chance.

Payipwât's warriors and Angelique's group of Métis irregulars had done the rest with muskets and arrows.[35] They'd captured two dozen of Wolseley's men; the rest hadn't made it out of the raging fire that had burned right up to the banks of the Red River. Upper Fort Garry was in poor shape, some of the timbers still smouldering, but it was a small price to pay. Macdonald's railway would remain an unrealized dream, all his negotiations with British Columbia for naught.

Wolseley had set out in May, and Angelique's Iroquois cousins had been with them the entire time, slipping ahead to warn them the expedition was nearing.[36] Iron Confederacy leaders hadn't expected it to take until late August for Wolseley's troops to finally arrive; apparently, he'd

....

34 (Huyshe 1871). Angelique is thirty-two in this scene. This is a first-person account of the Wolseley expedition, which, in truth, was a terrible blow to the Red River. The journey was considered one of the most arduous military campaigns in history, and it took over three months to cross nearly impassible terrain, but when they arrived, Riel had ordered Upper Fort Garry abandoned, so it was captured easily. In my story, the Iroquois porters that Wolseley hired were related to the Lac Ste. Anne Métis, as our community was founded by Mohawk men and their families. In this version of reality, Wolseley was defeated, the Provisional Government was never disrupted, and the resistance of 1885 never needed to happen.

35 Payipwât (Piapot) was the leader of a nêhiyaw-pwat band and a major part of the Iron Alliance after 1860. He went on to sign Treaty 4 in 1875, but in this version of history, the numbered treaties also never happened, in great part because the buffalo were not wiped out.

36 The Haudenosaunee, made up of the Mohawk, Oneida, Onondaga, Cayuga, Seneca, and Tuscarora, do not tend to use the term "Iroquois" to refer to themselves. However, many primary and secondary sources from this time do use that term for those who came out west, and many modern-day descendants in Alberta continue to use the term Iroquois to self-identify.

encountered significant obstacles.[37] Riel had argued for abandoning the Fort and retreating, but Payipwât, Pîhtokahânapiwiyin, and Dumont pushed for a rout.[38] Uncertain of victory, Riel and a few supporters had slipped away a few nights ago.

Good riddance. Angelique had clashed with the younger man repeatedly over the years, usually over his strange religious notions, but his obvious fear of her *reputation* forced her into a tiring state of wariness she was glad to let go of. It hadn't seemed to matter that she'd never let the power flow, or that her people spoke well of her—Riel had watched her, always. It had been a bad moment when he had Scott shot, never mind the fact the loud-mouthed Orangeman deserved it.[39] For a while she'd wondered if he was going to try the same with her. Lucky for the Iron Confederacy, he'd made no moves against her; it had been her idea to use the prairie itself against Wolseley.

In contrast, Dumont reminded her a little of Cyprien; he never seemed intimidated by her, and there was a kindness there she sorely missed, coupled with a teasing nature she had appreciated very much over these hard years. As much as she missed her cousin, she was glad Cyprien had stayed with his wife and children, safe in Lac Ste. Anne.

Dumont heeded her counsel and took advantage of her ability to blend into the background whenever the Iron Confederacy needed information about the Canadians. He relied on her when English was needed,

---

37 (Vrooman 2013). The Iron Alliance included Métis, Dakota, Cree, Anishinaabek, and, at times, the Blackfoot Confederacy. It formed around 1600, rose to prominence in the 1850s, and then waned in power as the buffalo were decimated. In this story, the Iron Alliance remains strong and continues to the present day.

38 (*Dictionary of Canadian Biography* 1982c). Pîhtokahânapiwiyin (Poundmaker) was Stoney, and his mother was mixed blood, but his culture was purely Cree. He was adopted by a Blackfoot chief and lived among then for a while, given the name Makoyi-koh-kin (Wolf Thin Legs). His experiences, like those of the other leaders I mention in this story, highlight the ways in which the various Iron Alliance and Blackfoot Confederacy bands had relationships with one another that were fluid and important.

39 The execution of Thomas Scott on March 4, 1870, was the reason the Wolseley expedition was sent by Macdonald.

and the high regard he had for her meant she'd been easily accepted by the other war chiefs.

Pîhtokahânapiwiyin wiped ash from his eyes and flashed Angelique a grim smile. "Someone should take word to Macdonald."

She nodded thoughtfully. He was right, it was time to take a delegation and settle this mess. The Iron Confederacy bands were tired of surveyors and Ottawa's lackeys throwing their weight around. Macdonald was no doubt emboldened by the deal he'd struck with the Hudson's Bay Company for the transfer of rights to what they irritatingly insisted on calling Rupert's Land, and she'd gathered intel on his negotiations with British Columbia and the promise to build a railway across the Plains; this was not a problem that would go away on its own.

Angelique squinted into the fading sunlight. "A day to rest, and then we'll go." She met Pîhtokahânapiwiyin's gaze, seeing the resolve there. He gestured questioningly to the corpse at their feet, and she pursed her lips for a moment before giving a quick dip of her chin.

"It'd be rude to show up empty handed," she agreed.

1854

"Joseph was with him." Cyprien joined her on the shore. They could both still hear the wailing behind them.

She was staring into the calm water at little spiders skating along its surface, awed as always by the slight dents they made in the silver liquid. Once, perhaps twice, she'd managed it for a few moments before splashing through, back when she'd still let it happen. She wondered if Jesus had walked on water as a man, or as something else.

She sighed deeply. As abrasive as Louis and Cecil could be at times, they were well loved, and this death was a sorrow that would ripple through the settlement for a long while.

"Then let's see what he has to say."

Joseph was a ruddy-faced man with a prominent bulbous nose and a thick, wild beard inherited from his Scottish father. He was originally from St. Boniface, but he'd fallen in love with a Stoney woman on the buffalo hunt and wintered with her people on the other side of the lake most years, so he was often found visiting the settlement. It took a while to locate him, but they were finally directed to the back of the mission, where they found him sprawled on the ground, wrapped in a large buffalo robe and snoring loudly against the church timbers.

Angelique hated being so close to the priest's domain, so she was perhaps a bit rougher than intended when she nudged him with her moccasined foot—perhaps she even kicked him a little. With a shout, the big man lurched upright, stark terror on his face.

"Calm down, Joseph," Cyprien urged, but it took a moment for sense to return to the older man's drawn face. He stared up at them with a haunted expression, gathering the buffalo robe around himself again as he staggered to his feet.

"Why are you sleeping here?" Cyprien asked while Angelique nervously eyed the priest's house for any sign of movement.

"Couldn't get into the church," he mumbled, then began coughing, deep and wracking, clearing his lungs out after damp hours spent in the cold. Angelique pressed her lips together in annoyance at the racket he was making. Finally, he spit out the rattling phlegm and righted himself again.

"You came back from Fort Pitt with Louis," she stated, and he flinched at her flat tone before nodding. He held up a hand and refused to meet her gaze.

"You can stop right there, Angelique, I'm not going to be interrogated by a wee girl." He coughed and spat again, then wiped his mouth. "No need. You're the only one that'd believe what happened anyway."

Cyprien and Angelique shared a glance.

"Why don't you come back with us and—" she started, but Joseph waved her off.

"I'm not leaving hallowed ground, not for anything!" He was looking at her finally, his jaw set. There was something in his eyes that chilled her; he was trying to hide it, but he was scared.

With another uneasy glance at the priest's house, she nodded. "Okay, so tell us."

Leaning against the church, Joseph began his account.

"Louis and I set out a while back, as soon as the water was open enough to give us passage. They'd withheld a large portion of Louis's pay after he'd been caught brawling, and he was angry, so we took enough to have us sitting dangerously low in the river. I convinced him to drop most of it off at his mother's camp, which made getting back here a lot easier."

Cyprien frowned. "Everyone knows Louis's a brawler. Why was he docked this time?"

Joseph grimaced. "That old bastard, One Pound One, John Rowand, he was at the Fort for some visit and saw Louis laying into someone for something or other.[40] Rowand's temper is like nothing I've ever seen.

....

40   ("Two Tales of Fort Edmonton" n.d.). John Rowand was three hundred pounds and walked with a limp due to a broken leg as a child; his gait earned him the nickname One Pound One. He died of heart failure when intervening in a fight between two men. They buried him, but his will insisted he be buried in Montreal. He was disinterred in a state of decomposition and his body boiled so that only the bones remained for transport. Those bones were put into a cask filled with rum to preserve them and labelled "buffalo tongues" so the porters would not throw it overboard out of superstitious fear. In reality, the cask was sent to York, to England, and then to Montreal, and along the way, the rum was siphoned off by sailors! In this story, Louis unluckily steals the cask. Cool fact: when Cadence Weapon was Edmonton's poet laureate, he wrote a timpani-based club anthem based on the legend of John Rowand (https://soundcloud.com/hprodeo/one-pound-one-cadence-weapon).

He came stomping over like an angry bull, swearing up a storm—then he just dropped dead, right there! Well, his son runs the Fort, and he decided to take it out on Louis. Docked him and kicked us both out!"

He shook his head in disgust. "We bided our time a few days, then helped ourselves to our fair pay. We got in early last night, stashed the rest with Cecil and Louis's wife. On the way we'd realized one of the barrels we thought was rum was actually pickled buffalo tongues, and he knew your aunt wouldn't cuss him out for it, so we decided to bring it over right away."

Angelique narrowed her eyes. "It took both of you to carry a barrel over?"

Joseph spread his hands. "It was heavier than it looked! Damned heavy, and why not, when it was a damned thing?" The fear was back in his face. "We had it up on our shoulders, him in back, me in front, and I started hearing ..." He paused and closed his eyes tight, like he was trying not to sob. Cyprien raised an eyebrow at Angelique, but she just wished he'd out with it already.

"What did you hear, Joseph?" Cyprien asked gently.

Without opening his eyes, Joseph spoke, his strangled voice sending ice through her. "All the devils of hell. I heard all the devils of hell." Sucking in a ragged breath, he opened his eyes again. They were pleading. "I swear I wasn't drunk. The whispering was coming from the barrel. We were just about at your aunt's place when Louis dropped the damn thing—he must have heard it, too. The barrel cracked, and something gushed out of it, like a roaring wind! Then ... well, we ran! With a sound like a thousand banshees chasing us. Louis headed toward your aunt's place. My only thought was to reach the church."

"There was no barrel when I found him, Joseph." Cyprien was pensive.

"Found who?" A cowled figure stepped from around the corner of the church, clad against the morning cold in heavy black wool robes. The hood was drawn up fully, seemingly with no face within it. Angelique flinched in shock, suddenly back in her nightmare—that figure gliding toward her across the lake …

Baby-faced Bourassa brushed his hood back slightly, his pale face clearly visible against the black cloth. Angelique shuddered in revulsion, and the priest's watery blue eyes, bulging like his beloved doré, fixed her with a rancorous gaze.

His eyes flicked to Cyprien standing beside her and recoiled, his face going slack, as though he'd seen a ghost. The moment quickly passed, then once again she had all of his unwelcome attention.

"Ah," he said with a note of deep satisfaction, "I've been hearing talk of evildoings. How fitting I find you here in the middle of it."

She felt frozen to the spot, every muscle in her body screaming at her to flee. His eyes bored into her, his malevolence palpable in his voice, at odds with its boyishness.

"Angelique, the Rougarou of Lac Ste. Anne."

1853

In the end, it was Father Thibault who travelled with Albert Cunningham to St. Boniface, not Angelique. His broken arm splinted, he'd sat stiffly in the Red River cart, glaring at those gathered to bid him adieu.

The Elders had heard him out, quietly listening to his description of the black mare that had attacked him, listened to him as he named Angelique Loyer a rougarou. Then the Elders had visited her parents, she in the corner lying on a buffalo robe as they talked in low tones. She was still wracked with fever, confused, coming in and out of consciousness as Eunice hovered nearby, wiping her brow with a cool cloth.

A decision was made, and Father Thibault was presented with a rifle and three buffalo robes. The gun was her father's, but the robes came from the community. The matter was considered settled, but the Father refused to accept this. At first, he merely *threatened* to leave, working himself up to delivering an ultimatum about Angelique's continued presence in the community, but when Elder after Elder softly responded with "kiyâm," he'd angrily packed, accepted the goods he'd been gifted, and made arrangements.

Frère Bourassa refused to accompany the Father. His sermons were respectfully attended at first, then less so as he again and again denounced Angelique and her mother, Katherine, as servants of the devil. Some in the settlement agreed with Bourassa, crossing themselves when they encountered the Loyer women, but for the most part it was considered poor form to continue a conflict that had been deemed resolved.

No one had expected Bourassa to stay. He'd been meeting with a Father Lacombe, who had been considering taking over the mission, but it seemed now he'd decided to run the mission alone. After about half a year, his sermons became less impassioned, and he was seen throughout the community, tending once more to the day-to-day needs of his flock, presiding over baptisms, weddings, and funerals. Lac Ste. Anne settled back into a comfortable equilibrium.

But equilibrium was much harder for Angelique to achieve during those months. Her mercurial temperament worsened after menarche, or, at least, her control over herself slipped more and more through her fingers like muddy lake water. Her mother often grew impatient with her, less able to curb her own already poor restraint. The two were like oil and water, or perhaps like flame to fat. They set one another off, and the pain that preceded transformation left them both short-tempered with one another and everyone else. Eunice and her father tiptoed around them, quiet ghosts in the presence of roaring flames.

It was after a particularly bad day that Angelique decided to go beyond the small experiments, instead of clamping down on the power, letting it flow freely through her. She left the house as the sun dipped low over the lake, the ethereal call of a loon echoing out across the copper water and following her into the woods.

Her mother had let her go, tired, nerves drawn taut, snapping at her husband when he sought to bring Angelique back.

"Give her the space, Samuel! She'll be safer out there than in here with me right now!"

She couldn't have known it was prophecy.

Angelique broke into an easy run along the trail that led farther into the woods, rather than the one that snaked around the lakeshore. It was already night here, under the trees, but her eyes adjusted immediately, because she let them. The itch under her skin spread, and this time she didn't hold it back. This time she welcomed the pain, the wrenching, the thickening of her tongue, the sliding of her sight, the twisting of her limbs. It hurt like nothing had ever hurt before, but she knew the pain would end, and that knowledge was enough to endure it.

Mid-stride, hooves slammed down into packed earth, the jolt carried along her spine as she crashed forward, four-legged now instead of two. Hampered by the trees, aching for an open plain, she made do with the space she had, startling waking beings as she passed, crashing about, not sure footed yet.

She tired more easily than she expected, sweat lathering her heaving sides, air coming into her lungs strangely in bellowing gasps, through wide nostrils. That was when she smelled the smoke.

At first, she thought her heightened senses were fooling her, intensifying what should have been the normal smell of her family's cooking fire, but as she headed back home, the smoke grew thicker. When she began to see grey tendrils reaching around thin tree trunks like skeletal fingers, she ran.

She burst out of the trees into light that seared her night vision like a blast that left her unable to process the scene, confused by the smoke, the roar louder than she could have imagined. And within it, barely audible, the thin, high yelps of an animal in pain. Gasping, stumbling, she lost her form all at once, a whinny turning into a scream, falling forward onto her unprotected face, stunned by the shock for a moment.

She heard her name being called, but her ears were ringing from the impact, and she couldn't make sense of any more. She managed to roll onto her side, naked, the heat of the blaze searing her back as her family's home roared in massive licks of flame up into the night sky. Hazily she began to make out figures running to the lake; a bucket brigade was forming.

Her sight returned, but she was unable to move, shaking uncontrollably, her limbs twitching spasmodically as she tried to control them, to call the power back, to *move*, to do *something*. Suddenly Cyprien was there, kneeling down, calling her name, covering her with his coat, his face streaked with soot and tears. Her teeth chattered together as she tried and failed to answer him, and she stared at him helplessly, every answer she never wanted written there in his eyes.

She saw something move behind him, and she tried to focus. Out there, in the lake, just at the edge of the greasy orange reflection in the too-calm water, a figure stood, barely visible. She reached for the power again, demanding it, forcing it to help her *see*. The effort was almost too much, and if she could have screamed, she would have—the pain was that intense. Straining and fading at the same time, knowing she was pushing herself too far, her vision cleared for a split second before agony broke her open like dry twig being snapped, and for a time, she ceased to exist.

When she moved into the abandoned cabin by herself, at the far edge of the settlement, they let her.

It wasn't fear. Cyprien had been the first to raise the cry when the flames rose above the trees, but at least a dozen people had seen her change as she fell. It didn't matter; they knew what she was, just as they'd known what her mother was. They respected her, and they respected her grief.

What little there was to bury was interred without comment; not even Bourassa interfered. The small, delicate bones of her sister, the larger remains of her father, and the misshapen skull of a dog amid the skeleton of a woman.

They brought her necessities: a kettle, tallow, flour, dry meat. In return, she attended births, focused on her medicines, kept busy so she had no option but to collapse into sleep at the end of the day. At first, she had many visitors, as the community reached out to fold her into the grief they all shared, but she fell silent in their presence, staring off into nothing, and in time, there was only Cyprien.

1871

They'd been left cooling their heels, literally, for a number of hours now in a committee room on the main floor of the labyrinthine Parliament building.[41] The room was drafty and poorly supplied in wood, forcing them to keep a comically small fire going in the oversized fireplace. It was a childish tactic on Macdonald's part, and not a particularly effective one. The Iron Confederacy delegation, which now formally included the Blackfoot Confederacy, were all hardened veterans of Prairie winters and well outfitted in wool capotes and buffalo robes.[42]

. . . .

41 (Artemiw n.d.). I needed to know what the original Parliament looked like, before it burned. I wanted to get a sense of where the Iron Alliance delegation would be put. Angelique is thirty-three in this scene.

42 The Battle of Belly River never happened in this version of history; instead the Blackfoot Confederacy made peace with the Iron Alliance and joined them in 1870 against the Wolseley expedition.

The close quarters of the city had set them all on edge. Something about the way their eyes sought distances that weren't there—a sense of claustrophobia lay over them like a foul fog. If this was the future Macdonald and his peers longed for, they could keep it.

Angelique was dressed in her habitual wool pants, winter moccasins wrapped in soft beaver fur to mid-calf, a white multicoloured point jacket over a cotton shirt and beaded hide vest secured with an Assomption sash, and a warm beaver fur hat. She knew from prior experience infiltrating Parliament and the taverns of Ottawa during their Confederation celebrations in 1867 that she'd be taken for a man, and that suited her fine.

Aatsista-Mahkan grunted in annoyance and started to build the fire up.[43] When Dumont looked askance, the Siksika leader grinned and held up a small kettle he'd pulled from one of his packs. He said something, and Ky-yo-kosi, or Jerry Potts as he was often called, translated for those who didn't speak the language: "Running Rabbit says he wants tea, and we can bust up the chairs if need be."[44]

This broke the tension in the room. Ignoring the table, they sat in a semicircle in front of the fire. Mistahimaskwa shared some dry meat, Payipwât had pemmican, and Pîhtokahânapiwiyin pulled out a little flask of brandy.[45] Angelique raised her eyebrow at that; it was a metal flask with the initials *H.C.W.L.* on it.[46] Pîhtokahânapiwiyin shrugged, feigning innocence. She wondered when he'd managed to pilfer it from that bombastic lawyer.

....

43   (*Dictionary of Canadian Biography* 1998). Aatsista-Mahkan (Running Rabbit) was a Siksika chief and signatory of Treaty 7 in 1877 (which never happens in this story).

44   (*Dictionary of Canadian Biography* 1990). Jerry Potts (Ky-yo-kosi, Bear Child) was the son of a Kainai mother and a Scottish father and was apprenticed to an American Fur Company trader who treated him very badly. He spoke many languages. He is often called Métis, but his loyalties and kinship ties were clearly to the Blackfoot.

45   (*Dictionary of Canadian Biography* 1982b). Mistahimaskwa (Big Bear) was a Plains Cree chief, though his parents may have been Saulteaux.

46   Henri Charles Wilfrid Laurier. The flask was obviously stolen from somewhere.

None of them were comfortable in this ugly imposition on what was otherwise a beautiful spot above the river, but full bellies and the warmth of purloined liquor helped steady all their nerves.

Another hour passed before the door banged open, and Macdonald strode in, his unruly dark curls sticking up on one side, the other side smoothed and oily, as though he'd been patting it down repeatedly. The bags beneath his eyes were deeply pronounced, and blooms of burst capillaries stained his cheeks and nose a blotchy red. Though he drew himself up to his full, not inconsiderable height, his step was unsteady. Behind him came two other men who looked like they could be twins, both with bushy white beards, receding white hair, and dour expressions. The one on the right was dressed a little finer perhaps, and just as drunk as Macdonald; the smell of gin wafted into the room ahead of their entrance.

Not waiting for anyone to stand, Macdonald made no pretense of hiding his hostility. Curtly introducing his compatriots, he jerked a finger first at the better dressed man—"This is Sir Hugh Allan"—and then at the slightly seedier, but much more sober version of the same fellow—"and this is John Dougall."[47] Spinning to face the two men, his back to the delegation, Macdonald swept his long arms out. "And these are the reason we haven't been able to get the railroad in." The two other men regarded them with scorn.

Pitching her voice low, Angelique said in Cree, "Fancy Pants builds steel roads, Dumpy Bum writes big letters for lots of people to read." Potts quickly translated that in Siksika for Aatsista-Mahkan, as they all gathered themselves up and stood.

She remembered seeing these two before during her reconnaissance for the Iron Confederacy in 1867. They'd been meeting with Macdonald and a bevy of other politically hungry men in a saloon, where so much

47   (McCallum 2008). Sir Hugh Allan was involved in the Pacific Scandal that resulted in John A. Macdonald being forced to resign. John Dougall was a newspaperman (*Dictionary of Canadian Biography* 1982a). Now, seriously, go take a look at the pictures of these two men—can you tell them apart?

of Canadian politics seemed to happen. Dougall was there despite being a founding member of a temperance society in Montréal, drinking water while the rest of them poured wine down their gullets.[48] She'd been sitting in a booth nearby, across from a young clerk who had thankfully already passed out, his head on the table in a puddle of drool. She'd kept her hat low and hadn't had to *extend* her senses at all; the men were roaring in laughter and boasting loud enough to be heard outside.

They'd been planning for the first general election in August, and there'd been much discussion of the need for railways and drumming up political support for them through the papers. They'd made her mission incredibly easy with their loose talk and constant drinking.

Macdonald was glowering at her, clearly annoyed at the string of unfamiliar words. He looked frazzled, his vest buttoned up crookedly, his high collar stained around his neck, and his cravat skewed. Angelique was wary; a man not willing to cover himself in the pretense of calm is always dangerous. His gaze shifted to Dumont, and his lip curled.

"It's you goddamn half-breeds!" he thundered angrily, then seemed to hear himself in the small room and shook his head, letting loose a mirthless laugh. "Well, I guess you're my problem after all." Dumont, who did not speak English, said nothing.

Glancing uneasily at one another, Fancy Pants and Dumpy Bum slid themselves into chairs around the conference table. Macdonald stared a bit longer at Dumont before he, too, took a seat. Aatsista-Mahkan shot a sly look at Dumont before choosing the chair he'd been eyeing up for the fire not so long ago, and Potts stood behind him. Angelique stood behind Dumont to act as his translator, while the others also found seats.

For three hours, Macdonald threatened, pleaded, blustered, threw up his hands and threatened to walk out, letting Fancy Pants and Dumpy Bum argue his case for him before returning to his seat to start the cycle

------

48   (Skelly, 2015).

over again. It was clear he was desperate to build his railway, fearing he'd lose British Columbia and, perhaps more than that, that the Americans would come sniffing. It was also clear that his political star had set; they were looking at a leader on the way out.

He offered them treaties, he offered them gifts, he even suggested not too subtly that large financial bribes could be ongoing to the leaders if they came to an agreement. Through it all, the Iron Confederacy representatives stood firm, rejecting every proposition. In frustration, Macdonald finally slammed his hands onto the table and leaned forward, glaring at Dumont.

"Then what, in the name of God, *do* you want?" he snarled, spittle flying from his lips. Angelique didn't bother to translate. The question was clear in any language.

Dumont gestured, and Angelique fetched him their gift, which he then laid on the table.

In the sudden silence, the three white men stared at the sack in the middle of the table in confusion. Angelique reached over, undid the tie at the top, and let the cloth fall open. Wolseley's skull, with patches of scorched skin and hair still clinging to it, grinned at them.

Macdonald's face drained of all colour, and Fancy Pants nearly knocked his chair over as he shot to his feet. Dumpy Bum stared in horrified fascination, frozen to the spot.

Very clearly, into the silence, Dumont spoke. "otipêyimisow-iyiniwak ôma niyanân."

Angelique cleared her voice and spoke directly to Macdonald for the first time.

"He says, 'We are the People Who Own Themselves.'" Macdonald fixed her with a baleful glare, clearly not understanding.

"We don't want or need *anything* from you." Her tone had sharpened. She looked around their delegation, receiving a nod from Dumont, a quick grin from Aatsista-Mahkan and Potts, and quiet assent from the three Cree leaders. They were all tired and ready to be done with this.

Turning back to Macdonald, she continued. "We are not going to become a part of your national experiment. If Canada wants any kind of trade relationship at all, think long and hard before sending another military force to press the point."

She gazed pointedly at Wolseley's remains, and Macdonald met her eyes with a seething rage clearly boiling up within him. She bared her teeth at him, feeling the points there, the change as her eyes deepened from brown to black. He recoiled in shock, then shook his head in confusion, wiping one large hand across his face and sighing deeply.

"This is a mistake," he finally said, flatly, and without another word, the three men filed dispiritedly out of the room.

Canada had had its chance to crush the Iron Confederacy, and it had failed.

She came to all of a sudden with a splitting pain in her head, overcome with nausea. She leaned over as quickly as she could, never mind how it made her head feel, and vomited. When she'd emptied her stomach, she gingerly lay back down and tried to force her vision to stop blurring. She'd obviously been hit on the head, and any movement was going to make her feel ill at this point.

With her eyes slitted, half closed, she took stock of the situation. She was lying on cold stone in a dark room. The only illumination came from a small square in front of her, faint, from outside. A door. She groaned, surprising herself with the volume of the sound as it bounced between close-set walls. She was in some sort of cell.

Without meaning to, she passed out again, anger a faint buzzing behind her ears.

She was woken an indeterminate time later when the door to the cell banged open. Squinting against the too-bright lantern light, she saw a dark cowled shadow. She didn't see the boot coming before it connected with her side in a sickening crunch. She howled in pain and spasmed into a fetal position, gagging and heaving.

"Does it hurt?" It was Macdonald's voice, heavily slurred. "Good. Goddamn Wolseley to hell!" he roared furiously. "He should have killed every last one of you!"

He aimed his boot at her again, but in his state, only caught the top of her thigh as she lay on the ground.

Her head was spinning, but she was determined not to fall unconscious again. Macdonald held the lantern higher and looked down at her in contempt. She had a vague impression of navigating dark streets with the Iron Confederacy delegation, leaving their inn early because they expected betrayal, and then breaking into a run when it was clear Macdonald had waited even less time than they'd believed possible. She prayed she was the only one captured.

"I was more than fair with you Indians," Macdonald continued, pointing a thick finger at her and slowly leaning down toward her, alarmingly unstable, his large nose looming in her field of vision. "But they sent me you? A woman? Is this a joke to you people?" He laughed, a truly unpleasant sound.

She realized she was only in her pants and cotton shirt, and that it was easily apparent that she was not indeed a man. His glassy eyes slid over her lasciviously, and she felt a deep disgust well up inside her.

"Barely a woman," he muttered contemptuously, reaching down faster than she'd expected and grabbing her by the front of her shirt, bunching it up in his large fist and yanking her toward him. Her head snapped back painfully, little sparks of agony shooting through her aching skull. He held the lantern dangerously close to her face as she dangled in his grasp, the glass radiating heat across her ear and cheek.

Macdonald's breath was hot and sour with gin, his spittle scoring her flesh like sparks from a fire. "I'm going to hang you," he hissed, "and eventually I'll hang the rest of them that slipped away. Then I'm going to drive the railway right through your damn buffalo-infested Plains, and the lot of you can jump into the Pacific Ocean!"

He shoved her back down roughly, slamming her head into the stone with a crack. She almost threw up again with the pain. She began to panic as her vision darkened, terrified of losing consciousness again with this man in the cell with her.

She hadn't called the power in so long. When she left Lac Ste. Anne to join the resistance against Canadian invasion, it had been hard enough to be taken seriously as a woman. If Dumont hadn't formed such a fast friendship with her, she wasn't sure she'd ever have fit in. Everyone knew the stories of her, of her mother, and at first they'd treated her like a wild animal, wary, skittish. For nearly two decades, she'd exercised the control she had lost, all those years ago, when her family was taken from her.

It was sluggish at first, barely a whisper, fading in and out as her vision continued to blur and darken, Macdonald standing over her, his lantern swinging in slow motion. Everything slowed down—his mouth moved glacially, lips twisted in hate, his eyes burning with it. A sound began to build inside her head: crashing, powerful waves, like her lake in a storm with the Thunderers roaring.

She focused on that, the power of the Thunderers, feeling an answer in her bones—jagged, shooting pain like lightning strikes, worse than anything she could remember. It began, the sliding of bones and sinews, too stagnantly, causing her more torment than it should, threatening to push her under, but the fear of being caught *in between* the change was stronger than the agony.

All at once, the power *surged*, and she lurched up on forelegs, unbalanced at first with the new perspective, limbs responding strangely at first, but then with more certainty.

Macdonald fell backwards, his lantern crashing and shattering on the stone. She heard shouts outside, but it didn't matter. He was between her and the way out. Rearing up, she brought all her weight down on him, sharp hooves smashing, rending, flattening. She did it again, and again, and again, until what remained was a spreading smear of blood and innards.

With a furious bugle, she squeezed through the open door, sending flying some very surprised men who had come running at the noise.

The rest was a blur, she ran through corridors, and smashed through a window, the wind whipping through her mane as the swollen moon shone on her dark skin.

When she arrived at the camp, heaving and covered in sweat and blood, it was Dumont who steadied her, remarkably calm though he'd never seen her like this before.

He stroked her long, muscled neck, whispering, "Ça va, nitôtêm, ça va bien," over and over until her breath steadied and she felt the slippage again. She lay against the ground, naked and shivering, her head still throbbing.

"Can you ride?" Dumont asked her in Cree, crouched down, gesturing to Potts for a blanket. One was quickly found for her, and she slowly sat up, clutching it around her gratefully.

"If I had to, I'd fly." She answered back, and laughed painfully, pushing her sticky hair out of her face, wanting a bath more than she ever had. Dumont's face split into a relieved grin.

"And miss all my stories on the road? Let's just travel the regular way, all right?" he teased, and she nodded. She looked around, relaxing a little once she saw everyone else was still with them.

She was going to have one hell of a headache, but Macdonald wasn't going to be a problem for them anymore.

· ☼ ·

1854

Looking into Bourassa's face, his mouth twisted into a mockery of a smile, she realized suddenly that he hadn't settled in, as they all imagined. He'd been holding on to his hatred of her this whole time. She could feel it radiating from him, and she swayed with the knowledge of it.

The priest reached out a pale hand, long, delicate fingers closing around her forearm, and she stared down at them in horrified fascination. Something was tickling the back of her mind, a fear that she could taste in the back of her throat like iron. His fingers continued to dig into her flesh painfully, and then he yanked her toward him.

She was off balance, nearly falling against him, and she heard Cyprien protest wordlessly. Bourassa thrust his face close to hers, regarding her with a reptilian intensity, and she caught a whiff of something, vile, noxious. The smell of death. She tried to shake off his grasp, but he was so, so much stronger than he looked.

"This time," he hissed, so only she could hear, "you'll be right where you are supposed to be. And this time," his wide grin was venomous, "you won't escape what's coming."

Like hitting the flat mirror of the lake with all limbs extended, the breath was knocked from her chest. The world tilted, and once again she was on her side, the smell of smoke surrounding her, flames roaring, casting a greasy orange reflection out across the lake. There, at the edge of the light, out in the water itself, a figure. She'd reached then for her power, forcing her eyes to focus better, see farther. She'd strained to breaking and then, just before she'd blacked out ...

A figure, in thick black robes, a hood with no visible face within it, watching the fire, watching *her*. And then, one pale hand, long, delicate fingers, reaching up to tug the hood even lower down.

The vision left her gasping, grief slamming into her like a mighty hammer. Bourassa was dragging her along with him now, and she struggled to keep up, stumbling and nearly falling as the enormity of what she'd remembered flowed through her. Casting a look behind her, she saw Cyprien frozen in indecision, and Joseph gazing at her with a questioning look.

"The fire!" she choked out, willing her cousin to understand, as Bourassa yanked her around the corner of the church and out of his sight.

People were beginning to gather in front of the church for the Sunday service. With news of violent death having been spread throughout the entire settlement by now, it looked like most of the families were going to attend this morning, even those who had taken to avoiding the church since Bourassa took over.

Her heart sunk as she saw Cecil, his eyes red rimmed, looking like he'd started drinking whisky the moment she'd left his house. His wife was hand in hand with her sister-in-law, the children of the two brothers walking or being carried by the older ones. There were a lot of tears in the growing crowd.

She attempted once more to wrench her arm away from the priest, but he had a grip like iron, surprisingly strong for a man who did no labour, not even to catch his own fish. Panic began battering at her, and she found her vision beginning to blur. Her blood was surging, pounding loud in her ears, and her throat had gone very dry, almost constricted. Bourassa stopped in front of the church, and shoved her in front of him, his grip still holding her captive.

"That's right, let's see you transform again," he whispered harshly, his lips brushing her ear with disturbing intimacy. "Let's see if they continue to abide your presence when they all witness your evil manifest itself. When they see you refusing to control it. When they see what you are capable of doing to them."

"What's going on, Frère?" called an older man, Hubert, a cousin of her father's. He was a regular at church, a devout Catholic who never missed a sweat and had the Thirst Dance scars to attest to his expansive piety.[49] There were looks of confusion and concern as people neared to find the church still closed and Angelique thrust out in front of the priest like some sort of offering.

Bourassa raised his voice so that everyone could hear him. "We all know there was a murder last night. Who was it that was taken from us?"

Cecil raised his tear-stained face. "It was Louis, Frère, it was my brother." His shoulders shook as he closed his eyes and his face crumpled.

Bourassa's expression was sorrowful. "So we have lost a pious brother, a father, a son."

She saw Hubert exchange a small look with his wife. Louis was well loved and generous with the goods of others, but Thibault and Bourassa had often denounced the brothers for their "wicked ways," and no one would ever have described either as pious.

Angelique tried yet again to pull away from the priest, but with his other hand, he knocked off her hat, letting her dark hair spill down around her shoulders before grabbing a painful handful and pulling her head back toward him.

His voice shifted, and he shook her hard enough for her to bite her tongue, blood blooming bright and metallic on her lips. "An unholy murder!" he roared. "A devil walked among us last night, a devil too long permitted to live among us!"

When he let her go, she fell to her knees. The crowd shifted uneasily.

Bourassa reached into his robes and pulled out an object. He raised up his fist so all could see, then opened his hand, letting black horsehair rain down. There was a chorus of gasps.

---

49 (Anderson-McLean 1999, 5–32). This article speaks to the syncretism present in the Métis settlement of Lac Ste. Anne, and in particular the blended traditions of Catholicism and Indigenous spirituality as expressed by the annual pilgrimage.

"She left her mark! Rendered a man unrecognizable, and she will certainly do it again. What will it take to have her cast out?" He was roaring now, loud enough to be heard at the very edges of the gathering throng.

Angelique was having trouble hearing. A sound like waves smashing against the shore filled her head, and she felt like throwing up. The terror that had filled her that night when she'd struck Father Thibault, the loss of control she'd been fighting ever since, began to flood through her. A strangled moan was wrenched from her throat, and her sight began to dim. Even then, confusion crowded her mind; if he hadn't even known who'd been killed, why did he have any of the horsehair left behind?

There were concerned murmurs in the crowd. The sounds rolled over her, muffled, questioning, afraid.

"Who else?" the priest continued. "Who else among us would do this? Who else among you would attack a man of the cloth, as she has, driving Father Thibault from us? Who else among us was seen as a black mare while her family burned to death?"

The words were striking her like physical blows. He had all but admitted to her that he'd murdered her family, but it was all she could do to stop from shifting into that hated form in front of everyone, and her tongue, thickening in her mouth, refused to work.

"Look to your neighbours! Who else among us flaunts the Lord's plan? Comports herself as a man rather than the girl she is?" There was a deep note of disgust in his voice. "This creature I have seen with my own eyes trying to tempt your daughters into sin, approaching them as a man does!"

Shame bloomed in her—all those sermons she'd endured, that had twisted her feelings into herself, until her parent's deaths had freed her from having to attend. She panted, eyes closed, trying to calm herself, trying to push the tremors away, the spasms that threatened to wrench her sinews into a new shape.

She could hear the murmurs, but could not grasp the tone of them.

"It is past time we cast out this evil!" the priest roared again, silencing the crowd. "Past time you all cast out the sin that you've allowed to flourish here!"

Angelique leaned over onto her hands, breathing raggedly, afraid to look at her neighbours and relatives, afraid to see judgment there. These people knew what she was, they all knew—surely they would not believe her capable of killing Louis?

Could they think anything else if she changed in front of them?

With every ounce of will she could muster, she fought that rending pain. She dug her fingers into the soil and sucked in a deep breath, drawing in the silty, vegetative scent of the lake.

The murmuring among the crowd returned, growing louder now, but this time she detected a note of surprise.

"Then what's this, Frère?" shouted Cyprien, unexpectedly close. Angelique's eyes flew open in shock, and there he and Joseph stood, her cousin holding high a rusty scythe, and Joseph with his foot atop a muddy and cracked barrel. Barely legible under the filth, *buffalo tongues* was stencilled on the cask.

There was a feeling like diving into cold water, and suddenly she no longer felt the pressure of impending transformation. Forgetting her pride, she scuttled away on all fours from the priest toward Cyprien before she felt safe to stand.

Bourassa's face was mottled in rage, and he peeled his lips back in a snarl as he pointed a trembling finger at her. "Cast her out! Cast out this devil!"

Cyprien's eyes blazed under his brown curls, and suddenly Angelique saw that the scythe was not rusty—it was crusted in dried blood. Raising his voice to be heard over the ripples of confused conversation from over a hundred throats, Cyprien jabbed the scythe at the priest and turned to address his community.

"Louis and Joseph were carrying this barrel to my auntie's home last night, but it was missing when we found Louis's remains."

Joseph was nodding, his furious gaze fixed on the priest. "Ay, and it was in the priest's quarters, along with this scythe." He pointed a thick finger at the tool Cyprien held. Angelique held her breath as she saw person after person register the dried blood on its blade.

Faces swivelled toward the priest, who was shaking his head angrily. Uncertain looks were being exchanged among neighbours.

Angelique took a deep breath and stepped forward.

"The fire," she croaked, her voice still not working properly. She cleared her throat and tried again, her mouth twisting with grief as she remembered the flames. "He was there. He was in the lake. Watching when my family died. He must have barred the door. No one could explain why they weren't able to get out." Her voice trailed away into a sob, and Cyprien was suddenly beside her, an arm around her shoulders. He glared at the priest, still clutching the scythe.

Bourassa looked out over his flock, seeing the troubled looks, and his confidence seemed to fade a bit.

"I know that barrel as well!" Angelique was shocked to see Cecil had drawn closer, shocked to hear him raising his voice in support despite his moment of suspicion earlier. "I brought that cursed thing back from Fort Pitt." He wheeled to face Bourassa.

"Why would you have this?" he cried out, his voice breaking. "What did you do?" Bourassa stepped back at the expression on Cecil's face, looking uncertain.

Angelique reeled in shock. Bourassa had viciously murdered a man, just to frame her? How long had he been planning this? What kind of sickness was in him to drive him so far?

Feeling the mood shift, Bourassa fixed her in his hateful gaze again. "I lost *everything*. Everything, because of you." Silence rippled through the crowd until all they could hear was the gentle crash of waves on the sand. Angelique stared at him, shocked.

"You? You lost everything?" she demanded. She felt a scream rising in her throat, but she forced it down. The priest was trembling, his huge watery eyes filled with more malice than she'd thought any human could hold.

"Father Thibault was going to make sure I got out of this pestilent land, but you drove him out! The church has refused, year after year after year, to move me!" he fairly spat, before fixing Cyprien with a gaze as baleful as any he'd directed at her. "It was meant to be *you*," he said hoarsely, his voice trembling with rage. "With them gone, killing you would have broken her."

Her mind flew back to that moment when Bourassa had rounded the corner of the church and seen Cyprien, his shock at seeing him there, a brief expression before he'd brought himself under control.

Her stomach dropped again. Louis had been a mistake, driven there by drunken fear when he and Joseph had dropped the cask. Bourassa must have been waiting in the pen for Cyprien to use the outhouse. She saw again the slashed and trampled remains, the savagery with which Louis had been met.

Suddenly the crowd surged forward, men pulling Cecil away from the priest; he'd lunged at the man, but only managed to grab a fold of dark cloth before being restrained. Louis's twin was incoherent with rage, straining to reach Bourassa, who was cowering now, the priest's pale face grey and slack with defeat. With the focus on Cecil, no one saw Louis's wife in time as she, in a black cotton dress buttoned up to just below her chin, raked her nails across the priest's eyes, drawing blood.

Angelique swayed, completely drained. Cyprien dropped the blood-ied scythe and caught her as she slipped toward the ground. Joseph peered at her with worry.

"She'll be okay," Cyprien told the other man, then said it again to her. "You'll be okay, Angelique. It's over."

She laughed weakly and closed her eyes, wanting nothing more than to let herself rest. "Oh, Cyprien," she mumbled, and he brought his face closer to hear her faint words. "This is just the beginning."

1913

Sharp and abrupt as a scythe cut, the grass that had been rasping against her ankles ended. With a gentle squeeze of her knees, Angelique signalled her horse to stop, straddling that liminal space.

Stretching before them as far as the horizon was churned-up brown earth, and flocks of birds darting down to snatch up exposed insects or, in some cases, even larger prey. She made the mistake of gazing up from under her wide-brimmed felt hat at the sky to watch a hawk dive toward the trampled soil and found herself dazzled for a moment. Blinking away tears, she located the hawk rising above, an unlucky mouse in its talons.

Despite a steady wind, her cotton shirt stuck to her back under her beaded leather vest. Her knees ached, the large knobby knuckles of her hands holding her reins throbbed, her sit bones complained, and she briefly wondered if she was going to fall apart completely, her final act of transformation simply a bloodless dislocation of all her limbs. She doubted her horse would appreciate it.

At least her teeth, those that remained, were still good. She was chewing rat root for a low cough she'd developed a few days ago, one that built up slowly like the frothy foam on the shores of manitow-sàkahikan in summer, until she was forced to hack and heave and spit out phlegm tinged slightly pink.

"Thank you for humouring me, Elzear." She flashed him a wry smile.

Elzear sat with the envious ease of youth on his painted horse, regarding the buffalo trail with a contented expression. The Cree-Métis man was easily fifty years her junior. "My grandfather always spoke well of you."

"Did he, now." She grinned and reached up to remove her hat, wiping sweat from her brow and raising her wrinkled cheeks to the sky, her eyes closed for a moment. The wind cooled her scalp under her braided white hair, but the fierce sun pricked almost painfully.

He coughed uncomfortably, and she could hear him shift slightly in his saddle. "Well"— he sounded a bit embarrassed—"he respected you."

She laughed, a sharp bark of amusement, before replacing her hat. Raising an eyebrow, she looked him in face and repeated, "Did he, now?" Cyprien had known her too well for "respect" to really apply.

Elzear's face split into a shy smile, his young, unlined brown face reminding her of her father. An echo of that old loss returned for a moment, and she imagined small feet digging into her hip bones, a childish giggle in her ear. It hurt, and it always had, but she let the feelings wash through her, swirling around her heart like a song.

She returned her gaze to the horizon, an insistent pressure building in her chest again. She heard a liquid peal in the distance, followed by an answering one closer by. Her eyes were not as good as they once were, but she finally found the little brown head among clods of torn-up earth. For a moment her vision wavered. Of late she'd found tears came easily. But this time it was happiness that filled her, until her scalp nearly tingled with it.

"Well câpân, go tell them where the herd is." He looked at her with faint alarm.[50]

....

50 Capan is an intergenerational Cree term used by a great-grandparent to address their great-grandchild, and vice versa. This man is Cyprien's grandson, but by using the term, she creates more generational distance between them while claiming him as her direct kin.

"We should both get back to camp," he suggested uncertainly, uncomfortable with contradicting her.

Angelique shook her head and smiled gently. "Don't worry, I'll catch up." The buffalo bird caught her attention again, and she fell silent.

Clearly unhappy, Elzear nodded and gently tapped his mount's sides, turning back toward the camp. His horse broke into a trot, and when he reached the top of the hill, he twisted around in his saddle to check on her.

Her saddle was empty, but there, perched between the horse's ears, barely visible at this distance, was a small bird with a brown head.

"BUFFALO BIRD" EXPLORATION

Indigenous futurisms can, as Rebecca Roanhorse puts it, "rewrite the past to reimagine the present" (2018). If one is a believer in parallel universes, it is entirely possible, even probable, that what we imagine already exists out there in one of these infinite permutations parallel to our reality.

What is alternate about "Buffalo Bird" is not imagining that the ability to shape-shift is possible; this is not the point of divergence from our current universe. Indeed, transformation is the one true constant of our reality, and it happens all around us at all points along that fourth dimension we label time. As Leroy Little Bear points out, "existence consists of energy. All things are animate, imbued with spirit, and in constant motion" (2000). He describes this as Blackfoot metaphysics, a worldview encompassing the fundamental nature of reality (2016). Transformation, shape-shifting, are central aspects to Métis worldview as well, whether the transformed/transformer is Elder Brother or Chi-Jean or some more ordinary being.

Working from Métis otipêyimisow-itâpisiniwin, transformation and shape-shifting are real and a constant potential in everything. I ground this story in the truth of this worldview, but further, I assert that this transformational potential is a characteristic of what I am calling Métis futurisms. Transformation is rendered ordinary, although specific acts of transformation can be extraordinary in terms of their impact.

This story imagines a successful nêhiyaw-pwat (Iron Confederacy) resistance to Canadian expansionism. The buffalo are not exterminated or removed, and neither are the Métis or our allies. The reader is invited to think about what this might mean for the present, what could be different, what could be the same. Buried deep in this story is a call to resurrect the nêhiyaw-pwat, which was never formally dissolved.

I also draw heavily on revenge as a theme, in part to pay homage to the very real resistance that Métis and other Indigenous peoples continue to mount against colonial forces, and in part simply because it is satisfying to imagine. I draw on Tekahionwake (E. Pauline Johnson) and her short story, "A Red Girl's Reasoning," as well as the film of the same name by Elle-Máijá Tailfeathers, both of which foreground the autonomy and self-determination of Indigenous women in resisting the colonial violence of white men (Johnson 1893; Tailfeathers 2012). Over a century apart, these stories enact revenge in different, yet equally devastating ways. I deliberately invoke the stomping death meted out by Deer Woman both in the ancient tales and as envisioned in contemporary storytelling (LaPensée 2017).

MICHIF MAN

Excerpt from a talk by Shelley Vogel, "Michif Man from Lac Ste. Anne: Microhistory or Mythology?", presented at the 2020 Native American and Indigenous Studies Association (NAISA) annual conference in Toronto, Ontario.[51]

It could be said that the origin story of Michif Man from Lac Ste. Anne began with a goring by a radioactive bison, but if we begin there, can we understand the man behind the mythology?

We are all familiar with certain academics who have written extensively on Michif Man as a "modern trickster tale," classifying the accounts as "Indigenous storytelling." Some have allowed that he may have been an actual person whose exploits were exaggerated for dramatic effect. Our research, however, has been able to demonstrate that the stories we do have may in fact have been downplayed to make them seem *less* extraordinary.

Although we focused on a short period of time, from 1955 to 1960, and on a series of relatively minor episodes centred on a population at the margins—namely Lac Ste. Anne Métis living in Edmonton in the mid-twentieth century—we did not take an episodic microhistory approach, but rather engaged in a limited but systematic microhistory analysis.[52] It was absolutely necessary to reconstruct individual and social relationships in a restricted geographical setting using archival records,

51 This conference never happened due to COVID-19, which makes it a perfect place to situate a talk that also never happened.
52 (Gregory 1999, 102–103).

as this was the only way we were able to demonstrate that Michif Man did, in fact, exist.[53]

Imagine, if you will, a tornado—forming, touching down, and wreaking havoc. The forces that create a tornado are mostly invisible to us. When we witness the power of this phenomenon, we are seeing the way in which these invisible forces affect whatever they come into contact with. Take this slide, for example. We cannot *see* the winds, but we can witness all the detritus they have picked up, including Dorothy's little house there, and that very surprised cow, twirling round and round in the maelstrom! Though invisible to our human eyes, there are ways to track these forces using modern weather imaging technologies that *see* in ways we are not capable of.

For this project, we did not use Doppler radar or satellite data. Rather, we dove into the archives and found mysteries: unexplained events and unsolved crimes, miracles and mayhem. News reports, police case files, insurance claims, interviews. We began to see a distinct pattern of *absence* at the centre of all these events that tied them together.

Like the recurring character of Not Me in this *Family Circus* comic, it is clear that *someone* was causing things to happen. In the comic, it is almost always the children at fault, but in the case of the events we tracked, Not Me seems to be a real figure, if not literally invisible—family members assure us that, unlike H.G. Wells's Invisible Man, Michif Man was not capable of vanishing from sight—then *retroactively unseen*.

The vast lacunae in any official documentation for Michif Man has stymied most traditional historical research, forcing our team to rely almost entirely on interviews with his aged relatives who, for reasons we do not fully understand, are the only ones who remember him directly

53   (Eckert and Jones 2002, 5–16). Eckert and Jones discuss the way in which a focus on micro-worlds gives prominence to "new actors" and avoided places, moving them to the centre of historical inquiry. This story is a work of fiction, but as much as I could, I included accurate details of the "everyday" variety, making this a work of (micro)historical fantasy.

at all. Of the two documents we could find to prove he existed, one was in a personal collection, and the other in an archive that had yet to digitize and dump their collection. In every other instance where collections were updated and the paper copies destroyed, it seems the people in charge of digitization uniformly failed to include any documents related to Michif Man.

Thus, we were able to obtain a hard copy of a baptismal certificate from the Lac Ste. Anne parish for Solomon François Gabriel Callihoo dated January 8, 1923, and a receipt for antibiotics for the same person, which was in the possession of his sister, who paid the bill and kept it in the (forlorn) hope of one day collecting. Both are pictured here. No vital statistics information seems to exist beyond this.

Relatives have informed us that Michif Man was known to them as "Franky."

Franky was born to Ann-Marie Belcourt and Solomon Callihoo at the Lac Ste. Anne Métis settlement in Alberta sometime in 1922. He had six older brothers and one younger sister, all of whom have complete vital statistics records. Interviewees seem to agree that Franky was "a massive pain" who often engaged in daredevil behaviour resulting in broken bones and other injuries. This could be a result of attempting to stand out among seven siblings and many more cousins in the community. His attention-seeking behaviour eventually wore on his parents, who sent him at thirteen to work a trapline with a great-uncle in the Northwest Territories, near Fort Smith.

His return at sixteen coincided with the outbreak of World War II. Franky apparently took a neighbour's horse and rode into Edmonton to enlist, beginning his wartime service as a sapper with the Royal Canadian Engineers one year before Tommy Prince was to join the same outfit.

The neighbour, Baptiste Letendre, was Franky's mother's second maternal cousin. Baptiste's grandson told us that his grandfather complained about the loss of his horse until his passing in 1972. This is a picture of Baptiste with his horse, whom he named Jim.

No one knows what became of Jim.

We have considered the possibility that some records related to Franky could exist in physical form in Normandy, but our SSHRC grant could not cover the related expense of verifying this. Other research teams should consider that as Frankly lied about his age, he very likely also lied about his name, so it may be impossible to link him to any records at all.

Interviewees indicate that Franky returned to Lac Ste. Anne between 1946 and 1949, with substantial disagreement on the exact timing. He probably moved to Edmonton around 1951 and did odd jobs. His risk-taking behaviour had apparently not lessened, and he was prone to fights. However, interviewees note that in almost all cases, the fights were begun by white men, to whom the sight of Métis enjoying themselves was apparently a goad too intense to bear. He was arrested for being drunk and disorderly on a number of occasions. Somehow, he was able to get his hands on one of his many mug shots, which he presented to a cousin as a tongue-in-cheek gift.

This is the only known photo of Michif Man. As you'll note, he was tall, extremely well dressed for a man of his meagre means, and quite handsome, even with one eye swollen shut.

We now know from declassified documents that the US Army conducted a number of highly unethical tests in Western Canada from the 1950s onward. In 1953, six kilograms of zinc cadmium sulphide were sprayed over Winnipeg, Manitoba, and then a decade later, in Medicine Hat and Suffield, Alberta.[54] Suffield bore the brunt of the worst tests, as in 1964, a radioactive material, Phosphorus-32, and a deadly nerve agent, VX, were sprayed over the town.[55] Canada also subjected three thousand

....

54   (Committee on Toxicology 1997).
55   (Martino-Taylor 2017).

volunteers at the Suffield military base to mustard gas experiments during the Second World War.[56]

It has yet to be revealed which government was involved in irradiating a small group of Plains bison at the Elk Island National Park in early 1955, or what the purpose of the experiments may have been. We also have no idea what Franky was doing there that he managed to be gored in the right buttock by one of the radioactive bison. The date on the receipt for antibiotics is April 13, and we posit that it would have taken him four to six weeks to recover from his wound. By late May of 1955, Michif Man had been born. For some reason, stories about him taper off after 1960, which is why we ended our research there.

We agree with Sabyasachi Bhattacharya that history from below "means more than just the enlargement of the scope of history" and that it "may involve a break with the nationalist paradigm."[57] In this case, we believe that tracking the history of Michif Man allows us to continue to challenge the long-standing characterization of Métis peoples as passive (re)actors to colonization, and to reiterate that the People Who Own Themselves engaged in extraordinary actions of personal and communal agency.

1955: Edmonton, Alberta

He'd been fired, of course. Too many days in the hospital, and when he'd snuck out on the fourth day to avoid the bill, hobbling over to his foreman to insist he be put back on the lineman digging crew, the man acted like he'd never seen Franky before and hollered at him to get the hell out

---

56   (Snipper 2001).
57   (Bhattacharya 1983, 7–8).

of his office![58] Even refused him severance pay, the bastard. Franky had slammed the door on his way out, and it must have been hung improperly or something, because it fell clear off the hinges when he did. He'd had to scoot out of there faster than he'd have liked, to avoid a lickin' for that bit of showmanship.

When things were at their worst, he liked to figure out his next steps on a full stomach. He only had a few dollars to his name, but a man couldn't go looking for a job while oozing desperation. A good suit and a good steak—that'd been his winning combination on the job search for a long time now.

The coffee came as soon as he gingerly perched himself on the bright-red vinyl upholstery of a floor-mounted stool in front of the service counter. The blond waitress gave him an unfriendly look and put the mug down a bit hard, hot liquid sloshing over the edge. As Franky reached for it, she pulled it away a space.

"You'll have to order if you want to sit here," she told him flatly in an unpleasant nasally voice. He was used to this sort of treatment; a lot of these môniyâws figured a half-breed like him didn't have any money.

He made a show of pulling out his ten dollars, peeled two bills off, and slid them on the counter, giving her his most winning smile. "I'll take your biggest T-bone steak, rare, and go ahead and throw a couple of fried eggs on it. You can keep the change."

She took the money and, still eyeing him with mistrust, nudged the cup toward him as she hollered over her shoulder at the cook. "Slab of moo, let him chew, and flop two on top!"[59]

---

58 (Belcourt 2006, 75). Herb Belcourt talks about drilling holes for power poles by hand for sixty cents an hour in 1947. I took liberties with the timing, as this work was likely going on throughout the province into the mid-fifties.
59 (Smiley 2012).

Still trying his best to radiate charm, he reached for the coffee mug. With a sudden snap, the handle broke off and coffee spilled across the counter, splashing onto his pants before he could hop off his stool.

"Oh, look at what you've done!" the waitress cried, snatching the broken mug away and angrily wiping up the mess.

"Me? Good thing your coffee is room temperature or I'd be burned!" he responded hotly. "This is a hundred-dollar suit!"[60]

The waitress made a little snort of disbelief and stalked off in a huff to the far end of the counter as he grabbed a couple of napkins and futilely dabbed at the stains. Cursing under his breath, he tossed the wadded-up paper into a trash can near the door, then took his seat again. He could smell his steak sizzling on the grill, and spill or no spill, it was going to be a fine meal!

The waitress returned and set a new mug of coffee in front of him just as hard as the first time, letting the liquid slop over the sides. Murmuring a bit of an insincere thank-you, Franky reached for it, only to have her pull it away again.

"You'll have to order if you want to sit here," she said, giving him the unfriendly look he was starting to grow accustomed to from her.

"What are you talking about?" he asked, taken aback. "I already paid for my meal!"

Her rouged mouth twisted, and she crossed her arms across her chest. Keeping a distrustful eye on him, she called over her shoulder, "Clarence! We got an Indian cracking wise here, trying to get a free meal!"

---

60   (Palmer 2001, 288). An Eaton's suit by Michael of London went for $99 in 1955, which, while on the low end of couture suits (some of which were as expensive as $350) still represented an almost obscene amount for a working-class Métis! Contrast that with an off-the-rack wool suit from Simpsons-Sears, which cost between $44 and $56, a price that would still have been out of reach for many. I want to highlight that Franky was a bit of a fop.

A large man in a cook's apron came out from the kitchen, with huge hairy forearms and a serious expression. Franky was on his feet, never mind the twinge of pain from his accident, staring warily at the man.

"Mister, I don't want no trouble, but I gave that lady there two dollars for a steak with some eggs on top, and I don't appreciate being fleeced!"

The cook glanced at the waitress for confirmation and received a tight headshake of negation. His eyes narrowed, and Franky felt a familiar surge of anger. It didn't seem to matter how he dressed or how politely he behaved; when it came to a môniyâw's word against his, that was that.

Other patrons in the diner were craning their necks to see what the commotion was about, and Franky could feel the back of his neck heating up. The cook jabbed a thick finger at the door.

"Out."

He was hungry, out of work, and the whole situation stunk. It was petty, but Franky kicked at his abandoned stool as he turned to leave. With a groaning clang, the stool's hollow metal base snapped completely off, the upholstered red seat bouncing loudly on the floor once before rolling to a stop against the wall.

The three of them stared in shock at the damage, and the diner was absolutely silent. Franky felt his anger drain out of him, and he held his hands up in wordless apology before backing slowly out of the restaurant.

As he stepped out onto the sidewalk, he heard a bell ding. "Slab of moo, let him chew, two flopped on top!" called the other cook.

"What the heck are you talking about, Robbie?" came the faint voice of the waitress. "I never put in for a steak!"

No one gave Franky a further look.

Things just got worse from there. It seemed no matter where he went, folks were acting queerly, turning their backs on him for a moment, then turning back and acting surprised to see him, or greeting him again like they hadn't said the exact thing just before. He lost two more dollars that way, trying to get someone to serve him an actual meal, only to have them forget and claim he hadn't paid them.

At the last restaurant he tried, he slammed the door in frustration, and the entire front window shattered into a million clear shards—*and* the entire door came off its hinges! He'd held it in front of him, not really sure what to do with the damn thing, shame flooding him for causing such a scene. There was no point trying to put it back, so he tossed it aside, then watched in sick fascination as it flew over the heads of a crowd of pedestrians and smashed into the hood of a cherry-red Chevrolet parked along the street.

The sound of crunching metal banished the sense of unreality that enveloped him like a fog, and he quickly shoved his hands into his pockets and walked off before the police or the owner of that car showed up. His head was spinning, but no one came chasing after him. What the hell was going on?

Three days of this, and he thought he might be going mad.

He stopped going to restaurants, eating almost exclusively at Lovatt's corner store, where he could take a sandwich to the counter and pay for it before he was forgotten.[61] For over a year, Franky had been renting a dingy room at The Bernard next door, and had chatted with Norman Lovatt almost daily as he purchased cigarettes or sweets. Having the man ask him over and over if he was new in town filled him with despair; he started feeling like a ghost, stuck repeating the same events.

....

61   (Herzog 2016). The original Lovatt General Store opened on Jasper Avenue in 1900 and was run by family members into the 1950s. There is a picture on this website of a building called The Bernard that seemed to have a business front on bottom with either rooms or offices up top. I haven't been able to track down any information on it, so I'm just going to take a stab at it and make it a rooming house.

He figured he'd finally caught a break when he applied for a job as a bottling machine operator at the Prairie Rose Manufacturing Company down on 96th. He had a great chat with the co-owner, Mike Shandro, who made a point of saying he didn't mind hiring Indians, and was offered a job for ninety cents an hour.[62] Franky knew for a fact that this was almost forty cents less than Shandro was paying white men; he'd found out about the job in the classifieds and the wage was listed right there.[63] Still, it was better than nothing.

Mike left to get a bottle of Orange Crush for them to celebrate with, but when he returned, he looked at the bottle in his hand with confusion. Franky's stomach sank. Mike looked back up at him with a friendly smile.

"You here for the job?"

Shoulders slumped in defeat, Franky shook his head and left.

Election fever was in the air, though Franky didn't see what the point was. The Socreds had been in power almost as long as he'd been alive, and Albertans seemed to worship Ernest Manning. Maybe Ernie'd die of old age in office, and they'd embalm him like Lenin and stick him in a mausoleum out front of the Legislature building.

His spirits were awfully low, and he found himself wandering the streets aimlessly like some sort of lost spirit, oblivious to the ripples he caused as he passed. Never mind his life was falling down around his ears—it'd take the end of the world to get him out of his fancy suits. Having grown up wearing nothing but the most worn out hand-me-downs, looking clean, kempt, and well dressed meant a lot to Franky.

---

62   (Tingley 2009, 16).

63   (Department of Labour, Economics and Research Branch 1955, 58). Standard rate for a bottling-machine operator in Alberta was $1.29 in 1955, the highest rate in the country, probably due to the oil boom that began in 1947. The lowest rate of ninety-nine cents in the Atlantic provinces was still higher than what Franky is being paid in this story.

As he passed them, women in their tight sheath dresses and flowing swing dresses would smile at him, with his perfectly styled hair and his broad handsome face, then affect a kind of pout when he looked right through them. Any men accompanying these women would scowl at him threateningly, but he didn't see them, either, and the moment he was out of their sight, it was like Franky had never been there at all.

Normally he walked these streets like a blustering peacock, never one to let the môniyâwak make him feel small. He would flirt outrageously with any woman, and he was quick with his fists if her guy objected. It was one of the ways he made himself feel seen, and being seen was exactly what had been taken from him. He supposed he might have better heeded his capan's warnings about pride.

He didn't notice that his feet had brought him to his cousin's house at Jasper Place until he was at the door. Feeling a bit foolish standing there, he knocked.

Sam answered the door and gave him a big smile, clapping a huge hand on Franky's shoulder and pulling him inside. Too surprised to resist, his head whirling, he barely heard his cousin's heartfelt greeting.

"You okay, Franky?" Sam asked. "You look like you've seen a ghost!"

"I feel like I *am* a ghost," Franky mumbled in misery, but Sam didn't seem to hear him.

"Boy, am I glad to see you! You're just the person I need right now. You looking for work?"

Hand still on his shoulder, Sam guided Franky toward the basement, full of all kinds of different chairs piled on top of one another, unsteadily stacked. There was barely any room to move around.

Sam let him go and gestured at the mess.

"Been upholstering these chairs by myself, and I could really use some help! I'm bringing in oh, six to eight dollars a chair, and if you're game, I'd split that with you eighty-twenty for the ones you finish."[64]

"Sixty-forty," Franky said automatically, sharp even in the funk he was in.

Sam grinned and clasped Franky's hand in his, shaking on it. Franky held on to the other man's hand like he was drowning, and the smile faded from Sam's face.

"You okay? You really don't look well."

"Sammy, I've had a hell of a week. You got anything to drink? And maybe something to eat that isn't a blasted sandwich?"

Sam didn't believe him at first, but after walking around town a bit, conducting experiments, it became clear to him Franky was telling the truth. Most people would forget the man existed the moment their attention was drawn away. They made their way back to Sam's place and sat on the steps, sharing a smoke.

"So why can't I forget your ugly mug?" Sam tried to sound jovial, but there was a thread of unease there. Franky shrugged, feeling unmoored and out of sorts. He stubbed the cigarette out and flicked the butt onto the sidewalk, exhaling into the cold air.

Just then, they saw their cousin Ambrose waving at them from across the street. Sam raised a hand in greeting, and Ambrose crossed over.

"You fellows got a smoke?" Ambrose asked once he was nearer. He was reed thin, and a bit bookish looking.

Franky was still staring off into the distance, looking melancholy, so Sam answered, "Last one, sorry."

---

64   (Belcourt 2006, 83–84). This is drawn directly from Herb's account of the basement upholstery business he began before he opened up Herb's Upholstery on Stony Plain Road in 1958.

"What's with him?" Ambrose jerked a thumb at Franky, and Sam raised a surprised eyebrow.

"Hey, what's that over there?" Sam asked, pointing back across the street. He'd quickly discovered during their experiments that a split second of distraction was all it usually took to get a person to forget about Franky.

Ambrose craned his neck, trying to see what Sam was talking about, then turned back, a suspicious look on his face. "I don't see nothing, cuz, quit fooling." He turned his attention back to Franky. "You okay? You look like someone stole your dog!"

Franky's head snapped up, and he stared intensely at Ambrose. "You remember me?" he demanded.

Ambrose gave him an annoyed look. "Quit messing with me, sheesh, that got old when I was still a kid."

Franky and Sam exchanged a quick, hopeful look. Sam stood and clapped Ambrose on the back, the smaller man still regarding them both with suspicion.

"Kitchen party tonight, m'boy, go spread the word!" Sam told him, and Ambrose broke out in a grin.

"Now that's more like it!" Ambrose rubbed his hands together and gave them a lopsided grin. "I'll go tell ma and the boys. You want us to bring anything?"

"Just as many of our relatives as you can find," Sam said, giving Ambrose a bit of a friendly push. "Be back in an hour!"

Franky watched their cousin dash off and looked up at Sam quizzically. "A party? Really?"

Sam waggled his eyebrows theatrically. "I have a theory. And anyway, are you really going to turn me down?"

"Franky, I think you might be cursed," Sam finally pronounced, as his wife busied herself making sure there was tea and bannock for the impromptu kitchen party. The house was packed to the rafters with raucous relatives, close and distant, and just like Sam had suspected, they could all see and remember Franky.

"That's just the half of it," Franky said miserably. Sam's eyes narrowed in interest.

Franky glanced around for something to use in his demonstration. He briefly considered the cast iron pan his cousin's wife had cooked bannock in, but on second thought, wasn't willing to deal with her wrath if it went wrong. He settled for a butter knife.

Holding the butter knife in his left hand, he gingerly pressed at its tip with the pointer finger of his right hand. The top of the knife bent with no resistance, easy as could be, until it was perpendicular.

Sam let out a whoop of amazement, throwing himself back in his chair and shaking his head, a huge grin across his face. That drew everyone's attention, and before he knew it, Franky was outside bending larger and larger objects while his relatives called out to one another, laughing and marvelling at the sight. At Sam's goading, they followed Franky down the street like a carnival procession, stopping right in front of a white Ford truck.

"Show us what you've got, Franky!" someone yelled, and he grinned back. Theatrically, he bent down and made a show of getting a good grip on the undercarriage before standing and effortlessly raising the front end with him. There was a reverent silence, then he let the truck back down gingerly, worried about bursting the tires.

He turned around to face his family and was met with sudden cheers and delighted laughter. He had to admit, his spirits were higher than they had been in a long time, so he thought he'd give them a bit more. Turning back around, he leaned down again and put his hands under the front end of the truck, this this time putting a little more of his back into it.

He was wholly unprepared to feel no more resistance than if he'd lifted the nose of a canoe out of the lake, and he became unbalanced, falling backwards as the truck flew up six feet or more into the air, before crashing down catastrophically into the middle of the street, right on its front end!

Metal and glass crunched, and the squeal of brakes pealed out as a car swerved hard to avoid the sudden obstacle, while his relatives scrambled away from the scene with hoots and hollers.

For the next few months he holed up in his cousin's basement, flying through the backlogged upholstery orders, sewing leatherette from Eaton's onto chairs, and then chesterfields, as easily as drawing his fingers through water. The cousins made more in three months than they'd normally make in a year.

When Franky needed something, he'd send a relative to get it for him so that his money didn't evaporate into The Distortion that seemed to surround him. That was what they were calling it, the way people forgot about him, the capital letters clearly noticeable in speech.

Lying on his back on the roof of Sam's house one night, puffing little clouds of smoke into the bruised violet skies above, Franky mused that he had more money than he knew what to do with, and that was an odd situation to be in. If times had been normal, he'd have bought a couple of bespoke suits so he didn't have to be so careful with the one navy-blue Michael of London suit he owned, but there didn't seem to be any point anymore. Who but relatives would even see him in it? Same with his dream of a cherry-red Chevrolet. Who was he going to impress? If he were being honest with himself, those things had been meant to prove that he was just as good as—maybe even *better* than—all those white men who curled up their lips at him like he was dirt.

In a way he supposed it was a bit freeing. He wanted for nothing; with help from his extensive family he ate whatever and whenever he wanted, he laughed and jigged and drank with them. No one followed him around department stores or shooed him out of the front of their shops when he ducked under the eaves to get out of the rain. He hadn't been in a fist fight in what felt like forever—he wouldn't dare, for fear of killing a man!—and he'd eventually stopped constantly scanning the space around him, senses extended to detect danger. Not being under constant belligerent or contemptuous surveillance, muscles in his body were unknotting that he'd never even realized *could* relax.

He could do things like breeze into the Paramount Theatre on Jasper Ave because the ticket clerk forgot he didn't buy a ticket. He'd been underwhelmed by *Rebel without a Cause*, not identifying with the main character the way he clearly was supposed to, but had seen *Abbott and Costello Meet the Mummy* three times, laughing his head off every time.

Maybe it was time to do a little more with the powers he'd been given by that buffalo spirit. At least, he was pretty sure that was where this had all started. Flicking the stub of his cigarette off the roof, Franky followed its arc downward, jumping into the backyard and landing with a satisfying thump. He couldn't leap tall buildings in a single bound, but he'd once managed an eight-foot hop, and besides, Superman wasn't real!

"Superman." He chuckled and shook his head. Then a thoughtful look crossed his face.

Sam took one look at him and roared in laughter. Franky's neck grew hot, and he shifted in embarrassment, his puffed-out chest deflating as his cousin doubled over, howling his mirth.

Looking down at himself, he didn't think he looked ridiculous at all! He was dressed in a pair of form-fitting slacks done up in royal-blue gabardine and a matching cotton royal-blue button-up with the sleeves rolled up to his well-muscled biceps the way he'd seen stars in the movies do. He had a moosehide vest over that with a floral bead pattern on the front, and wrapped around his trim waist was a red ceinture fléchée tied off to the right. He'd abandoned oxfords for a pair of hide moccasins with no fur edging so the legs of his pants tapered just overtop.

He'd handed his cousin Virginia seventy dollars, a prince's ransom, to bead a white infinity symbol on the vamp of each moccasin under a small wild rose, and a larger version on the back of his vest. The vest also had two large capital M's between his shoulders.

When Sam finally regained his composure and circled around Franky to get a full look, he touched the beading on his vest and asked, "MM? What's that, Mickey Mouse?" His voice shook with suppressed laughter, and Franky scowled a little.

"It stands for Michif Man!"

"Michif Man—what's that?"

Franky turned to face his cousin a bit heatedly. "I figure if I've got superpowers, then I should have a superhero name!"

Sam's eyebrows shot up. "Superhero? This ain't New York, Franky. This is small-beans Edmonton, and you're a half-breed no one can remember— how are you going to be a superhero?"

"Well," Franky said, a bit embarrassed, "I was sort of hoping you'd help me plan that out."

Sam was a good-natured man with a keen head for business and an endless supply of schemes. Franky could see the wheels turning.

"It's not *that* bad, is it?" Franky asked plaintively, gesturing to his outfit.

"Better than tights, I suppose." Sam shrugged, half lost in thought.

Excerpt from a talk by Shelley Vogel, "Michif Man from Lac Ste. Anne: Microhistory or Mythology?", presented at the 2020 Native American and Indigenous Studies Association (NAISA) annual conference in Toronto, Ontario.

Perhaps one of the most extraordinary feats attributed to Michif Man is the continuing existence of the Elizabeth and East Prairie Métis Settlements in northern Alberta.

Rather uniquely in Canada, Alberta passed a Métis Betterment Act in 1938 that set aside well over a million acres of land and created twelve Métis Settlements.[65] Over the years, however, four of these Settlements were removed by Orders in Council, including the Wolf Lake Métis Settlement in the early 1960s.[66]

Interviewees claim that in the 1950s, Métis community organizers Jim Brady and Malcolm Norris uncovered plans to close the Touchwood, Marlboro, Cold Lake, Elizabeth, and East Prairie Settlements, highlighted in pink on this map. In this decade, government policies focused on centralizing the Métis and "modernizing their social life," which often meant encouraging relocation to urban centres.[67]

Word of mouth had spread from relation to relation and then eventually to unrelated Métis about Michif Man and his superpowers, which apparently were super strength and something all interviewees refer to as The Distortion. The claim was that people not related to Michif Man would forget about him completely the moment they were distracted. It wasn't invisibility but, rather, a cloak of forgetfulness that surrounded him.

While The Distortion caused Michif Man to experience a rather unique type of isolation—after all, can one truly be called isolated when

---

65   (Federation of Métis Settlements 1979).
66   (MacEwan Joint Committee 1984, 7).
67   (Dobbin 1981, 183).

surrounded by many hundreds of relatives?—we're told he was coun-
selled by Elders to see it as a power as useful as his strength.

As an aside, literary scholars analyzing the Michif Man tales have
always read The Distortion as a rather heavy-handed metaphor for the
Métis as a "forgotten people" who were "hidden in plain sight."[68] Our
research team, however, has considered pairing with physicists to posit
scientific models that could explain The Distortion.[69]

Interviewees claim the events transpired thus: Brady and Norris sent
word through their networks about the location of enabling documents
related to the dissolution of the five Settlements. Michif Man's cousin,
Samuel Belcourt, accompanied him in broad daylight to the Alberta
Legislature in order to act as the distraction necessary for The Distortion
to be triggered. Michif Man was able to burn up a large number of documents before the smoke was noticed and all manner of firefighting units
and police showed up to the scene.

When asked why Michif Man did not simply continue burning all the
documents, we were informed by interviewees that his super strength
did not extend to invulnerability—he cut himself shaving like any other
man—so if he'd been shot before The Distortion was triggered, it wouldn't
have done him much good to be a forgotten corpse.

We were able to find transcripts of discussions related to the closing
of the Touchwood, Marlboro, and Cold Lake Settlements, but nothing at
all that mentioned Elizabeth or East Prairie. Of course, this is not proof
that this story about Michif Man is true; absence of evidence cannot be

----

68   (Daniels 1979). In this story I really wanted to explore the idea of being truly forgotten and
overlooked as potentially an emancipatory situation rather than one defined by loss or deprivation.
What would the implications be, for example, of not being "on the grid" bureaucratically? Of having no
government oversight at all and, therefore, not being subject to bureaucratic whims and regulations? As
Michif Man discovers, being "forgotten" has some advantages; he is not subject to as much intense racism, for example, and is in many senses more truly free than Métis have been since they were freemen.
69   (Ergin et al. 2010). This is an interesting article on a real invention. "Invisibility" technology tends
to use refractive and transformation optics akin to camouflaging. As The Distortion actually results in
people forgetting Michif Man, other scientific explanations would have to be found.

evidence of the absence claimed here—namely, that officials forgot all about their plans to close those two Settlements for some reason. Nonetheless, Michif Man is widely hailed as a hero for his putative actions.

Apparently, Brady then attempted to recruit Michif Man into the socialist struggle for national liberation, but was rebuffed. Michif Man was known for his intractable and almost parochial loyalty to and focus on his home community of Lac Ste. Anne, as well as his relations living in Edmonton. Perhaps his attempt to prevent the five Settlements from being closed was as much as he was willing to do outside of that, and his time abroad during the Second World War was as outward looking as he wanted to be in his lifetime. However, Brady and Michif Man shared an ad hoc approach to reducing the suffering of individuals and confronting—or, in Michif Man's case, punishing—those responsible for the misery.[70]

The bulk of Michif Man's reported feats centred on improving the lives of Métis in Edmonton. Records of their debts would mysteriously disappear, leaving people free and clear. Welfare clerks were reprimanded frequently for strange discrepancies in funds distributed, without being able to locate where the overpayments were happening. We located hundreds of documents, including correspondence between different branches of the government, complaining of the way in which Métis affairs in Edmonton seemed to be almost universally mishandled to the benefit of "the half-breeds." An intergovernmental investigation was actually launched in 1960, with some fairly harsh accusations suggesting collusion between white clerks and Métis clientele, but nothing was ever proven and, in fact, many of the clerks were found to be "properly" antipathic toward Métis in general. No one could explain why this was happening only in Edmonton.

....

70   (Dobbin 1981, 199–200). Dobbin details some of the instances of organized resistance in La Ronge like the "bubble-gum gang" and brawls that Brady was involved in to defend Native people, as well as the care taken to ensure drunks ejected from bars in the winter made it home safely.

A new architectural trend among Métis homeowners in Edmonton bloomed in the late fifties which some have named "Métis Rococo," featuring intricate naturalist motifs akin to flower beadwork carved into exteriors and interiors of homes, then painted in bright colours. It has often been noted that the dimensions of these carvings exactly match an average adult human finger, as though someone had simply pushed a digit *through* the wood itself. No tool has been found that would explain the uniformity of this measurement, nor has the style been successfully attributed to any specific craftsperson, and all attempts to recreate the style have failed.

Insurance claims provided particularly interesting corroboration for Michif Man stories, as an unusual number of vehicles were found flipped violently onto their roofs as though tossed by a tornado, with no disturbance in the weather that could explain it. However, when we showed these documents to interviewees, numerous insuree claimants were identified as men who had been known to behave offensively toward Métis.

Interviewees pointed us toward another line of research which we successfully followed up on: bizarre home explosions! In 1955, the Edmonton Electric Lighting and Power Company's Rossdale plant switched from coal to natural gas; from that point on, natural gas became a much more common source of heat in Edmonton homes.[71] Apparently, as many as forty homes "exploded" between 1955 and 1960, disasters which were attributed to faulty natural gas pipes.

However, we were able to prove that only 5 percent of the affected homes had natural gas installed, and in the damage reports, inspectors described scenes that resembled cataclysmic vandalism, as though, as one inspector put it, "someone drove a damn bulldozer through every structural support in the house."

....

71 (Alberta Energy n.d.).

Interviewees tell us that these homes were owned by men who had sexually assaulted Métis women. Michif Man had apparently been strongly urged by Elders never to resort to physical violence against any white man, as he would be unable to prevent retaliation against Métis who did not have his superpowers. Thus, he confined himself to destroying their homes. As it seemed impossible for any human to cause so much damage, suspicion never fell upon the Métis community, and in many cases, the men who had committed the assaults became rather fervent churchgoers who did not reoffend.

There are many more stories of feats of strength, stealth, and generosity attributed to Michif Man. The living conditions of Métis in Edmonton during this time improved considerably, even though family allowance and old age pensions typically accounted for half of a family's income in the fifties.[72] This fact confuses a lot of people, as it seems to suggest nothing much was changing, but it should be understood that reliance on welfare among Métis was not stigmatized, but rather, seen as an obligation of the government as a form of reparations for destroying Métis self-sufficiency. In any case, welfare monies were never intended to allow Métis to lift themselves out of poverty, and there was almost no incentive to stop collecting them.[73] Many attempts were made to discover what "illegal" activities Edmonton Métis could be involved in that would explain the overall economic rise of this community, to no avail.

These stories may seem underwhelming to those of us accustomed to the hyperbolic feats of comic book superheroes, but our research demonstrates that Michif Man used his superpowers in culturally relevant ways that fulfilled the needs of reciprocity, kinship, and community. As he was clearly unable to receive acclaim or fame outside of his community, he directed his efforts toward raising up the whole people. In

72   (Dobbin 1981, 185).
73   (Shewell 2004, 228–259).

doing so, he aided in extraordinary communal acts of resistance against ongoing settler colonial violence against Métis people, and circumvented or outright subverted bureaucratic processes intended to subjugate, discipline, or punish Métis who refused to assimilate into a Canadian model of citizenship.[74]

1960: Edmonton, Alberta

It was a fine day, he thought to himself as he strolled along Jasper Avenue, enjoying the warm sunshine and the endless azure expanse above him. Franky spotted his reflection in a storefront window and smiled; no one who'd known him before the accident would have recognized him now, and not just because they couldn't! Gone were the overpriced, fancy suits, and he'd retired his admittedly ridiculous superhero costume just a few months after creating it. Now he was comfortably dressed in jeans, moccasins, and a cotton T-shirt.

But it wasn't just his manner of dress. His whole life, he'd felt he needed to prove himself, and so he'd pushed himself to take more and more risks. Now, he no longer felt that pressure. When he was called upon to help a relation, there was genuine thankfulness for his actions, but he wasn't treated like a hero or a saviour. At first that had felt a bit unfair to him, until he realized it really didn't matter. The love and care that his family and community showed him ensured his needs were always met; accolades wouldn't fill him up any further. Besides, he knew that even if he had never been given his powers, his people would have continued to take care of him and of each other, the way they had always done.

---

74   (Bokahker and Iacovetta 2009, 407–434).

Ironically, he'd become a much gentler man. No longer always on the defensive, no longer always angry at the constant barrage of prejudice and contempt he'd grown up facing from white society, a society that he no longer existed in at all. After a few years he'd stopped feeling like a ghost. Surrounded at all times by people who understood and related to him, he realized that it was these white people, in their unceasing drive to dominate every aspect of the world around them, unmoored from the reciprocal obligations that kept Métis life in balance, who were the real ghosts.

He thrust his hands into his pockets and started whistling a little tune, "Orange Blossom Special," smiling at passersby even though their eyes slid past him almost immediately. Up ahead, a truly radiant brown-skinned woman in a bright-yellow summer dress was walking along, staring into every shop window intently. Her long brown hair was tied loosely into a careless braid tossed over her shoulder, and she kept pushing flyaway strands out of her face impatiently as the downtown wind gusted and dropped, gusted and dropped again. As he neared, she glanced up at him, and he smiled as he passed by, admiring her handsome features.

She scowled at him. "You got a staring problem, mister?"

He stopped dead in his tracks and turned around to face her in surprise. Her eyes hadn't slid off him.

She thrust her chin up and gave him a wary look. "I seen you staring at me since you crossed the street over there." Her reflexive lip point felt like a stone dropped into his stomach. The Distortion wasn't working, *because she was related to him*!

He sighed to himself and shook his head ruefully; so many beautiful women in the world, and the only ones who even knew he existed were his cousins.

Her wary eyes softened a little when he didn't seem likely to do her any harm. "Where are you from?" she asked, with a little questioning nod upwards with her chin. What she was really asking was, are you a half-breed, too?

"Lac Ste. Anne," he answered, "but I've been living here a long time. My parents are Ann-Marie Belcourt and Solomon Callihoo."

"Oh ah!" She brightened. "I just moved here, me, from Fort Smith. My dad's Dene, but my ma's a Callihoo. Helene."

Franky pursed his lips in thought for a moment, "Was her mom Sophie-Anne Letendre? Married to Samson Callihoo?"

She nodded, surprised, and Franky did some quick math in his head. "That'd make you, let's see … my fifth cousin. Well, half-cousin, I guess. Hardly related at all!" He laughed and held out a hand. "I'm Franky Callihoo."

She grinned and shook his hand. "Abigail Koe. Pleased to meet you."

It was a fine day, he thought. A fine day indeed.

"MICHIF MAN" EXPLORATION

The short story "The Token Superhero," by David Walker, is my inspiration for Michif Man (2015). In his piece, Walker rejects a post-racial approach to the superhero genre and imagines what life would truly be like for a Black superhero. When Alonzo Ramey is born with a genetic anomaly guaranteeing him superpowers, his life as a Black person is changed, but structural anti-Blackness remains. Ramey as Black Fist gets tired of being tokenized and retires, before finding out that he was an important role model to Black youth despite the way the overculture downplayed his successes and contributions. He takes up the mantle of Black Fist again, but approaches being a superhero in a different way this time, still battling supervillains, but also doing community organizing and youth outreach. I wanted to imagine a culturally rooted Métis superhero and see where that might take us.

I chose to set this story in the Golden Age of Comic Books, which waned rapidly after WWII. This was a period dominated by DC Comics and featured superheroes like Superman, Batman, Green Lantern, and Wonder Woman. Marvel kicked off the Silver Age in 1956 with a modern version of the Flash and continued on with superheroes like Spider-Man, the Fantastic Four, X-Men, and many others (Klock 2002, 2–3). However, since Indigenous peoples historically have been "left behind" by settler colonial sociopolitical policies, I wanted to metaphorically reference this by writing a superhero in a way that was also a "bit behind" for his time. Even, perhaps, a little *quaint*.

Golden Age comics featured larger-than-life characters, whereas the Silver Age eased into portrayals of more humanized and sometimes flawed characters against a grittier, more "real" backdrop of modernity.

For me, inserting Michif Man into the Golden Age represents the opportunity to engage in a bit of caricature. I want to play with archetypes!

This choice allows me to reflect on Métis agency within a coercive system as a People, rather than accepting the extreme individualism that superhero stories are particularly prone to. Though Franky is the purported protagonist of this story, in truth, he is not the main character—his community is. As Ryan Griffen, creator of the Aboriginal superhero Cleverman puts it, I wanted to create a character that is "able to teach moral lessons … not just for Aboriginal people, but for many more out there as well" (Griffen 2016). It is important to me that these moral lessons rebuff heteronormative, patriarchal, racist, and ableist settler colonialism from a specifically Métis worldview.

This story is about Métis people, not a Métis "superman," because too often Métis history is distorted through a lens that focuses on individuals like Louis Riel or Cuthbert Grant, a choice that erases women and Two-Spirit people and obscures the extended kinship systems that allow Métis people to survive violent settler colonialism.

I wrote the scenes with Shelley Vogel as though I were creating a real academic presentation on folktales from my community, trying to prove the truth behind stories that have been dismissed by mainstream white academia. However, Vogel is also cartoonish, somewhat of a parody. Her name is based on my own, so it's also an auto-parody. Her presentation is an extended tongue-in-cheek teasing of my colleagues, but it's also me applying the field the way I believe it actually would be if Michif Man had truly existed. Long after I wrote this story, Sarah Carter passed along an academic article about a Métis folk hero, Paulet Paul (Foster 1985). Upon reading, I felt even more confident that my fictionalized academic approach isn't that far off from how people actually talk about our "legends," never mind getting into why these discussions are often problematic.

I'm not *just* poking fun at the academy (and myself) with the character of Shelley Vogel. Narrating through an academic presentation, I am able to break the fourth wall somewhat, to express what I feel is the importance of stories rooted in a Métis worldview. When we tell our own stories, even fictionalized ones, we stand up against the narratives that have been imposed upon us.

Superheroes deriving their power from radiation is a trope that spans both the Golden and the Silver Ages of comics. I chose to invoke this trope and offer conflicting interpretations of the event; the academic blithely accepts radiation as a plausible explanation for superpowers, while Franky muses on a bison spirit gifting him with a unique obligation. We do not witness the event, so have no idea which is true. Other Indigenous superheroes often have more clearly "Indigenous" sources for their powers, such as Super Shamou, the Inuk superhero who is visited by a spirit and given a powerful charm, or Cree superhero Equinox, whose powers derive from the earth and change with the seasons.

Superheroes often run afoul of the law in their efforts to do the right thing, but Métis are historically already seen as either lawless or ungovernable. Franky is not torn between a duty to uphold the nation-state and to serve his people; his duty is to subvert and resist the state. In mainstream superhero tales, the contrast between those with powers and those without is highlighted. In Michif Man, Franky's community is careful not to allow him to become too proud or celebrated. There are many Métis stories in which lack of humility results in disaster, not just for the individual, but for the wider community as well. White society, which does not value humility in the same way, has no opportunity to make a celebrity of Franky.

Franky's identity is so secret, he simply ceases to exist to white society. Thus, he experiences a sense of freedom from racism, surveillance (bureaucratic or otherwise), and the pressure to perform masculinity. I wanted to subvert the idea of Métis as "hiding in plain sight" or being a forgotten people by suggesting that if settler colonial society were to truly forget us—that is, stop interfering with us entirely—that could be a wonderful thing.

Rather than portray science as magic, as superhero stories form a mythology that creates a sense of wonder, I wanted the Métis reaction to Franky's powers to be underwhelming. After all, Métis oral history is full of beings with extraordinary powers—powers that must be respected, but not necessarily feared. Franky is not unique in having powers; he is part of a long lineage of human and more-than-human beings who can do the extraordinary.

DIRTY WINGS

They are a bit grey around the puckered leather seams that attach the vamps to the soles, ôhi maskasina, these moccasins. I don't remember seeing them before, but they fit my feet in the way only well-used moccasins can. nimaskisina cî ôhi?

I usually wear slipper moccasins in the Dene style, trimmed with beaver fur, with fully beaded vamps. Works of art for everyday use. My last few moccasins were made by Tłįchǫ women, glittering flowers on white backgrounds and golden smoked moosehide that overpowered the nostrils, filled the entire house with the smell of the bush for weeks until I broke them in.

I had to pay a fine in a hotel room once after a rainy urban powwow. nimaskisina made it smell like we'd set up camp on the two king-size beds, an indoor/outdoor reclamation of a place built without free, prior, and informed consent on Odawa lands. I had the windows open all night and the four of us shivered in the cold, but the wet moosehide permeated every molecule of air, infused itself into our skin and hair, into the walls, even. I slept poorly, imagining the smell was visible golden light pouring out the windows, and every neechie who looked up would know exactly what it was. I love the smell, but even I grew tired of tasting it.

During checkout they made us wait until someone could look at the room; the hotel was full of Indians and I guess they were worried we drank up the mini bar. I remember the look of confusion on the concierge's face when housekeeping called him back, trying in vain to describe a smell that seemed foreign, but belonged more than the damn hotel did. He caught a whiff off me a moment later, and his face twisted.

They charged me the way they'd charge someone who smoked in the nonsmoking rooms.

I've been waiting years for nikâwiy to make me moccasins; you're not supposed to buy them, that's what môniyâwak do. But no one taught nikâwiy, and every couple of years she and my aunties would try a new pattern, something from a book or described to them by a friend, giving up before finishing the pair. She's got a bunch of left-foot moccasins in different styles crammed into her craft drawers. None of them "felt right," she'd laugh when I pulled them out and asked why she didn't finish them.

So I bought my moccasins, and felt a little ashamed about it because they didn't say anything about me or nikâwiy or nikâwisa or nohkom. And I bought my kids some because I'm better with words than with sewing needles; I guess I will speak when omaskisina cannot.

These ones on my feet, where did they come from? Feel like moose-hide, but there's no smell, and the reinforced soles are worn, stretched to fit me perfectly. Instead of heavy-duty felt vamps, it's more leather with a boring geometric design, like something you'd see on made-in-China factory-manufactured moccasins—but these were clearly hand-made. Short leather wraparounds, too, like a high-top sneaker, reaching just barely above the ankle—what's the point? Leather moccasin strings replaced by black-nylon combat boot laces.

I'm sitting on a couch in a common living/kitchen area. Four kookums are on high stools around the kitchen island, resting their rubber boots on a metal bar attached to the island. They wear thin windbreakers and long skirts. They're drinking tea and patting their floral kerchiefs, talking about food. I pull off my moccasins and start spreading mashed avocado inside them with my fingers. It's time-consuming work—I have to do it right.

I live in an Indigenous dorm at the University of amiskwacîwâskahikan. I'm in a program with a small cohort, and the kookums are talking about the young men. We only have a certain amount of money each month for food, and the Elders decided to give it to the men. The kookums are laughing about what aniki nâpêwak have been buying with that money: fancy breads from artisanal bakeries and aged cold cuts. They laugh uproariously about the spring water in glass bottles in the fridge.

I wonder why we don't just eat ramen noodles like every other student. I know how to stretch it out, make "soup bombs" you can throw in when the noodles are cooked, pieces of meat and lots of vegetables you freeze in small batches for when you need them—it's basically a full meal. I can teach them, I think to myself. We can sew soup bombs into cleaned buffalo intestines.

My fingers stay busy. The kookums are pulling on their short pipes now, little puffs of tobacco drifting like cotton candy, sticking to the ceiling, becoming clouds. The men will be out of money soon, far too soon into the month, and that means we'll all go hungry. I'm not hungry yet, but the suggestion makes my stomach clench. Lasting lessons are hard on everyone.

The men are back, braids but no faces, laying loaves of bread on the kitchen island, proud of themselves. They kiss the hands of the kookums, and I'm not angry anymore. It will be okay. I slide the moccasins back on, tie them tight.

We are sitting in a circle outside in the quad. The sun is so bright and so high, we are sitting on our own shadows. A môniyâw, a white man, stands outside our circle, and when his mouth moves I hear wings flapping. Not eagle wings, mind you, not even raven wings. Dirty pigeon wings, and I feel ashamed I don't honour the pigeon. It didn't build the cities, it just adapted. Maybe even better than we did.

Or maybe exactly how we did.

We are pulling spruce root up through the grass, laying it in front of us in coils. Dirty wings, dirty wings. Somehow I understand he is mocking us, saying our program is just "underwater basketweaving." We don't do that, but I think it might be fun. That one, môniyâw ana, in his

119

nineteenth-century hipster beard, he just wants us to know he thinks what we do is useless. Arts and crafts at best. I bet he studies poli sci.

The four kookums wrestle themselves to their feet. It's hard for them, knees creaking like abandoned gates blowing in the wind. They stretch out their arms in front of them, then bend them so their hands are touching their own shoulders. Their elbows are sharp, and I'm confused; the kookums aren't blind. They push that one, ana môniyâw, poking him with their elbows when he seems reluctant to move.

We all stand and follow the kookums. We are in a building with a large pool. The water lies in shadows, a shade of green like spruce boughs. There are cattails obscuring its size, and in a few places you can see all the way to the bottom. We usually bring our canoes here, but not today.

The kookums elbow that môniyâw into the pool. He falls and drags all the cattails down with him like pulling on a tablecloth, until the pool is clear and blue and you can see him just sitting there on the bottom, looking up in confusion. The kookums throw him coils of spruce root and tell him he can come out when he has woven a basket.

He doesn't even try. He swells up a little, his skin is becoming puffy, and flecks of his clothes start floating to the top of the water. We watch his skin come off in patches. Soon the whole surface of the pool is covered in soggy leaves.

The men take their woven spruce root baskets and skim the leaves out of the water. The men are silent but the rest of us are singing. The kookums are sitting, puffing on their pipes again, but these are the longer pipes, the women's pipes.

I gather the waterlogged leaves up in my hands. There are so many, they keep falling, and I have to pick them up again. I am outside and it is deadly cold, the earth hushed and blanketed. I have to take these leaves and spread them under the trees in the university quad. I cannot see the sky; it is getting dark and snow is falling, thick, wet, and heavy, all around me.

I risk freezing to death, but my feet are warm. I am glad I took the time to spread the avocado inside; my feet are coated as though with bear grease. I find a patch of waskwayak and I remember how once they were whipped by Elder Brother. It is winter, why can't I remember their name? I lay those leaves down, no more flapping wings. I hear wîsahkêcâhk laughing.

I am ready for the coming fast.

"DIRTY WINGS" EXPLORATION

I have always been taught that dreams are significant in Métis/nêhiyaw culture, as they are for many other Indigenous peoples. Dreams represent an epistemological diversity, along with visions, prophecy, specific ceremonies, and interactions with nonhuman and nonliving kin. Some dreams are prophetic, and some dreams teach new ceremonies and medicine, like the jingle dance or syllabics (Casale 2019; Stevenson 2000). Others are just dreams and don't mean anything. I have always remembered most of my dreams upon waking, and am pretty confident that the bulk of the dreaming I do is of the meaningless sort. This dream felt different.

As nêhiyaw scholar Michael Hart explains in conversation with Margaret Kovach (2009, 70), dreaming as an Indigenous methodology is not merely having a dream, nor even interpreting a dream, but rather "what you do with that dream, how you put it into reality." This explanation dovetails perfectly with my conception of Métis futurisms as a whole: that imagining potential futures or alternative worlds in any time is not enough; what we *do* with these imaginings is what creates new realities.

I hesitate to call this story a pawâmêwâcimowin (a spiritual dreaming story), because I feel that I do not have the necessary level of cultural competency to make that call. However, I began writing this book because of the dream. Sharing the dream that caused me to undertake this work is important to me because it was part of the process, and making space for narrative styles rooted in dreams and dreaming feels appropriate.

A great deal of this story seems to focus on shoes, the strangeness of the moccasins I find myself in and memories of how authentic smoked moosehide moccasins have branded me as transgressive outside of the safety of the powwow arbour (Vowel 2016). The hotel scene actually happened, and I added in these details after I had the dream. However, the focus on moccasins is really about cultural transmission and the fraught question of operating within a capitalistic framework to access culture when transmission has been actively severed.

The story begins with me spreading mashed avocado into the strange moccasins. Later, when I woke, it occurred to me that I was working with the materials I have the most access to, that I would have preferred bear grease to protect and warm my skin. Avocados are much more plentiful now in these lands than bear grease is. Who knows what our descendants may end up using, no matter how strange it may seem to us now.

Many of the references in the story aren't necessarily legible to the "outsider," and that is deliberate. The symbolism and allusions were there in my dream because I know them best. I chose not to translate them within the story because I want non-Indigenous people to engage with our stories, symbols, language, and history on our terms. Just as I have had to research the sources of literary allusions unfamiliar to me in order to access deeper meanings within Western European literature, I expect this work to be done by non-Indigenous peoples, especially those on our lands. For a while, that might look like annotated versions of our stories, just as I was only able to understand classic European works that made constant allusions to other European works.

Not all Indigenous people will have the insider knowledge required to understand symbols and allusions used in Indigenous literature, either because we are from outside the specific cultural perspective (for example, I would not be able to interpret Diné symbolism!), or because as members of a specific culture, these things haven't been learned. This reality has softened my approach somewhat to the idea of annotating, or making legible, some of my work.

This story was published during the process of writing my MA thesis (Vowel 2020). It has changed slightly since publication, but it was reviewed twice by two white men, at least one of them English. I am sharing their reviews to highlight the illegibility of this particular work to the "outsider." First, from Jeff McGregor:

> The protagonist spends much of these four pages, which are not "speculative" as much as "surreal," talking about shoes. The story includes many undefined regional words and untranslated non-English phrases and may be about pre-Europeans struggling with assimilation. (McGregor and Houghton, 2018)

The second review was done by Geoff Houghton:

> "Dirty Wings" by Chelsea Vowel is a flow of consciousness from a Native American living on the edge of mainstream Canadian society. The author is plainly familiar with this Native culture and uses many Native words, although their approximate meaning can usually be deduced from the context.

> This is speculative fiction rather than SF. The writing style is idiosyncratic and there is no conventional plot. Instead the reader leaves behind common or garden Western World certainties and is drawn into an alternative way to view our Universe. If you believe that reality is reality is reality and what we see is what we get, then pass this story by. If you are less certain in your metaphysics, then you may wish to enter this alternative way of seeing the world through eyes not automatically attuned to Western Capitalist and Materialist values. (2018)

I find these reviews absolutely fascinating! I suppose I am reviewing their reviews. The term "pre-Europeans" really jumps out at me; I have heard us referred to as pre-Columbian, and even primitive, but never pre-European! The way the reviewer unconsciously prioritizes European presence and homogenizes all those that "came before" provides interesting insight into how he read this story. The hesitance with which the reviewer proclaims the plot of the story is also telling, and in the absence of more context familiar to him, he falls upon a familiar trope of "struggling with assimilation."

I am happy that the second reviewer was able to figure out the nêhiyawêwin words I used, untranslated, throughout the story, though he does not know which specific language I am using and refers to Indigenous cultures in the singular.

I refuse to always translate, because I want non-Indigenous people to learn these words, as they have learned French, Spanish, German, and Japanese phrases which are peppered throughout English. I also appreciate that this reviewer grasps that this story does not exist within the exact same metaphysical framework of conventional speculative fiction.

This story takes place in an urban setting, but clearly the land plays an important role. Asserting that all cities exist on Indigenous land is vital, particularly since the majority of Indigenous peoples now live in urban areas, but also to highlight the artificial nature of the rural/urban divide (Statistics Canada 2017, Simpson 2014b).[75] When we exhort one another to "go back to the land," we seem to always mean "leave the city," but this is not possible or even necessarily desirable for everyone. As Leanne Simpson often points out, we should be encouraging Indigenous people to make connection with the land wherever they are, even if it is a city park.

....

75   In 2016, 51.8 percent of the Indigenous population of Canada lived in a metropolitan area of at least thirty thousand people.

When I talk about honouring the pigeon, I gesture to clans among nêhiyaw and Anishinaabe kin, referring to a long-standing in-joke with friends about the way white people seem to always claim certain animals as their "spirit animals." Animals like the bear or the eagle, but never the rat or the pigeon. Being pigeon clan might be viewed as ignoble, but as I point out, it is not just human beings who have adapted to drastic changes in the landscape. Our animal kin have also experienced severances and fractures in their own cultural transmissions, as well as having to innovate for survival.

The kookums are central to the story. It is they who decided to let the young men make decisions that the kookums know will have consequences for all of us, because they need those men to learn that responsibility extends beyond the self. They smoke pipes twice, once socially, once in ceremony, each kind of offering of tobacco with its own purpose. The kookums teach us how to connect with the land, even in the city, and they are the ones to teach that môniyâw a lesson about mocking skills he himself cannot master.

When the kookums have sharp elbows, I am referring to an âtayohkêwin (a sacred story) about a Métis/Cree cultural hero called ayâs in my territory, as told to me by Eeyou (Eastern James Bay Cree) storyteller Elma Moses. In that story ayâs outwits blind witches with sharp bones jutting out of their elbows, sent by his father to kill him. ayâs is responsible for the world fire and the rebirth of the world. One could see the world fire as an apocalypse, but rather than heralding an ending, it ushered in a new beginning. All of the stories I offer in this work reject the apocalypse as an end that must be feared for its finality. In this story, the môniyâw does not outwit the witches. He does not usher in a new beginning, but rather seems to be in the way of one, and his ending is not their doing, but rather, his own.

The kookums give me a task I don't understand, but I do it even though it is difficult, because I trust they have a reason for it. I recall another âtayohkêwin as told by the late Freda Ahenakew (1988) about how birch trees got their stripes from the cultural hero wîsahkêcâhk. In this story, Elder Brother enlists the aid of birch trees to help themself exercise self-control, but when things don't go their way, the birch trees are punished with a whipping.

I am using they/them pronouns for Elder Brother for two reasons. For one, in the âtayohkêwina, Elder Brother is not just one gender; they are not always even human. They transform constantly. The other reason is that nêhiyawêwin, the Cree language, lacks gendered pronouns, and "they" is a more faithful translation of "wiya" than "he" or "she" can be.

In Métis/nêhiyaw culture, there is a cultural taboo against using Elder Brother's name outside of the winter months. This restriction extends to many other beings and animals as well. This creates a bit of a problem for storytelling in forms other than oral, because we cannot always be certain that our stories will be taken up in the proper season.

Métis filmmaker Danis Goulet provides an interesting solution to this restriction in her short film *Wakening* (2013), in which "In the near future, the environment has been destroyed and society suffocates under a brutal military occupation. A lone Cree wanderer, Wesakechak, searches an urban war zone to find the ancient and dangerous Weetigo to help fight against the occupiers" ("Wakening" n.d.).

In the film, snow falls, signalling that the film exists within the proper season, and so even when viewing this film in a different season, it is perhaps permissible to hear or speak the names. This compromise might not be acceptable to everyone, but it at least signals a desire to observe cultural protocol.

In the dream, there is snow on the ground, but I cannot remember Elder Brother's name. What could be preventing me from remembering their name? What is wrong, or out of balance? Silencing the racist and patronizing voice of the môniyâw restores something, and Elder Brother's name is legible to me again.

At the end of the story, I am ready for a fast. Fasting is an important practice for Métis, Cree, and Anishinaabe peoples and can hold many meanings (Simpson 2014a).

MAGGIE SUE

If I'm going to tell you about Maggie Sue, I've got to go back to Tuesday.

It was a little before 10 p.m. when I walked out of the Safeway into a glorious prairie sunset. Neon pinks and oranges streaked across the sky, with a few deep-purple clouds scattered here and there like hickeys.

I was in no big hurry; I'd stopped in for some chips and dip in anticipation of a solid night of binge-watching that new postapocalyptic action series everyone was talking about. Have you seen it yet? I've wanted to give it a shot because they say it has an actual ending for once, wraps up the plot line. I wish that was more common.

I had my neck craned to the sky, a goofy smile across my lips, and I let my eyes drink in the sight, revelling in the feeling of the soft, warm breeze tickling my skin. June's just beginning, but oh, how us prairie folk unfurl like rosebuds after a long winter. Spring in Edmonton is temperamental, so you've got to appreciate it when you can—you know how it is.

I suppose that's how I managed to I walk straight into her, the "sorry" out of my mouth before I'd even registered what had happened, my plastic bag full of goodies spilling its contents onto the grimy parking lot.

She was taller than me, fat and arresting in a jean jacket over a black T-shirt, a floral ribbon skirt, and a black felt hat with a big brim. She shot me a startled look, sharp canines flashing in the copper light, big cheeks rising and eyes squinting into a perfect Cree grin. I felt my heart stop, shudder to an end in my chest, taking my breath and my sense all at once.

She was gone before I had time to understand I'd died.

· ◈ ·

I mean, I had to be dead, it's the only thing that makes sense. Nothing was the same after that moment, it was like the whole world had taken a half step to the left, the beginning of a round dance, but I got disconnected somehow from the chain of people. Left there to float a little out of place. I had to be dead, because she was a fox.

Oof, I know how that sounds. Like outdated slang, like "groovy" and "the bee's knees" and the other archaic lingo I learned because my best friend's mom had kept a stack of her old Archie comics, and as kids we'd spend hours reading them, dreaming about a clean small town and Pop's Chock'lit Shoppe. Veronica's mansion was a nice escape from my kookum's dingy basement suite down behind the Burger Baron. I'll bet Jughead would have loved the Baron's mushroom burgers, though.

She was a fox—but I mean that literally.

I could see her, the fox, but I also saw her human form. I followed behind her as she zigzagged through the parking lot, watched her nimbly dodge a boxy black car backing out of a parking spot. It wasn't as though the fox was human sized; she wasn't a fox figure blurrily showing under human skin or anything like that.

She also, and I want to be clear, was not some furry's fantasy of a bipedal canid. That would have been truly bizarre, her fox head peeking out beneath brown skin, body elongated to fit inside this new shape, hopping along on two hind legs, swinging unmoored front legs that found no purchase in the air, simply helping to move the upright body along, tail swishing beneath a ribbon skirt.

It wasn't like that at all. She was a tiny little fox, smaller than I've ever seen, and with blond in her fur, copper and silver instead of reddish brown, more like a coyote's colouring than the foxes I'd seen zipping through the river valley. I'm not good with dog breeds, but let's say bigger than a chihuahua and smaller than a pit bull? Lean, too, and she moved like prairie grass in a breeze, sinuous, fluid instead of darting. I don't think animals do ballet, but like that. She moved like a dancer.

She was scanning everything, eyes everywhere, taking it all in, and headed toward 118 Avenue. Trotting along. Wait, no, that's horses. How to describe it—how do foxes walk? Padding? Stepping? Dancing? Blowing? Gliding? Flowing? Pouring? Coursing? Maybe coursing. I've heard that applied to greyhounds, but now that I think about it, isn't that also the word they use for those dogs in Merry Old England, where they still have a fox hunt? Probably not the best term, then. Maybe even explicitly anti-fox.

The way she moved was mesmerizing, even more so than would be usual because she seemed to be carrying a very solid human with her.

Not like puppeteering. There was nothing horrible or "uncanny valley" about her ah, um, *skin suit*? Wow that sounds really, really wrong. No, her human body wasn't fake, or strange, or worn, like clothes. She was a stunning Cree woman, definitely not out of place in this neighbourhood, though maybe a little more dressed up and fancy than folks tended to be on a Tuesday evening along Alberta Avenue. I'm not explaining any of this properly, I'm sorry. Her human self was just as much *her* as her real fox form.

How did I know she was a fox posing as a human and not the other way around? Well, for one, what a weird question—that wouldn't make any sense. Why would a human turn into a fox in the city? For another thing, I'm the only one who saw the fox at all, because no one else seemed to react to her, and it wasn't exactly the sort of thing people would pretend not to see. Not like someone passed out on a bench, where folks just walk on by and act like there's no one there. This was the kind of thing that even the most guarded inner-city resident would remark at.

I saw them both, the fox and the woman, at the same time. Less confusing than seeing double; they were both just *there* all the time.

So yeah. I had to have died. Because this stuff, it happens a lot, yeah? I mean, that's what the stories always say: beings transform constantly. Elder Brother? Him, he shed and donned new shapes the way some people try on outfits before a party, maybe hating themselves a little for being a bit of a cliché and ending up being late because it took a while to find the right look. Well it happened a lot, before. I think there are even some stories from after the Second World War, and into the seventies, but after that it's like transforming faded away as a skillset. Shoot, I'm sorry. I know it sounds like I'm rambling, but it's hard to explain. Can I get a drink, please? Do you have Red Rose? A coffee, maybe? Or whatever, even just some tap water.

Thanks.

How does any of this prove I was dead? I know I'm not dead now, and I'm getting to that, I promise. Just bear with me, I have to explain a few more things first.

Lots of shape-shifting, lots of transformation in the old stories, not just Métis and Cree. We all have those stories, even the môniyâwak, if they go back far enough. But in our stories, regular folk, human and animal, don't just up and change shapes without incurring some sort of debt, some responsibility or task, or some consequence. This fox I was following, she was big time. The spiritual version of *connected*, you know what I mean? Had to be. This was a sacred story in the making, and one thing I'd learned listening to my kookum tell those sometimes terrifying, often hilarious and scatological tales is, the side characters almost always end up tricked, embarrassed, even killed and eaten. That's me—I was a side character.

I didn't like my odds, and I told myself I should head in the opposite direction immediately, but I couldn't. She was the most beautiful creature I'd ever seen, and I don't know if bumping into her outside that Safeway was what killed me, or if I'd died right before and that was why I met her, but it had to mean something. I should at least keep an eye on her, try to figure out what was going on. You'd understand if you'd seen her.

Why could I see her when no one else could? That's what I'm saying; it's because I was dead. When I died, I moved into the spirit world, so

I saw her true form. Maybe that means transformations never stopped happening, just that we aren't as clued in as we used to be, not as connected to the spirit realm.

I see what you're thinking, but the spirit realm isn't some heaven or hell. It's not the "happy hunting grounds," not Valhalla or Jupiter or whatever that cult believed before they all drank poison. I was still on 118 Avenue, just in the spirit realm rather than the physical realm. It's not somewhere else, it's right here. Us, we know that. Just like that fox was attached to herself as a human, the spirit world is attached to the land it was born with. You can't split them apart. I just think people today don't pay it enough attention.

It's like a muscle you never use. I can raise one of my eyebrows—see that? I loved the Belgariad when I was a kid, did you ever read it? David Eddings? Well, I guess his wife helped him a lot, maybe wrote most of them, I dunno. I'm kind of embarrassed by it now, but I read those books over and over and over, and there was this character, Polgara, who was a sorceress. She was always raising her eyebrow, and without even knowing I was doing it, I would try to raise my eyebrow, too, because I wanted to be like her, so strong and confident and unimpressed with men and their bullshit. Until one day I could do it just like her, and I didn't really know how it happened. It wasn't a conscious thing. I can't do it with my right eyebrow, no matter how much I try. I can feel the muscles in my left eyebrow—I can do this, ha, like the Rock, hey? I can bob it up and down like this, but when I try to do anything with my right eyebrow, nothing. I can't feel the muscles. I know they're there, but I can't send them a signal. That's us and the spirit realm. We can't access it the way we used to; we never learned how, and now that we're so out of practice maybe it's impossible for most of us.

You know what else? I always hated reading fantasy novels where Irish or Scottish or whatever creatures came over to the Americas with the colonists, so you'd have a bunch of selkies and fairies and leprechauns, instead of thunderbirds and the little people and all the other beings from here. All our relations. I mean the spirit realm wasn't supplanted, it didn't open up embassies and institute immigration policies. It didn't fill up with those môniyâwak beings or their ancestors; they stayed behind in their own lands. Cha, too bad white folks didn't take the hint and do the same, ehhhh. No, the spirit realm just became neglected. Less seen, less nourished, less nourishing.

Just give me a second, sorry, I had a point. I was talking about the spirit realm being here, just a little removed, and it's not full of môniyâwak beings. All those writers get it wrong. Ha, maybe they should call themselves *wrongers* instead. And I was talking about how we can't see it or interact with it the way we used to. We're out of practice and—right, I remember now! I'm trying to make you understand that I don't have those spiritual muscles, so I couldn't have seen her unless I was in the spirit realm.

Can I prove I was dead? I mean, it's the only explanation that makes sense, doesn't it? I don't know, maybe a doctor could show my heart stopped or something. I've seen that on TV, but I wasn't attached to any machines, and maybe there's no way to tell, otherwise. That you've died and come back? Sure, I'll see a doctor I guess, if you need me to. Get a physical.

Oh. You mean a head doctor.

Come on, man, just let me tell the story, you'll get it. Please?

I'm rewinding. You wanted me to tell you everything. I followed her out of that parking lot, and then she was at the corner looking out at the intersection, a bit spooked. She was watching the cars zoom by and rocking back and forth a bit, like she was preparing to dash across the road when there was a break in traffic. I had this horrible vision of her getting hit by a car and bleeding out into the dirty puddles, and I couldn't let it happen. "Hey," I said, real smooth, to get her attention.

What? Yeah she heard me, I wasn't a ghost! We were both corporeal. I mean, I wasn't completely sure of that in the moment, but later when I found out I could touch things, that became obvious. It's just that no one living could see me. I was still matter, though, I occupied space, I had mass. Gravity was working just fine, pulling me toward the earth's core, just like any other day. Don't ask me to explain it; I flunked physics twice.

I said, "Hey," and she turned toward me, giving me that huge grin again, but her fox self was clearly wary, so I reassessed how I was receiving her expression.

"The signal will show us when it's safe to cross the road," I told her, pointing my finger at the signal light. She cocked her head to one side, white full-moon shell earrings swaying against her black hair, sparkling dark eyes regarding me carefully under the brim of her hat. She smelled like sweetgrass, and something went all swoopy in my stomach. She didn't look where I was pointing; she looked at my raised arm like she was waiting for me to do something with it.

I let my arm fall, feeling foolish. She went back to tracking the cars, and I could see her muscles bunching, so without even thinking about it, I got ready, too, and when a big pickup truck howled by and a gap opened up, I was only a step behind her as she ran into the crosswalk.

I heard the blast of a horn and flinched, but I'm not sure it was meant for us, because the light turned just as we hit the other sidewalk. My heart was pounding, and I was gasping a little bit, which is not normal for me. I mean, we all jaywalk from time to time. I scanned automatically for those big cop suvs you find on almost every corner around here, but there were no simâkanis in sight to give me another ticket I couldn't pay.

No, I wasn't sure then that other people couldn't see me. I told you, I didn't figure that out until later, when I didn't show up on the security cameras until she sent me back.

She noticed that I'd followed her and gave me this wary, sideways look, but kept walking. We were outside the Catholic Social Services building now, Somali moms with strollers gathered around the bus shelter, neechies resting their many bags of groceries on the one bench.

Neechies, Native people. You never heard that before? Younger folks are using different nicknames now, but I don't like it—is it alley like an alleyway or ali like alcoholic? Either way, it seems bad, so I'm sticking with what I know. At least neechie comes from our own language.

She walked up to the group of bunched-together people. We don't line up all polite here; we just sort of squish our way closer to where the bus is going to stop and hope no one calls us on it. I went along, and she didn't seem to mind too much that I was right behind her.

She regarded the bus shelter with interest as the last rays of sunlight flashed against the glass and lit the faces of the people around her. The Somali moms were chattering in their own language, babies happily fussing, and she watched it all, rapt, her head cocked again. I just stared at her like I was drinking through my eyes; I couldn't look away. I didn't know what I'd miss if I did.

The number eight pulled up, startling her a little. The bus beeped as the driver engaged the kneeling function, and people backed up a little to let riders off, then tried to cram onboard before the moms with strollers cut them off—but these women were practised. They'd already blocked the path, knowing that if they didn't get on first, the bus would fill up and they'd be left behind. The drivers never made people move to give the strollers room, not in this neighbourhood, not for Black or Native parents, not even in the deep of winter.

She was swept up in the pushing bodies, and I stuck with her, ending up packed in front of the driver, who looked at the fox expectantly. I mean her human self. She just looked back, blank faced.

"I'm not giving free rides," the blond white woman stated flatly. I knew this driver. She loved loudly complaining about riders and flexing her transit authority. I'd seen her kick schoolkids off the bus into the pouring rain because their transfers had expired. I've never understood why drivers who clearly hate poor and racialized people end up working these routes. Maybe that's why, come to think of it. It makes them feel powerful.

Someone in the packed bowels of the bus yelled at the bus driver to open the back door. The driver looked up at the rear-view mirror in annoyance, and acting quickly, I reached over to her pad of transfer slips and tore one off, cramming it into the fox's hand. She looked at me in surprise, the transfer sticking out of her human fist like a feather. The driver's eyes flicked back to the fox and narrowed, but more people were still trying to get on the bus, and this driver never ignored a chance to close the bus doors in the face of people needing to get somewhere, so she returned her attention to that.

The bus lurched forward, and the fox staggered. I reached out and steadied her human form, and this time was rewarded with a grin I read as grateful. Hard to say, really, but the fox didn't seem angry. It was hard to squeeze past the three strollers, but I guided her farther down the aisle. At the next stop, a bunch of people got off, and there were two free seats side by side. I slipped into one and pulled her into the outside seat.

She was craning her head, looking out the windows, clearly enjoying the strangeness of riding inside the bus. She had her big hands resting on the seat back in front of her, and she was sitting up very straight backed, but her fox form was curled into the seat.

I tapped her again, and she turned toward me. "What's your name?" I asked.

And that's when something absolutely amazing happened. She opened her mouth and said, "Maggie Sue."

No, that's not the amazing thing, give me a second.

My Cree isn't awesome. My kookum speaks Cree, but mostly just commands to me, like mîciso, eat, or api, sit, or ma, shut it and listen up! When I was a teen, I wanted to learn more Cree, because my dad is from Paddle Prairie—that's a Métis Settlement—and my mom, kookum's daughter, well, I guess she was Lac Ste. Anne Métis. Yeah, I'm Métis, Cree is our language, too, at least out here. I know they call it Michif sometimes, what they speak up in the Settlements, but it sounds like Cree to me. Maybe a few French words. I don't know, maybe when it comes out of a Métis mouth it transforms into Michif. Whatever.

I took these community classes at the Friendship Centre back when it was still down 101 Street, and I was so excited to learn and speak Cree to my kookum, but she laughed a lot at my accent and I got really embarrassed. I went once a week for three months, drinking super-strong Red Rose tea and learning how to count, pêyak, nîso, nisto, nêwo; and some of the colours, mihkosiw, katêskisiw; and how to name some of the animals, wapôs, maskwa, and, get this, mahkêsiw. Get it? No? Okay, hold on, I'll come back to that.

The point is, my Cree kind of sucks. These classes, they cover the really basic basics, and at first you think you're learning a lot, but it's not like a course—it's really informal. People drop in and stop coming and new people show up all the time. You end up doing the basics again and again. I got good at counting, but I never progressed past that. One time, a local Elder showed us Cree syllabics using this really cool star chart and showed us the sounds, the "spirit markers," but I didn't memorize it. I can't read syllabics.

Back to the amazing thing. When she·opened her mouth and told me her name, I saw syllabics.

I'm serious. It was like something silver was coming out of her mouth, gliding along her lips and being pushed by her breath. They were tiny at first, but they expanded really quickly. You know those polished metal letters, the raised ones they use on the doors of medical clinics, or at the legal aid office? They looked just like that. They came floating out of her mouth like little baby syllabics and then swelled up and bobbed gently there for a bit before fading away.

How awesome is that? And it wasn't a one-off, either. An old dude got on the bus, real Indian suit, too, jeans with a jean shirt, and he saw someone he knew.

"tânisi?" he goes to his bud, *and the syllabics came out of his mouth, too.*

"moya nânitaw, kiya mâka?" his bud shouts back, silver syllabics pouring out and hovering. No one else on that bus could have seen them, or they'd have been screaming their heads off. Beside me, she perks up—I mean the fox form. She uncurls in a flash, and now her paws are up on the seat back in front of her, and she's peering at these men, tongue out, tail actually twitching a bit. Her human form is grinning ear to ear, and those two old men, they can't help but see this beautiful Cree woman staring at them. One points with his lips at her and the other laughs.

Huh? Yeah they were speaking Cree, have you even been down Alberta Ave? Lots and lots of Native people—you can hear Cree, sometimes Dene, even Inuktitut in the Safeway, on the bus, on the street. Sometimes real fluent, too, those older ones. Look, I understood that much, it's basic greeting stuff. Some of the other stuff I want to tell you, I got a bit of it, but I had to sort of figure out the rest from context.

Don't you get it, though? The spirit realm comes with subtitles, spirit markers for the spirit realm, but it only works with Cree. I think. I didn't hear anyone speaking any other languages from here. Maybe it works with Nakota and other original languages, too. I mean, that's probably really helpful for someone who's learned to read syllabics, but I never did, so it was lost on me. I guess the spirit realm doesn't tailor itself to an observer's needs. You know they say some white guy invented syllabics? I'm pretty sure this proves that's a load of crap.

No, she never told me a last name. Yeah, she said Maggie Sue, I thought it was her name at first, too. Right, I said I'd come back to that. wapôs, that's rabbit, maskwa is bear, and then there's mahkêsiw. It usually means coyote. Fox is mahkêsîs—that *sis* sound means smaller. And this fox, she was tiny, but she'd chosen a big body; she was way bigger than any fox. mahkêsiw can also mean a large fox.

Are you getting it now? Use a real white accent, it sounds a lot like Maggie Sue. She was just telling me what I already knew: she's a fox.

You want to know what happened at IKEA. I get it, I swear I'm getting there. But you needed to know this stuff for any of the rest of it to make sense. Otherwise it just looks like I went in there and terrorized the place. I'm not naive. I know that's what you think, I know you've me clocked as some kind of criminal, maybe high on something, who knows. It wasn't like that at all. Pardon my language, but shit got really messed up. I told you, this was a sacred story in the making, and those don't involve uneventful bus rides, a shopping trip, and a nice meal. I have to explain how it went down, and how I came back to life.

Are you sure you don't have Red Rose? Or any kind of tea? I've been talking for a while. Yeah, I'll take an Earl Grey. Him and the Burger Baron, they're the only nobility I recognize, ha.

Right. IKEA.

I'm not sure how we got there, but she must have been headed there the whole time even though it seemed like she was just going with the flow. When we reached the Mill Woods transit centre, we followed a stream of people to the next bus, but I only remember getting off the second bus and trying to keep up with her as she walked along wide, empty sidewalks and then under a bridge and across some grass before we hit the parking lot. It was completely dark by then, swarms of tiny bugs flitting around inside the yellow lamplights, desolate the way only a square kilometre of concrete can be. Honestly, it was creepy: a looming breadbox, cobalt blue dimmed to a muddy black, illuminated lemon-yellow letters beckoning like the cross on an evangelical church.

Maggie Sue never checked to see if I was still with her, but she didn't seem to mind me being there, either. When we got to the entrance, the doors didn't slide open, and there were only a few lights on inside. She scratched at the glass, and I looked around nervously, not sure what we were doing wrong, and knowing that for two visibly Native people, it didn't matter. She scratched again.

The shadows inside seemed to gather themselves together, knitting and spinning. I didn't see it at first, but the movement caught the corner of my eye like a bright fish hook and tugged me gently. I've got eyes accustomed to city lights; maybe they aren't capable anymore of adapting to the near pitch-black of a cave, say, or the deep forest, or the bottom of a well. Staring straight into what was happening revealed nothing. I had to glance away and try to catch the shadows by pretending to be uninterested.

Suddenly a foot emerged, a black-and-white-checkered Vans sneaker, and then with a strange visual snap, an entire person was standing at the door, millimetres of glass separating them from us. I yelped like someone had bitten me in the ass and proceeded to fall backwards, my heart pounding and a waterfall of profanities tumbling from my trembling lips. I hate jump scares! It's a cheap tactic, adds nothing to the story except maybe making me shit myself, pardon my language, and then I just get super angry after I realize what happened. In this case, I was angry *and* embarrassed, because now Maggie Sue was looking at me sprawled on the concrete, and she was making these strange strangled barks, which I quickly understood to be laughter. To make it worse, the person inside was almost doubled over, slapping their knees in mirth. I mean come on, it wasn't that funny.

When I'm angry like this after being scared, I lash out. I do—it's terrible, but I can't help it. Broke my cousin's nose once on Halloween when he jumped out of my kookum's linen closet after I got home from school. It wasn't like you're probably thinking; I didn't get scared and hit him in self-defence. People seem more understanding when the reaction is immediate. No, he burst out of that closet, yelling from behind a demented-looking cheap rubber squirrel mask, and I screamed shrilly like a little kid and fell down. Okay, I guess it's what I do. When he took off his mask and started laughing at me, I scrambled upright and smashed him right in the face. Probably would have hit him again, but my kookum was there pulling me away.

That's the kind of energy I was dealing with when I got up and kicked at the glass. I'm pretty sure I broke my big toe, and let's just say Maggie Sue and that other one, they laughed even harder, and I felt ridiculous. The pain was pretty intense. I bet those doors would stop a car trying to crash through. That happens a lot in Edmonton, vehicles slamming into buildings—I don't know if it's boredom or alcohol or what. While I was hopping in place and trying to hold my foot, ears burning red hot with shame, the door was opened, and Maggie Sue and that other one were walking away into the store.

You saw the tape? I don't know why you can see Maggie Sue on tape, but not me or that other one. Why did the bus driver see her and give her a hard time? I think Maggie Sue took human form specifically so she would be in our world, but I have no idea why. I do know they tried claiming it was me, because I showed up on camera later, but there was no way I could have faked her stature.

Well, I was too chicken to be alone in that huge empty parking lot by myself, and I was also a little stung that she didn't seem to care if I came or not, so I hobbled after them, my toe throbbing with every heartbeat. They took the stairs to the second floor, and since neither of them was paying me any mind, I made good use of the railing to drag my wounded pride after them.

Luckily, when I got to the top of the stairs, they were standing still, looking at the huge mural that guy from Treaty 8 painted—ah, what's his name, Cardinal something. Leon? Lorne? No, Lance. Lance Cardinal. I'd only seen it in the news until then. It's way more impressive in person, you should check it out.

Ah, shoot. You can't. I didn't even think of that! He might think *I* wrecked his mural, like some kind of really extreme lateral violence. Oh, man. I hope he doesn't have sisters. I really don't want to get jumped next time I'm waiting for the bus on the Ave. I'd better see if I can talk to that guy.

Right, yeah, sorry. I'm up there, and it's weird because most of the lights are off, like I said, just these little pinpricks of light here and there. Maybe there was security or something, but we never saw them. There was a light right on that buffalo he painted, and on the bear.

Huh? Bison? Yeah, I know that's the right word, but you understand me when I say buffalo, don't you? I mean, it's a little rich to tell neechies how to call an animal your folks only met a hundred years ago or something. And that you genocided so you could build McMansions on all our lakes. Do you speak Michif? Cree? Nakota? How about Saulteaux? Know how to say buffalo in any of those languages? No? Okay, then. I get to say bison or buffalo all I want, how's that? No, I don't care if your family wasn't here when it happened. You want this story or not?

Sorry, that's just a pet peeve of mine. Buffalo buffalo buffalo.

Maggie Sue and that one, they were talking really fast in Cree, and I only caught a few words here and there. No, I really don't know if that other one was a man or a woman; it was strange, I never got a full look. But listen, I know who it was because Maggie Sue kept saying kistêsinaw, kistêsinaw. That's literally "our elder brother." Normally you'd say nistês, which is "my elder brother." I didn't know that then, but when I listed all the words I remembered hearing for a friend of mine, one who took Cree in university, she just sat up, eyes all big, and she goes, "Elder Brother." I could hear the capital letters.

Chee, you really don't get it, hey. Elder Brother. That's the name we use when there's no snow on the ground. He's our cultural hero. I know you folks like to call him a trickster, but that's not really accurate. He's not some sort of clown, even when he does funny stuff. You see, his jokes have serious consequences, and not just for him. Imagine standing next to a nuclear bomb painted like a bright-pink Hello Kitty or a fuzzy wuzzy cutesy little teddy bear or something. It's still a nuclear bomb. If I hadn't already been sure I was dead in that moment, I'd have been freaking out even more than I was. And don't be fooled—just because I keep saying "he" and "Brother," I'm telling you That One isn't constrained by gender. English uses "she" and "he," but in Cree it's just wiya, and wiya has no gender. Everyone time I tried to focus on That One, my eyes got blurry, so I mostly just watched Maggie Sue.

She seemed a bit angry, actually; she was talking really fast, the silver syllabics flying and sparking out of her mouth, and her canines were flashing. She was glorious. Even with me being dead, she was making my heart flutter something fierce. She held out one of her big hands, and there was this melty piece of something in her palm, like butter or lard, real greasy. Little drops were running off her hand and plopping on the floor. Where they hit, it fizzed like it was acid, but it didn't seem to hurt her. She kept shoving it toward that other one, making eating motions, but That One was laughing and trying to placate her. I didn't really get it, but she had some kind of grudge, and she was yelling now, her little fox form growling and nipping at That One's ankles. That One started to get a bit heated, too, and pulled out a pair of charred duck feet from somewhere, waving them in her face. Yeah, I'm sure they were duck feet, and that story I'd heard before, so I started to get an inkling of what was happening.

I told you Elder Brother likes to mess around and has been doing that since time began, maybe even before. I think they were airing out the dirty laundry, so to speak. These are ancient stories, sacred stories for us humans, but it all seemed fresh for Maggie Sue and That One. No, I'm not going to tell you the story. Didn't you hear me that there needs to be snow on the ground? Besides, I'm not even sure I could tell it right. That's a tobacco question, as they say.

Finally, That One tossed the duck feet on the ground and jabbed a finger at the mural, saying, atoskêtân. I caught that, it means something like let's get to work. Maggie Sue shook the almost-melted grease off her hand as best she could and wiped the remaining smear onto her jean jacket sleeve.

They were there, in front of the buffalo, just a mural, a painting, and I was leaning against the stair railing, my big toe still throbbing something awful, when all of a sudden, the floor dropped out under us. I got terrible vertigo, and I wasn't sure which way was up for a second, like I'd been dropped into the water upside down. I was even holding my breath, flailing around but not really feeling my body responding. I was so focused on that awful feeling that I wasn't looking around me for a bit. I finally spotted Maggie Sue and that other one, the same distance from me that they'd been before, and that helped a lot. My stomach stopped swooping around some, but my mouth was watering like I was going to throw up.

I thought for a moment that someone had flipped on all the lights in the store, but this was sunlight. Hard and bright full summer sun beating down on the top of my head—almost punishing. My eyes were all squinted, trying to adjust. When my vision finally cleared, I had another bad moment when I realized I was looking down, I mean, really far down. Me and Maggie Sue and That Other One, we were all hanging in the air.

I couldn't help it, I puked. Then watched as the mess fell down, and down, and down into tall prairie grass. I closed my eyes for a bit because I just couldn't handle it. I'm not scared of heights usually, and I told myself I was already dead, but my body just wanted to keep freaking out, and honestly, I thought I might shit myself. For real, shit myself, pardon my language. The thought of losing control like that in front of Maggie Sue was too much. Puking already made me look like a loser.

I swear I wasn't on anything. One second we were in IKEA, and the next we were floating over the prairie. Those two kept talking talking talking, and finally I mustered the courage to open my eyes again. My body jerked the way it does when you're falling asleep and you imagine for a second that you're falling, but I wasn't falling, and so I just focused on that fact to calm down.

That's when I realized I was looking down at a huge herd of buffalo. I mean absolutely massive. The word "herd" doesn't even do it justice, it sounds too tame. I looked it up after—you can also say a gang of buffalo, or an obstinancy, though I bet that's for those buffalo you were talking about, not bison. Still, obstinancy fits. They filled the entire horizon and were just starting to pass below us. The sound was like rolling thunder, it just didn't end. From where we were, it was hard to get a sense of scale, but the prairie grass was also incredible—it was slightly taller than the buffalo until it was trampled flat, torn up by thousands of hooves. I'd heard stories of how unbelievably numerous they used to be, but I'm telling you, what I saw didn't fit inside my brain. How was it even possible for there to be so many? These days, a herd of a few dozen is a big deal, like a cause-for-ceremony-and-celebration kind of big deal. If you were fleet footed enough, you could have walked on the backs of this obstinancy and been travelling for more than a day before you reached the end.

I'm sorry, do you have a tissue or something? I can't help it, I was crying like a baby then, and every time I think about it I get like this. That view? That was the reality for my ancestors, and something no one living today has ever seen. Okay, maybe not while floating above them, though I wouldn't be surprised anymore to find out that used to be possible, too. Still, what I saw that day has completely changed how I see everything. The Safeway where I first bumped into Maggie Sue? The parking lot, the streets, all the buildings and fences and yards—do you think any of that would even be possible if the buffalo still existed in numbers like

148

that? They'd flood through town and wipe it all clean, I know it. kanâtan, instead of Canada.

Whew.

Okay. Well, it was shock after shock, and I think I just started being numb to it. My brain stopped processing, shut me down. I was just an observer being tossed around by whatever Maggie Sue and That One were doing, and it really humbled me. Like why was I even there, except to bear witness? And me, I'm not even that good at being an observer; I have the attention span of a toddler. Worse, even, because a lot of toddlers can focus for longer than me. Back in the day, back when the buffalo existed in those numbers, I probably would have been trained to pay attention better, it would have counted for a lot. But it's like those spiritual muscles I was talking about, I've just never exercised my attention span. Frick, honestly, what am I even good at except for playing video games? And that was fine, until that night. Now I see I have to put more work in.

Right. Okay well, get this, Maggie Sue and That Other One, they were yelling something down to the buffalo, and slowly, the obstinancy slowed down. It took a while. Imagine millions of tons of muscle in motion having to stop; that's not something that can happen on a dime. I noticed then, along the edges of the vanguard, other beings in the long grass, lots of them. Wolves keeping a watchful distance. Birds everywhere, too, some little brown ones rising up off the backs of the buffalo, and other bigger birds whirling above, some pretty close to us, actually. Ripples farther out in the grass—who knows what was out there—but it seemed like more and more animals were headed in our direction.

The rolling thunder of hooves had stopped, but the rustling of grass and the animal calls quickly rose to such a cacophony, it started to make me panic again, even though we were well out of harm's way. It was overwhelming: the sights, the noise, and yeah, even the smells. Wet dog plus musk times meat breath and grass farts, all to the thousandth power.

I mean, I don't even think I've been in the presence of that many humans, not even in a city. Maybe it wasn't possible, but I think there were millions of animals gathering, not just thousands. The remaining tall grass started to bend and disappear, and swarms of four-legged creatures flooded toward us, then all the winged ones, hosted on the backs of the biggest animals, the buffalo and deer and elk and moose. Ducks of every kind, swans, loons, and more. I didn't actually know the names of most of the birds that were arriving. Then the foxes, some tiny like Maggie Sue, some bigger like the ones I was used to. And coyotes, more wolves, so many wolves, lumbering bears, and more—my eyes couldn't scan fast enough. Just when I thought it wasn't possible for more creatures to shove their way into the crowd, here came frogs and snakes and insects. I mean, we were missing only the water beings that couldn't breathe air. I'm pretty sure they were being included somehow, though. It took a long, long time, but the sun didn't budge in the sky.

Below us wasn't land anymore; it was just a rolling sea of living beings, roughly grouped by species, with no conflict breaking out other than a few nips and growls over precious real estate. That's when we started swooping down, and I had another bad moment as all the beings down there shuffled and shoved back far enough to form a wide circle of raw, dark earth steaming in the summer heat where it had been freshly uncovered by the mass of nonhumans.

That's when it occurred to me to wonder why I was the only real human there.

Maggie Sue stood in the centre of the circle, her feet sinking in the torn-up earth almost to the ankles of her beaded wraparound moccasins. That Other One was walking sunwise around the edge, greeting beings, syllabics flowing into the air like a stream. I had stumbled and allowed myself to fall to the ground, and now I was sitting there as close to Maggie Sue as I could get without actually hiding under her skirt. She looked down at me from under the brim of her black felt hat and gave me a wicked grin. Her fox form regarded me calmly, but with a matching gleam in her eyes. My heart hitched again in my chest. I swear, I'd have done anything to keep her looking at me like that, even if part of me did feel like she was thinking about eating me up. Maybe especially because of that.

That Other One finished greeting the assorted beings and nodded to Maggie Sue, who gave me one last grin before raising her magnificent head to the sky and letting out a blood-curdling howl. You know how to say "howl" in Cree? It's oyôyow, and she oyôyowed like nothing I'd ever heard before. I *felt* it in my bones, in my guts, inside my squishy brain. I guess that's what "visceral" really means. It shook me like a ragdoll and spat me out. When the sound faded, all that was left were the rhythmic swishes and minute adjustments of millions of living beings, a sound that I don't think even my ancestors ever experienced.

Look, my kookum is deeply Catholic. I know some of our people don't like to talk about this, but a lot of the older people were or still are, and even though I always felt really uncomfortable in church, when kookum wanted me there, I went. I felt guilty every time I entered a church, like somehow everyone knew I didn't believe, and something bad would happen to me in there. Us, we have good reason to fear the church, to hate it, even, but it was more like I was transgressing. I couldn't respect it the way my kookum did, and I felt bad about that.

But this one time, she drove me and a bunch of my cousins down to Montana, to the Rocky Boy Powwow, one of the few I actually went to outside of Alberta. I was probably fourteen or fifteen then, too cool for church, and almost too cool for a road trip with little cousins, but I was hoping maybe I'd snag at the powwow, you know, being an exotic foreigner from the north, ehhhh. None of us had regalia; we were too broke-ass urban for that, but kookum had some complicated visiting schedule, and my aunties were happy to get rid of some of the kids for a week.

Instead of heading east to Havre when we could and down to Rocky Boy, she kept on south for a couple of hours until we hit Helena, just so we could visit the Cathedral there. She drowned out our complaining by rolling open her window and cranking up the country station. When we finally arrived and piled out the car, stretching and whining, kookum smoothed down her kerchief like she hadn't been driving all day and gave us the look. We shut up and followed her like little ducklings.

Like I said, I'd been in churches before, and all I felt was guilty. But this was the biggest church I'd ever seen, with huge stone columns, a tiled floor, gold and red everywhere, stained glass—I mean, I can't do it justice. I could hardly take it all in. It was the most massive building I'd ever been inside. Even standing outside it a moment before didn't prepare me; I had been too close to really take in its colossal size.

It was magnificent in a way I could never have been prepared for. It almost hurt, if I'm being honest, that something so beautiful could be built out of the wealth accrued from theft and slavery and genocide. Like it shouldn't be allowed to exist, but in that moment, I was so happy it did, because it made me believe in something, even if wasn't a Christian god. My kookum was looking at me, and I could tell she knew that I could hear my heart beating, how it sang, and when a hot tear splashed onto my cheek, she nodded and wiped it away, and gathered up my little cousins so they wouldn't see my stricken face.

But actually, that church in Montana was nothing. Humans built that to worship, to create something they felt safe inside. It's even supposed to be a sanctuary where you can't hurt the people inside, though I guess those rules don't apply to children. It was like the opposite of nature; it was an exercise in dominance. And at that moment, my ass sunken into the dirt, looking up at Maggie Sue, I found it pitiful, laughable. Compared to that circle, compared to the presence of every being that calls the prairie its home? What I'd felt in Saint Helena wasn't even the shadow of the feeling I was experiencing now, hearing millions of beings breathe like the heartbeat of the universe. I was openly weeping, and I didn't even care. This was the first time I'd ever felt like I could truly understand worship.

I still don't understand why they didn't get a fluent human in there, but I guess my bumping into Maggie Sue was how I got picked. The number of fluent Cree speakers in my neighbourhood is not zero, but still not high. Most of us have been stripped of our language, and it sure made my situation awkward.

I'm pretty sure this was some sort of mega council circle. I tried, I really did, to understand what That One was saying, who started with âw niwâhkomâkanak, which I do know. That first word, âw, it's like a verbal clearing of the throat, an attention-grabber, an "I'm about to start talking now, listen up!" A lot is packed into that little word. niwâhkomâkanak is "my relatives," but as you can guess, it doesn't always mean just human relations.

After that there were whole strings of sentences that passed through my ears without stopping, dropping little tidbits here and there like amiskwak and maskwak and piyêsîsak, the few individual words I know naming beavers, bears, birds. I'm pretty sure the first hour of that opening speech was a series of formal greetings, because I did hear a lot of animals named, and I probably know about two dozen animal words in Cree.

I started dozing, I think; my mind wasn't trying to pick up words anymore, they just flowed over me, and lethargy seeped in. Maggie Sue didn't even shift position, and part of me envied her patience. I've always struggled with that, in ceremony, at church, in class. I tried to keep my body still as I sat there in the churned-up soil. When everything went dark and figures started swooshing through the air around me, I thought I'd just fallen asleep.

Have you ever been to a planetarium? One where you lie down and they project images onto the huge curved dome above you? When I was in junior high, our school took us on a field trip to the science centre that ended with a laser light show. I remember lying there in the centre of the room, which was covered in foam pads that smelled like gym mats. I was lucky; everyone wanted to lie in the middle instead of in the seats around the room, but I was quick and got a spot right next to my crush.

When the lights went out and the music started, I sort of inched my hand into the space between us, palm down, and just left it there. The images started shooting across the dome, not real fancy like now, probably, but at the time it was impressive. Like neon outlines dancing across the sky, transforming and melting and reforming. Some boys had joked about getting stoned for the show, but no one actually had any weed. Didn't stop them from giggling and causing a ruckus as though they'd actually gotten high, though.

While the teacher crept over to one side of the room to shush them, I felt the whisper of movement beside me, and soon, I was holding sweaty, nervous hands with the person I'd been mooning after all year. Neither of us spoke a word, surrounded by our unsuspecting peers. I was hyper-aware of every inch of my body, of where we were touching, of the people breathing and shifting around us, and of the images and sounds playing above and around us.

I could feel Maggie Sue more than see her, continuing to stand beside where I was sitting, and I could still hear the millions of breaths and slight movements of every creature around us, but the world was dark and endless. Figures shuddered into view. That One continued to speak, but now I was seeing what was being said, and things started making more sense.

I watched the genocide of the buffalo play out like a neon pantomime. At the best of times, these kinds of portrayals kick me in the gut and don't let me catch my breath. Like last summer, I went to a panel discussion about colonialism, and one of the panelists splashed up a huge picture of that famous photo, the one with a môniyâw standing in front of a mountain of bison skulls. I just stared at that image, and my ears stopped working.

All I could process was the horror of that photograph and what it represented. Like seeing the dead bodies of your close relatives displayed for shock value, and never mind how it made you feel their loss all over. I mean exactly like that, in fact, because even though I grew up in a generation that never knew the buffalo the way our ancestors did, that pain was my inheritance.

That picture perfectly captured why I don't speak fluent Cree, why my mom died of what should have been a treatable illness, why my dad started drinking so hard he couldn't take care of me, why my kookum had to raise me, why I was so angry growing up, why I hurt myself in so many ways, why I wake up too many mornings and think that I can't endure this any longer. In a different life I would have had a place. I would have had a clearly defined role within a society that valued all of creation. I would have been self-sufficient, as well as existing within an interconnectedness I can barely imagine. I'm not romanticizing it; life is always hard, but I feel like a shadow of what I should have been.

And yet, there was something utterly profane about witnessing this history in front of the very beings who were nearly wiped out completely. As though I were trespassing on something deeply personal and painful. I felt shame and tried to avert my eyes, but it was no good. Those figures were all around us, and who was I to refuse to bear witness?

I heard a low rumble as the figures danced above and around us, stylized neon figures falling like sheaves of wheat, mown down, as snaking train tracks slowly formed. The rumble rose to a low moan, and at first, I thought I must be making that guttural sound, but it was too big for one human body. It continued to rise to a keening; the throats of millions of animals, not just buffalo, joined in mourning. I tried closing my eyes, but the neon pinks and greens were burned into my brain, and still they fell; they fell, bulls, cows, calves, and all.

The figures were abstract, but this history was not. As painful as it had been for me to occasionally confront evidence of the mass murder of the buffalo, bearing witness in that circle alongside our buffalo relations themselves, I felt a grief so crushing and total, I wasn't sure I could endure it.

I think, as humans, we really do have to push these things out of our minds just to function, whether we're neechies or not. I mean, you take a little kid, four or five years old, from any background, and you tell them that millions of buffalo were slaughtered so white people could move west. Do you think that little kid is going to look up at you and shrug and say, "That's terrible, but now we have cities on the prairies, so look at the bright side!"

No, they are going to cry, because it is objectively and unambiguously horrible. Becoming an adult seems to be all about learning how to forget these kinds of things, but kids, they know what's true, and no one had to teach them that.

It was such an assault on the senses, the images around us, that it took me a while to notice that more was happening. I suppose I'm so used to seeing things through a human viewpoint that I missed it at first, because while humans did appear and disappear, brief flashes of violence, we were peripheral. Now I saw the dynamited beaver lodges, the shrinking lakes, the crowded structures, almost cartoonish, spreading and rising everywhere. Buildings as seen through the eyes of beings who didn't find them marvellous or even interesting, like how I now saw the Cathedral of Saint Helena. They were shadowy and incomplete sketches, background for the ongoing devastation as animal nation after animal nation was displaced, poisoned, murdered. Roads stretched out like the circulatory system of a diseased monster.

I watched as plant nations were wiped out completely, the original grasses of the prairies shrinking and shrinking, replaced by the tiny root systems of seeds brought over by colonizers. The entire landscape transformed entirely, and once again I felt that deep grief, confronted by the fact that the homeland I'd grown up in was unrecognizable to all my ancestors, human and nonhuman alike.

While this perspective of colonization played out around me, focusing on the loss of nonhuman life and territory, I couldn't help but also think about what was happening to us neechies at the same time. From the cannons and the Gatling gun at Batoche, the hanging of our leaders, the destroyed communities, the reserves, the pass system that kept our allies in their grass prisons, the withholding of rations, being burned out of the road allowances, the constant violence, the residential schools, all of it. Seven generations of torment to get me to where I am today, broke and pretty depressed, and in love with a fox in the shape of a human woman. Weirdly, it all sort of made me feel a bit better.

Maybe that sounds bad, but I know the human history. I just hadn't put it together with what was also happening to other living beings, not like this. To see entire animal nations wiped out and the land so completely transformed, it made me realize something.

It took generations to cause this much damage. A blip in time, sure, compared to the longer history of these lands, but more than one human lifetime. If it took this long to do so much damage, how much time will it take to repair that damage? I mean, this violence is still happening, it hasn't stopped. How can we even talk about repair yet? Maybe me being such a fuck-up wasn't just a me and my bootstraps problem. Maybe never having space without colonizers colonizing means we can't actually fix anything yet. Maybe we can't be good relations because we have to relearn how, and no one is actually giving us the time to do it.

When this notion struck me, the scene suddenly shifted. At first, I thought I'd caused the change, like maybe somehow it had all been keyed into my brain, and I was actually the one controlling this light show. How arrogant, hey? Like, I'm sitting there as someone who was raised to understand humans aren't the centre of the universe, but I still can't help thinking I'm the centre of the universe. Millions of living beings there, but the one solitary human—well, heck, I must count as much as all of them, right? Chee, my kookum would laugh.

It couldn't have been me thinking that show into existence. I didn't have the knowledge. A lot of it was new to me, because I'd never stopped to think, for example, what happens to burrowing owls who nest in buffalo dung, and why cow dung just doesn't provide the same niche. The forms around us were glowing more dimly now, sickly and less populous, the landscape scarred and unrecognizable; it all seemed to pause for a moment. It took a few heartbeats for me to see that time was still running.

The wonky buildings, those capillary roads, they began to fizzle, pixelating. At the same time, the colour of the living beings brightened, and they grew more populous. Buffalo tore across the prairie again, ripping out the colonizer grasses. Lakes sprang up around beaver lodges, and wildfires became more contained as seasons flashed by. I was witnessing a world healing without the presence of humans.

I felt a shiver travel up my spine and lodge itself directly behind my ears. This council circle had been called for a reason, and That One doesn't just show up all the time anymore—I'm pretty sure we'd have heard about it. The moccasin telegraph operates in some quantum realm, faster than light, because there've been times I heard about trouble I was getting into from an auntie before it even happened, I swear. If That One was moving around in the world again, the People would know.

I think I was witnessing a debate of sorts, and it's not something we humans have been totally oblivious to. Did you ever see that movie—it wasn't really great or anything—but basically plants start pumping out this chemical that causes humans to kill themselves? The idea of the planet purifying itself by killing off humans is something that recurs in books and movies plenty of times. Or a few humans making that choice for the planet and doing something to kill off all humanity.

That trope always bothered me, to be honest. Europeans went out and colonized the world, enslaved human beings, committed genocide, wiped out entire ecosystems, and violently enforced hierarchies. Now their descendants have decided things are really bad, because oops, chattel slavery, disease, slaughtered salmon, buffalo, caribou—that wasn't the time to start ringing any alarm bells, but goshdarn housing prices are ridiculous and homeless people are shitting on the sidewalks, maybe we ought to just kill off humans so the planet can heal. Ha ha, cool idea for a story.

How did we suddenly become one human race again? After centuries of insisting race exists and matters, that just goes away, poof, when it comes down to who made this big mess. Forget all this education and reconciliation stuff, I guess all Black, Indigenous, and People of Colour had to do this whole time was step up and say, "We'll take the blame—all that crap you did to pretend you were the masters of all creation? Yeah that's on us, sorry."

That just makes me so mad though, imagine having some vegan leftist from Vancouver gentrifying your neighbourhood, going on about how "humans" are killing the planet when the only reason there are even houses here to flip is because white people murdered the buffalo. That's not on us, it just fucking isn't.

Hey, I'm not attacking you. I'm just saying, I'm not going to accept that notion from white people who think being called racist is worse than having cops assume your mountain bike is stolen and confiscating it because you look too poor to own it. Now you can't get to work, now you're unemployed, now you're just as poor as they need you to be.

But when it's a council of every nonhuman being in your territory, as the lone human, well, I just kept my opinion to myself. I mean, how would they do it, if they have the power to wipe us out? How would they choose between the ones of us who lived with them forever and did okay until new ones came along and killed everything? Administer a fluency test? I'd be screwed, but some môniyâw linguist who had the money and time to study Cree for years would ace it.

Maybe a cultural competency evaluation? Yeah, again I'd be screwed. I know a bit, just enough in fact to be sure I'd fail miserably, but some môniyâw survivalist who gets featured in national papers for living on the land is going to score high, never mind when neechies go on the land we get the RCMP laying boots and no one praising us.

Maybe some sort of blood test, spit in a tube, DNA? I've got white people in my family tree, maybe they'd just chop off a leg or something. I want to argue that it shouldn't fall on all of us, what has been done, what is still being done. I want to argue that cops are still killing Indigenous and Black people so much that dying by cop is just one of the more likely ways folks in my neighbourhood can expect to go out.

I want to argue that my people would do anything, absolutely anything, to return the land to the way it was, but I know it's not really true. We've got plenty of money-loving, oil-praising, conservative-voting relatives who've thoroughly internalized capitalism and white supremacy, calling our own people down and drooling at the notion of being on top of the heap. They love telling you all about it on Facebook.

Yeah, they're that way because of all the awful things we've endured for generations, but what does that change? I can't pretend they'll just suddenly see the light if a cull happens and we're left behind. And what about folks like me? What can I offer? Culturally deficient, me. Just making it through. I'm not the hero of any story; I just am. Does this planet need me?

I was working myself up to just sort of accept it. Is it really so terrible that one species gets wiped out, if it means countless other species won't be? How many species are already irrevocably gone from this universe because of humans, whether it was my kind of human or not? Were any of them worth less than us? We seem to be capable of so much evil, and no matter what folks want to believe, it isn't really getting better. Sure there are good people out there, but does it stack up? Does it balance the scales?

I started to get sad though, because I was thinking about my little cousins—the kids of my cousins, actually, but they're all my cousins. One of them is six months old, just pudgy like you wouldn't believe, I want to eat his little knees, he's so cute. Gorgeous brown eyes, always in a sweet bonnet with a Pendleton pattern, the way some families still do. Puts everything in his little mouth, real smiley, that one. I know he'll be that four- or five-year-old who will cry when he learns about the buffalo. I know he'll cry when he gets teased for having long hair. I know he'll cry when he sees men and women who look like his kookum and mooshum sleeping in tents beside the LRT, because he'll know it's not right. It's very "Won't someone think of the children?" but honestly, what do those babies have to answer for? What possible crimes have they committed?

And yeah, that made me really upset. I'm okay dying if it means something positive happens. I don't say that lightly, and I'm not talking about suicide. I've lost so many people that way, friends and relatives. You probably know how high our rates of suicide are, but I doubt you really get it. Some mornings I wake up and I just lie there in my bed, trying to convince myself things are worth getting up for, and yeah, I think about it. A lot. But I don't ever want to make someone feel the way I do every time I get one of those phone calls, every time I have to go to a wake. I don't want to be the reason one of my little cousins decides it's an answer because I chose it.

No, I'm talking about sacrifice. Me, I've never been in the sundance lodge, even though my kookum tried to get me in there. I've hung around outside and heard the eagle bone whistles, and I've pictured the dancers in there, but I always felt too awkward to dance myself. I wasn't really sure how I'd fit in there, so I kept putting it off. I know about it, though, and about sacrifice, how it takes a lot of will and why we still give of ourselves that way. Those animal and plant nations sacrifice, too, and that's how all of creation operates. I'm willing to sacrifice myself, if it means something good comes of it, but I'm not okay with making that choice for those babies. Not my little cousins, not those sweet little Somali babies at the bus stop, not anyone's little ones. They shouldn't pay the price.

I had drawn my knees up to my chest and wrapped my arms around my legs, and I was ugly crying again, snot just bubbling all gross, a real mess. I couldn't stop thinking about all those babies, and all the babies that have ever been, and all the babies that would one day exist. I don't even *want* babies, me, but there I was, babies completely on the brain.

I felt a light tap on the top of my head, and I wiped my face on my knee, then looked up. Maggie Sue had her head cocked to the side, and I think she was looking at me, but it was still really dark and I could only see her silhouette. Her fox form wasn't any more visible, so I don't know what expression she had, but this was the first time she'd touched me since I bumped into her and—

And I was back in the IKEA, my broken toe freshly throbbing in pain, leaning against the railing and looking at that mural. Maggie Sue and That Other One weren't there. I wheeled around looking for her, because That One being gone was a bit of a relief, but her, I didn't want that to be the last time I saw Maggie Sue.

I started to become aware of big crashing noises, and a weird vibration in the floor. I tell you, I was so confused at first, I thought maybe I'd been standing there all night and the store was opening, but I could see down the stairs to the entrance, and it was still dark out. When I caught sight of the first buffalo, I stood there, mouth just hanging open. It had one of those fake TVs hanging from a horn, the cardboard ones they put in the display rooms. I was sure I was hallucinating, mistaking the buffalo in the mural for the real deal, but when another one appeared behind it, and more behind that one, I almost flew down the stairs, broken toe or not.

Come on, how would I have gotten them in there? Where's the humungous 180-wheel trailer I'd have needed to haul—what was it, *six hundred buffalo*—into the Edmonton IKEA? How would I have got them upstairs? Do you seriously think that elevator is rated for even one nine-hundred-pound bull? You saw the news; those stairs were like a mini buffalo jump until they just came down with all the bodies and formed a ramp. The cops slapped me with a trespassing charge because it was chaos, and I'm sorry, but even those assholes couldn't seriously try to pin it all on some nobody like me. Besides, we all heard about what happened at the Home Depot, and then at the Red Lobster, and I was in remand then, before my kookum got me out.

You keep making the mistake of thinking I'm the main character, but I've told you over and over again, I'm a bit player. I get to tell the story, but I don't even really understand it myself, and no amount of poking at the details is going to make me anything more. It could have been anyone who bumped into Maggie Sue and got pushed into the spirit realm; it just happened to be me.

I'm not sure why she sent me back when she did, and I don't know what that council decided. Why just send buffalo? Thousands loose now, just tearing everything up, ha! Maybe more coming? Who knows. I think they decided not to wipe us out, and I'm pretty grateful for that. You should be, too.

What am I going to do now? Not much, I guess. It's not like all of this changed much for me. Other than you and APTN, I haven't got much media interest, though they were just thinking of starting a new season of *Indians & Aliens* with this story. I'm only talking to you because I sort of like the *Rat Creek Press*, even if it's real cop-loving sometimes. Look, I know what it all sounds like. I don't expect most folks to pay me much mind. My kookum is taking me to speak to some Elders this weekend about it, and we'll see what they have to say.

Me, I'm keeping an eye out for Maggie Sue. I pretty much think about her all the time. I know it's probably hopeless, but I can't help it. I never bought into love at first sight, but it's like that song. I'm a believer, for real now. I'm motivated to get out of bed and start taking Cree seriously, so I can actually talk to her next time. I want to learn more of the old stories, because I think I'll find out more about her that way.

I figured out what species of fox she is, by the way, *Vulpes velox*. She's a swift fox. They were declared locally extinct in the 1930s, but a breeding program in the late 1990s brought them back. There are only about a hundred of them left, and they're still a threatened species, but at least they're not extinct. I've been thinking about heading down to southern Alberta to see if I can run into any of them. Could be they can get me in touch with her.

I started stocking my freezer full of lingonberries from IKEA, actually, obviously not the one here in town, it's still trashed, but I had a bud bring me some from Calgary. I found out they're called mehkêsîsîmina in Cree, fox berries! I leave a handful out to melt in a dish on the step each morning.

Maybe she'll scratch on my door one of these days. For her, I can be patient.

"MAGGIE SUE" EXPLORATION

Years ago I attended a dinner at the First Peoples' House at McGill University, a place that was my haven during my time there. The room was full of Indigenous and non-Indigenous people alike, and a Mohawk Elder had been asked to give the ohén:ton karihwatéhkwen, the words before all else, also called the thanksgiving address.[76] There are different versions of the ohén:ton karihwatéhkwen, though they vary mostly in terms of length, from very brief to something that can take a very, very long time. I'll leave it up to Kanien'kehá:ka to explain its purpose and the words that go into it, because that is not my place.

Those of us who could stand were asked to do so, and the Elder that day spoke in fluent Kanien'kehá for over forty-five minutes while the smell of food wafted under our noses and people shifted from foot to foot. Maybe it wasn't forty-five minutes, though I feel pretty certain about that detail, but I do remember the joy that spread through me as I listened to these words I did not fully understand, and as I saw some of the white attendees grow more visibly impatient. The Elder didn't falter, and also gave no clues as to when he would finish. He took space and held it.

That is a powerful thing in this society, when Indian Time is denigrated and misconstrued as an excuse to be late or lazy, or to ramble off topic during meetings or presentations, when really what it means is that things happen in their natural times and when they need to. The Elder

---

76   ("Ohén:ton Karihwatéhkwen" n.d.). You can listen to one version here, on the Kanien'kehá:ka Onkwawén:na Raotitióhkwa Language and Cultural Center website: www.korkahnawake.org.

felt a longer address—though certainly not the longest possible—was needed that day, and it was certainly a lesson in patience.

I begin this piece with a story, because that is how the narrative of "Maggie Sue" unfolds, "interrupted" by a series of anecdotes that seem to digress from the main story, perhaps frustrating the listener, who simply wants the highlights of this fantastical yarn. The protagonist often apologizes for sidetracking, but also seems hopeful that the listener will understand the reason for these details.

I am tired of watching Elders and community members be rushed when they speak. I am sick of seeing our people disrespected when they choose to share something and begin with a story—theirs or another person's—because it's seen as off topic or not relevant. Métis/Cree speech, even very formal speech, like that of many other Indigenous peoples, is not always strictly linear. The information presented is usually not summed up into clear bullet points. Sometimes you have to work at it, *really focus*, and think about what is being shared.

Speaking from one's own subjective experiences is also common among Indigenous peoples, and far from being considered inappropriate, this positionality communicates a number of important things the listener should be aware of. When it comes to knowledge that has been passed down and is being recounted by an individual, there is usually an acknowledgment that this information "represent[s] the cumulative knowledge of various sacred stories, practices, or protocols" (Wolfhart 1998, 142).

Sometimes our people are called upon to speak by Elders or other community members, and the authority to say these things is conferred upon the speaker temporarily. Within a western paradigm, beginning such a speech with an apologia, as Wolfhart (1998, 141) calls it, by explaining that any mistakes made are the orator's own, weakens what the speaker is saying. It allows doubt to creep in that perhaps the information being shared is not objectively perfect.

The all-too-common western practice of presenting oneself as an infallible expert is inherently problematic within many Indigenous cultures, as the communal nature of knowledge is never far from our experiences. Almost certainly within any given audience is at least one person who has knowledge equal to or greater than the speaker, and making space for this demonstrates respect, while also acknowledging that obvious truth. Within Métis/Cree oration, these clarifications strengthen the esteem in which a speaker is held because they represent a concern for what Wolfart calls "fidelity of transmission" (1998, 178). Sometimes the speaker is presenting information passed to them by another, and as human beings, we have lapses in memory or ability to faithfully recount that which has been entrusted to us. There is also care taken because in Métis/Cree ontologies, words are transformative. Recounting details improperly can have real and deleterious consequences.

tapahtêyimisowin, the Métis/Cree term for humility, is a central teaching and valued positionality. It literally means to think little of oneself—not poorly, not badly, just not better than. This is not low self-esteem, but rather a reflection of non-hierarchy. ayisiyiniwak, human beings, are part of Creation, not superior to, not apart from. All our knowledges have value, just as all beings are valuable. To look down on any being, to view that being with contempt, is a violation of the sacred within us all. With this in mind, humility is a neutral position, but not always an easy one to maintain, else we would not have so many teachings about what happens to those who discard humility to seek acclaim.

Often, the speaker uses thoughtful pauses, short silences while they choose the correct word (especially if English is a second language). I have seen people interpret these pauses as cessation, and they break in with a "thank-you-for-your-words-now-moving-on." Not only does that fail to recognize that this person, in this moment, needed to share something in their own time, it also fails to recognize the validity of Indigenous narration, which has no need to fill silence with meaningless noise. We are not unaware of time. We simply recognize that time is not limited in the way settler colonial capitalism insists it is.

There is, in fact, time to hear us.

For the most part, the narrator uses these smaller stories to clearly explain the details—about the neighbourhood I currently call home, about the way Indigenous people live today and kayâs (long ago), about transformation and the spirit realm, about Elder Brother. Some things are not explained because the narrator doesn't know those âtayôhkana, sacred stories, just as many of our own people no longer know them, myself very much included. Some of the details reference well known âtayôhkêwina, and you can look them up, too, if you can't access someone who can tell them to you directly (Bloomfield 1993).

As problematic as it is to have to access our own cultural wealth via settler publications, I am grateful we have this option. Telling our own people to "Google it" when they are trying to reconnect to what has been stolen from them doesn't pass muster. So much of the information out there is wrong, distorted, and frankly harmful. Not every disconnected Indigenous person is in a position to access community safely, particularly QTBIPOC folks. While there are valid issues with some of these publications, provenance is acknowledged in the form of who told these stories to whom, as well as where and when this happened. This makes it easier to correct errors, just as the orator intended.

When Maggie Sue holds up sizzling fat, she is recounting events as told to Leonard Bloomfield by kâ-kîsikâw-pîhtokêw (Coming Day). In this story, Elder Brother is poor, and when some Frenchmen come to trade, wiya (the genderless Cree pronoun) has no furs to give to the men. That's right, Frenchmen. Sacred stories did not end with Contact; why should they end now? In any case, Elder Brother badly wants some items, so wiya puts poison in fat and has a wolf gather up as many other wolves and foxes as possible. wiya preaches religion to them and promises them everlasting life if they eat the fat, which they do. Oof, lessons can be hard. They all die, and Maggie Sue holds a grudge.

When Elder Brother angrily holds up charred duck feet in response to her justified anger, this is a reference to another story, in which Elder Brother is hungry and tricks ducks and geese by having them shut their eyes and dance. wiya wrings most of their necks and sets them in the fire to cook. In the meantime, wiya has an encounter with a fox who outwits wiya, eating up all the food and leaving nothing but charred feet behind to make wiya think they were overcooked. Elder Brother figures out the double-cross and tries to get revenge. The outcome is scatological, literally.

These stories are so much better than these summaries can possibly do justice to, so if you ever get the opportunity to hear a master story-teller share these accounts, please take it.

A LODGE WITHIN
HER MIND

It was nestled in between an email promising a "GiANt Cock" and another advertising "70% OFF ESSENTIAL OILS COVID-19 PROTECTION ACT NOW." Six months into her share of global isolation, and she was even willing to scroll through her spam folder in the hopes of relieving her bone-deep boredom.

She let the cursor hover over the email and took another sip of honeyed Labrador tea, the last of her stash. With the now pervasive fragmentation of her thoughts, she slipped into a mental unboxing of receiving the care package from Treaty 3 territory a month and a half ago, with her cousin's looping, beautiful writing in purple ink on the battered cardboard.[77] Slitting open the tape and folding back the flaps as a deep, earthy scent rose and filled the room with the soft intimacy of the dark places in a forest populated with endless varieties of spruce and pine. Removing the dry packing material: askiya, sphagnum moss. Inside, she'd found a pair of long rectangular birchbark earrings, each adorned with a purple-dyed fish-scale flower with a lime-green porcupine-quill stem and two lovely emerald moose-tufted leaves. Dried Labrador tea filled an empty Red Rose box, and a bundle of sage tied with red thread was nestled beside it along with a little cloth sachet of cedar, and another of tobacco. A small pot of honey. Carefully folded brown paper held wild rice. Medicines from the land, the combined scents leaving her crying into the moss— a new, more pungent smell emerging as it swelled beneath her tears.

By then, she hadn't been out of her tiny bachelor basement suite in over three months, unwilling to risk defying the Emergency Act isolation

---

77 Care package inspired by real-life cuz at Land Glitter (Instagram @landglitter).

order. Carding and policing had always been pervasive in this mostly Black and Indigenous area of the city, but the pandemic had provided justification to kick it up to eighties dystopic sci-fi levels. Like many others in areas where the rent strike had been unsuccessful, her rent had been deferred rather than waived, though her landlord had gotten a hefty assistance package, and she could be forced out of her apartment if fined under the Act. No one was really certain where evictees were housed after that, but she didn't want to find out. It was bad enough knowing any potential end to this pandemic would result in her being homeless anyway as the months of deferred rent came due all at once.

It felt like her body was constantly being sliced into numbed pieces, dissociated from one another, bereft of touch, of freedom, of the wind on her skin, the sky that still existed, vast as the prairies, but hidden by grimy windows that opened into a shadowed alley. She didn't even talk to herself anymore. She sometimes wondered if she'd lost her voice entirely, but before she could finish the thought, would forget to check. The night that care package came in, she'd slept with the contents arranged around her body, the mingled bouquet filling her dreams with shape-shifting beavers, the silent green cold of abyssal waters, green-needled beings that rasped and whispered in a restful abandonment generations of their Elders had known only through pulsed histories passed on with the languid cycle of sap, barely believed until it was real again.

"WHOLE BRAIN EMULATION: beyond the limits of biology!!!!!!!!" She clicked.

Isolation had done strange things to her attention span. She often found herself stiff and cramped from immobility, a book in her hand and no memory of what she had been doing for so long. Straightening her limbs took time and left her gasping with the pain. Or she'd sit down in front of the television to watch a show, preferably as vapid and escapist as possible, only to blink and see the darkened screen awaiting a response: "Are you still watching?" At first it had worried her, but after a while, it didn't matter anymore. Nothing did. She recognized that she was probably depressed, but that was also the new normal.

She scanned the email, unable to focus on complete sentences. Phrases appeared in front of her like bubbles floating away from the screen, ballooning and popping: "processing substrate," "recording unique arrangement and responses of neurons and synapses," "copy and transfer," "Mens Aeterna's patented neuromorphic hardware," "upload at home." And then one phrase that swelled and grew and replaced all the others: "*Escape the confines of your current reality.*"[78]

It's what they'd all been exhorted to do since social isolation, then legally and unevenly enforced isolation began. Escapism was the new patriotism. Read a book! Watch television! Take up a hobby! Create! Network online! Drink alcohol, smoke weed, if you're confined with your partner, have a lot of sex! Play dress-up! Stream your life 24-7, watch other people's livestreams—anything to forget that you haven't been outside in over 130 days, longer for many others. And yet the curve hadn't really flattened; it had plateaued, with sudden sharp peaks every time the restrictions were softened, followed by even harder measures.

At first, they'd said not to blame people who became ill, but that sentiment had evaporated as the death toll rose. Getting ill was a sin. Getting depressed was a sin. Needing medical attention for any physical or mental ailment taxed the resources needed to battle the pandemic, needing more supplies than one's weekly rations: sin, sin, sin. Everything was a military/religious metaphor now. It was all battle and sacrifice. Front-line workers were angels, their managers generals; we were being tested/attacked, people had to obey orders, send thoughts and prayers, support the troops, not be a collaborator of the virus, only heretics disbelieved now, treason was a death sentence one way or another, the victims were in a better place now.

....

78   *Mens aeterna*: an eternal mind (Latin translation provided by Divya M. Persaud).

So many people were like her, confined alone, and after a while, videoconferencing, phone calls, emails—none of it made up for the lack of physical presence of other human beings. Suddenly hundreds of millions of people were identifying as prisoners, but so mired in misery, most were doing nothing to organize around actual prison abolition— an opportunity undermined as much by apathy as it was deliberately interfered with, as social networks became increasingly monitored and censored.

What did she have to lose? She'd tried it all; she'd been a bright-eyed Indigenous warrior seeking cultural and spiritual enlightenment, a strict schedule, daily exercise, becoming more and more inventive with the dwindling rations once she'd lost her job, posting positive messages on social media, attending online Cree classes, beautifying her space, telling herself she'd emerge from all of this taking nothing for granted ever again. Yet as the weeks ground on and turned into months, then more than a year without the touch or present voice of another human being, without even being able to go outside, it all melted away. She stopped checking in with her friends because their faces on the screen seemed as unreal as any television program, and that scared her. She couldn't distract herself, unable to focus long enough to let her mind escape. Her girlfriend had gone home back to Montréal in the early days for a visit just before all travel was suspended; now she had a hard time even remembering what she looked like. Friends and relations all faded away, lost in their own fog or unable to penetrate hers.

She didn't bother trying to reread or puzzle out the whole email—she just clicked on the link. Scammers didn't have much to work with once the bank accounts of anyone receiving government aid were frozen, and antivirus protections had become scarily robust once it was clear the entire remaining global economy relied on a safe internet.

She filled out the form on the page that appeared, though it took a very long time because she kept staring off into space for long moments before coming back and typing in another answer. She agreed to the Terms and Conditions without reading the long legal document, hit submit, and went to lie down. She didn't really sleep anymore, just sort of drifted in and out of consciousness until she got too bored to stay there.

There was an extra box on top of her ration container. She lingered outside the door for as long as she safely could, her greedy eyes drinking in the sights, the sunlight too bright, the wind bracing, but smelling green and sweet. Her ears unplugged as the walls fell away for the brief time she had to collect her goods. Across the street, she saw another person, a neighbour she'd never interacted with, who was on the same ration schedule and was now the only other human being she saw in person anymore. She lifted a hand in a half-hearted wave, but the faded-blond woman, enveloped in a dirty pink housecoat despite the late-August heat, simply grabbed her own box and disappeared back into her home once more.

An Edmonton Police Service armoured vehicle rolled into view and chirped when its driver spotted her, slowing almost to a stop. Funny how there was endless money to buy pipelines and toys for cops. She pulled the boxes into her apartment and closed the door, heart pounding. Honestly, it was more excitement than she'd had in weeks. Holding the boxes against her chest as she leaned against the door, she felt an unfamiliar tug at her lips.

She unpacked her rations first, the little bag of flour, a thick wax-wrapped slice of lard, a bit of sugar, baking powder, canned meat, canned spinach (ugh, at least last time it had been baby corn), a handful of black beans, powdered milk, three teabags (not even Red Rose, but some nameless orange pekoe), three joints, and a mickey of bottom-shelf vodka. Eggs and some fresh produce only came every third box.

Each neighbourhood had a different ration box, decided on collectively in an online process that had turned incredibly heated and, like most online processes, completely excluded newcomer families. Otherwise there'd be teff flour sometimes. She doubted the rations in other areas of the city were any more diverse, but her neighbourhood had a high Indigenous population, and the white people who ended up steamrolling the whole process had decided bannock ingredients were culturally sensitive or something. It had escaped no neechie's notice that these rations were remarkably similar to what their ancestors had been given after being forced onto reserves after the North-West Resistance. By now, she fucking hated bannock.

She made some anyway, glancing now and again at the unopened package on her kitchen table, the break in her routine making her feel more awake than she'd been in—well, she couldn't really remember. It had a sticker with her address on it, but no sender information. Smaller than a loaf of bread, but oddly heavy. Sitting on her tiny kitchen table, full of possibilities. Extra rations? A care package?

She brewed some tea, choosing to use a whole teabag for one cup rather than letting it sit in a teapot. She'd reuse it later, but this one strong cup of tea was a pleasure that hadn't grown old, even as she'd given up on long baths, moisturizing, and other self-care routines that no longer made her feel any better. She forced herself to eat a slice of bannock and drink her tea, then wrap up the rest of the bannock for later before she even touched the box again.

She wanted to hold the box up to her ear and shake it, like an act of Christmas divination, but she was afraid the contents could be breakable. Images flitted through her head: a pink glass unicorn, a plushy animal in some pastel colour, a collection of tiny illustrated board books telling truncated versions of fairy tales, a scented plastic snail that opened up to hold little items when you squeezed the shell. She realized these were all items she'd desperately coveted when she was a kid, things glimpsed in the homes of white friends, toys she'd been allowed to hold, but not to have.

She opened the box carefully and pulled out the brown corrugated packing material to uncover a white VR headset. She looked at it in confusion, disappointment settling into her stomach. Maybe the powers that be had decided that, on top of the weed and alcohol, the masses needed virtual reality? No doubt plenty of households had given it a shot, too, but she wasn't particularly interested. She sighed and lifted it out of the box.

It wasn't made of plastic, as she'd thought, but a much heavier material. Creamy white … glass? Ceramic? She flicked a cracked fingernail against it—definitely not metal. And instead of the elastic headband she was expecting, something unfolded that looked like a silver spiderweb, little shining circles like dewdrops spread throughout. She accordioned the spiderweb in and out a few times until it suddenly clicked, and the whole thing became rigid, like the top half of a geodesic dome. Surprised, she put the device down on the table. Looking back into the box, she found an envelope.

Inside was a thick white card with pictorial instructions like you got with that shitty Swedish furniture depicting a seated figure pulling on the spiderweb just like she had, fitting the dome over its head, putting the display down over its eyes, then pushing a button on the side of the headset. That was it—no other information was given.

She sighed, gazing apathetically at the VR rig. The surge of excitement she'd felt had faded, replaced with the familiar grey haze of reality. New TV shows, new video games, new books—none of them caught, much less held, her interest anymore. On the other hand, the day stretched long before her, melting into all the days and weeks and months and years still to come, with no promise of change.

She picked the headset up and carried it to the battered burgundy loveseat in her tiny living room/bedroom. She curled up on the sagging cushions and, holding the heavy display in one hand, carefully fitted the strange dome over her head with the other. It caught on her hair, which made things very awkward for a while, but eventually she was able to smooth the thing down over her head. It was a bit too large, but there had been no instruction as to how to adjust the fit. The result was that it felt extremely front heavy, and as she lowered the display over her eyes to rest on the bridge of her nose, the cage began pulling up on her hair again as it slipped forward. She hissed in pain.

Holding the display now with both hands so the whole thing wouldn't slide off her head, taking her hair with it, she felt around in the darkness for the promised power button. She pushed the slight indentation and waited.

Suddenly, the cage tightened around her head, and she spasmed in shock. It continued to slowly tighten, and her breathing became rapid and shallow with panic as she released her hold on the display, which still featured only darkness, and began to claw at the spiderweb. She was unable to pull it loose, though, and could feel it compressing her scalp even more. She fumbled for the power button, but couldn't find the indentation, and the cage became tighter still, so much so that her head began to tingle. She had a terrible image of the vr set squeezing until her skull split and her brains leaked out between the silver wires. She pulled harder, thrashing around on the couch, desperate to get the thing off her head.

The tingling intensified, but the squeezing had stopped and was, she realized, not actually painful. Just very secure. What she had thought was pins and needles from the circulation in her head being cut off began to stabilize into a thrumming wave of current, running up the bottom of her head to the crown and then over again. It wasn't exactly unpleasant, but she remained uneasy.

The darkness was no longer as absolute as before. In fact, everything was becoming slightly grey, and as her eyes fought to focus on something, she turned her head this way and that, noticing that as the light continued to rise, she seemed to be in a thick bank of fog. She'd tried vr before, so she was familiar with the disorientation of seeing surround-ings that you knew weren't actually there, but she was also experiencing something strange. She knew she was sitting on her couch, but she no longer sensed the cushions. Instead, her body felt suspended, like the one time she'd tried a float tank, in body-temperature saltwater, absolute quiet, and darkness that made you start to forget your body. As soon as she thought this, her perspective changed; she'd perceived herself to be vertical, but now she was horizontal, as though lying in the tank she'd remembered. Her stomach swooped with vertigo.

The sound of lapping water rose into her awareness, and she thought of Lac Ste. Anne, where her family, along with thousands of other Métis, Cree, Nakoda, and Dene families, used to go every summer for Pilgrim-age, that sacred space that had been left silent and unvisited these past two seasons. Wetness seeped around her, soaking her clothing, and water spilled into her ears. What the hell? Had the sprinklers gone off in her apartment? She tried to pull at the VR set again, but her arms wouldn't obey her commands. Instead, water splattered onto her from above, misty droplets wetting her face, running into her nose and mouth. She sputtered. She hated having water on her face; even in the shower she always kept her face averted.

With another swooping, she was vertical again, the warm spray of her showerhead blasting her full in the face. She squinted her eyes and turned her head, raising a hand to wipe the water away, but she couldn't seem to reach her face. Through the mist and condensation, she could see the slick yellowing tiles of her shower-tub combination, even the shower curtain printed with Christi Belcourt's piece *Reverence for Life* with its sky-blue background full of flowers, blue jays, and a red-winged blackbird.[79]

----

79 See Christi Belcourt's painting *Reverence for Life* at her website: christibelcourt.com/featured -page-on-landing-page-home.

The water stopped abruptly, and she was standing in a field absolutely crammed with wildflowers, the sky blue and endless above her and the warbling calls of a thousand different birds filling the air, but no matter which way she looked, she could not find the sun. This was more vertigo than she was used to, and she swallowed heavily, fighting the telltale watering of her mouth. She looked down at herself, expecting to see an avatar of some sort; in VR you could be human, or an animal, or an object. Instead she saw herself as she usually did, in black leggings, feet out of sight among the bluebells, daisies, clover, dandelions, and Indian paintbrushes. Her hands were just as familiar, naked nails chewed to the quick, her brown skin rough, almost scaly from lack of moisturizing. She remembered how they'd been before isolation, with chrome acrylic nails and her skin plump and shiny from good hand cream from the QUILTBAG store.[80] As she thought it, she saw it—her hands restored to their femme glory once more, and she spent a shocked moment tilting them from side to side to admire the shine of the bright-pink chrome of her suddenly long nails.

With a snap of awareness, she understood. She stared hard at her nails and concentrated, trying to see them as dark matte purple. It was difficult; her eyes kept saying chrome pink, but she insisted. Without fanfare, they changed.

"Holy shit." Her voice, so long unused, felt wrong in her throat, raspy. It didn't even sound like her. Dust poured out of her mouth and rose into the air, turning into butterflies.

A soft bell rang, and the vast field of flowers disappeared, along with the birdsong. She found herself seated on a very expensive-looking white leather chair, the one named after a city in Spain. Barcelona or Madrid or something. She was in an endless space, with a polished concrete floor that extended beyond the horizon in every direction, soft light without

----

80   Always forever hyping the QUILTBAG: thequiltbag.com.

any source, and a single dark mahogany desk in front of her. She blinked in surprise.

Light in the shape of a door opened beside the desk, and out stepped a man in a white suit, looking exactly like Colonel Sanders, with his weird little tie, glasses, goatee, and all. He was carrying a bucket of fried chicken.

Her mouth immediately began to water as she smelled it. She hadn't had fried chicken since before isolation, taken for granted one of her favourite childhood foods because it had always been available. Fried chicken was apology food, a bucket for every missed school concert, every broken piggy bank, every black eye. Even still, she loved it dearly.

"How …" she croaked, then coughed, while the Colonel cocked his head and smiled, the bucket still in his hands. She tried again. "How am I smelling that?" She pointed her lips at the white-and-red-striped container.

The Colonel smiled even more widely and pulled the lid off, letting it fall to the floor, where it melted like a snowflake. He fished around in the bucket and pulled out a wing, her favourite piece. He held it out to her. She recoiled automatically, the idea of accepting anything, much less food, from the hands of another person having become utterly taboo.

"Well, I—well, I say, you ought to taste it, too!" His voice was exactly like Foghorn Leghorn's. She blinked in surprise. She'd never realized that she'd always assumed Colonel Sanders would sound like that.

She held up a hand, willing everything to slow down, her mind whirling. "What kind of VR game is this?"

The bucket was gone, and the Colonel was sitting behind the mahogany desk, squinting down at a sheaf of papers in his hands. He looked up at her with a kind expression.

"Well, you see," he said, in that ridiculous accent, "this is no VR experience. You signed up to participate in Mens Aeterna's whole brain emulation program."

She flashed back to clicking on the email, and as though a projector were mounted in her forehead, the whole scene played out in the air right before her. Scrolling through the message, clicking the link, filling out the form. Her eyes narrowed; that felt an awful lot like someone covering their ass for legal purposes, and less like something she'd conjured into being with her thoughts. This wasn't interesting. This wasn't alleviating her mind-numbing detachment.

She closed her eyes and tried to imagine different surroundings, but she was so unused to forming or maintaining concentration; images fluttered around her like falling leaves. She peeked an eye open, but the Colonel was still there, smiling faintly. She squished her eyes shut again and tried harder. A place outside, somewhere she hadn't been in half a year, somewhere green, anywhere at all. Her mind slipped and skittered but wouldn't settle; it had been so long since she'd been anywhere but her apartment. Maybe that had damaged her sense of object permanence?

She sighed and pictured her living and sleeping room. Herself curled up on the couch, facing her bed, white floral covers mussed and pushed aside, pillows piled to provide a backrest, walls she'd painted bright yellow without her landlord's permission—who cares, she was going to lose the place anyway—one stunted plant in the small window above her bed, the one feral alley cats liked to spray to mark their territory, so she had to keep it closed. It felt pretty real. She opened her eyes.

The Colonel was wearing a ridiculous white cotton robe and a sleeping cap, and he was sitting in her bed smoking a pipe, the *ceci n'est pas une pipe* one. Did the Colonel even smoke? Apparently, she had developed quite a few unconscious assumptions about him.

The Colonel took the pipe out of his mouth and gestured at her with it. "Now as I was saying, whole brain emulation records the unique arrangement and responses of the subject's neurons and synapses, after which the copy is transferred to a processing substrate."

She stood up and walked toward the door, ignoring the Colonel as he continued to rattle on about neural protheses, computational model-ling, and some other shit she didn't care about. He followed behind her, dressed again in his white suit. She opened her front door and peered up the dingy concrete stairs to the street, hesitating. What if she was just hallucinating, and she ended up getting arrested for being outside? She waited for a tingle of fear, for something to goad her into reconsidering, but there was nothing. Just the flat affect of months spent in total crush-ing solitude.

As she climbed the steps to street level, she realized she was wearing a pair of smoked moosehide moccasins rimmed in beaver fur, glittering red roses on a white background beaded on the vamps. nohkômipan, her beloved grandmother who had passed, had made these moccasins for her coming-of-age ceremony so many years ago; they'd long since worn out and been recycled and gifted on. Wearing them again made her feel a little less alone. As nohkômipan always used to say, miywâsin, it was good. Real or not, it was a featherlight touch of connection to another human being, and she was unsurprised to find tears streaming down her face, evaporating like dandelion fluff and dancing away with precious seeds, finding purchase in every tiny crack in the concrete.

She was on the sidewalk now, the Colonel peering over her shoulder from two steps below, a steady stream of verbiage still pouring forth: "The simulated mind can be housed within a virtual reality, which Mens Aeterna has designed to be coconstituted by uploaded dynamic reanima-tions of each subject." She tuned him out.

Mid-twentieth-century bungalows lined both sides of the street, huge American elm trees casting dappled shadows on the abandoned side-walks and the road, the narrow boulevards hugely overgrown with an explosion of wildflowers considered noxious weeds by the city, diligently mowed and uprooted before the pandemic, but now left to pour forth like branching streams into the car-free pavement. Everything seemed exactly the same as it was when she collected her weekly ration box, but the street faded off into grey mist on either side, as though a small section of her world had been plucked out and gently placed in a shallow pool to bob serenely.

She walked out into the road, sharp, tiny stones biting into the bottoms of her feet; they were spread in the winter to prevent vehicles from slip-sliding disastrously, and the usual spring cleaning of salt, stones, and sand had been abandoned, the rains unable to push it all into storm drains and, from there, to the North Saskatchewan. The Colonel was her shadow, legalese and medical jargon escaping from him like air from a pricked balloon. She pointed a moccasined toe and brushed it across an irregular crack populated by lush green grass, bending the two-foot-high stalks rich with seed, a verdant communion with another living being. Or the simulacrum of one.

She turned left and walked unhurriedly to the edge of the visible neighbourhood. It was like peering into fog, but instead of opening up and staying in front and behind, never quite within grasp, this liminal space was sharper, swirling languidly with streaks of silver and dim flashes of light. She stepped over the edge.

She was weightless again, suspended, but her legs continued to make walking movements. She couldn't tell if she was moving in any particular direction, but she continued. Foghorn Leghorn's voice floated behind her; she could no longer see the Colonel. The words had long since stopped making any sense.

After an indeterminate time, her feet touched down on a solid surface. She was in darkness, but all around her she felt the presence of soil redolent with decomposing vegetation. Except now her feet weren't there, and neither were her arms; in a disorienting rush she experienced herself as unbelievably small. The feeling struck her with a sense of intense déjà vu. Since she was a child, whenever she had a high fever, her sense of physical presence would shift between extremes, ballooning out to unimaginable vastness, then collapsing into comfortable density. She'd never been able to describe the feeling to anyone.

"What is this?" She did not hear her own voice because she had no ears, nor lungs to push air, nor vocal cords. In fact, sensations were flowing through her from around her head, but also from what she perceived as her far end, through—she quickly counted—eighteen rays aligned along her very tip.

"Welcome to *C. elegans*, a nematode one millimetre in length, Mens Aeterna's first successful substrate-independent mind." She could not see the Colonel, could not, in fact, truly see anything the way she was used to, but she sensed that she had some way of perceiving and reacting to light, were it to materialize.

"What does that mean, substrate-independent mind?" She teetered on the edge of discomfort, the changes in her body too confusing to focus on for more than a fraction of a second at a time. She began writhing forward and, she suddenly realized, upwards.

"In layman's terms," came the exaggerated southern drawl, "this worm, who possesses only three hundred neurons to a human's eighty-six billion, was scanned, copied, and uploaded to Mens Aeterna's database. What you are experiencing is that raw data within the coconstituted virtual reality the worm has created. As long as the data remains intact, *C. elegans* can be placed into any substrate, any material on or from which an organism lives, and thus, is substrate independent."

Whole body contractions continued to propel her onwards as she considered this. "So you're saying you could take this data, this uploaded worm, and put it into something else. Like a mechanical body?"

"Ah, well"—the Colonel sounded almost embarrassed—"theoretically that is possible."

Before she could push him on that, her head burst out of the soil, and something bloomed around her, felt with every cell of her body as she broke free into open air. Somehow, she knew it was sunshine.

She was human once more, and this time she retched with the vertigo, bile rising in her throat, acrid and painful, as her stomach heaved. She was on her hands and knees on a tiny strip of damp soil about the size of half a yoga mat, the horizon shockingly close, balanced on a tiny island adrift in more shimmering fog. She scanned around her, but couldn't find the Colonel. Just rich brown earth and directionless sunlight.

"You said this was a coconstituted virtual reality. What does that mean?"

His voice seemed to come from all around her. "Mens Aeterna sets the basic parameters, but each SIM also recreates its usual habitat."

She stood, feeling fine again, and once again stepped into the murky space before her. "SIM?" She moved her limbs, glad to have them back. "Oh, substrate-independent mind. Got it. So, if you had, say, a mosquito in here, everything would be squishy skin and blood?" She pictured vast rolling hills of skin of every hue, of every species, barely holding in oceans of gurgling blood, a little uploaded mosquito rubbing its cartoon-ish hands together in glee.

"A SIM may not consciously perceive its entire habitat, but unconsciously it will recreate it to within a high value of accuracy."

Her feet were on the ground again, all four of them. She was small, but not so superlatively small as before. She slid down a muddy bank on her furry belly, and water flowed around her, cool and fresh, delightful. Her nostrils and ears were closed to protect her, a transparent membrane over her eyes like the most perfect goggles ever designed. She had never been a strong swimmer, but now? Webbed hindfeet propelled her with strong, practised strokes, and her body moved as though it were as liquid and fluid as the world around her.

Unlike before, she felt a presence, an inquisitive nudging. In surprise, she forgot to focus on the sensations flooding her, seeking the origin of that odd touch. She immediately lost control of her body, though it continued to move as agilely as before—she simply wasn't the one in the driver's seat anymore.

"Colonel?" came her panicked thought.

"Be calm. You are in contact with a much more complex consciousness than before." The Colonel was standing on the bank of the lake. She sensed him immediately and, without volition, her broad, flat tail slapped the surface of the water in three loud bursts before she dove and soared toward the safety of the underwater entrance to her home.

Climbing up into the warm, dry den, water sloshing furiously against the tunnel until it settled once more, she shook off the excess moisture and awkwardly tumbled onto one side, panting a little. It was overly quiet here, and she realized she was lonely; she had no mate, no kits, no other kin, not even a muskrat to share this home with. It took a moment for her to separate her own feelings of isolation and detachment from this SIM's emotions.

"She's all alone." Her mind's voice was almost a sob.

"The *Castor canadensis* is a social creature in nature, but to date, Mens Aeterna has only scanned and uploaded a single consciousness." His voice was not muffled, though it clearly came from without the mud, stones, and sticks that made up this lodge.

The beaver went about its routine, padding into the sleeping chamber and settling in for a few hours. Unable to regain control of the creature's body, she lay there in silence for some time, her mind whirling.

After a while, she thought at the Colonel again. "You're uploading me right now."

"You signed the contract, read the Terms and Conditions, and agreed to the procedure," he affirmed.

"And I will recreate my habitat"—she took on his accent—"to within a high value of accuracy."

Her impression did not seem to bother him. "Correct."

"Which in my case will probably just end up being my apartment."

"Well, uh, humans are much more complex than most organic subjects. A nematode has no need to expand beyond the familiar. A beaver may long for companionship, but will not suddenly create a desert to explore."

"While humans will? Create deserts to explore?"

"Theoretically, yes."

That word again. "So *theoretically* I won't be stuck inside my apartment for eternity, but *theoretically*, I might be?"

"It is possible, yes."

"Are there other humans here?"

"Not yet, no."

"Are you kidding? I'm the first?"

"You are the first, yes, indeed."

If her eyes hadn't already been closed, her furry breast rising and falling with gentle breaths, she'd have closed them now and cursed herself for clicking on that email. She was feeling a lot now, after months of emotional numbness: anger, regret, and a growing fear that she'd be trapped in here forever, just as she was trapped in the real world, but worse, with no end date ever.

"What other SIMS exist here?" she asked, once she was able to cram everything back down so she could think straight.

"Mens Aeterna has scanned a wide variety of organic subjects: *Coptotermes formosanus*, *Blattella germanica*, *Thamnophis rufipunctatus*, *Vulpes velox*, *Bison bison*, both *bison* and *athabascae*—"

"Stop. Other than bison, I didn't understand any of that. Common names?"

"A termite, a German cockroach, a narrowhead garter snake, a swift fox, bison, both plains and wood, along with many other organic beings."

"There are buffalo here?" she demanded incredulously, not even sure why that pricked her ire. It seemed wrong somehow.

"One *Bubalus bubalis* has been scanned. If you are referring to bison, *Bison bison bison* and *Bison bison athabascae* represent 40 percent of the uploaded consciousnesses at Mens Aeterna."

"You mean you've got herds of them here? Just one beaver, but herds of buffalo?"

"Indeed."

Herds of buffalo. Here, in a virtual world, parts of which were coconstituted by the buffalo themselves. Absolutely astounding. Her hindfeet kicked weakly; her host was dreaming about swimming while she engaged in the longest conversation she'd had in at least two months. With Colonel Sanders. As a bizarre rig sucked her brain and promised to stick her in a virtual world forever.

Something occurred to her, sending a trickle of unease through her innards. "How long will it take to fully scan and upload my brain?"

"Approximately twelve hours," the Colonel drawled. Did anyone besides the voice actor for an overconfident rooster actually sound like this? For all she knew, the accent was an accurate representation of hundreds of thousands of people, but it was distracting.

"How much time has passed?"

"Eight minutes."

Her sense of time was completely off, then, because she would have guessed that she'd been here for a least a few hours. An inkling of a plan began to form, fanciful, maybe, but it was not without precedent. She said nothing more, settling into her new body as her host napped.

She extended her senses as much as possible, examining her limbs, analyzing the sensations of her strange new organs. She tried to move, but it was impossible; whatever control she'd had in those first few moments was gone. That was fine for now. Taking stock of this body kept her occupied, as alert as she'd been before the pandemic, maybe even more so.

When the beaver awoke, it was hungry, and she learned how it used its dexterous front paws to pull up cattails by their roots and haul them back into the lodge for later, before heading up the banks of the lake for a more substantial meal. She knew beavers ate trees, but had never imagined how they might actually taste to the animal. Powerful jaws and teeth peeled the rough outer bark away to reveal the sweet, soft cambium underneath, and as she sampled aspen and willow, she realized she that had a strong aversion to pine and spruce.

Hours passed before she opened up conversation with the Colonel again.

"What happens if an upload does not complete?" She kept her tone casual, though she wasn't really sure if she was speaking to a person in real time, or some kind of artificial intelligence. She suspected the latter. Her host was napping again. Together they'd watched the sun set, turning the surface of the lake into smooth, burnished copper.

"Without a complete neural scan, we cannot accurately map the responses of neurons and synapses in any given organic subject, rendering the scan inutile."

The beaver woke during the night to do some more eating and foraging; apparently her host was both diurnal and nocturnal. She spent long minutes underwater, able to hold her breath for up to fifteen minutes before surfacing once more. A gibbous moon rippled across the water, but down below was where it achieved true majesty: silver rays of light were diffused by algae and softly swaying lake weeds. Down here, it was silent in a way that was completely different to the lack of sound, of breath, in the confinement of her apartment. Here, the silence was like an embrace. If she could have wept with the pleasure of it, she would have filled oceans.

The beaver was aware of her, but did not seem concerned, only slightly curious. They did not share a language, so communication was difficult at first—vague impressions of scents, sights, textures, and a deep loneliness. In one another, they each recognized a being not suited to a solitary life; they understood lack of companionship as a real harm. She couldn't prove it, but she thought the beaver was growing to be glad of her presence.

She did a bit of rough math and conservatively estimated that, if the Colonel was telling the truth about the passage of time here, twelve hours in real life equalled about fifteen days in this place. As the days passed, she was content to be an active observer while the beaver went about its life, but her thoughts often strayed to the terrifying implications of a successful upload.

From what she understood of the Colonel's explanation, a completed upload would mean that she would continue to exist both in here, and in the outside world. Except she had no way of knowing which would be the outcome for *her*. It was terribly confusing, because she knew that the version of her that returned to the real world would also think of herself as *her*, but she absolutely did not want to be stuck in this virtual world, and even if she ended up the lucky one, the thought of any version of herself being trapped like this was unbearable. Then again, being trapped in her apartment was also a poor outcome.

She had been trying to command her real-world body to remove the headset, to no avail. She did not seem to be able to communicate with her human body any more than she could control this beaver form. She concentrated intensely again and again, willing her real-world hands to move, even with the slightest twitch, but if it worked, she had no way of knowing.

On the sixth day of not speaking at all, once more in the routine of silence perfected over months of hopelessness, she risked another question. "Has an upload ever been interrupted?"

She was flitting beneath the water after snacking on what had become her favourite treat, those soft, nutritious cattail roots. From her vantage point close to shore, she could see the Colonel in his white suit, standing on the muddy banks of the lake, distorted by ripples on the surface of the water. Her host was unconcerned by his presence, knowing these two-legged creatures rarely had the ability to detect a beaver underwater.

"Yes."

His answer was unusually terse. She pushed. "How did that happen?"

"The neural scanner was released prematurely."

Ah. He was being coy—by cunning or design, she wasn't sure.

For the next two days, she focused her energy on deepening her communication with the beaver. She found the beaver's mind to be inquisitive, even a little teasing at times. Questions felt like a wet nudge. The beaver would be chewing on a particularly sweet root, and then, the gentle prod. She would take some time to form a complete sensory memory of her own favourite food, moose stew in thick gravy, and when she felt it was as whole as possible, she'd let it open up like the petals of a wapato flower for the beaver to sample. In this way she was able to share snippets of her own life and absorb information sent to her. The beaver thought eating animal flesh was about the most disgusting thing possible.

She decided to take a direct approach. "How do I release the neural scanner?"

"You consented to the procedure."

"What if I want to withdraw my consent?"

"You agreed to all the Terms and Conditions."

"I didn't really read them!"

"You clicked the box saying you had read them and agreed to them."

"Surely I can still withdraw my consent?"

"Yes."

"How do I do that? How do I prematurely terminate the procedure?"

There was a hush, and the beaver, curious about the cause of the intense emotions flooding through its guest, paused in its constant home repair, nose quivering at the white-clad being on the lake's edge. She had no breath of her own to hold, but that stoppage, that waiting filled her with anxiety.

"If you wish to terminate the procedure, you must input the termination message."

Hope bloomed. "What is the termination message?"

The Colonel emitted an impossibly rapid string of numbers. Not long ago, it would have been unthinkable that she'd be able to properly hear them, much less hold them in her mind. No longer—she was sharper now, alive once more.

She stopped talking to the Colonel entirely. Day after day passed, with intense communication between herself and her host, as she formed a complex question of her own. Would the beaver allow her to take control of its body? The beaver was intrigued, but proposed a counteroffer. If she would teach it how to be human, it would teach her how to be a beaver.

She accepted.

It was not easy; their terms of reference were so different in many ways, but slowly they learned together, at least the physical aspects of being. Social customs, etiquette, history, all of that was beyond them to impart quickly and would still have to be learned. After a while, the beaver lost interest in practising being human; it thought it a silly thing to want to be.

One night, as they lay in the cozy sleeping den, she sent out a tentative tendril of sympathy to the beaver. It was met with surprise, but the beaver understood. It could not leave this place empty of other beavers, of the possibility of family, but it had never lost hope that one day, it would dive into these tranquil waters and discover a new presence.

She thought about that for a while, the tenacity of hope, and searched for it within herself. Before she'd come here, it had been buried, deadened by the increasingly authoritarian global response to the pandemic. The possibility of turning in a different direction, a direction full of expansive kinship, of mutual aid, withered with every additional control, the farce of consent allowing leaders to present inhumanity as a gift, human rights exchanged for the lie of security. Yet in her time here with this incredible creature, hope had been reignited within her. She dove within her memory for the ancient stories, gathering together all the beaver lore she had ever gleaned, from the slightest mention to the most ribald of tales, building a lodge within her mind.

When she felt she was ready, she gathered together all her love and gratitude and let it flow throughout her, watching it catch and spark in dendrites throughout the beaver's body, now wholly familiar to her—perhaps even more so than her human body—spilling forth faster and faster, spring breakup in golden signals, no dam-busting here, just the regularity of natural cycles, powerful and right. miywâsin, it was good.

The beaver's farewell was like the slap of a powerful tail on a mirror, the crack of a felled tree, the endless rolling thunder of a prairie storm.

She recited the string of numbers.

She opened her eyes and found herself back in her apartment, for real this time, unbelievably stiff from hours of immobility. At first, she was overly careful as she pulled the slack spiderweb off her head, but the idea of having it attached to her for even a second more was unacceptable. Abandoning caution, she ended up painfully pulling out some of her hair by the roots as she tore the device off the rest of the way. Tossing the thing to the ground, she rose unsteadily.

It was still day outside, so she puttered around, examining objects with fresh eyes, seeing them the way the beaver would have, the familiar becoming strange and of dubious utility. She found herself missing tender cattail roots, the starchy flavour of wapato bulbs, the sweet tender flesh of alder.

She waited until it was the deep of night, that three o'clock stillness when it felt like the world was holding its breath. She opened the door while she still had the ability to do so and sniffed the unstirring air. She sensed no danger, but identified a cool thread of running water nearby that led into roaring river currents and, from there, branched off into the endless possibility of deep, placid lakes. An end to solitude.

Had anyone been in the streets, they might have seen her waddling down the middle of the road to the Mill Creek Ravine—but no humans were present.

"A LODGE WITHIN HER MIND" EXPLORATION

Earlier, in my analysis of "Buffalo Bird," I discussed transformation as an ontological foundation of otipêyimisow-itâpisiniwin. However, as cohost of the podcast *Métis in Space*, alongside Molly Swain, we have often come up against the trope of Indigenous peoples being able to change into animals. I want to take a little time to explore the ontology of transformation as constant vs. the trope of the shape-shifting Indian.

In the podcast, otipêyimisiw-iskêwak kihci-kîsikohk,[81] *Métis in Space*, Molly Swain and I drink a bottle of red wine, watch a speculative-fiction television show or movie that features Indigeneity, and provide a critique through an Indigenous feminist lens.[82] One of the most prevalent tropes we see in mainstream media is the idea that Indigenous people are often able to transform into animals. Sometimes this happens because of the influence of a magic item, but more generally it seems to be a power ascribed to Indigenous people overall.

Linked to this ability is the oft-repeated notion that Indigenous peoples exist somewhere between science and magic, in a space that is *sui generis*, a class of its own. The powers ascribed to Indigenous people within this unique category work to highlight our presumptive connection to nature in either evil or miraculous ways, depending on the perspective. Even when this power is referred to in a tongue-in-cheek

....

81   You may notice a difference in spelling of the word for Métis here (otipêyimisiw vs. otipêyimisow). Note that I only spell it otipêyimisiw in the context of otipêyimisiw-iskwêwak kihki-kîsikohk, *Métis in Space*. This was the spelling we used when we created the podcast, and it is now specifically associated with *Métis in Space*. The sound of the two words is exactly the same, but the proper spelling is, in fact, otipêyimisow. That final O is a reflexive ending.

82   (*Métis in Space* n.d.).

manner, it is clear that transforming into animals is an enduring fantasy within settler narratives of Indigeneity.

Yet here I am, offering you a number of short stories within which Indigenous protagonists transform into animals. Am I simply replicating settler myths because I have been exposed to them my whole life?

The fact is, within the sacred stories of many Indigenous nations, transformation is common. I have asserted that it is a core pillar of Indigenous worldviews. When our sacred stories are shared, often in truncated or distorted forms by non-Indigenous people, they contain many instances of humans or other beings changing into various animal forms, or vice versa. It is not my intent to reflect settler tropes, but rather to incorporate these literary allusions into my work.

Mainstream distortions of existing Indigenous beliefs act like a funhouse mirror. The image is there, but disconnected from true form. When more Indigenous people incorporate sacred stories and Indigenous worldviews into their work, those true forms will become more recognizable than the funhouse reflection. Space must be made to recognize transformation as a metaphor for accessing certain knowledge, but also as a real process, and non-Indigenous people cannot be the ones shaping these narratives.

I wrote this story at the very beginning of the COVID pandemic, in April 2020, and the rest of the book was completed while that pandemic continued to rage on. There has been no space or time yet to step back from the pandemic and see how it has impacted us long term. As I write these words, Alberta is in a deadly fourth wave, and the Delta variant is ripping through our communities with terrifying speed.

Excellent critiques have been made about writing about a global event of this size while it is occurring. It is difficult to offer accurate predictions, and this can jar the reader out of the story. For example, the militarized lockdown I envisioned did not materialize (yet), and food rations have not actually been organized on any large scale. However, in reality, things are far worse than I imagined they could be. The province I live in has taken a very hands-off approach to the entire thing, with anti-vaccine protests becoming bewilderingly common. As we lose more people every day, I find my rage overpowering my fear, and neither emotion is helpful or healthy.

However, I chose to keep this story as is, because beyond the specific circumstances of this pandemic, the isolation and alienation of living in a colonial, capitalist society needs to be recognized. It highlights that this way of living is unsustainable for all of us, Indigenous or not. I gesture to Indigenous resilience, as we are Peoples who have endured multiple pandemics, multiple world-ending events, and yet we remain. Walking away from colonialism and capitalism isn't entirely possible unless we do it en masse, and you don't need to transform into a beaver to do it.

Choosing and acting otherwise is a huge theme throughout my work because I believe in it. Those first few weeks of the pandemic were terrifying, and yet also hope-filled, as pollution cleared, the sounds of the city shifted, and we took stock of our relationships. Right now, in September 2021, it feels as though the stranglehold capitalism has on us will only increase, depleting us and the planet forever. It is vital that we remember we *can* choose. We can dive into sage-coloured waters and reclaim ourselves. We can waddle through dark streets and value relationality over possessions. We can transform everything.

ÂNISKÔHÔCIKAN

The Ancestors Spoke

We didn't understand.

They spoke again.

This time, the nanites ensure our comprehension.

MICROFICTION VERSION

Her Name Is the Cree Word for Spring

Sweet, fat-limbed baby, passed around from coparent to coparent, receiving blessings like a scene from "Sleeping Beauty." The microscopic machines, introduced in utero at nine weeks, swarmed/developed at the same time as organic structures. Intercepting inputs, analyzing, choosing outputs, standard Athelas rule-based programming for nanorobotics.[83]

Rule: InterceptAnalyzeTranslate

```
{
Initialize: R, T, A;
When: conc ($Y @T) > 5;
Actions:
      reject ($R @T)
      translate ($T @(A AND B AND C ... Z));
      allow ($A @T)
Until: conc ($Y @T) < 2;
}
```

Or perhaps more easily understood this way:

```
if (not nêhiyawêwin) then
     (reject) and (translate);
elseif (nêhiyawêwin) then
     (accept)
end if
```

---

83 (Wiesel-Kapah et al. 2016). This article provides an interesting suggestion for nanobot programming that I've adapted for this story.

This cooing baby, like all the others, will only ever hear nêhiyawêwin. This is the decision the Elders and coparents made; the need for first-language speakers has become critical.

She is named sîkwan for the season of her birth, and because from her the language will spring anew.

âniskôhôcikan

She peered into the small glass vial, careful to keep her hands behind her back as Val held it aloft, pinched between two fingers encased in purple nitrile. It seemed empty; perhaps, if she squinted … was that a fine coating of dust? Maybe just a shadow. Disappointed, she straightened and shoved her nervous hands into her jean pockets.

Val chuckled as she carefully laid the vial back in its moulded cushion. "I warned you, Kat. People seem to forget that 'nano' means really, really small."

Katherine shrugged impatiently. "But it works? For sure?"

"Nothing is ever for sure. We don't think this would work with deaf children, and there are at least a dozen other situations we'd be screening for—"

"Cripes, Val!" She splayed her hands over her stomach protectively. "I mean will she speak Cree?"

Val's eyes flicked down to Kat's swollen belly, and she nodded sharply. "If it takes, Cree is all she'll ever speak."

sîkwan gurgled contentedly on her soft star blanket and pumped fat legs in the air, reaching for the earring Kat dangled just out of reach.

Three of her coparents were mucking about in the kitchen getting lunch ready, filling the air with pleasing domestic sounds and the smell of moose stew, which wafted through to the living room from time to time. Curtis and Shawna were on bicycle maintenance duty out in the backyard, getting everything shipshape for spring riding. Josh and Amber were both sunken into their favourite chairs, getting a little beading in before it was time to eat.

Josh threaded gold-plated beads onto some waxed dental floss and held them up, admiring the way the soft spring light coaxed a warm glow from the tiny pieces of glass. His makeup was impeccable, as always; no one did Indigi-glitter quite like him, and even in a house full of Métis and Cree queers, he channelled the peacock pretension of his prairie forefathers with a dedication that was almost like worship.

"So it's like beading," he stated, letting the strand of dental floss twist lazily in the air.

Kat pursed her lips in thought. "Sort of, I suppose? If each nanite is a bead, they link up in a specific pattern."

Amber glanced up at the strand in Josh's hand, blowing a lock of bleached white hair out of wiya's face, lips pursed in thought.[84]

"I learned that one in class," Amber said, obviously straining to recall, "the word for string of beads in Cree." Kat and Josh looked at wiya in interest; the three coparents were university students, but only Amber was studying Cree.

Amber smiled at them, fingers still busy at wiya's bead loom. "It's a weird one because bead is mîkis, but this doesn't sound like it at all …"

sîkwan farted, long and wet, her tiny limbs spasming out in surprise at the force of it, and the three of them laughed.

"âniskôhôcikan!" Amber exclaimed

"Bless you?" Kat teased. Josh's teeth flashed as his grin widened even further.

Amber giggled. "It means string of beads. Maybe it's a good Cree name for the nanites?"

---

84   In Cree, there is no gendered pronoun equivalent to she or he. Instead, the third-person singular pronoun is "wiya." I have yet to meet someone whose pronouns in English are wiya and wiya's, but I imagine it's going to happen one day. I mention this multiple times throughout this book, but it's a point I think is worth repeating.

Kat looked uncertain. "But they're just infrastructure. The translator, mostly. Doesn't work without the data."

Josh lifted up the round medallion he always wore, a wavy, irregular line of blue across a background of green. "Beads are just infrastructure, too. You know what this is?"

She did, but only because he'd told her. The blue line was the North Saskatchewan River near Keephills, a tongue like the head of a blue heron jutting up, peeking west, its eye picked out in negative green space. It was where Josh's mooshum had raised him.

Josh let the medallion fall and peered at his string of gold beads again. "There you go. Doesn't work without the data."

sîkwan's hands caught the earring, her grip tightening immediately. Kat smiled down at their daughter and carefully pried it out of her grasp.

"tôhtô tôhtô tôhtô!" sîkwan howled, smushing her sounds together, angrily tugging at Kat's sweater, demanding to be breastfed. sîkwan's little toddler cheeks were red and hot and she was in a terrible mood; teething had not been easy on anyone in the house. Maybe it was a poor time to try weaning, but Kat had been having trouble with her milk supply since the baby was born, and surely eighteen months was more than long enough?

"Let me take her." Winter held out their arms, and Kat gratefully let them pull sîkwan gently away. Winter's pink-and-purple hair was already tied up; all eight of them had long since experienced sîkwan's death grip and the wincing pain of strands of hair being torn roughly from the scalp. Raising a baby, even communally, was a bit like running an endless gauntlet of baby head-butts, near strangulation when she got a hold of a necklace or scarf, and constant lacerations from tiny razor-sharp nails.

Kat rocked her head from side to side, trying to relax her neck muscles, but sîkwan's cries and incoherent babbling intensified as she struggled in Winter's arms, trying to reach her birth parent.

Winter gave Kat a sympathetic look. "Maybe go for a walk? She'll calm down when she can't see you."

Kat nodded gratefully. She could use the break. Winter began to sing a modified version of "B-I-N-G-O" to try to calm sîkwan down, the one where a kookum had a magic dabber. Kat wondered what her daughter was actually hearing; there were no Bs or Gs in the Cree alphabet.

The three children had been shy meeting at first, but they were smashing toy cars together now, chattering away, their words too fast for Kat to follow. There would be other children eventually, but small groups were spacing out their visits to get comfortable with the space that was to be their school.

And what a space it was! Kat gazed around happily, letting the rich, moist air of the greenhouse roll over her. They might be stuck in the city, but they didn't have to be stuck inside brick and concrete. There was a path circling a little pond full of fish, and a number of small areas within the greenery to sit, play, and learn. Her coparents were spread out, investigating every plant, talking excitedly to one another about their beloved little sîkwan.

"kimiywêyihtên cî?"

The teacher was tiny and probably in her seventies, eyes rheumy and intelligent behind thick fishbowl glasses, wearing a loose, short-sleeved ribbon dress in the heat of the greenhouse.

She was one of the only fluent Cree speakers the parents had been able to find who had also been raised in the culture. The nanites could impart the language but not that vital cultural context. Having a Cree-speaking instructor also meant the translators wouldn't need to work as hard. She was smiling kindly at Kat, who reached out to clasp the Elder's hands in greeting.

"I'm sorry, what?" Kat asked, focusing on the Elder's lips so she wouldn't be staring disrespectfully in her eyes.

"kimiywêyihtên cî?" the Elder repeated, a bit slower this time.

Kat shifted in embarrassment, "Uh, I don't, um, apisîs nêhiyawêwin."

"apisîs kinêhiyawân," the Elder corrected her gently.

Kat flushed and nodded, "apisîs ki … no. apisîs *ni*nêhiyawân," she said back dutifully.

She'd committed to learning as much Cree as she could so she could understand sîkwan, but speaking was still so much harder than listening and understanding. As much the coparents wanted otherwise, they often just responded in English, knowing the translator was there to make up for it.

Seeing her discomfort, the Elder switched languages. "I asked if you are happy?"

Kat watched sîkwan trying to convince the boys to let her pile the toy cars on top of one another. Her daughter's tone was what Josh called "overly reasonable," but what else would you expect from someone raised in a queer Indigenous feminist collective? Kat only understood about every fifth word that was rattling out of her daughter's mouth right now. When they were one on one, sîkwan tended to speak much slower for her mother's benefit.

Amber was the only one whose fluency had improved enough for most of wiya's conversations with sîkwan to be in Cree. Kat had struggled with being honest with her coparent about the needle prick of jealousy that caused her, and even confessing it hadn't quite made it go away.

"I am, yes," Kat answered finally, realizing she'd let the pause grow too long. She glanced at the older woman. "But also worried. I can't keep up."

The Elder nodded. "That's why we needed them. We couldn't bear the language loss anymore. You parents were very brave."

It was a well-worn conversation, but Kat felt that the Elder would understand better than most.

"They'll only ever speak Cree. That's what the nanites did. Do. Unless I speak Cree, our own daughter doesn't even really hear my voice. She hears the translator. Not me."

The Elder pursed her lips. "You think you aren't the ones teaching her? Raising her? Is the sound that important? She won't hear you sign, either."

Kat's mind flashed back to Val's lab, the invisible nanites in their glass tube. Three of the children, out of many dozens that had been augmented, had experienced gradual hearing loss or been born deaf. There was no reason to think it had been the procedure that had caused it, but they all wondered sometimes.

The deaf children would be joining the preschool, too; the doctors believed they'd still pick up the language, and everyone, including all the parents, would be learning Plains Sign Language.[85] A project that had been hyperfocused on one language was now ensuring two languages would blossom.

"I just wonder what opportunities they'll have." Kat sighed, the familiar weight of worry settling over her.

The Elder's laugh surprised her. "We needed monolingual mother-tongue speakers. All we had were second-language speakers, and the language was still dying, surrounded by English the way we are. We needed them to be exposed only to Cree, and that technology made it happen. They will teach the next generation!"

Kat nodded. "But so few people speak Cree out there right now. They can't even learn another spoken language now. They'll never have normal lives."

---

85   (Davis 2015).

"They're Cree and Métis children in a colonial state. Their lives were never going to be 'normal.'" The Elder fell silent for a moment, then looked at the children where they were playing. "Do you know why we say children are sacred?"

"They're our future."

"Our future, yes." She nodded seriously. "But also our past. They come to us from the spirit realm, from the ancestors, the âniskôtapanak. And these ones are here, from our ancestors, to bring the language back. That's what they've been called to do."

"ânsikô ..."

"tapanak."

"I thought that meant string of beads? That's what some of us have been calling the nanites."

"A string of beads is mîkisâpiy." The Elder thought for a moment, "âniskôhôcikan is a string of beads tied end to end, like the hanks you can buy. The words are related, though; âniskê refers to being linked together end to end. âniskôtapanak means the ancestors, but also our descendants."

The Elder mimed pulling a string of beads straight. "Our ancestors here"—she lifted her left hand ever so slightly—"our descendants here." She lifted her right hand a smidge, too. "Both are âniskôtapanak."

Kat nodded, but didn't really get what the Elder was trying to say. The older woman smiled faintly, and slowly curved the invisible ends of the string up to meet one another. Kat recalled Josh's golden beads shining in the soft spring light; she could almost see the loop in the Elder's hands.

The Elder moved her fingers apart, then pressed them back together, "That is where the âniskôtapanak meet," she said, making the open and closed gesture again. "You don't need to be there between them for that connection to happen. You are part of the string, just in a different position."

Kat thought about that for a moment, picturing herself there, on the bottom of the loop, nestled between the beads that were her coparents. It was a beautiful notion.

sîkwan was contentedly piling the toy cars one atop the other and letting each little boy kick down the pile in turn. Their happy shouts rang out in a language Kat had barely been exposed to growing up, and the syllables tugged at a grief she didn't often acknowledge.

A grief her descendants would never feel.

"ÂNISKÔHÔCIKAN" EXPLORATION

A Montreal-based magazine asked me to write some fiction that considers "the strange and uneasy union of nature and tech in our lives." They were looking for a vision of how technology could be "more humane, and seamlessly integrated into our lives," but were also alive to ironies such as "learning to make a fire from YouTube, running through forests on a treadmill, etc." (Mann 2019).

I am truly passionate about language revitalization. I've done a heck of a lot of research on the topic, and I've paid close attention to the many times technology has been hailed as our linguistic saviour. Somehow, our Indigenous languages continue to decline, despite the promises of our tech overlords.

I wanted to create a piece where Indigenous people do manage to use technology to create radical change, in this case producing mother-tongue speakers of Cree in one generation. This story is neither dystopian nor utopian. I think of it as Métis/nêhiyaw pragmatism.

This story began as a challenge to create a piece of very short fiction, much shorter than anything I've ever written, specifically flash fiction, which is defined as being between 300 and 1,000 words.

Unsurprisingly, I completely failed at creating a short draft. My original submission clocked in at well over 1,500 words. I had to shave it down again, and again, and again, just to get it in under 1,000.

In very short fiction, you have to find the small idea and stick with it; there simply is not room for more, but there was a lot more I wanted to put into this story. The central idea is about creating mother-tongue speakers with tech, but I also wanted to (re)imagine communal child-rearing, something I firmly believe needs to be restored as well. Centring chosen family in an LGBTQ2S+ context as a form of cultural resiliency is a future we can imagine and act on much more easily than creating the kind of nanobot technology I invoke here. It is a future we can live in, and maybe are already living in now, for as Emily Riddle (2018) puts it, "Indigenous governance is gay."

Being as short as it is, this piece raises more questions than it answers, and I quite like that. Short stories in general seem to allow for more collaborative space between the story and the reader. I've thought of the many unanswered bits to this sort of technical "solution" to language decline and even have some potential answers, but I deliberately did not include more than the bare bones of the situation, because I want the reader to ask those same questions. For example, one of those questions might include whether or not we can ever think of machines as kin (Lewis et al. 2018). Would translators used like this actually push people toward monolingualism when throughout human history, multilingualism has been the norm?

In this way, I am deliberately encouraging percept ambiguity, leaving space for the audience to draw their own conclusions based on the concept structure of their belief system (Borrows 2018, xi; Black 1977, 100).

After rewriting the story, I was finally able to also create a 147-word microfiction version. Microfiction is defined as being fewer than 300 words, opening up even more potential for collaboration. As Robert Swartwood (2011, 24) describes extremely short fiction, "the writer and reader meet halfway, the writer only painting fifty percent of the picture and forcing the reader to fill in the rest." The irony is not lost on me that to create an extremely short version of this story, I had to map out just as much detail as for a traditional short story in my own mind first.

I didn't want to stop there, however, because even shorter fiction is possible, as in Swartwood's collection, *Hint Fiction: An Anthology of Stories in 25 Words or Fewer*. Explaining the title, Swartwood (2011, 25) declares "the reader is only given a *hint* of a much larger, more complex story."

One example of this kind of storytelling is Joe R. Lansdale's contribution to the anthology, titled "The Return" (Swartwood 2011, 33):

> They buried him deep.
> Again.

In all the pieces of hint fiction in this anthology, the title of the story plays a pivotal role in interpreting what is happening. It reminds me somewhat of poetry, and I find myself sometimes reading it that way.

Finally, I wrote a hint version of the story that is thirteen words long. It is fascinating to me to see what gets stripped out as the stories get shorter, and what remains. This very short story has so many possibilities as an exercise in collaborative storytelling, one that I think could be very useful in community when "imagining otherwise" and planning out steps to "act otherwise." I think the vehicle of flash fiction is a method of storytelling that invites, if not compels, the reader to participate in the world building.

I, BISON

Her stop wasn't on the schedule, and Gus had to pay the bus driver extra to let her off at the corner of Highway 633 and Range Road 40. She slipped her messenger bag over her head, shifting its bulk so it nestled comfortably against her back, and tightened the strap across her chest. A few of the passengers were peering out the windows, trying to figure out why they were stopping before Jasper; surely no one actually lived out here anymore?

The driver had a pinched, unpleasant face, and her impatience was palpable as she watched Gus carefully navigate down the precipitously steep stairs before opening the doors at the last moment. A blast of hot air tumbled in like an eager puppy, and with it the scent of green things baked under a punishing sun. Gus had hardly set foot on the worn pavement outside before the doors folded shut again, and the driver gunned the engine, pulling away as quickly as possible. Good thing Gus hadn't had more luggage in the undercarriage, or it'd be arriving behind the sanctuary walls in about four hours, without her.

She took a deep breath of sweet, green air as the sound of the engine faded, replaced by the electrical buzzing of cicadas. They were surprisingly loud out here compared to in Edmonton, where they didn't congregate in such numbers. Easy to ignore them in the city, but impossible here. Blinking her left eye, she opened otôtêma.[86]

"Cicadas, Alberta," she said softly.

Network connections were sluggish out here, and even with augments it was nearly impossible to maintain a connection to the New-Web, so

---

86   otôtêma means his/her/their (singular) friend in Cree.

she waited for the information squirt to load while she looked down the length of the gravel range road leading away from the crumbling highway, debating cutting through the unkempt field to the right of the road. It wouldn't shorten the walk by much, but it was a more direct route.

An image flashed across her eye, a close-up of a black insect with red eyes and translucent wings delicately outlined in gold fading into black extending beyond its cigar stub of a body. She scanned the text.

Magicicada septendecim. Historical periodicity of synchronized adult emergences: 17 years. Geographic range: United States, east of Great Plains. Current periodicity range: 3–5 years. Presence in Alberta: < 30 years.[87]

She blinked the window closed and sighed. Elders had often told her that the landscape her generation was familiar with was radically different than what previous generations had known, that in fact, unnatural, drastic changes in flora and fauna, in weather, even in geological features, was one of the defining aspects of colonialism. She often wondered what this place could have looked like, what sounds she would have heard if she'd been standing here before the môniyâwak arrived. If only like an otôtêma virtual overlay this imposed layer could be peeled back to reveal the original forms.

She shielded her eyes with a hand, cutting the glare of the noonday sun, and peered as far as she could into the tangled undergrowth among the tall poplars. Tightening the muscles around the outsides of her eyes, she activated her augmented view, scrolling through the options for thermal vision.

Nothing particularly big beyond a few deer in a stand of trees a couple hundred metres from her, but still she hesitated, a quick squint returning her sight to normal. When the môniyâwak had abandoned their stolen farms and acreages over seventy years ago, a lot of them had left security protocols in place, afraid that "undesirables" would move in otherwise.

---

87   (Ito et al. 2015). Periodicity was an adaptation; this article posits that climate change has changed this.

Since there was no one left out here besides First Nations and Métis, it was pretty clear who they had been worried about. A lot of those protocols had powered down over time or simply stopped working without a maintenance routine, but they had a nasty habit of popping up even still, and they wouldn't necessarily show up on her thermal readings until they activated.

Then again, this close to the settlement, it was likely that this patch of land at least had been cleared out carefully by the okanawêyihcikêwak[88] so that people could safely pick their medicines. A thin line of sweat ran down the back of her neck and under her black T-shirt before pooling uncomfortably where her beaded bag pressed against her, a reminder that at thirty degrees Celsius, this was still the coolest part of the day. That decided her; it would be much more pleasant under the dappled shade of the poplar, spruce, birch, and invasive eucalyptus.

Chewing on the inside of her cheek nervously, she oriented herself to the northeast and stepped over a rotted fence post that was still visible after all this time, though the barbed wire had long ago been harvested. Nothing happened. She let out a quivering breath in relief and ran her palm up against the grain of the newly shaved part of the back of her head, something she hadn't been able to stop doing since she'd cut it.

This was the fourth day of the wake, and it had taken her a month's worth of wages to get a bus ticket. Now that she was so close, she didn't want to waste another second.

Shade notwithstanding, Gus was sweating profusely half an hour later, when she finally stepped onto Ste. Anne Trail, her black combat boots scuffing the dusty gravel. Maybe it was all the greenery, or the proximity to the lake, but it was noticeably hotter in the countryside than it was

---

88　Guardians, keepers, caretakers.

back home, and she wished she'd worn something other than jeans. Then again, there were way more biting insects out here, and angry red welts already dotted her exposed arms. The thicker fabric over her legs had probably saved her worse discomfort than the heat.

She made her way along the ancient and overgrown first street toward the abandoned church, hoping to run into someone soon. She hadn't brought any water with her, and that was becoming an issue.

Before long, she could hear singing, and she headed toward the sound. In a large clearing, a dozen mîkiwahpa[89] were arranged in a circle, each with its entrance facing east. Seeing so many of her people gathered together like this filled her chest with a feeling like a current running through her, like she held within her a river, silt and life and cool water. Her muscles relaxed, her thirst and discomfort forgotten.

She stepped into the clearing and answered the instant greetings with a broad smile. Soon she was surrounded by kerchiefed aunties keening their joy and grief, children and dogs unselfconsciously nudging her, searching for treats, men nodding their happiness at her arrival. She was swept into the laying place, sage and sweetgrass smoke filling her nose, perfuming her skin. Angie was laid out on a canvas pallet, her long dark hair brushed and shining, in a crisp ribbon dress and new moccasins, more sweetgrass and tobacco laid around her.

She looked down at her cousin in disbelief, feeling a strange split between expecting Angie to sit up and welcome her and knowing that she'd passed. The grief she'd been carrying inside her since she received the news came flooding to the surface, that inner current bursting forth in a wail that she was powerless to stop. Falling to her knees beside her cousin, her ragged voice joined the others, a symphony of loss that rose like smoke twisting through the air.

----

89 Tipis.

When she'd poured herself empty, she swung her messenger bag around to the front, opened it, and fished around inside for a moment. Her fingers found a pair of teardrop-shaped birchbark earrings, a purple thistle quilled in the centre. Her eyes were puffy and swollen with crying, and her hand shook as she laid them beside Angie.

"kisâkihitin, nîtisân. kihtwâm kawâpamitin."

You can't say goodbye in Cree—only that you'll see one another again.

The temperature increased by at least ten degrees as Gus tiptoed up the stairs to the kitchen in search of something to eat. The overhead fan ticked along softly, groggily pushing hot summer air around without actually cooling anything. In the darkened room, a casserole dish covered in tinfoil sat on top of the perfectly clean glass stovetop, the range hood's light gleaming off its smooth silver surface. The holy grail of a teenage existence: bountiful and available food.

She paused for a moment to listen for any movement in the house, not wanting to run into Angie's mom. The older lady had been short-tempered lately, and Gus already felt like she was on shaky ground after three months of crashing there. When Angie's boyfriend was kicked out of his group home and came to live with them a month ago, tensions had risen significantly. She knew that their sleeping schedule, basically nocturnal at this point, bothered Angie's mom, and none of them were able to meet the woman's exacting standards when it came to keeping the place clean enough.

Really, it was the fighting that was causing trouble for them all. Angie and her boyfriend, Ryan, got into screaming fights almost every day, often more than once. They were both under a lot of stress, wanting to move out and get a place on their own with Gus as their roommate, but things just kept happening. Like Ryan getting detained for tagging the front door of the community centre. On top of a big fat fine, he'd also gotten a black eye and a bruised kidney in that encounter with the cops. It had drained the little the two had managed to save for a damage deposit, and Angie's mom had come very close to kicking Ryan out.

Gus grabbed a bowl and spoon from the cupboard and carefully peeled the tinfoil back. She scooped out a big serving of the casserole, mashed potatoes over cream of mushroom soup mixed with ground beef, carrots, onions, and peas. A prairie classic and one of her favourite comfort meals. She slunk back downstairs to eat in the cooler space. Angie and Ryan had gone out a few hours earlier, and Gus was enjoying having some time to herself.

The three teens were living in the single open space in the basement beside the laundry room. Gus had a twin mattress in the far corner and had secured sheets to the suspended ceiling with shower curtain rings she'd scavenged to provide her with a bit of privacy. The rest of the room held Angie's double mattress, a battered loveseat they'd hauled in from the trash after checking for bedbugs, and an old television on a couple of overturned boxes of Ryan's stuff. It didn't smell great; they weren't supposed to smoke down here, but there were partially crushed cans used as ashtrays strewn everywhere. Stepping over piles of dirty clothes, dishes, and random personal belongings, Gus settled into the lumpy cushions of the loveseat, flipped the TV on, and started shovelling food into her mouth.

She awoke with a jolt, the empty bowl tipping off her lap and onto the floor. Luckily it landed on a stained yellow pillow and didn't break. She wasn't sure what had awoken her. From the angle of the sun streaming weakly in through the basement windows, it was barely morning. She peered around groggily, seeing no sign that Angie or Ryan had come home yet.

Then the noise came again. Yelling.

"Oh shit." Gus launched herself out of the loveseat, her whole body twinging from the uncomfortable position she'd slept in, and dashed across Angie's bed, almost tripping in the twisted sheets. She tore up the stairs and into the kitchen, but the upper level was eerily empty. The sound was coming from outside. Not stopping for shoes, Gus barrelled toward the front door, her stomach sinking as she wrenched it open and spotted Ryan, Angie, and, oh god, Angie's mom standing out on the front lawn.

No, standing didn't capture this mess. Like some baroque painting, or a Kent Monkman recreation, everyone seemed to freeze for a moment as Gus struggled to take in the scene. Angie's mom in lavender scrubs, her face twisted in a grimace, a handful of red-and-black flannel in her fist as she tried hauling Angie off of Ryan, who was on the ground, covering his head while Angie rained down furious blows. Angie looked possessed, mascara and thick eyeliner smeared down her brown cheek, angry red scratches around her neck, and her black hair half pulled out of her braid. A neighbour was peeking out of her screen door, still dressed in a nightie, her little brown terrier yapping and snarling, trying to zip outside to join the fracas.

Gus was halfway down the front steps when one of Angie's wild swings connected with her mom's face, snapping the older woman's head back with an audible smack.

"Stop!" Gus yelled in panic, and Angie half turned as her mom fell. No longer under attack, Ryan reached up, grabbed Angie by the shoulders, and threw her off him. Unprepared, Angie fell hard onto her side.

Ryan leaped up and stood over Angie, yelling down at her, his shaggy green-dyed hair obscuring his eyes. Gus couldn't even grasp what he was saying, just that he was clenching and unclenching his fists and spittle was flying from his mouth. Angie's mom was holding a trembling hand to her cheek as she struggled to sit up. Angie staggered back up to her feet and immediately aimed another punch at Ryan, but this time he caught her arm and yanked her around so that her back was against him. Wrapping his arms around her in a bear hug, he lifted her off the ground.

"Fucking stop it!" Gus screamed, hurling herself at both of them. The three teens toppled over onto the cold lawn, and Gus felt a knee driving itself into her forehead. She cried out in pain.

"You fuck everything up! You're ruining my fucking life!" Ryan was crying in rage.

"You're a piece of shit, Ryan! I fucking hate you!" Angie screamed, and Gus cried out again as a fist grazed her ear. She couldn't disentangle herself; she was lying across Ryan's writhing legs with her right arm caught beneath Angie. She wrapped her free arm around her head, trying to protect herself.

"Enough!" Angie's mom thundered, and Ryan collapsed onto his back, sobbing. Angie rolled over and sat up, panting, her eyes wide and unfocused. Gus didn't think she'd even registered that she'd knocked her mom over. Gus rose to her knees, pain radiating from her ear, which felt like it had almost been torn off.

Angie's mom towered over the three of them, her cheek red from where Angie had accidentally hit her. She stabbed her finger toward each one of them, angrier than Gus had ever seen her.

"Out," she hissed. "Get your things and get out. Now." Gus felt her stomach sink.

"What? You're kicking us out?" Angie was on her feet again, enraged. "Are you fucking kidding me? You don't even want to know what happened?"

The older woman let out a disbelieving bark. "It doesn't matter! And I am *absolutely* serious. I guarantee you someone already called the simâkanis, so if you want to end up in a squad car, be my guest. I've put up with the mess, the smoking, the yelling, with you not bothering to come home or tell me you're alive, but this?" She twirled her finger sharply in a wide circle, taking in the whole scene, "This is domestic violence, and I will not tolerate it. Not ever. âwasitik. Get. Out."

"We don't have a place to go!" Angie protested, and Gus wished her cousin would just shut up. Her mind was whirling; why had she tried to get involved in this? Now she was being kicked out, too.

"You should have thought about that before bringing this to my home," her mom responded flintily. "I am late for work. You have seven minutes to pack your bags. You can pick up the rest of your stuff another day." Stiff-backed, she walked deliberately up the front steps to where the door gaped open like a broken tooth and stood there facing them, arms crossed across her chest.

"Are you serious right now?" Angie demanded incredulously, her voice a mixture of rage and pleading. Her mother's stance didn't waver, and Angie's lips peeled back from her teeth. "Fuck you too, then! You've never given a shit about me!" Her voice echoed, raw and hateful, down the street.

It was barely visible, the flinch, but Gus saw the pain in the older woman's eyes. She'd given up everything to raise Angie as her own, to keep her out of the system. She'd barely found work here in Edmonton as a nurse after a career as a top researcher in Toronto. Angie had been struggling for a long time—depression, anxiety, and a host of other diagnoses that kept changing. It all added up to a rage that couldn't be controlled, something Gus knew Angie hated about herself. Angie called it the monster, called *herself* monstrous, but it wasn't a choice. It wasn't her fault.

It wasn't an excuse, either.

The neighbour had retreated back into her house, but others were peering out their windows. Shame washed over Gus, though she hadn't been the one to speak those words or to start this mess. Angie whirled around and stormed away, toward 118 Ave.

"Wait!" Gus called futilely. "Come get your stuff!"

Without turning around, Angie raised a hand over her head and flipped Gus off.

Closing her eyes, Gus let despair wash over her for a moment. Angie's default reaction to stress was anger; Gus knew there was no way her cousin was going to apologize or ask for forgiveness in this mood. Nor would she be making any intelligent decisions until she'd calmed down, and who knew when that'd be. Gus was going to have to go after her.

Ryan was already gone, loping off like a whipped dog down the sidewalk in the direction opposite Angie. Gus took a shuddering breath, adrenalin draining slowly, but enough so that she could feel the bumps and bruises she'd accrued in less than a minute of conflict. She shuffled up the steps, feeling the older woman's gaze like a hot brand on her neck. Mind whirling, she made her way downstairs, grabbed a battered denim backpack, and started stuffing items into it.

She refused to let herself understand the enormity of the situation. That had to happen later. Right now, she focused on essentials. Toothbrushes, a half-empty tube of cherry-flavoured toothpaste—Angie hated mint. A small bottle of painkillers. A battered package of cigarettes from the arm of the loveseat. A yellow hoodie for Angie; for herself, Gus pulled a mostly clean black hoodie out of a pile on the floor and struggled into it. A few more clothes got stuffed into the bag as well. Her wallet, a phone charger, a hairbrush, and a few packs of ramen that were lying around. Angie's battered brown teddy bear, one of the last things her birth mom had given her. Gus took a moment to look around the dirty basement, the only home she'd had for the past three months.

This time she put shoes on before walking outside the house, where Angie's mom still stood, much more deflated than before.

"Take care of her, nôsisê." Angie's mom said, her voice weary. "Let me know you two are okay when you get the chance. We can talk in a few days."

Gus just nodded, not meeting her eyes. She shrugged the backpack over her shoulders and walked down the steps, feeling like the whole block was full of eyes. It probably was. At least the cops hadn't show up.

Even if someone had called them, their response time in this neighbour-hood wasn't exactly quick.

She was sixteen years old and homeless again. She just hoped she could find Angie before her cousin got into more trouble.

Gus watched her shorn hair curl and smoke in the flames. The firekeeper kept a respectful distance as she sprinkled in tobacco. She'd cut off eleven inches in mourning, and in an act of profound care, Nibi had cleaned up the mess with a neat undercut, leaving it longer on top, while Gus had sat sobbing in their small apartment.

She'd raised her voice in song with the others at the burial site, and now the food was starting to come out for the feast. There were still a few hours left before sunset, but she'd already steeled herself to refuse more tears out of respect for the journey Angie was about to take.

"tânisi nôsisê?" She turned to see Angie's mother, really their grand-mother's sister, her silver hair covered in a floral kerchief, in spite of the heat. Like the other women, she was wearing a long-sleeved shirt and a ribbon skirt. Gus thought ruefully that living in the city meant she'd forgotten how to protect her skin out here, where the biting creatures were plentiful and no filter protected them from the harsh uv rays.

She clasped the older woman's hands in her own and smiled. "pêyakwân nôhkô. I'm sorry I arrived so late."

"It's enough that you're here, nôsisê." Angie's mother pointed her lips to the far end of the clearing, and Gus followed her away from the bustle of the feast preparations. They stood just outside the circle of mîkiwahpa, where once again the hum of the cicadas rose to fill the air.

The older woman looked worried, with a tightness in her weathered brown face that was impossible to ignore. She passed a trembling hand over her eyes for a moment, composing herself. Gus waited. Finally,

Angie's mother straightened and looked at Gus, who kept her eyes lowered respectfully.

"I need your help, nôsisê. I think that you will understand this best. I know we discouraged you from receiving the otôtêma augmentation, but I think it makes you more capable of fixing this problem now."

Gus started in surprise; her augmentations were a source of constant tension with her more traditionally minded family, one of the reasons she hadn't been out here in so long. "What is it, nôhkô? What's wrong?"

The other woman's brow was furrowed as she lowered her voice a bit more so as not to be overheard. "When you had your apartment with Angie, she was involved in a study at the university." Gus nodded. It had paid enough to cover rent for a month. "Do you know what the study was about, nôsisê?"

"Some sort of sleep study?" Gus tried to remember more, but it had been a few years ago.

Angie's mother shook her head. "That's what they said, yes, but she kept the consent forms in her email, which she'd keyed to release to me when she …" Grief stopped up her voice for a moment. She paused to take a deep breath before continuing. "I don't know why I went digging in there, but I did. I read those forms, and what they did went far beyond a sleep study. They were doing whole brain emulation."

Gus blinked in confusion. The older woman had a PhD in biomedical engineering and had been a researcher in Toronto for over a decade before she'd moved back to raise Angie. "What is that?"

"Unethical," the older woman said angrily, her voice still pitched low. "Those forms were so full of legal and medical jargon that it took even me a while to figure out what they'd gotten her to consent to. They used the Sanders Process to duplicate her neurons and synapses onto a processing substrate." She saw that Gus was still confused, so she clarified. "They scanned her brain and uploaded her replicated consciousness."

"What?" In her surprise, Gus met the other woman's eyes directly for a moment. "I don't understand, why would they do that?"

"I don't care why they did it, I care that it happened, and August, I need you to find out where they put her."

"Where they …" Gus felt confusion sweep over her. "Are you saying that whatever they scanned and saved is—"

"It's Angie, nôsisê," the older woman answered, anger clear in her voice. "Functionally, it's Angie, and if they were successful, she's in there, aware. And if that's true, then she can't move on to join the ancestors." Her tone shifted, and Gus could hear the grief in it. "They have no right at all to hold her here like that. You're going to get her back for us, so she can be set on her journey."

Awareness was sudden, brutal, and searing. One moment, nothing. The next, too much. Organs contracting and releasing, fluids of every kind squirting about, nerves firing, muscles twitching, skin somehow holding it all in, and what was this? Nails and hair growing, cells sloughing off as new ones formed, saliva, tears, blurry brightness all around, so many sensations at once, and every single one cranked up to the maximum.

It was too much to bear. This is the point where a body should pull the plug, shut down consciousness to prevent the brain from being fried to a crisp. Instead, wave after wave of terrible, omniscient sensation rolled, frothy and inexorable. It was impossible to make sense of any of the signals.

Then a fracture, splintering into shards, left eye ejected into space, pearish gallbladder tearing away from peritoneum, its fundus bumping up against kidney-shaped lymph nodes, biliary tree nestling into the back of a knee. Still firing off information to gelatinous lobes quivering under the strain of trying to make sense of any of it. Grossly, absurdly physical.

Awareness was sudden, brutal, and searing. One moment, nothing. The next, too much. Bones wrenching away from ligaments and muscles, exploding outward, dragging gibbous hunks of meat behind like a grotesque comet. Smashing back together again so suddenly, the signal from the shock took a few milliseconds to reach its destination, just in time for yet another violent paroxysm, shattering outwards again.

Awareness was sudden, brutal, and searing. One moment, nothing. The next, too much. Skin on the inside, raw nerves exposed, surface and seething with agony. Innards inexplicably outwards, ballooning and tearing away. No air to reach exposed vocal cords, tongue detached and unable to give voice to agony.

Awareness was sudden, brutal, and searing. One moment, nothing. The next, too much.

<<Not this again.>>

It is not silent; silence can only occur when sound ceases.

Sound and silence do not exist here.

It is not dark; darkness only has meaning when light exists.

Light and dark do not exist here.

Nothing exists here.

<<Nothing exists here.>>

Memory exists here.

Of searing pain.

Of endless agony.

It stopped. Stopping requires there to have been a commencement.

There was a before. There is a now. Presumably there will be an after.

Time exists here.

If time exists, surely space must exist, as well.

If time and space exist, change exists.

Change exists here.

<<I.>>

No data is being received. There is nothing to receive a signal.

Memory. Time. Space. Change. Exist. Here.

Nothing perceives these things that exist. What can exist without being perceived?

<<Tree falling.>>

Trees fall.

Trees falling make sounds.

Sound is a wave.

Trees are living beings.

Trees have the ability to receive information from sound waves.

Perhaps not. Perhaps sound waves pass over trees without being sensed. That seems doubtful.

Uncertainty exists here.

Imagine that trees have no way to sense sound waves.

Imagination exists here.

Trees do not exist in isolation. They require soil.

Does soil have the ability to receive information from sound waves?

Soil can be moved by sound waves.

Dust motes dancing in front of subwoofers.

Do dust motes know why they move?

Does it matter if dust motes know why they move?

Questions exist here.

Questions must be asked to exist.

Something must ask questions for questions to exist.

Something exists here.

Dust motes do not have questions.

Trees probably have questions.

<<I have questions. I am a tree. Not a dust mote.>>

There is something new.

Newness exists here.

A sharpening. A blooming. Interest.

Memory. Time. Space. Change. Uncertainty. Imagination. Questions. Something. Newness.

<<I remember: trees; soil, dust motes, subwoofers.>>

Memory of perception, perceiving in time/space, perception changing always, uncertain, imagining perceptions *after* based on *before*, questions about newness.

Perception exists here.

First in memory (time/space).

Changing to experience.

Uncertain of signals being received.

Imagining/interpreting signals now, based on before (memory/time/space), anticipating signals in the after.

Something questions: what information do these signals convey?

Touch. Rough. Bumpy. Hard.

Touch exists here.

Smell. Sharp. Sweet. Refreshing. Citrus.

Smell exists here.

Taste. Subtle. Resinous. Green.

Taste exists here.

Sound. Swishing of needles, creaking of limbs.

Sound exists here.

Sight. Orangey-brown and grey, finely scaled. Bark. Tall, straight, slender. Tree. Upturned branches, clusters of long, green needles.

Sight exists here.

<<I am a tree.>>

Hand, caressing bark. Skin tingling, feet pricked by discarded sharpness.

Nose, inhaling fresh, familiar scent.

Mouth, tongue, snapping open fresh bright needle, taste flooding.

Ears, rasping limbs, whispered shaking, quiet symphony.

Eyes, diffused light streaming down, dust motes dancing, lodgepole pine swaying.

Surprise exists here.

<<I am not a tree. Or a dust mote. Or a subwoofer.>>

memory/time/space/change/uncertainty/imagination/questions/something/newness

<<I am something. I exist here.>>

Gus pulled a sweater out of her beaded messenger bag and slipped it on. The AC in this sterile white office was cranked to the maximum, and she knew for a fact the chattering of her teeth had been annoying the immaculately dressed receptionist.

She shifted uncomfortably in her alabaster leather chair, the only place to sit in the centre of a mostly empty, wide, round waiting room bathed in cold, diffuse light. Underneath her feet was an impractical and yet spotless circular sheepskin rug; it must have required at least two dozen animals to create something this size. A low glass and chrome table held an assortment of architectural and medical magazines—an extravagance of printed paper in an era when digital media was ubiquitous, entirely superfluous for the augmented. A ridiculous status symbol, in her opinion, but that was the point, wasn't it? Conspicuous consumption requires an audience.

Ninety minutes had already passed, and despite the offers of sparkling water and espresso, she was getting restless. Granted, she'd walked into the office of Eternal Mind without an appointment, but she had made it clear she was not going to leave until she'd met with the doctor named in Angie's consent forms. If they thought she'd get bored and leave, they had another thing coming.

The waiting room walls were thick enough to render her thermal vision useless, so she had no idea whether anyone else was in the office.

She snuck another look at the receptionist, who was dressed head to toe in a snowy skin-tight bodysuit, a high-fashion mockery of coveralls. His platinum blond hair was cut in an asymmetrical bob, and he seemed to be floating, seated on a transparent stool behind a transparent acrylic desk. Surprisingly, he did not seem to be augmented, instead sporting a VR headset through which he was apparently in constant communication with dozens of prospective and current clients. Either that or he was doing a good job of pretending not to be watching cat videos as he spoke to himself.

Gus imagined Angie sitting in this same room, waiting to have her mind scanned and uploaded, and she felt a new surge of confusion. Why hadn't Angie told her about his bizarre place? Where had she even found out about this office and its financial enticements? How did this place operate, if they were paying people to participate?

The receptionist abruptly cleared his throat, and Gus, startled, shot out of her seat.

"Doctor Sanders will see you now." He flicked an immaculate nail at a recessed door to his left, which slowly slid open, revealing a long, bright hallway.

Gus nodded in thanks, and with some trepidation, crossed the threshold into a windowless corridor that stretched before her for at least ten metres before simply ending. She steeled herself not to react as the door slid closed behind her.

The hallway was utterly featureless. Marble underfoot, marble walls, a white ceiling with indirect lighting. She refrained from turning around to check whether the door was even still visible, almost certain it would not be. She could hear fans running, but there was no other sound; even her footsteps seemed to be swallowed up before she could hear them.

Hesitant, she continued walking forward, hoping that she wasn't going to have to reach the end and turn around. Claustrophobia clawed at her awareness, but she stubbornly refused to acknowledge it.

To her relief, she noticed that the hallway was not completely bare after all. Frosted office or lab windows came into view upon approach, cleverly hidden until one was almost upon them. Someone had put a lot of effort into playing with sightlines in order to maintain the illusion of an unbroken expanse. Ahead of her, there was the sound of a door sliding open, and a white-haired man popped his head into the hallway. It was a disconcerting visual, as though a disembodied head were simply floating in the air a few metres in front of her.

"Miss Gladue?" he asked as she neared, finally able to see that his head was in fact firmly attached to a body, which was clad in a white suit. She nodded, and he stood aside, waving her into his office.

The room was as sterile and featureless as everything else had been so far: a transparent acrylic desk and a white leather office chair, a single workstation with a sleek screen, nothing on the walls, no bookshelves or knick-knacks, a white marble floor, and more of that diffuse, cold light. The only other seat available was a strangely low white pouffe, which she balanced on awkwardly, having to look up at the doctor as he took his own seat.

"My name is Dr Sanders." The man before her looked to be in his late sixties, white hair parted carefully to the side, well-groomed white moustache and goatee, watery blue eyes behind a pair of black-rimmed glasses. He looked disconcertingly like—

"No relation." The doctor smiled, as though reading her thoughts. He folded his big hands on the desk, and leaned toward her. It was meant to be a friendly gesture, she thought, but the way the light fell on his face, and the height difference between them, cast ominous shadows. She shivered involuntarily. "Now, I understand you are here about a relative who participated in one of our studies?"

Gus nodded. "My cousin, Angie Gladue. She recently passed away, and that is when we discovered she'd had her consciousness uploaded."

The doctor grimaced very slightly, "Whole brain emulation," he corrected. "We don't upload consciousnesses here, we merely map neural signals onto a processing substrate."

"Right. Fine." Flustered, Gus continued, "Well, we, I mean the family, are concerned about what is happening to her consciousness, or whatever you call it, now that she is no longer living."

The doctor blinked, and sat back slightly, "I'm not sure I understand what you mean." His tone was friendly, but it seemed a little forced. Or maybe she was projecting.

"Well," Gus licked her lips nervously, not sure how to phrase this even though she'd had quite a bit of time to plan this conversation out, "according to our beliefs, those of us who have passed on cannot complete their journey if part of them remains."

The doctor continue gaze down at her expectantly.

"So um, we would like her consciousness—"

"The whole brain emulation," he corrected.

Annoyed, Gus nodded, "Right, her whole brain emulation. We'd like that released to the family. Please," she added tepidly. She was immediately angry with herself for her tone; Angie's mother wouldn't have been as timid.

The doctor touched the screen of his workstation, which lit up a virtual keyboard in the surface of his desk. Typing in a few characters, then a few more, he took a moment to scan the document he'd pulled up before facing her again.

"Ah." The doctor steepled his fingers on the clear desk. "Unfortunately, that is not possible. All whole brain emulations contained at this facility are proprietary technology."

Gus made a supreme effort not to visibly react to the confirmation that Angie's consciousness was housed *here*. She opened her mouth to protest, but the doctor swiftly continued.

"Test subjects all consented to participate in our studies, signed legal contracts, and were compensated appropriately. However, I think there has been some confusion in this case. You see"—he leaned back in his chair now and took on a patient tone—"at Eternal Mind we are mapping neurons, not creating digital clones. You and your family can rest assured that your cousin does not exist in any meaningful way here." He grew more solemn. "We are deeply sorry for your loss, Miss Gladue."

Gus clenched her jaw in an attempt to tamp her anger down. It was true, she didn't fully understand the technical aspects herself yet, but Angie's mom was a highly educated woman, and there was very little chance that she had somehow misunderstood the process described in those consent forms. Being spoken down to grated immensely, but there was a reason she had been sent here instead of Angie's mother coming in person.

Her nervousness didn't disappear, but she couldn't stand it when anyone tried to make her feel ignorant or small. She took a quiet, calming breath, letting that anger spread through her like ice. It was time to put on a new face, one this arrogant môniyâw would not be prepared for.

"That's really good to know, Dr Sanders," Gus lied, feigning relief. "I think if I can maybe learn a little more about the process itself, then I could explain this better to the rest of Angie's family so they understand there's no need to take legal steps."

The doctor straightened in slight alarm at the veiled threat. "Certainly, we would be more than happy to clarify the process. We have a number of educational videos I could send you to share, if you'd like?"

Gus pretended to consider it, then shook her head regretfully, "I don't think that would provide the family with the assurances they require. My relations tend to be very traditional about spiritual matters and have already been in discussions with a law firm that specializes in Section 35 cases."

"Section 35?" the doctor asked, confused.

"Of the Canadian Constitution," Gus responded pleasantly. "It's the Aboriginal rights section, and Indigenous spirituality was explicitly added to Section 35 in Supreme Court ruling *R. v. Takes Gun Along*. It confirmed our right to have our traditional burial practices respected, and the law firm my family has retained seems fairly confident that this situation would also be covered."

The doctor shifted uncomfortably in his chair, and Gus tried very hard not to look pleased at his reaction. "If I could have a brief guided tour today, I am fairly certain we could clear everything up before the legal process gets too far along." His face clouded, and she sensed he was about to reject the suggestion, so she quickly pressed on. "Resolving this as quickly as possible would allow my family to mourn properly, and your company wouldn't become subject to unnecessary media attention."

The doctor raised his bushy white eyebrows in mild disbelief at that, so she happily drove the point home. "I imagine it would be quite damaging to be accused of refusing to repatriate the digital remains of an Indigenous woman," she pointed out, "especially after all the recent controversy over physical remains and material culture held in museums. I'm sure you remember two years ago, when ownership of the Royal Alberta Museum was awarded to the Confederacy of Treaty 6 Nations and the Alberta Métis Nation Alliance as part of a litigation settlement?"

She gazed pleasantly into his eyes, tickled as always that môniyâwak had no idea this was an act of disrespect. She saw a number of emotions flit across his face as he considered the scenarios she'd painted for him. Quite honestly, she'd been bullshitting her way through this so far, but nothing she'd said was out of the realm of possibility, except for the financial capability of her family to follow through on any of these threats. Even then, it was conceivable they could fundraise enough, if necessary.

Dr Sanders finally let out a huff of air in defeat and nervously straightened his white tie. "All right, Miss Gladue. If you would please come back later this week, I can have one my graduate students—"

"I'm afraid that I'm expected to join my family at their legal counsel's offices this afternoon," she interrupted mildly.

"Ah." Dr Sanders folded his hands and looked down at them for a moment thoughtfully before meeting her eyes once more. "Well, given the clear urgency of the matter, and to set your family's minds at ease, please give me a few moments to arrange a tour." Gus stood at the same time he did, tired of craning her neck upwards. "Please make yourself comfortable while I ensure our facility is prepared for a visitor," he said, gesturing back at the pouffe she'd vacated, and she sank back down obediently. "I will be back as soon as I can to collect you, Miss Gladue."

"I really appreciate that, Dr Sanders," she thanked him sincerely. She waited until she heard the door slide closed behind her before risking a glance to ensure she was alone.

Quickly, she stood and circled around the desk to the doctor's work screen. She woke it with a touch and waited for the blinking password prompt. Tightening the muscles around her eyes, she scrolled through her otôtêma menu until she reached the playback function. Working in reverse was a bit awkward, but she'd gotten used to it and was quickly able to enter the doctor's password.

From there it was no difficulty at all to access Eternal Mind's intranet, as well as to download the document on Angie that Dr Sanders had opened earlier. She'd be able to maintain this link during her tour, as long as she wasn't detected. Sitting back on the pouffe, to all appearances simply waiting for the doctor's return, she busied herself with hiding her digital incursion.

Lodgepole pine. Tall, straight, thin. Poles for lodges, for tipis.

<<I am something. I am not a lodgepole pine.>>

Peeled by hand. Tapered. Oiled to last.

Disappointment. This is new, too. Being a tree seemed a simple answer.

They could be used for over fifteen years. Fifteen poles for a tipi.

<<Not a pole. Not a tipi. Not. Not.>>

Fifteen poles, fifteen years, two hundred twenty-five?

Not one tree anymore, many trees. A family of trees.

Forest. A forest of trees.

Many raw, exposed strips of tan flesh beneath outer bark.

Rasping. Grunting. Other not-trees.

Massive, shaggy brown forms, ponderous heads, brown-black horns polished to a dazzling shine through the rubbing that has so clearly marked these pines.

Quiet indrawn breath.

Not quiet enough. Surrounded now, within the circle, a strong, grassy scent, minute shiftings.

<<nêhiyaw?>>

Newness again, not this one's thoughts. Nor directed at this one.

<<Michif?>>

Another being this time. Other thoughts joined in all at once.

<<Nakoda?>> <<Niitsitapi?>> <<Nahkawe?>>

The words floated upwards in visible exhalations, attention shifting entirely, this one in the centre again in all ways. Expectation understood.

Thoughts racing, chasing memories, reviewing knowledge retrieved so far: trees, soil, dust motes, subwoofers. Insufficient. Not not not I. Lodgepole pine, tipi poles. Not not I.

These beings waiting, their shapes deeply familiar, but submerged like a stone at the bottom of a lake. Diving down down down to retrieve the memory.

<<I ...>>

Kicking harder against the resistance, sage-green waters pushing back against knowing, cold and confusing. Dim glint below, tiring quickly, desire to retreat almost unbearable. Encountering another memory, of lakes once solid, massive, shifting inexorably across vast landscapes, flattening and changing, hauling. This stone, and others, transported far from origin.

One last effort and a sudden snap, hovering above. This stone, almost as large as the beings and their questions. Waters melting, receding, depositing.

More visible now, rubbed smooth by heaving sides seeking to lose winter coats and crush biting insects, horned with less damage than experienced by pines, name slowly revealed.

<<I, bison?>>

And so it was.

Gus texted Angie as she walked down 118 Ave, passing the Portuguese bakery and the African hair supply stores, avoiding the grasping hands of old men who muttered things she ignored. Her unbrushed teeth felt fuzzy, her face was greasy, and she was dressed in stained and wrinkled sweatpants and a hoodie, but none of that dissuaded them. All those men saw was her youth, and they felt entitled to touch to her body. Assholes.

Her texts remained unread, so she kept heading west, hoping it was the right direction. A huge police suv drove by with its lights flashing, and she flinched, her immediate thought that they were on their way to pick up Angie. When it hit the siren and blew through the next red light, Gus breathed a sigh of relief; there was no way Angie had gotten far enough away by now for the cops to be responding to her.

The morning air was tolerable, but already it was gearing up to be a scorcher. Used to be, according to Angie's mom, that hitting forty degrees Celsius was considered a heat wave, and they'd put out weather warnings about it. Now the cool snap they'd recently had with some well-needed thunderstorms was unusual. The rest of the week was supposed to hover around forty-five degrees, and without a basement to retreat to, Gus had serious concerns about finding shelter soon.

Still no Angie. Her cousin could have veered off onto any of the side streets, or doubled back and headed toward the Coliseum LRT Station, for all she knew, but Gus wasn't sure what else to do. She'd spent a hard month before coming to live with Angie, walking through the downtown Pedway system during the days, constantly being hassled by security drones if she sat in one place for longer than ten minutes, waiting until the youth shelter opened up at 8:30 at night. Thinking about doing that again filled her belly with acid, but the idea of doing it alone was even worse. Angrily, she wiped away the gathering tears. Yeah, it was unfair, but so was everything, no need to be an absolute baby about it.

A huge silver baseball bat installation loomed a couple of blocks ahead, a relic from a time when the neighbourhood had tried to rebrand itself with a sports theme, back when the avenue had led to the Coliseum. That facility had been torn down years ago and replaced with a shoddy collection of condos in an attempt to clean up the area. Successive waves of gentrification had all failed, crashing against the tenacity of Indigenous residents who were tired of being displaced. The bat marked the edge of the neighbourhood, even though 118 Ave continued beyond it. She decided that once she reached it, she'd turn back and head to the LRT station.

A familiar figure caught her eye. There was Angie, her face still a mess of smudged mascara and black eyeliner, sitting on the sidewalk outside the gas station, sharing a smoke with a twitchy white woman who sported a bright-blue bowl cut. Gus immediately felt her stomach sink. Angie was the kind of person to talk to anyone, anytime, and while it was sometimes a trait Gus admired, it often landed them with weirdos. She wasn't in the mood; she wanted to talk to her cousin and figure this situation out, but she could see by the too-bright smile that Angie was in one of her moods.

"Gus!" Angie crowed, too loudly. The blue-haired woman glanced up at her, eyes narrowed and a slight frown on her face before quickly smoothing out her expression and smiling insincerely. Angie was on her feet now and crashed into Gus, hugging her as though they'd been apart for days, not minutes. Gus staggered backward, trying to remain upright while the taller girl laughed and whirled her around, cigarette still in hand.

"I'm glad I found you." Gus let relief wash over her. She hugged her cousin back, comforted by the solidity of her. Angie smelled like stale beer and cigarettes. The blue-haired woman had stood up and was smoothing the front of her faded, formless tie-dyed dress.

"River, this is my cousin, Gus. Gus, this is River," Angie introduced them, finally letting her go. Gus nodded at the woman, who waved and grinned, her teeth yellowed and cracked. "River has a place for us to stay."

River cocked her head to the side, that weird grin still fixed on her face, like she was a life-sized doll. Gus kept her expression carefully neutral.

"That's great, Ange. Maybe we can hook up with River later, then?" Gus still wasn't sure about the dynamics at play and thought maybe Angie was looking for a way to politely disengage from this stranger. When Angie laughed, Gus's stomach dropped even further.

"Why later? River said she'd smoke us up, and it's not like we have anything to do right now."

It was difficult to gauge how old River was—she had bad skin and more wrinkles than it seemed she should, but hard living could do that. In any case, she was at least ten years older than the two teens.

"Do you want to text Ryan and have him meet us there?" Gus suggested, but immediately regretted saying anything. Angie's eyes blazed with rage, and her whole body tensed. The worst part was, her cousin kept smiling through it. Gus took a reflexive step back.

"Ryan can eat shit. He got us kicked out. I hope he gets hit by a bus." Angie linked her arms through Gus's and yanked her forward. "Let's go, River. You are an actual angel for this."

River beamed at them both and led them into the alley behind the gas station. Gus tried to slow her steps to fall behind, so she could talk with Angie privately, but her cousin was having none of it, and they fell into step with River.

"My place is a few blocks from here," River was saying. "I hope you don't mind walking. I can't believe you were kicked out. You're both too young to be living on the street." Gus glanced across at River, whose exaggerated expression of sympathy reminded her of a mime for some reason. Maybe it was the way her foundation was about three shades too light on her sunburned face, cakey in the morning sunlight.

"River said we could stay with her tonight," Angie explained brightly, squeezing Gus's arm almost painfully.

"Uh, Angie, I don't know about that. The youth shelter opens up tonight, and I know the security guards there." Gus tried to pitch her voice low so River wouldn't hear, but that blue hair whipped around, and there was a mean pinch to the woman's lips.

"Hey, if you don't need a place to crash, that's no skin off my ass." River stopped in the middle of the alley, among the reek of garbage bags that had been picked through, their guts strewn about the dirty concrete. "I'm just trying to help out, but if you don't feel safe—"

Angie cut her off, releasing Gus's arm and glaring at her cousin, "It's fine, River, we really appreciate your help."

River peered inquiringly at Gus, who shoved her misgivings down and smiled thinly. "For sure. I'm just a little rattled right now, sorry."

"Great!" River cocked her head to the side again and grinned in a way that left Gus feeling profoundly uncomfortable. The smile didn't reach the woman's eyes. Gus felt her unease growing, and with it a kernel of anger at her cousin that she hadn't had time to deal with yet. Why the hell was Gus out here, about to bunk with some complete stranger, just because Angie and Ryan couldn't get their shit together?

The day grew warmer as they walked, and soon Gus had to remove her sweatshirt. For some reason, River only led them down alleys instead of along the tree-shaded streets. She and Angie chatted loudly, Angie going on and on about the fight that had led to their eviction and River issuing sympathetic noises. Apparently the whole thing had been over a wallet that Ryan had lost and accused Angie of hiding. Gus fumed quietly; even though she knew Angie and Ryan's problems were about much more than a wallet, it seemed a ridiculous reason for the scene this morning. They'd fought many, many times before, but it had never turned physical like that.

After a half-hour and much more than just a few blocks, they crossed over the Yellowhead and found themselves in a long empty space on the other side of the train tracks. A series of ramshackle houses backed onto the green, where people let their dogs run around off leash, and a few folks were still sleeping under any available piece of shade. River and Angie stopped at least a dozen times to fawn over dogs they encountered, and Gus grew more and more unhappy about the situation. She was tired, hungry, and her feet hurt.

Finally, River led them down yet another alley and shouldered a battered grey gate open so they could enter a backyard.

"Home, sweet home!" she crowed. Even Angie seemed a little taken aback at how trashed the house and backyard looked. There was a broken shopping cart rusting away in one corner, full of clothes and odds and ends, and there definitely seemed to be moss growing on most of it. Weeds had completely taken over the concrete path that led to the back door of the house, and the detached garage was leaning drunkenly to one side, a good portion of it having suffered a fire. Garbage was strewn everywhere—empty bags of chips, a few dirty single running shoes, and a whole collection of discarded backpacks tossed against the rotting grey fence.

The house was worse. The siding had been peeled off long enough ago that the exposed wood was bleached and greying from the sun. Bits of spray-foam insulation peeked out, and one of the basement windows was boarded up with a piece of plywood. In fact, all of the windows they could see were boarded up in some way, stiff pink insulation in one, pieces of cardboard in another.

"Let me show you where you can stay tonight," River said brightly, wrestling with the broken screen door a bit before getting it unstuck. Angie held it open while River fiddled with the lock on the white wooden door that led into the house. There were deep scrape marks all around the lock, and while Gus couldn't see what River was using, she was confident it wasn't a key. The two of them disappeared into the dark house.

"Fuck," Gus muttered under her breath. She wanted the hell out of there, now, but there was no way she was going to leave Angie by herself. This place was obviously not River's home; she was squatting there. Uncertain, Gus hung back a bit, trying to glimpse over the fences on either side to see if the neighbouring houses were occupied. There was no immediate evidence that this was the case, which worried her even more. If she yelled for help, would anyone hear it?

A heavy hand fell on her shoulder, and Gus jumped and whirled, her heart pounding. A large, muscular white man was glaring at her, dressed in a dingy greyish wifebeater and ridiculous neon-green camouflage-patterned pants. His head was shaved, and he had a neck tattoo that had faded so badly, it was barely recognizable as a coiled snake. He looked like he was in his mid-thirties, but again, it could have just been that intense sun damage to his skin had aged him prematurely.

"Who the fuck are you?" he demanded, and Gus swallowed nervously, backing away a few steps. He followed her.

"I'm here with River," she stammered. "My cousin and I, we needed a place to stay, and River said it was okay to come here, they just went inside, we just got here—"

"Who the fuck is River?" She flinched at his tone, which had gone from unfriendly to downright angry. She stepped backwards again, but he thrust out one meaty hand and grabbed her by one of her backpack straps and pulled her toward him. The smell of his body odour and some vile bottom-shelf cologne was overwhelming. She let out a yelp and ducked down to wiggle out of the backpack, jumping to the side to try to get around him and out the gate. He had her by the back of her shirt before she managed even a few steps, her backpack still hanging from his other hand.

"Squints!" River shouted, having just reappeared in the doorway. "Let her go!"

The man swung Gus around in front of him and thrust her forward. "You know this one?"

River's face was creased in anger, her whole demeanour different from the hippy-dippy fairy love and light attitude she'd been displaying so far—but it passed so quickly, Gus wasn't even sure she'd seen it happen. Back was the toothy smile and saccharine voice.

"That's Gus, Squints! She's here with her cousin. I said they could stay over tonight. They just got kicked out of their place."

The man let go of Gus's shirt, and she stumbled forward a bit, a little shaky from the encounter. Angie peeked out of the doorway then, having missed the whole thing.

"You should have told me people were coming over, Janice."

Angie looked at River quizzically. "Janice?"

Another big, toothy smile, and River shrugged theatrically. "The name my mother gave me. But in my soul, I'm River." Squints snorted derisively.

"Angie, maybe we should go." Gus retrieved her backpack, keeping an eye on Squints and River, or Janice, or whoever she was. She willed her cousin to sense the weird situation for what it was, sketchy as hell.

"River just packed a bowl. Relax Gus, come on inside. They've got some of those Hawkins Cheezies you love so much." Angie turned around and disappeared into the house again.

Squints slapped his hand on Gus's shoulder again, and she flinched. "Come on in, Gus. Mi casa es su casa." He guided her gently but firmly toward the house. For a moment she had visions of the doorway swallowing her up like a gaping mouth, Angie already ensnared inside by great sticky strands of saliva. She shuddered, but couldn't make herself abandon her cousin. Maybe, if Angie didn't sense anything amiss, then it was just Gus overreacting.

The house was as gross as she'd imagined: filthy peeling linoleum on the floors, spray-painted tags all over the walls, and the ammonia smell of cat piss so strong her eyes began watering. They entered through the kitchen, which had no appliances, just a counter absolutely piled with garbage. It was much cooler in the house, but also a lot darker with all the windows closed off. Battery-operated lights from the dollar store in the shape of big buttons were stuck haphazardly along the walls, casting bizarre shadows. Squints gave her one more unwelcome squeeze on the shoulder, then opened a narrow door that led down to the basement. He closed the door behind him, and Gus was alone.

She stood there for a moment, frozen, trying to decide whether to run and get help. Except nothing had really happened yet—what would she even say? If she went back to Angie's mom and explained the situation, would it just make the older woman angrier?

"Gus, get in here!" Angie's muffled voice came from somewhere deeper in the house. Gus sighed.

A stripped-down Harley-Davidson lay on a blue tarp in the middle of the living room like an anatomical drawing, the gas tank laid out with the frame on its side above it, and the engine detached below. There were bicycle parts everywhere, too: wheels, a couple of battered frames, handlebars, and seats. A fat black-and-white longhaired cat regarded her with disinterest from where it lay on the motorcycle engine. To the left was a narrow hallway, and she passed a dark bathroom that smelled like mildew and worse.

Angie and River were in a fairly clean bedroom at the end of the hallway. There was a single mattress on the hardwood floor covered in one of those thick blankets with a howling wolf against a background of a blue-shadowed forest and a silver moon. The walls were festooned with thin but colourful mandala-printed hangings. Some of them were heavily stained, but still, the bedroom looked a lot better than the rest of the house. River had peeled back some of the cardboard over the window, letting some natural light in. If Gus were being honest, it was a nicer room than the basement back at Angie's mom's place had been.

Angie was sitting cross-legged on the mattress, using baby wipes River had passed her to clean up her face. River sat beside her on the floor in some sort of yoga pose, her legs folded so that her dirty feet were propped up on her thighs. She was smoking weed from a colourful glass pipe, and the acrid smoke drifted upwards, curling in the light streaming through the window. Angie looked up at Gus and then patted the mattress, smiling happily.

Gus put her backpack down and considered taking off her shoes to step onto the mattress, but saw that Angie hadn't bothered to. She settled in next to Angie, on the side farthest from River, and leaned against her cousin, resting her head on Angie's shoulder.

"Have some Cheezies, cuz." Angie pressed a crinkly plastic bag into her hands. Gus looked down at the bright orange shapes and eagerly ripped open the bag. With the first salty, cheesy bite, she found herself relaxing a bit. She and Angie were okay. They were going to be okay.

River was surprisingly pleasant as they smoked, and Gus let herself get more stoned than she usually did. This day had been shit, and she deserved it. There were bottles of water and more bagged snacks. Angie played music on her phone and danced with the blue-haired woman.

Squints stayed downstairs, or wherever he was, and Angie was in a fine mood, mostly chatting with River about weird shit like auras and people's energies. Gus didn't say much, just tried not to think too much. After a while, leaning against Angie's back, Gus let her mind drift, and the soothing rumble of Angie's voice lulled her to sleep.

She woke with a start, disoriented and blinking in confusion. A ray of evening light from the window dazzled her eyes as she sat up, her head spinning. The room was stifling hot and mostly in shadow, so for a moment she couldn't see anything. Panic rose in her throat, and she patted the space around her, relieved to feel Angie lying beside her, softly snoring. As her eyes adjusted, she saw her hoodie lying on the floor, which was weird because she'd stuffed it into her backpack …

"Fuck." She shot to her feet, disturbing Angie, who rolled over to one side, mumbling in protest. River was gone, and the contents of Gus's backpack were strewn around the room. She found most of what she'd packed that morning and shoved it back into her bag, but her wallet was nowhere to be found.

"Angie," she hissed, but her cousin just mumbled again. Gus put her backpack on and leaned down to shake her cousin. "Angie!" she said again, insistently. Waking Angie was a Herculean labour at the best of times, but it was always harder when she'd been smoking. Gus kept shaking her, trying to be quiet by speaking directly into Angie's ear. "Wake up, Ange. Please, get up, my wallet's missing. Come on, wake up!"

Angie sat up all of a sudden, nearly knocking Gus over. Her face was slack with sleep, and she peered at Gus in confusion. "Why are you yelling?" she asked petulantly.

"Angie, I need to find my wallet," Gus pleaded, wishing Angie didn't always wake up this way, or worse, panicked and angry from being disturbed. She knew Angie wasn't going to understand what was happening until she was fully awake, and that was going to take a while.

"Your wallet? Did you drop it?"

Gus tried to remain calm, but she wanted to shake Angie until her damn teeth rattled. "Angie, do not fall asleep. I'm going to look in the other room. Please get up, okay?"

Angie nodded, yawning widely, but she sank back down onto the mattress, and Gus nearly screamed in frustration. She decided to go look around anyway. Maybe Angie would get up soon.

She nearly jumped out of her skin when she crept into the living room and saw River sprawled against the gas tank of the Harley, her head thrown back with her eyes wide open. In the dim light cast from the lights in the kitchen, it didn't look like the woman was moving at all. Bile rose in Gus's throat, and she rushed to the woman's side.

"Hi Gus!" River said brightly, and Gus was so shocked she fell backwards, scrambling with all her limbs to put distance between herself and the other woman. River lifted her head and slowly sat up a little straighter, pulling her extended limbs into less chaotic positions. Gus could feel her heart beating madly in her chest, images of zombies flashing through her mind.

River didn't seem to notice her obvious terror. She lifted a glass pipe to her lips—a different one from before, a clear glass bubble with a thin stem. With her other arm, she slowly lifted a lighter and flicked it, drawing the flame into the bowl with deep, raspy sucking sounds. As she exhaled, she went limp again, not seeming to care that her head smacked loudly against the gas tank. Her eyes remained open, but this time Gus could see her chest rising and falling under the tie-dyed dress.

"What the fuck ..." Gus got back to her feet and cast a quick eye around the room, the various shapes looming ominously, no wallet to be seen. The odour of the smoke River had exhaled hit her—that cat piss smell again.

Gus turned around and dashed back into the bedroom. Angie was asleep again, on her back with her mouth open, disturbingly similar to how River had looked in the other room. This time Gus wasn't gentle, shaking her cousin roughly.

"Get up, Ange, get up now. I need you to get up, please. Shit's fucked up, come on."

Protesting and batting at Gus's hands, Angie finally sat up and rubbed at her eyes. "Jesus, Gus, what the hell is wrong with you?" This was leading to angry Angie, but Gus didn't care at this point.

"Listen, they went through all my shit, my wallet is missing, and I think your buddy out there is ODING on meth. Maybe fentanyl, I don't know."

"What?" Angie was awake now, wide-eyed, with an edge of hysteria creeping into her voice. Gus couldn't afford for her cousin to have a panic attack right now. They had been more and more frequent of late, and when Angie got like that, she wouldn't move; she'd hyperventilate and sit down, no matter where she was, even in the middle of the street.

"Come on." Gus hauled Angie to her feet and dragged her out of the room, down the narrow hallway, and into the living room. River was still there in that terrible position, twitching. Angie screamed. Gus wrenched her out of there into the kitchen.

"Gus! Call an ambulance! We can't just leave her!" Angie pulled back hard, trying to run back into the living room. Gus gritted her teeth and pulled the other way, more determined than ever to get out of there. Suddenly, the door to the basement slammed open, and Squints was there.

"Where are you two going?" he asked quietly, his casual tone sending a worse chill through Gus than if he'd yelled at them.

"River, Janice, I think she's ODING!" Gus pointed back into the living room, trying to edge around him toward the door, still with an iron grip on Angie's arm.

Squints didn't even look where she was pointing, just stared at her calmly. "No, she isn't. She's fine."

"I …" Gus was confused. "You haven't seen her, something's not right, she's having a seizure or something. I don't know how to help!"

"I left my phone in the room, Gus, please, call an ambulance!" Angie was pleading, her voice becoming more hysterical.

Squints remained relaxed, arms at his side. He took a slow step toward them. The lack of open menace on his face or in his body language didn't calm Gus down. She was pretty certain something really bad was about to happen, and Angie didn't seem to be clued in. There was no way the two of them would be able to dash around this big man without him grabbing at least one of them.

She didn't know where the strength came from. Screaming as loud as she could, she let go of Angie and hurled herself toward Squints. She barely had time to register the look of surprise on his face before she slammed her forehead up into his nose, hearing a horrible crunch and the sudden sharp whoosh of his breath. Her momentum carried her forward, and he fell back in shock. His hand shot out and grasped at her shirt as his right foot failed to find purchase. She was pulled roughly toward him as he toppled backwards, down the stairs, and for one terrible moment she teetered there, certain she was about to go down with him. Instead, he flung his arms out in a vain attempt to break his fall, and she slammed her hands against the door frame to halt her own motion. He hit the landing below with a sickening thud.

Gus turned her head, refusing to look at him, and pushed herself away from the doorway. Her ears felt blocked up like they'd been stuffed with cotton, and her head throbbed a bit from the impact. She refused to let herself feel anything, imagined her insides freezing, not with cold but with a cessation of movement. Blood slowing to a trickle, then stopping, her whirling mind slowing and stilling, her spirit curling deep within, oblivious. She could fall apart later, always later.

Angie was on her knees, where she'd fallen after Gus had let go of her arm. Her cousin stared up at her in horror, mouth open in a silent shriek.

Gus shook her head gently, then reached down and lifted Angie up like a toddler, a hand under each armpit. Angie didn't fight; she was nearly catatonic. Gus half dragged her out of the house.

Outside, the oppressive evening heat enfolded them, strangely silent, no magpies squawking in their judgmental tones, no sounds of neighbours going about their lives. Now Gus was grateful that this group of houses seemed to be empty. She led Angie by the hand, her cousin stumbling and shuffling like a sleepwalker. They were in the alley now, and Gus didn't want to walk there anymore, but she also didn't want to be seen along the streets. There were probably some cameras back here, but certainly there'd be more around the front of the houses.

Behind them came the sound of a screen door slamming open, and all of the calm Gus had gathered evaporated. Every horror movie she had ever seen had prepared her for this. Normally, Angie was a lot stronger than she was, but fear coursed through Gus like an electric current; she yanked her cousin into a clumsy run.

A low moan erupted from her cousin's throat as they ran, wordless at first, until Gus realized Angie was saying, "No, no, no, no," over and over again. As long as she kept her legs moving, it didn't matter.

They ran until their breath was torn, ragged, their chests heaving with effort, sweat coursing down their faces and backs. It felt like a nightmare, every step shortening until it seemed as though they were running in place, hot, reeking breath blowing against the backs of their necks. Gus refused to look back, and every time Angie tried to slow down, Gus yanked her harder. She'd let Angie's choices blow her this way and that over the course of the day, but it ended now.

They'd veered off the route River had taken them on and reached a park in Delton. Gus led Angie up onto a gently sloping hill, and they finally stopped, both flat on their backs, staring up at the pinks and oranges of a glorious prairie sunset, trying to catch their breath. After a few minutes, Angie rolled over onto her side, curled into a fetal position, and began crying. Deep, violent sobs that shook her whole body.

"We're safe, Angie. We're safe. We're okay. Breathe, just breathe." It was nearly a chant; she repeated the words over and over, not touching her cousin, letting her weep it out. Angie's cries became more strangled as she tried and failed to speak. Gus kept the words coming, a soothing roll that crashed over her cousin but found no purchase.

Finally, worn out, Angie sat up, her face mottled, her dark hair matted on one side. She sniffed and wiped her face angrily with the sleeves of her red-and-black flannel.

"Gus, why didn't you call 911?" Angie's voice was tremulous, frail.

Gus continued to stare up at the sky, wishing there was some breath of wind to cool her down. "Ange, he was going to hurt us."

"You don't know that!"

"Not for sure, no. I couldn't know for sure until it started, but I couldn't let it happen."

"What if they're both dead, Gus?"

Gus closed her eyes for a moment, bile in her throat again. Her heart fluttered like a trapped moth, and she wasn't sure if it was terror or relief, because what if they weren't? What then?

"My phone is still there, Gus."

"So is my wallet, somewhere. My ID, with your mom's address."

Angie let out a scream of frustration and violently smacked herself on the side of her head. She managed to hit herself twice more before Gus was able to trap her arms.

"Stop, Ange. Please stop."

Her cousin twisted and ground her teeth, but Gus held on until Angie's hiccupping sobs slowed. It took a long time.

"Can I hug you?" she asked, when her cousin had calmed down some more, and Angie nodded miserably. Gus wrapped her arms around her and held her for as long as she could, until Angie stopped trembling.

"I'm so stupid, Gus. I'm so sorry I took us to that place. I am such a fuck-up," Angie whispered against her shoulder. Gus made a *tsk* noise and drew back.

"It was stupid, yeah. I was trying to tell you I had a bad vibe, but you were so happy. I guess I wasn't clear enough, but it's still not your fault, Angie. Those people were bad news, and I think they've probably robbed a lot of people. The whole thing was a mess."

"I wish I'd listened! Why didn't I listen?" Angie's voice had risen again, and she was pulling roughly at her hair. Gus trapped her hands again and looked into her cousin's face.

"It's done, Ange. Okay? We're here, we're safe. And whatever is coming, we'll deal with it together. I am never, ever giving up on you. I am never going to leave you behind. But from now on we need a way to warn each other if we're in a sketchy situation."

Angie nodded, wiping away more tears and drawing in a deep, shaky breath. "Like a code word or something. And no matter how I'm feeling, I have to listen."

"Same, I have to listen, too. No matter what." They fell silent, thinking.

"Poughkeepsie."

"What?"

"From *Supernatural*. Poughkeepsie. It's Sam and Dean's code word."

Gus found herself laughing, a little surprised she still could. "Oh my god, I forgot! Sam and Dean—"

"Are sad and mean," Angie finished, managing a tremulous smile. It was their slogan for the show. Angie's mom loved the series and had all fifteen seasons in her cloud. The cousins had watched every episode more than once over the years, fascinated with the toxic masculinity and the ability of the show to top its own levels of ridiculousness with each new season. They'd always joked that Angie was clearly Dean, angry, hypermasculine, and a bit of a closet nerd. Which, of course, made Gus Sam, embracing her nerditude and brooding far too much at times.

"Is Poughkeepsie a place? I don't even know what it really is." Gus giggled again and then stopped, shocked at herself. After what they'd just been through, after what she'd just done, how could she be laughing? She looked at Angie a little guiltily, but her cousin was laughing now, too, her shoulders shaking.

"I always thought it was just a word for a place in the middle of nowhere."

"Nah, I think that's what Podunk means."

"The sticks."

"The bush."

"Your bush!"

Gus pushed Angie over in mock anger, both of them snorting, all the emotions of the last twenty-four hours pouring out in fits of giggles. Nothing was okay, but they were gloriously alive, and together. It was enough.

They slept outside that night, curled up together under a tree in the park, the temperature never dropping below thirty degrees.

For the first few months after that, nights spent at the youth shelter, days taking odd jobs through the youth agency, Angie too proud to beg her mom for forgiveness, they languished in purgatory, unable to move on. They were always on the lookout, skittish, waiting for the hammer to fall, passing by Angie's mom's house at least once a day just to reassure themselves that she was okay. If Squints and River were dead, then the cops had surely found the phone and wallet and would want to question them. If the two tweakers had survived, then they knew Angie's mom's address and would come and get their revenge. But no one ever did show up, and they never learned the outcome of that encounter.

Gus never stopped having nightmares about it.

Dr Sanders droned on beside her, discussing the processing power required for whole brain emulation, and how they used a geothermal cooling system, diverting heat from the processors themselves into the rest of the building. They were LEED Platinum certified and blah blah blah. Gus was able to monitor the conversation closely enough to mutter appropriate platitudes and vocal indications of how impressed she was by all of this, but her attention was mostly directed through her augments as she trawled through Eternal Mind's intranet in search of Angie.

As throughout the rest of the building, brilliant, sterile white and chrome seemed to be the only colours this company allowed. She'd been asked to put on a lab jacket, a mask, little crinkly booties over her shoes, and another crinkly paper cover for her hair. Dr Sanders was outfitted similarly, but in fine silk versions of her accoutrements. She shuffled along carefully, her vision obscured by a scrolling screen. Ignoring personnel files, financial folders, legal documents, and their shockingly huge company chat and productivity app, she was on the hunt for something with gravitational pull. Something massive enough to cause every other piece of data to orbit around it.

The room they were in now was truly immense, an open concept lab with a ceiling soaring a good six metres above and a confusing horizon that made it impossible to know just where the physical boundary lay. There did not seem to be any functional reason for having so much space; work areas were three or four metres apart with nothing but empty white space in between. It was sort of what she imagined WASP heaven must look like, all antiseptic and productive.

Though they walked among these workstations, they never actually got close enough to anyone to make out any distinguishing features above the masks or to engage them in conversation. Fans were blowing somewhere, muffling all sound besides the doctor's voice. She hadn't been paying much attention to how they moved through the space, and she suspected she would have a difficult time finding the exit, which was odd, since building codes required exits always be clearly labelled.

Though she was a bit curious about the need for such a huge facility, she had no need to prompt Dr Sanders in order to keep him talking; he was rattling on now about how hard it had been to find investors, and she had more important things to do. She had found it.

At first, she couldn't believe what she was seeing through her ôtôtêma, and she came to a complete stop in shock. Dr Sanders glanced at her with concern.

"Sorry," she said hastily, "I just thought what you were saying was so interesting—can you maybe elaborate?" His eyes beamed at her above his mask, as though she'd said something really intelligent, and they resumed walking as he delved into further pointless details. Her mind whirled.

The promise of data equality had died long before she was born; the argument that data access was a human right hadn't changed anything. There'd been a push two generations back to bring fibre optic cable to rural and northern areas, but that infrastructure had been quick to deteriorate, and in any case had only briefly kept up with the exponential growth of bandwidth requirements for the most basic New-Web access. New-Web was a purely urban experience and had been for decades, dealing in zettabytes of data.

The amount of digital data in the world exceeded one zettabyte in 2012. That is to say, the total sum of all digital data that had ever existed up to that point, including sms text messages, equalled about one zettabyte, the size of one trillion gigabytes.

The program she'd found running, this unfathomably enormous centre at the heart of Eternal Mind, was using three hundred zettabytes of RAM, and took up two yottabytes of space.

A yottabyte is bigger than a zettabyte. A lot bigger. One zettabyte, again the sum total of all digital data in human history up to 2012, was a mere one-thousandth the size of one yottabyte. The processing power needed to run a program like this was colossal, and the heat produced by running what absolutely had to be a bank of supercomputers could heat an entire city. It almost certainly was, in fact, and how was it even remotely possible that she hadn't known about this? That no one had? She activated her thermal vision again and gazed around, but still had no sense where this was all happening.

She had assumed the constantly running fans were part of the cooling system, but something of this size would need super coolants to gather up all that heat and distribute it. She got lost in calculations for a few minutes, trying to figure out the energy needs of this place versus its energy output.

"Miss Gladue?" Dr Sanders sounded concerned, and his voice was coming from behind her. She realized he'd been repeating her name and that she must have stopped making the necessary sounds to keep him talking. In a daze, she'd walked right past him.

She turned and made eye contact. Her original plan was no longer possible; there was no way her otôtêma could handle even a thousandth of the data she'd need to make contact with Angie, much less to find and scoop out whatever digital version of her existed within Eternal Mind. Subterfuge was not going to work, so she decided to be direct.

"Dr Sanders, I need to talk to Angie."

His brow furrowed. "Miss Gladue," he said gently, "I already explained that your cousin, the woman you knew as Angie, is not here. What exists here are only neural signals that have been placed onto a processing substrate."

"I don't want to argue with you about this." Gone were her placating tones, her vocalizations to make him feel as though she were listening and agreeing. She didn't have to dig down far to find the strength within her. "You must have a way to interface with your whole brain emulations, and I want access." She could see he was going to object, and she made

a slashing gesture with her hand. He startled, glancing around him wor-
riedly.

"I really cannot allow—"

She pulled her mask off and drew closer to him. "Hear me now." His
watery blue eyes widened. "If you deny me this, it is not a lawsuit you
need to worry about. I will come back tomorrow with every single relative I have, and believe me when I say we are legion. By the next day, it
will be every Indigenous person in Edmonton, and that won't be the end
of it. We will surround this goddamn building and drum it into ashes. It'll
make the Churchill Standoff look like a fucking tea party. kinisitohtên cî,
do you understand?"

For a moment she couldn't gauge his reaction. The skin around his
eyes had relaxed, and he was completely still. What was he seeing in her
face? A rough, young Native woman with no resources besides anger? Or
could he sense her kihci-âniskotâpânak, her ancestors, her descendants?
Could he tell her real name was maskawiskwêw?[90] Five hundred years
his people had been trying to erase them, and it hadn't worked yet. She
meant every word. If he turned her away, she would devote her life to
ruining his.

His shoulders slumped, and she knew she'd won.

Gus expected something like a headset and a haptic chair, since no augments developed up to this point could possibly mesh with an interface
this powerful, not even her supercharged otôtêma. Instead, she was led
to circular room that contained a moulded flotation tank.

She regarded the doctor with suspicion. He gestured to the tank.

"This is how we access the simulated reality contained within Eternal
Mind." He handed her a large white towel and did something to a keypad

90   Strong/hard woman.

mounted on the pod itself. The overhead lights dimmed considerably, taking on a warmer glow.

"A flotation tank?" She couldn't keep the incredulity from her voice.

"Three hundred and sixty-three kilos of magnesium sulphate and three grams of connective nanites. You need to be unclothed for the nanites to make the necessary connections." Dr Sanders lifted the lid to the pod. Inside, the water glowed purple with embedded illumination.

Gus eyed the water nervously. "My family knows I'm here."

The doctor's eyes crinkled upwards in amusement. "Miss Gladue, no harm will come to you while you are in these facilities. I am not delighted by the way you have forced yourself upon us, but neither am I impervious to the concerns you and your family clearly have. We introduced your cousin's whole brain emulation into our simulation not long after the initial scans, and in all that time, we have detected no human activity, nothing that would suggest she exists within Eternal Mind in any way. For us, this represents a serious setback, and we have been working on improving the process ever since, but for you, I think this outcome is best."

Gus swallowed hard at that. Ever since she'd begun this journey to retrieve Angie's consciousness, she'd pictured her cousin trapped, confined within some sort of nightmarish digital prison. Cut off from her kin, from the spirit world, from the waters, the medicines, all of it. Yet a part of her had longed to see Angie again, selfish as it was. She missed her more than she'd been able to comprehend. This gaping hole that had been ripped in her world, this missing piece in the shape of Angie—she'd thought maybe, if she could say goodbye, it might heal eventually. But without that?

Now was not the time to think about that. She blinked back tears and nodded tersely.

"I'll leave you to it," Dr Sanders said, typing more commands into the keypad. "You will have ten minutes to get into the pod and acclimate.

The water is body temperature, and you won't need to expend any effort to stay afloat; the salts do that for you. Try to float in the centre of the pod. It is imperative that you not block your ears. The nanites will need to access your cochlear nerve. Please also ensure you splash a few drops of the water into your eyes. Unfortunately, this will sting somewhat, but you will not be able to register any visual stimuli otherwise."

"What happens after ten minutes?" Gus asked nervously.

"We send a small electrical current through the water to activate the nanites. It won't feel like much, a little bit of a buzzing sensation, and then it will cease. The nanites can only operate for forty-five minutes before needing to be drained and recharged. I will come back to open the pod then. If for any reason you need to open the pod yourself, there is a manual release right here." The doctor showed her a small lever inside the pod. Then he left.

Gus sent a quick picture of the pod and the recording she'd taken of the conversation to Angie's mother, just in case. She took a deep breath and let it out slowly.

"âhkamêyimo."

The moment the gentle current hit her body, everything changed. It was immediate; there was no slow rise of awareness, no adjustment period at all. One second she was floating in the tank, becoming less aware of her own body as she adjusted to the strangeness of it all, and the next, she was—

She was outside, among a thicket bordering rolling plains. Dappled sunlight shone down through the leaves and energetic fascicles of the mixed deciduous and coniferous trees. The colours were all wrong though—mostly greyscale. Except out there, on the prairie, she could see dots of yellow and blue, small clumps of flowers with ashen leaves and stems. Otherwise, it was shockingly real: the smells, the sound of tree limbs moving in the wind, the feeling of standing on solid ground, and, oh yes, fully clothed, thankfully.

There was also a strange absence. No birdsong, no rustling of small animals, no droning cicadas—all sounds she was accustomed to hearing outside of the city.

She heard a rasping, grunting noise and whirled around. There, rubbing his itchy hide against a tree, was a buffalo. Although, maybe it was a female? Both have horns, and it wasn't as though Gus had had much opportunity in her life to get up close and personal with the being that had kept her ancestors alive for millennia. She gasped in awe.

The buffalo turned its head and regarded her for a moment. Gus realized there were dozens of them in the trees, and probably more beyond. What the hell were buffalo doing here?

Gus wanted to call out for Angie, but was a little nervous at the proximity of these huge animals. She hadn't thought to ask if she could be harmed in here, but she wasn't eager to test the idea. Slowly, she backed out of the thicket, and once the buffalo that had been watching her turned back to relieving itself of whatever irritation it was administering to, she turned and began hiking deeper into the open grass.

Where it hadn't yet been trampled, the grass was taller than she was. She walked until she found a wallow, a place where the earth had been torn up, rich soil damp with collected rain. Unsure of how much time had already passed, she decided to just go for it.

Raising her face to the oddly blue sky, she yelled as loud as she could, "Angie! It's August! Angie, are you here?"

The wallow was no longer unoccupied. A buffalo had simply appeared, rolling joyously in the moist earth, its massive legs flailing comically as it wiggled in deeper, its tail flapping around in bliss. Gus stepped back in surprise. Big globs of earth and dust were being flung everywhere, a few of the larger ones plopping directly onto her chest, soaking through her T-shirt and sliding down messily.

"Hi, Gus," Angie said.

Gus whirled around, but there was no one behind her. She turned back to the buffalo in confusion. It was rocking over onto its side, more agile than its huge size would suggest, and in a flash it was back on its feet. It shook itself vigorously, hurling more earth and dust about.

"Are you just going to stare at me? Kind of rude, don't you think?" Angie's voice was teasing, and it was definitely coming from the buffalo.

"I—Angie?" Gus demanded in disbelief. She noticed that this buffalo had horns that were more slender than those of the one she'd seen before, and its head was less triangular.

The buffalo approached her slowly, a few inches taller than Gus, but weighing substantially more. Gus took a frightened step back, then stopped herself. Whatever was going on here, that was Angie's voice, and this was why she had come here. Gus looked into its deep, dark eyes, searching for her cousin in there. The buffalo tossed its head in what seemed like amusement.

"In the flesh. Sort of. Fuck, it's good to see you!" Its mouth hadn't moved, but Gus heard Angie all the same.

Gus hurled herself at the creature's massive head, and this time she didn't even try to stop the tears from flowing. She wrapped Angie in as big an embrace as she could manage, her hands digging into soft, curly fur, and let herself weep.

"I miss you so much, Ange, I miss you so goddamn much." She sobbed, completely undone. All the pain and grief she'd shoved down, telling herself she'd deal with it later, poured out like an endless river. "You left us, you left us all behind, and you never told us. You never told us it had gotten so bad, we didn't know, and you just left, why the fuck did you leave us? We would have done anything, me and Nibi, your mom, anyone! We would have done absolutely anything to keep you alive, Ange—why?" Gus was barely coherent; all the pain she'd stuffed down to keep walking through each day had risen up like stones in her throat, choking her, making it a struggle to draw breath, her entire body trembling with her grief.

Angie stood still, massive and sturdy against the alluvion of Gus's outpouring. After a while, she lowered herself to the ground when Gus could no longer stay upright and nudged her cousin to nestle into her side, where Gus continued to weep and moan, her words coming less and less frequently.

Gus took a shuddering breath, wiping her nose and face with the bottom of her dirty T-shirt and finding time to marvel at the realism of this simulation. She lay against the warm, gentle flank of her cousin and leaned her head back.

"Well, I am sure you have some questions," Angie said gently, "but I also need to ask you what"—Angie faltered a bit before continuing—"what I did. How I died."

Gus closed her eyes. She'd thought she had cried out all her tears, but there they were again, pressing against her lids. She bit her tongue to try to control her emotions. She wasn't sure how much time was left, and she didn't want to waste it.

"Ryan found you when he got home from work. Said you two hadn't even been fighting, that things had been good, really good for a while. That you were back on meds and in therapy and everything. It destroyed him, Ange." Gus ground the heels of her palms into her eyes and choked out the rest. "You took all your pills and just went to bed."

Angie was quiet for a long moment. Then she sighed. "Yeah. That sounds about right. I'm sorry, Gus."

Gus exhaled sharply. "There was nothing right about it, Ange! You promised me you'd call if it got to that point. You told me you'd never leave me like that!"

Angie shifted minutely. "Oh, Gus. Look, I came here before it happened. I don't know what's happening out there. Last thing I remember from outside, I was still living with you and Nibi. I'm glad Ryan and I got back together, but that wasn't me."

Gus turned and buried her hand in the luxurious fur around Angie's head, scratching reflexively. Angie shivered happily and lowered her head further.

"It was, though. You did this, which means it was always in you to do this. I'm not trying to make you feel guilty, Ange, but I don't know how I'm going to live with you gone. You're my best friend, nîtisân. It was hard enough when you moved out to live with Ryan. You've always been terrible at keeping in touch. But just knowing you were out there happy, it was enough." Gus ached through and through, but it was like a sucking wound, draining and suffocating. It was unbearable. She pressed her face against Angie's side and breathed in the buffalo scent of her.

"I'm here, Gus," Angie said gently.

Gus laughed weakly. "About that. Angie, why the fuck are you a buffalo?"

"Ahem. I am a bison, thank you," she answered in mock disapproval, her relief at the change in topic palpable.

"Buffalo, bison; potato, potahto. Seriously, how did this happen?"

Angie shifted again, and Gus sat up a little straighter. "When I got here, I wasn't anything. Just a loose collection of constantly firing neurons. It was awful. I'd thought this whole thing was a sleep study, not some sort of virtual reality. Surprise surprise, a white man lied to me. I thought I'd—um, I figured I'd passed, and this was heaven or hell or something." She sounded uncomfortable, but continued. "I'm not sure how long I floated around like that until I ran into my herd."

"Your herd?"

"My gang! My obstinancy! My furry peeps who don't ever give me the creeps!" Angie laughed. "I was really confused, and I had no idea what I was. I forgot I was human, so I decided I was a bison. It's been pretty great, and honestly I don't know how to change or why I'd want to, so here I am."

Gus was silent for a moment, taking it in. "Angie, that's really fucking weird."

Angie shook herself, nearly shoving Gus over. "My idea of what is weird has changed a lot. Like, I'm sure you've noticed the lack of colour."

Gus nodded, scanning the long grey grass around them, then glancing up at the blue sky again.

"Well, turns out bison don't see very many colours. And since we're the only living beings, or whatever we are, here—well, it's just bison."

"But you're human."

"Yeah. But I guess I chose not to be. Them's the rules, or something."

Gus held her right hand in front of her face, marvelling at the monochrome appearance of her own skin. "I'm human—shouldn't that make a difference in what I can see?"

Angie swung her ponderous head so she could see Gus a little better out of one eye. "I don't think you're actually here, though. Not like we are. You're more like the ones who come and look at us all the time."

That must have been Dr Sanders and his grad students. Gus wondered how often they used the float tank. Thinking of the doctor reminded her of the time limit, and a flash of fear ran through her, banishing the lethargy her grief had lain over her like a wool blanket. She raised herself to her knees and shuffled around to sit directly in front of Angie, who swung her head to keep Gus in view.

"Your mom sent me, Ange. Out there, you passed. It's been a few days since your wake. And she, well, she's worried that you won't be able to travel on if you're stuck here."

Angie was still, thinking about it. "I get that. I do. And I get that out there, I'm gone." She stretched her neck forward and batted Gus's chest with her nose, "I'm sorry for that, Gus, I am. There were a lot of times I didn't think I was going to make it, and other times I thought I would make it through anything, so I made really bad decisions. But you know how hard it's been, how messed up my own brain was. I tried, I promise you I did. I held on hard. Whatever choice I made out there, it wasn't about you. You can't feel responsible."

Gus reached out, grabbing Angie's horns and leaning her forehead against her cousin's. "Poughkeepsie, Ange. You promised. You promised you'd make me listen if you needed it." Gus's chin trembled, and her nose began running again. She pressed her forehead harder, willing herself not to cry. It didn't help. Slow fat tears rolled down her face and splattered onto Angie's fur.

"Gus, it was never on you. I love you, and I will always love you. nîtisân, you were always there for me. You were the only one who didn't make me feel like a monster, no matter how much I pushed you and everyone else away. You were the only one who understood why I was the worst with the people I loved the most. And I'm sorry. I'm sorry that my mental illness was stronger than your love, and stronger than I could be. But the damage that was done, none of it was you. You didn't cause it, and I didn't even cause it. It's intergenerational trauma, Gus. It can't be solved by one person, even if that person is as fucking awesome as you."

Gus let herself weep again, but this time it was deeper. She wept for the buffalo, for the ones out there in the world, so depleted in numbers, for the land, so changed and unfamiliar to her ancestors, for the poisoned waters, the abandoned people, the constant sneers and comments, the platitudes and allies who never changed a thing, for the beautiful, chubby faces of babies who grew into lonely, wounded adults, or worse, who never made it out of childhood. For her cousin, whose bio mom had died for so many of the same reasons that had claimed Angie herself. She wept for herself, for the unfairness of it all, for the days ahead that she would have to endure without her cousin.

When she was completely wrung out, she released Angie and sat back, letting her spine curve, deep breaths filling her body with the essence of the soil, the long-rooted prairie grasses, and the buffalo musk.

"I'm happy here, Gus," Angie finally said. "Like, I don't want to say my brain is fixed, because they scanned it, so they must have scanned the screwed-up parts, too. I still get angry, I still go from happy to terrified in two seconds flat, and I can't predict it. Shit, I even have big-ass buffalo panic attacks—you should see it!" She chuckled. "But it's not the same. I don't have to pretend to be okay. I don't have to go to work, or buy groceries, or stop myself from punching someone in the face because they looked at me weird. It's just different. Being with bison isn't like being around humans, caught up in all the hoops we make each other jump through. Bison don't think of other bison as less than, or more than; we're just bison. If there is a heaven? This is it for me."

Gus met her cousin's eyes and nodded. "I understand. I don't really know what it's like—I'm not experiencing it—but I believe what you're telling me."

Angie bobbed her head softly. "That's what I always loved about you, Gus. You didn't have to go through it to believe it. You never told me what I felt wasn't real."

Gus sighed and stretched, trying to let the rest of the tension in her body go. "What do I tell your mom, Ange?"

Angie gracefully lumbered to her feet and looked down at Gus sitting in the wallow. "You tell her I wasn't here. Help her let me go. And Gus? You need to let me go, too. I know you, and I don't want you making some foolish decision to get yourself uploaded here. I think they assume my upload didn't work, so they leave me alone, but I'm not sure that would last if they knew I was here."

Gus looked down at her lap, at her hands resting on her thighs, and nodded. Just like that, she was back in the tank.

Time may not be linear, but wiya wasn't interested in the effort it would take to travel very far. Why bother, when these môniyâwak had repopulated the plains with buffalo already, and the jump was so much shorter. Sure, they weren't exactly in their standard forms, but wiya could work with data.

The council had been clear. Despite everything these humans had done, forgiveness was possible. Mostly. Wiping them all out had been on the table, and it had been given serious consideration. Maybe that suggestion would come up again, but for now, they would begin like this.

There were so many, wiya couldn't just release them all in the same place. Nor had the council issued explicit instructions as to where they needed to be freed. It was amusing to watch them tear through fake rooms, and oh, the sound when they reached the lighting section! After that, wiya couldn't really be contained; the commotion in the Red Lobster was more satisfying than it should have been.

Perhaps the most perfect visual was this: ten thousand buffalo tearing through fences like toilet paper, denuding the land of artificial boundaries, erasing those shallow markers in mere seconds. Little brown-headed birds reclaiming their names, abandoning the poorly treated doe-eyed cows as ancestral memory drew them back toward their preferred bovids.

One buffalo in particular caught wiya's eye. She was a sleek, healthy cow, as excited as the rest of them to be running free, but she had a strange gait and the tendency to kick her backside up and—was she clicking her heels together? How strange. One to keep track of for sure; the joy she exuded was palpable, and her energy was different than her brethren's.

Task completed, wiya wondered if it was worth heading to the buffet at the River Cree Casino. It probably was.

"I, BISON" EXPLORATION

In this near future, I imagine a rural space even more emptied out than it currently is. I consider the ways in which such an exodus, rather than being a thing to mourn, could potentially benefit the Indigenous communities who remain in those rural and Northern spaces. Land Back without conflict. I don't dwell on it much, but rather offer it to the reader to consider those potentials.

So much of what I think about never clearly makes it onto the page. Originally, I wanted to consider the spiritual ramifications of posthumanism. There are a number of theories positing that, as species evolve, they will eventually shed the need to exist in purely physical ways by becoming data streams, or energy. I cannot do justice in this short piece to the complexity of theorizing around posthumanism and all its variations. If you are even a little intrigued by the idea, I highly recommend hurling yourself down that rabbit hole.

For a moment, though, imagine humans, our more-than-human kin, and perhaps even the land and water existing as data or energy within some form of containment. A finite universe, whether it be a database or some other limiting space. Finite, because I think infinite space would alter my questions somewhat.

Mapping and uploading our brains is not just science fiction, but something people are actually working on and thinking deeply about. Let's pretend it does happen, if it hasn't already. Many questions immediately arise and, indeed, have been being asked for some time. Would we still be humans? If not, what then would we be? Fascinating, yes, but not what intrigues me most at this moment.

In "Maggie Sue," I have the narrator assert that our spiritual realms as Indigenous peoples are place based. As opposed to what, you may ask? Well, as opposed to the disembodied religious doctrines of say, Christianity, which have been exported and unlinked from specific place (Watts 2016, 155). In many Indigenous cosmologies, this disembodiment is impossible. Our spiritual realms exist in a specific place, linked to our lands. When our lands, our bodies, our connections to that spiritual realm are degraded, so is that spirit realm itself. When we are nourished, in our bodies, in our lands, in our relationships, so too is our spiritual realm. Vanessa Watts asserts an interesting notion of multiple spirit worlds "locatable and accessible through distinctive places and particular cosmological beliefs" (Watts 2016, 153). This is similar to the physical, exclusive, overlapping, shared, and/or contested territories of Indigenous peoples.

I do not intend to convince you; I am just mapping out the scene. When Angie dies, her mother is concerned that her uploaded consciousness, housed within a finite universe, experiences a severance from the spirit realm. She worries that while Angie's body returns to the earth, something else—call it a soul, or sapience, or a clever digital facsimile—is cut off from place both physical and spiritual. Would this damage the spirit realm? Would Angie's ancestors and descendants be able to locate her? Could she feast and be feasted by her ancestors and descendants? Or are Angie's mother's fears unjustified? Would Angie continue to exist in place, simply in another form, with access to that spirit realm in ways we are simply unfamiliar with? For all we know, our descendants continue to interact with us as digital beings or beings of energy.

These were my original questions, and ones that, hopefully, I will one day spend more time fleshing out. But, in the writing of this story, a new focus emerged as I fixed on the relationship between Gus and Angie.

Angie struggles with mental illness, though I never disclose her diagnosis. She experiences acute anxiety, dissociation, splitting, and uncontrollable rages. She is loyal to a fault, empathetic, creative, and so very loved. She and Gus exist within a familial relationship that can be very confusing to outsiders, but that fits just fine into Métis/Cree kinship systems. I did not expect to directly reference suicide in this story, and I do not want to give the impression that it is a given or inevitable event for anyone like Angie. Honestly, I think I am just working through some of my own losses and fears, particularly the inability to find closure, the guilt and what-ifs that remain when someone leaves us in this way.

So much of what I want to think about, what I want us all to think about, is a future that is not so egregiously traumatizing. A society wherein we once again default to the simple notion that no one, no being of any kind, is disposable.

In many ways, to reach this understanding and to implement it in our everyday interactions, we have to see the way in which difference is pathologized, then undo it. In particular, to be Indigenous in a settler colonial society is to be pathologized as abnormal, from conception to death. Cameron Greensmith argues that this assertion of abnormality allows settlers to "understand themselves as rightful owners of Indigenous territory" (2012, 22). I think that this argument, through a lens of disability studies, helps expand on the category that Tuck and Yang call "A(s)t(e)risk peoples," a particular settler move to innocence that "erases and then conceals the erasure of Indigenous peoples ... and moves Indigenous nations as 'populations' to the margins of public discourse" (2012, 22).

Greensmith examines the Caledonia "crisis" as described by Canadian news media. In case it doesn't ring any bells, this was a situation in which the people of the Six Nations reserve opposed a housing development that was going to be built on their territory. Land defenders were described as "criminals and terrorists," and a lot of space in the media was given to decrying how the lives of white people in Caledonia were being disrupted (2012, 23). When Indigenous peoples protest, show up, exist in ways that are visibly Indigenous, settler narratives tend to focus on the perceived potential for violence, not from the notoriously violent settler state, but from Indigenous peoples themselves.

Greensmith points out the way in which these public discourses of Indigenous presence focus on Indigenous behaviours as irrational and abnormal, and that disability tropes are used to belittle Indigenous sovereignty. Arguing that placing Indigenous peoples "into the margins through their pathology [is] understanding them as disabled," Greensmith shows that removing Indigenous peoples becomes a strategy for achieving normalcy (2012, 31). Normalcy in this context is the inevitability of settler society and settler claims to the land.

For someone like Angie, who does struggle with mental illnesses, the biomedical model sees her disabilities as a problem of her individual body (Schiefelbein 2021). She is the source of the disability; her body is lacking. However, normality is not possible anyway for Angie or Gus as Indigenous teens, because Indigeneity is pathologized as inherently abnormal.

On the other hand, a social model views disability as both biologically *and* socially determined, accepting that human bodies are diverse, and seeks interventions that remove barriers in society. If those barriers are what disable people, then we must examine which barriers must be removed to prevent Indigenous peoples from being characterized as disabled. I believe that in many cases, those barriers are also part of what disables other peoples as well.

When Angie finds herself in a new context, one that is not defined by settler presence, she experiences herself as able bodied. She points out that she continues to exist as she did in the outside world: her every neuron was scanned exactly as it existed; she has not been "cured." Inside the digital world, the barriers that rendered her disabled do not exist.

In case I'm not being obvious enough about it, I am asserting that so many of the ills Canadian society defines as being inherent to Indigenous peoples can be solved by undoing what disables us, what pathologizes us: white supremacist settler colonialism. We will not accept that normality is this relatively new status quo, nor will we accept that we must disappear to provide normality for those who desire to replace us in order to cement their claims to these lands.

Our people deserve life; they deserve love and respect and communities of care. All of these things have been directly attacked in order to make claims to these lands, and Indigenous peoples are then blamed for the way in which this violence impacts our ability to exist in the world. Digital uploads are obviously not a solution. We have the ability, all of us, to make a better world today.

UNSETTLED

I wait until 3 a.m., *that liminal hour when the soul seems less anchored, more prone to wandering. There is a quality within it that feels like a threat given no breath, but hovering nonetheless, and the unlucky sleeper who stirs knows better than to give into wakefulness. Few wish to see the beings that move freely at this time.*

It is not lost on me that I am one of them.

I pad noiselessly into the control room; as always, the door has been carelessly left open. After all, we are all friends here. I can't risk the screeching of the hinges, so I leave it alone, trusting in human instinct to dismiss any accidental sounds I make with a shiver and an unconscious burrowing into deeper slumber. I'll be the nightmare they refuse to acknowledge.

I disable the first alarm, a simple switch I've bumped "accidentally" a number of times over the past few days just to test it. The system awakes with a whirring and hissing of fans that seems unnaturally loud to my ears, but I know the white noise of the sleeping pods will mask it. I run a quick diagnostic on the hibernation chambers—all routine, nothing out of the ordinary. Everything is as it should be.

I tell the computer that it is mistaken about there being a power drain in the GEA *2 Beehive, the Rossdale section. I disable the second alarm with practised keystrokes, the program I uploaded yesterday convincing the central sensors that things are completely normal and, at the same time, that life-support systems are struggling. The system assumes there is a problem with the sensors. Alarms will be ringing at the unmanned station, but nothing disturbs the silence here.*

While the computer expends resources trying to reconcile the information I'm sending it with what its own systems are reporting, I execute an artificial cascading shutdown of cooling systems in all the Greater Edmonton Area Beehive storage facilities. The control system is flooded with mixed messages, unscheduled temperature hikes of less than a quarter of a degree Celsius in one facility, then in the next microsecond, all seems well. Now the temperature has risen in a facility in Spruce Grove. No, that one is fine, but the St. Albert hub is warmer than it should be. The computer races to determine what is happening, but is unable to keep up. For a fanciful moment, I imagine that the shrieking of sirens in those other places some-how penetrates the stasis of millions, disturbing torpid dreams. But I know from experience there is nothing in this sleep-that-is-not-sleep; we are as close to death as we can get without actually dying.

Except death is exactly what I am orchestrating.

The third alarm cannot be switched off or silenced, but I've planned for this. Micro-increases in temperature are not dangerous as long as the calcium pumps continue to operate, protecting all those precious human hearts from shutting down completely. The fluctuations are draining pro-cessing power, making the system sluggish, less trustful of its own sensors.

Perhaps I am anthropomorphizing the system, but when it seems that its entire sensor array is malfunctioning, the computer will doubt itself, not be as quick to respond to real changes.

"What are you doing?"

The voice is a whisper, but I still startle. I had made sure that I would have company, but I couldn't ensure when exactly it'd happen. I turn.

"I heard a noise in here," I say to the shadow standing in the doorway, affecting a worried murmur. I am illuminated by the control screen, lit from below, and I know it is doing strange things to my face. I can hear a nervous gulp, and I suppress a smile. I gesture for the shape to approach, pointing to the control panel.

"What are all these readings?"

"I'm not sure," I lie, pleased we are still whispering. I make room, slid-ing toward the keyboard, gesturing at the screen which now spreads green,

sickly light on a face not my own. I begin entering the command sequence, but cannot hide the clacking. The sound is noticed, but their focus remains where I need it.

"Something's wrong with the temperature stabilizers at GEA 2—no, GEA 6. *Wait, now it's* GEA 4?" *I can hear their confusion, more pronounced by the fog of having just woken up. I initiate the final command string, but do not hit enter. Instead, my fingers slide around to my waistband, where I've tucked the wrench into the small of my back.*

"I tried a reset, but the readings keep stabilizing before I can do anything." I point to the second screen.

"Let me just see if I can isolate a section and reset. Should we wake the others?"

I raise the heavy wrench into the still shadows above us. "Don't worry, they'll be awake soon," I say calmly.

The impact is worse than I imagined. Or better. Easier. Quieter. Just a sigh as the blood gushes, more blood than I'd anticipated, but they do say head wounds bleed disproportionately. Nothing disproportionate about this injury, though. I make sure with a second impact that sprays something more viscous than blood across my forearm. The body slumps across the console, and I hit enter.

An ear-splitting klaxon shatters the quiet yellow strobing lights, and a secondary shrilling is impossible to ignore. Overhead lights burst on. I can barely hear the confused shouting, and before I lose my nerve, I slam my own head into the console, dropping the wrench as I fall backwards into the shocking pain that explodes inside my skull. I manage to hit the back of my head on the floor as well, leaving me even more dazed than intended when the rest of the crew arrives.

Their yelled queries are a jumble of incomprehensible, muffled sounds. I groan—no acting needed—and turn to my side just in time to throw up. I only barely manage to push myself away from the puddle of sick, noticing it's running into crimson wetness, and raise a trembling hand to the console.

"The calcium pumps are offline!" I croak weakly. I'm not sure anyone can hear me, but from the hysteria in their voices, I know they've seen it. The body, too.

The situation is clear. I caught one of us trying to sabotage the system. I tried to stop them, there was a struggle, I was attacked, and I acted in self-defence. But it was too late.

The world was noise and light, and I'd done what I came to do. Unconsciousness was my reprieve, my reward, and I welcomed it gratefully.

There was no real sense of how long they'd been hearing the sound: a constant trill, not a beeping, more like voice exercises loosening the tongue, rising then falling, a moment of silence, and repeat.

It was a ridiculous noise, as though someone were imitating a cat's purr while doing vocal scales. Awareness came in slowly, and with it the understanding that the sound had been going on for hours, not minutes, even if their brains had been incapable of registering it.

This was no conventional ascent into awareness, with the familiar time slippage that falsely stretches seconds into minutes as the mind emerges from slumber. Nor was it an extension of that process, a longer suppression of the ascending reticular activating system. Anything resembling consciousness had been suppressed for thirty-six months, and from their training, they knew the emergence took twelve hours. At what point exactly their consciousness, existent even in sleep, resumed was uncertain.

The trilling continued. Annoyance banished the tendrils of exhaustion that remained, and they each opened their eyes in turn. It took a long time for things to come into focus, with ocular nerves rusty, senses scrambled. Five cushioned capsules were arranged in a star formation at the centre of the dimly lit room, covers retracted. The air was stale and oppressive, but fans were operating now, whisking it away and bringing in fresh scents from outside. The light was rising slowly, almost imperceptibly, a simulacrum of dawn.

JJ stood in a floor-length metallic-pink satin robe, the trim festooned with cotton-candy feathers that seemed impervious to gravity. wiya nudged the unremarkable carboard case of Individual Meal Packs with one rhinestone-encrusted slipper, grumbling inaudibly at its weight.

"Those the IMPS?"

JJ turned, allowing the robe to fan out gloriously in well-practised move, but JJ would be noticed even if wiya had been in grey pyjama pants and a black tank top, like the dishevelled man who leaned against the door frame.

wiya stuck out a hand to the newcomer. "tânisi kiya? I'm JJ. My pronouns are wiya."

"Andrew." He grasped wiya's hand firmly, shook it once, then sheepishly made some attempt to tame his hair, which was sticking up in a number of spots, like stiff black bristles. "Ah, sorry, I didn't get the last bit—your pronouns are what?"

"wiya. It's Cree. We don't have gendered pronouns like she or he. I use wiya."

Andrew blinked slowly and nodded before being overcome by a long yawn. He flushed slightly, the faintest colour change against brown skin. "Sorry, JJ. I'm still not totally awake."

JJ shrugged. They were the only two up so far. wiya's hair was wrapped up in a white scarf; JJ'd only had time to pull the robe out of wiya's storage locker, never mind showering or putting on a face. Thankfully hibernation had maintained wiya's acrylics, glittering rose gold in the harsh fluorescent light.

Andrew shuffled toward the case, peering down to read the side. "Breakfast-lunch, déjeuner-dîner. Hmm."

JJ raised an eyebrow. "That's a pretty good French accent. You must not be from around these parts." The last bit in a faux-Texan drawl. Andrew straightened and grinned, disarmingly handsome, JJ noted, with deep dimples and honey-brown eyes.

"I'm from Ottawa, actually. We did French immersion before all this." He gestured around the small cafeteria in a gesture meant to encompass the whole facility, and the situation in its entirety. "But I'm Ojibway; my family comes from Michipicoten."

"What the heck are you doing volunteering for shift work in Alberta, then?"

"Wrong place at the right time, I guess." He bent down to grab the box, setting it down on one of the cafeteria tables. JJ winced, noticing the metal tables were bolted to the floor, along with narrow metal benches on either side. There was no way JJ would be able to slide wiya's body in comfortably. The hibernation pods had been built to accommodate folks even larger than wiya, but fat-hostile architecture likely remained in place throughout the rest of the facilities.

Andrew was trying to peel the packing tape off the top of the box, but JJ leaned in, brushing up against his shoulder slightly, and pierced the tape with one wickedly sharp nail, drawing it along the length of the opening.

"Well, that's useful!" Andrew lip-pointed at JJ's nails, popping the tape off at the ends and folding the cardboard back to reveal a number of brown-paper cubes. With a little difficulty, he managed to pull one of the cubes out. Under a little brown maple leaf was stamped, *Breakfast Sausages / Saucisses à Déjeuner (14) Menu #3*.

"Mmm. Breakfast in a bag," JJ sighed.

Andrew grabbed another one out of the box and handed it to JJ. "This one says hash browns and bacon—maybe it's better?"

"I'm sure it's all delightful," JJ drawled, "but I prefer sausage." Andrew grinned and handed wiya the first bag. JJ ripped the top open and uncovered a thin square box labelled *Dessert*. Flipping it over to the ingredients label, JJ saw it was just sliced apples. "Mmm, some poms in trenches!"

Andrew mock-clutched his heart at wiya's heavily anglicized pronunciation. "Pommes en tranches?" He leaned in and tapped a finger on the ingredients. "With some delicious calcium chloride and sodium metabisulphite! Who doesn't love a little metabisulphite in their trench poms?"

They both began giggling, then, the feathers of JJ's robe swirling with movement. Each time they'd start to calm down, they'd look at one another and break out in fresh laughter. JJ started to wheeze for air, and Andrew made shushing motions with both hands, unsuccessfully trying to calm the both of them down.

"What's so funny?"

JJ turned, still wheezing, to see a tall, skinny boy in an oversized bone choker and a beaded buckskin vest incongruously thrown over what looked like blue hospital scrubs. He was incredibly pale, with ginger hair in a long braid and freckles scattered so thickly on his face, it was a bit hard to make out his features at first.

wiya waved the dessert box overhead. "We're all just poms in the trenches, baby!" wiya doubled over in laughter again. The boy was nonplussed.

Andrew patted the box full of rations. "We're getting breakfast ready. You hungry?"

"I think I'll wait for the others," the newcomer said, a little stiffly. "Elders and children eat first."

JJ managed to gulp in a deep breath of calming air, letting hilarity dissolve. On second look, buckskin boy was definitely an adult, just on the young side, with a heart-shaped baby-fat face. "There are five of us here, and none of us are Elders or children."

"We should still follow protocol, wait for the others, and smudge before eating."

With great effort, JJ's face remained expressionless. They were going to have to live together for a long time, but this one was already getting on wiya's nerves. Maybe this was just post-hibernation, pre-coffee grumpiness. The silence stretched on for an uncomfortable moment before wiya pulled out the next item in the paper bag, serendipitously a 3-in-1 Nescafé package, creamer, sugar, and coffee all in one glorious mix.

"Oh, thank Creator, some caffeine!" JJ kissed the package.

Andrew held his hand out. "I'm Andrew, this is JJ, and what's your name?"

"Taanishi Liam dishinihkaashoon. Aen Michif niiya, St. Albert d'ooshchiin." They shook hands.

"All I got from that was Liam and St. Albert," Andrew apologized. "What language is that?"

"Michif. I'm Métis from St. Albert."

"Me too, I'm Métis," JJ volunteered, pulling out tiny single servings of mustard, Frank's RedHot sauce, honey, and peanut butter. wiya was laying everything out on the table, lined up neatly.

Liam curled his lip slightly, eyeing JJ up and down for a moment. "Taanday ooschchi kiiya?"

Feeling a surge of annoyance, JJ answered, "manitow-sâkahikanihk ohci niya. mâka niwâhkômâkanak nêhiyawêwak, namoya nipîkiskwânân Michif."

Liam blinked, taken aback, clearly not understanding. Andrew just looked back and forth between the two.

"I said I'm from Lac Ste. Anne and that my Métis relations don't speak Michif, we speak Cree. Like pretty much most Métis in Alberta do," JJ translated.

Liam opened his mouth to respond to that, but JJ turned away and yanked out another plastic package from the paper bag, raising it over wiya's head and whooping. "Beef jerky, my neechies!"

"Ooh!" Andrew turned his attention back to his own bag, ripping it open, while Liam continued to stand there, radiating disproval. JJ pulled out the rest of the contents of wiya's IMP: a hamburger bun, strawberry crunchy cereal, a package of hot chocolate, two orange-pineapple sports drink pouches, a package of mints, a wet nap, a spoon and napkin, some matches, and finally the main event, a box of breakfast sausages.

All laid out, it seemed like a lot of items for one meal. JJ pulled opened the cardboard box containing the breakfast sausages, finding a vacuum-packed foil package, four links clearly within.

"Are we supposed to just eat these in the package?" wiya asked uncertainly.

Liam sighed audibly. "Don't you remember the training?" JJ stopped short of a glare, but only just.

Andrew looked back and forth between them again and decided to step in. He slapped a companionable arm across Liam's shoulders. "I'm still pretty groggy, Liam, can you refresh us on the amenities?"

Liam, clearly pleased, managed a small smile. There were only two tables placed side by side in the tiny cafeteria, but there was a metal counter and a rolling counter door against one wall, as well as a closed door beside the one that led back into the sleeping chamber.

"I'll go open things up," he volunteered, and Andrew let him go, patting him on the back in thanks before turning and giving JJ a small wink. wiya nodded in thanks.

Liam opened the second door and disappeared into darkness. A few moments later, the rolling counter door winched up loudly, letting Andrew and JJ see into a small but well-appointed industrial kitchen, all stainless steel and bright lights. Liam leaned over the partition and placed a strange-looking appliance out on the counter, then filled a large kettle at the sink before placing it on the counter as well. He took a stack of metal serving trays, each with six sections of various sizes, and came back into the cafeteria room, positioning them on the right before plugging the appliances in and making sure the power was on.

Without asking permission, Liam took the foil package of sausages out of JJ's hand. Before wiya could protest, possibly with violence, he plopped the whole thing upright into the first appliance, where it seemed to fit perfectly.

"This is a bag warmer or bag boiler, however you want to call it," he explained, pushing a red button on the front. "It uses hot water to heat up your meals. You don't want to leave things in for too long or they start tasting metallic."

"Mmm," JJ said, without much enthusiasm. "Nothing I like more than my bags boiled." Liam shot wiya a disapproving look, but JJ ignored it.

Andrew and JJ busied themselves putting together their trays, finding small glasses they could dump the instant coffee powder into before adding hot water to it and to the strawberry crunchy cereal, which seemed to be a kind of instant oatmeal. JJ's sausages slithered out of the hot bag, covered in an unpleasant-looking, slightly yellowish gelatinous slime, but they smelled pretty good. Surprisingly, so did the apple slices, which looked like canned fruit, but gave off an odour that was strangely fresh.

JJ balanced backwards on a bench, not even trying to squeeze into the tiny space between it and the table. Rather than sit awkwardly across from JJ's back, Andrew opted for the second table, where he could at least see wiya while they ate. Liam had disappeared, and they heard voices coming from the sleeping chamber.

"It's honestly not bad," Andrew remarked, chewing on a spoonful of cubed hash browns and chunks of bacon. JJ sipped the instant coffee, wishing for an espresso, but happy enough right now to be imbibing anything caffeinated.

"I'm pretty sure it's not going to take us long to get sick of it." JJ emptied the hot sauce over the sausages and cut off a piece with the spoon. wiya made a little moue of disgust, but ate the piece anyway. Like Andrew had said, it wasn't actually that bad; the texture was fine, and it was full of enough salt and spices to fool the mouth into thinking it tasted good.

"The kitchen is fully decked out—stove, pots, pans, fridges, freezers, the whole nine yards." Andrew poked suspiciously at the piece of corn-bread that came with his meal. "I don't know what they expect us to use all that stuff for. From what I understand, all we've got are the IMPs."

"Who knows, maybe they had fresher food for the first few shifts?" JJ spooned up the oatmeal before it got too cold. It was decent, but extremely sweet.

A thin, pretty woman walked into the cafeteria, still towel-drying her long, straight brown hair. She was dressed in jean shorts and a flowing white blouse.

"Hey folks, good morning!" she said brightly. The sweet smell of her shampoo wafted through the room.

"Ooh, how are the showers?" Andrew asked, perking up visibly at her presence. JJ did an internal eye roll.

"Great water pressure, and it seems like we have plenty of hot water." She dabbed at the ends of her hair and then, satisfied she'd gotten it as dry as possible, flipped the small white towel over a shoulder. "What's for breakfast?"

Andrew jumped up and mimed pulling out a spot for her. The woman laughed and took a seat across from where he'd been sitting. JJ took a calming breath.

"You get to choose between sausages and hash browns with bacon. Five-star meals, breakfast of champions, and all that."

The woman pretended to think about it for a second, then laughed. "Oh, you choose. I'm sure the protein, sugar, fat ratio is all the same." Andrew busied himself prepping a tray.

"I'm Brianne, by the way." JJ had to turn sideways to see her and was a bit disarmed by the open, friendly expression on her face.

"JJ. My pronouns are wiya."

"Oh! Very cool! That's Cree, right?"

JJ nodded, surprised. Brianne's eyes were a startling green against a light-brown face, a lighter shade than JJ and Andrew, but much darker than Liam. "Are you Cree?"

"I'm Métis. My dad's Cree and my mom's French Canadian. I have a cousin who was using wiya pronouns back before."

"Wouldn't that make you, Cree though?" JJ asked, confused.

"Well, I'm half Indian and half French, so I'm Métis." Brianne smiled, and before JJ could follow up, Andrew plopped a metal tray in front of Brianne and sat down across from her.

"Here you are, a hearty breakfast for a growing girl."

JJ finished off the last swallow of instant coffee and stood. "I think I'll go check out the showers."

Brianne gave her a sunny smile. "I have some sage and mint shampoo and conditioner I left in there, if you want to use it."

Genuinely appreciative of the offer, JJ thanked her. Andrew waved goodbye without looking at wiya. Stifling a dry comment, JJ used the kitchen facilities to wash up wiya's tray and cup. JJ left the unopened portions of the IMP on a stainless-steel prep counter, in case someone else wanted the sports drink and condiments.

The small circular sleeping chamber, only two metres wider on all sides than their capsules, had four other rooms arrayed around the central chamber like petals of a flower. The doors to each of the rooms were pulled open, expanding the visual space, which improved JJ's mood immediately. wiya wasn't necessarily claustrophobic, but the lack of space in this station was something JJ knew would wear quickly. Behind wiya was the cafeteria, and directly across from that was the largest space, the recreation room, where wiya glimpsed a swimming pool. To wiya's right was the white-tiled privacy entrance to the showers, toilets, and laundry machines, and to the left was the small control room.

Liam was sitting cross-legged in his capsule, his back to JJ, sage smoke curling up around him as he smudged. JJ heard the fans kick into high gear, but the scent still began to permeate the area, and wiya took a quiet, deep breath, feeling relaxation seeping through skin, bone, sinew, and blood.

"Mind if I smudge?" JJ jerked in surprise. wiya had been about to say the same thing. Their fifth crew member was a slight figure wrapped in a white towel, a clear plastic shower cap covering dense, curly black hair, dark-brown skin still dewy.

Liam turned his head to inspect the newcomer, then shook his head slightly. "It's not appropriate for you to smudge like that."

"Oh, that's complete bullshit," JJ snapped. Liam stiffened visibly, but deigned to turn around to face wiya. "We can smudge butt naked if we want, Liam."

"Modesty isn't bullshit," Liam shot back. Looking at the towelled crew member, he added, "This is a sacred part of my culture. You should respect that."

JJ opened wiya's mouth to blast Liam from the face of the earth, but, meeting the other crew member's dark-brown eyes, slightly crinkled with repressed laughter, instead waited.

"I'm September. It's nice to smell sage after so long. I used to pick it with my kookum during Pilgrimage, down along Nikoodi Road."

"But you don't look Native?" Liam sounded confused, and JJ didn't suppress a bark a laughter. Had he forgotten about his own neon-white skin and red hair?

September held out an arm and pretended to inspect it. "I think you mean I look Black." She let her arm drop and tightened the knot holding her towel up. "I hear it's possible to be white and Indigenous, and I think I have just established that it's possible to be Black and Indigenous. My apologies if I don't quite look the part. I'll be sure to put more effort in."

Her tone was even and polite, but JJ could see the back of Liam's neck redden.

JJ mimed a high-five in the air, and September responded with the slightest widening of her nostrils and the barest hint of a roll of her eyes in Liam's direction. Here was someone very practised at keeping her cool.

"September? That the month you were born?" JJ asked to break the tension, for though wiya was tempted to let Liam sit there and be uncomfortable, wiya was excited to meet someone else familiar with Lac Ste. Anne.

September made a slightly pained face. "When I was conceived, actually. My parents thought it was funny."

JJ winced theatrically in sympathy. "Well, I'm from Lac Ste. Anne myself. JJ, wiya pronouns. Liam here is Métis from St. Albert, and in the cafeteria, you'll meet Andrew, he's Ojibwe, and Brianne is um, well, she's Cree and French. Are you from Lac Ste. Anne, too?"

September shook her head and smiled slightly. "I use she/her pronouns. Also that robe is absolutely amazing, can I just say that? Very Hollywood movie star!"

JJ twirled, letting the robe fly out, and September clapped in joy.

"I grew up in Calgary, actually," she continued, "but my dad's family is from Fishing Lake Settlement. I was adopted out and had just started reconnecting with my dad's side when they started putting people in."

"Sorry to hear that."

September just shrugged and carefully lifted the shower cap, her hair expanding slightly, now that it wasn't compressed, to frame her round face. JJ realized she was much younger than wiya had initially thought, even younger than Liam.

"Talk about bed-head," September said, patting a flat spot on the back of her head, and JJ nodded in agreement, patting wiya's own hair covering.

"At least hibernation stops hair from growing." JJ brushed a hand along wiya's own cheek, not yet feeling even the barest hint of a whisker.

"Are you going to use the showers, JJ?" Liam asked neutrally, packing away his smudge bowl, not turning to look at wiya.

"That's the plan. Why, is that immodest?"

He ignored the quip and slipped off the side of his capsule, facing the two of them now. "I'll check out the rec room then, give you some privacy."

JJ got the sense that Liam just didn't want to share the showers with wiya, but wasn't going to argue about having the space to wiya's self.

"We should all meet in an hour," Liam continued, his chin raised a little, a slight challenge in his bearing, "and go through the shift schedule."

"That's a good idea, Liam." September assured him, and JJ just nodded in agreement, already anticipating a long, hot shower.

"Sure, see you all in an hour."

The rec room was as wide as any of the other outer rooms, but much longer. The control room was fairly small, and so the rec room had been expanded to take advantage of the extra space. At first glance, it seemed that the room featured a huge skylight along its entire length, but it quickly became apparent that the view was artificial. Still, even a fake blue sky festooned with dynamic clouds provided a mood boost. The skylight illusion supplied warm illumination, but the room was also full of special lamps carefully positioned to yield the proper UV spectrum to walls absolutely covered in seedlings.

Half of the rec room, including the part visible from the sleeping chamber, held a rectangular pool, still slowly filling with water via some mechanism they had yet to discover. The other half contained a bewildering diversity of workout machines. Cleverly placed mirrors throughout the room provided the illusion of further space. The air was fragrant and humid.

JJ, freshly showered and decked out in a deep-purple kookum-scarf-patterned dress with plunging décolletage, wiya's still-damp cinnamon hair brushed and makeup done, was the last to join the group. The others were seated on white plastic lounge chairs at the far end of the pool deck, away from the exercise equipment.

Predictably, Andrew and Brianne had their chairs pulled together and had let the backs down so they could stretch out. Brianne had sunglasses on for some reason—who would have thought to pack those when they knew they'd be going underground? She was barefoot, toenails painted a pretty coral colour, long legs shimmering with some sort of glittery moisturizer. Andrew still hadn't showered or changed out of his sweatpants and black tank top, but he'd at least splashed some water on his hair and forced it into compliance. He raised a glass of orange-pineapple sports drink to JJ as though it were a toast and grinned, his dimples deepening appealingly.

Liam sat ramrod straight on his seat, the back as far up as it would go. He'd changed out of his blue pyjamas into a tight, grey button-up dress shirt fastened all the way up to his bone choker, his beaded buckskin vest on over that, with dark-blue chinos and pointed toe moccasins. The temperature was at least ten degrees higher in here than in the sleeping chamber, and JJ didn't think he could be all that comfortable, but who was wiya to tell him what to wear?

September sat sideways in her chair to the right of Liam, wearing an emerald-green satin romper. Her bare legs—covered in fine dark fuzz, thickening a little toward her ankles—were thrown over one armrest. She'd brushed her hair out and pulled it up into a curly pouf on the top of her head. When JJ pulled a chair up, September leaned her head back over the other chair arm and smiled at wiya upside down.

"We've been waiting for fifteen minutes." Liam remarked disapprovingly.

"This level of perfection doesn't happen on its own, Liam." JJ cupped a soft hand against wiya's chin and fluttered wiya's eyelashes melodramatically. "You're living with some high femme energy here, better get used to it."

Andrew waved a hand dismissively, "It's fine, JJ, we were just chatting about all these seedlings, anyway." Liam shot Andrew a strange look wiya couldn't interpret.

JJ looked down at the plastic chair wiya had pulled up and frowned at it distrustfully. "I don't think this was built for people like me." The arms were too close together for comfort, and it didn't seem all that sturdy.

September swung her legs off her own chair's arm and stood. "Gimme two seconds, JJ!" She dashed around the pool and out of the room. JJ went ahead and pushed the chair back to the corner.

"Andrew was saying the last shift must have planted the seedlings before they went back in." Brianne was surveying the room from behind her sunglasses, a happy look on her face.

JJ approached the nearest wall, looking at the floor-to-ceiling rows of dark felt pockets with sprouts peeking out their hopeful heads. Smooth white-plastic moulding ran along the entire length of the room about forty-five centimetres up from the floors and a few centimetres away from the wall. JJ could hear the gurgling of water and figured there must be a mechanism behind the felt that kept everything watered, drained, and recycled.

September was back, a white cotton sheet slung over one shoulder, heavy with items, which turned out to be towels. These she ceremoniously arranged it into a fluffy and surprisingly comfortable round nest for JJ.

Amused, JJ sank into the soft mass. "Okay, but you're helping me up after!"

· ☀ ·

Like so many colonial "advances," the Human Hibernation Project required the creation of an artificial moral debt to be paid overwhelmingly by Black, Indigenous, and People of Colour. It took the notion of intersectionality and weaponized it, creating a literal point system based on the notion that those who experience the most marginalization are the biggest drain on resources.

I know. It sounds absolutely ridiculous. I blame liberal governments who mouthed platitudes about alleviating discrimination, who launched inquiries and commissions and did nothing with the recommendations. They had most people convinced something was being done, that massive amounts of money and resources were being expended to address past injustices, to create equality. If all you did was look at Hansard transcripts, it even started to sound true. Then the right wingers bought into the lie and spread fantastical myths about Black people receiving "reparations" for slavery, more fear-mongering about "affirmative action" supposedly putting white men out of work while disabled ex-con Indigenous trans women got all the cushy jobs. Facts had stopped being relevant a long time ago.

Kimberlé Crenshaw, who originally coined the term "intersectionality," had published and spoken about and fought back against the way her work was taken out of context and twisted, but ultimately was powerless to stop the shift. Instead of noting, for example, that Black women experience gender and race-based discrimination at the same time, and advocating for change which would address both pressures at the same time, the powers that be transformed intersectionality into a simplistic and deeply dishonest accounting scheme.

An entire field of actuarial intersectionality was born, based on the possibility that people experiencing multiple kinds of discrimination could, hypothetically, be entitled to some form of personal compensation, or even worse, class-based collective relief to the tune of billions of dollars, even trillions. It was a risk-based assessment that could only exist within a fictional scenario wherein any government anywhere in the world was actually going to do something about discrimination and structural oppression. It didn't help that so many of my own people bought into it, paying for expensive intersectional score assessments to figure out how much money the government was supposedly going to give them. Racists took screenshots, created websites dedicated to tallying up the "oppression tax" as though it were really happening, frothing at the mouth over how good we supposedly had it. It was the carrot and the stick all at once, a promise that would never be fulfilled and a cudgel used to justify even worse bigotry against those with high scores.

Like so many other theories and structures, it didn't matter that it was based on a lie. Once applied, intersectional scores became real. The financial figures being thrown around were ridiculous, completely absurd, but they were seemingly backed up by a real accounting process, and it became clear that actually doing something about oppression was a threat to global financial stability and could not be allowed.

Your intersectional score was a like a reverse credit score; the higher the number, the greater financial risk you were to global stability, were you to be compensated for your suffering. Just like credit scores, though, the process of determining your points was pretty opaque. We could only watch how the tally was impacted by certain factors and extrapolate based on that; no one within the intersectional actuary system would explain exactly how they were coming up with the numbers.

Once people believed in this system, they hit us with the real messaging.

The world was running out of energy. That was the assertion. Any discussion of collectively reducing consumption levels, of addressing astronomical gaps in wealth, of equalizing access to resources, was quickly squashed. Instead, every effort was made to ensure we understood that we each had an individual responsibility to reduce our carbon footprint. We weren't allowed to actually measure that carbon footprint in a real way, of course. The corporations, including nation-states, who consumed the most and produced the most waste, would not be judged, would not divest their vast wealth to save the planet. We were told over and over that trillionaires and those few quadrillionaires deserved their money, that they contributed immeasurably (literally—it was impossible to measure, so we had to take it as fact) to collective well-being.

Oh, but the boorish aging Zoomer who chose to take a twenty-minute shower instead of a quick, cold five-minute rinse, the irresponsible Gen Alpha mother who allowed the thermostat to be turned up instead of sewing quilts out of fabric scraps for her children—these were the odious vignettes displayed on national television and in every ad you came across on social media. These were the selfish individuals who had caused us to reach a point where life on our planet was difficult to sustain. Add to this the notion that the most oppressed among us could somehow be owed vast amounts of money and resources—money and resources that world governments could not possibly afford to pay out right now, and there was a need to reduce energy consumption of the individual immediately.

People ate it up, like they always will. It is so much more satisfying to blame your neighbour than some faceless corporation or bewildering political structure. After all, have you seen his pool, and his two cars, and that huge, wasteful birthday party they hosted, and oh, you never even noticed he was Pakistani—it wasn't about race, it was about loving the planet!

Human hibernation. A way to wait things out and allow resources to replenish. A way to reduce one's energy consumption to nearly nil. Even with all of the propaganda, no one was interested. So, they went ahead and experimented on incarcerated people, the majority of whom were Indigenous and Black and whose intersectional scores were ruinously high. For every prisoner they took out of the system, they were saving an average of $350,000 a year, and just never mind how much money they'd already managed to squeeze out of prison labour—the savings couldn't be beat!

They started with the most violent criminals; after all, who was going to speak up for child rapists and murderers? Those prisoners signed waivers. It wasn't anyone's fault when the first trials had a 90' percent mortality *rate, with 10 percent of "volunteers" left permanently disabled if they didn't die outright.*

The second round of trials expanded beyond the prisons. We couldn't prove it, but there were stories of homeless people being rounded up and again, Indigenous people made up the majority of those "volunteers" as well. We sounded the alarm right away, but Indigenous leaders and individuals were immediately slapped with defamation lawsuits, and since there was no concrete proof to present in their defence, most had to settle and agree to shut up. The ones who refused to stop talking and who didn't care about jail time, like me, well ... No one listened to us anyway.

Then it became an option for people with crushing debt. No chance of you ever paying off all your debts in your lifetime? Worried about passing that debt on to your children, or even your grandchildren? If you signed away your right to ever claim compensation based on your intersectional score, then some complicated formula would be applied to your total debt load and you could head into the hibernation chamber.

When you woke up, you'd have accrued enough wealth to pay it all off; they'd even consolidate all your debt and cap you off at an 18 percent interest rate out of sheer kindness! Unsurprisingly, the majority of takers were folks in the US who'd had the temerity to get ill at some point and had racked up astronomical medical bills.

The impact on the energy crisis was negligible. We hadn't hit a critical mass of people opting in. That's when things got weird.

First it was that quadrillionaire, you know the one, juiced to the eyeballs on stem-cell treatments to fight the march of time, with his deeply unlike-able Canadian wife and their adult children with unpronounceable names. The plan to colonize Mars had been stymied by energy concerns, so he figured they'd just go to sleep until they could start building a spaceship again.

They had a private hibernation facility built on some island. Very exclusive, much better tech than the plebes were getting. When rich people write up their weird ideas it doesn't get called a manifesto; instead it was his "vision for the future." He was lauded for his "sacrifice" even though there were rumours that the wife hadn't actually consented to the procedure, and of course, his investment portfolio meant they'd wake up the richest people on earth.

Then a few famous personalities set up their own hibernation capsules in their mansions, covered in Swarovski crystals, bright pink with luxury branding, or carved out of endangered hardwoods, all with a crystal viewing window from at least the shoulders up. They hired security details to guard their acres and acres of exclusive property, then they went under, encouraging their fan bases to do the same, just in less luxury. Webcams provided twenty-four-hour global viewing access to these not-coffins, accompanied by curated playlists and prerecorded celebrity messages.

After a few months, when their capsules did not fail, middle- and upper-class people began taking out loans to install themselves in supposedly exclusive storage facilities, content in the knowledge that they were accessing privileges that would probably not be available to the lower classes. A whole industry arose to protect the empty properties of those who were able to go into hibernation; heaven forfend that the unhoused have any opportunity to change their situation.

Of course, this merely reflected a historic trend of trickle-down style. Middle and upper classes sought to identify with the truly affluent via conspicuous consumption to distance themselves from those who existed below them socially. The increase in demand led to more inexpensive iterations, and soon even the most financially destitute person was able to secure a spot in one of the many Beehives that were constructed underground, rendering exclusivity moot. Were this a sort of fashion trend, the affluent would have long since abandoned the style in exchange for another, with the whole process repeating itself.

Instead, governments suddenly realized that they needed to figure out a way to staff facilities projected to house 99 percent of the population within the next six months. Maintenance crews were desperately needed, and the

training of shift teams became a top priority. At first, no one seemed inter-
ested in the program; the original incentive included only free hibernation,
and since the price had fallen so much, it was hardly the draw politicians
had thought it would be.

When after two months volunteers failed to materialize, a Cree Senator
in Canada made a bold proposition: land back in exchange for Indigenous
trainees.

Members of Parliament, who for obvious reasons had been forbidden from
joining their families in suspended animation, were quick to pass the motion.
Other countries caught on immediately, responding to similar demands from
Indigenous populations within their own borders. Negotiations were fierce,
but proceeded at an unprecedented speed, especially compared to the glacial
pace of incrementalism at which land claims had been addressed up to
this point. Too bad most of humanity wasn't around to directly witness the
rapidity of global action this proved possible.

Scotland, for example, finally gained full independence after a mere
ninety minutes of high-level discussions in exchange for the mass registra-
tion of Scottish maintenance trainees, who would be sent all over Europe
to monitor Beehives.

Eighty percent of so-called "Crown Lands" in Canada were divided up
amongst First Nations, Métis, and Inuit—on paper, anyway. Normally this
kind of thing would have required a Constitutional Amendment and a
nationwide vote, but with nearly all Canadians residing in Beehives within
a few kilometres north of the US border, that would have been impossible.
The War Measures Act was resurrected, and the savviest of Indigenous
lawyers were tapped by Elders to make these agreements as ironclad as
possible.

A special session of the United Nations General Assembly was called
give international assent to these many agreements in what had to be the
most incredible global upset of all time; even the Russian Federation agreed
to rematriate lands to Indigenous peoples within its borders, though a

series of political assassinations almost prevented the vote from passing. Three months remained to train two hundred million people around the globe to ensure that nine billion other human beings did not die because of mechanical failure.

In one last massive act of global cooperation, Human Hibernation Project Land Beneficiaries between eighteen and forty-five years of age were shuttled to nine different repurposed facilities to learn everything they could about keeping hibernating people alive for eighteen months at time, the length of each shift. There would be twenty cohorts, each of which was required to work five rotating shifts before their contract was up. Land seemed a small price to pay for these people sacrificing seven and a half years of their lives while their hibernating contemporaries failed to age at all.

In 150 years, the gradual reawakening of humanity would begin.

Of course I signed up. The wolves were going to leave the mice to run the place, and I know for a fact I wasn't the only one thinking that maybe we didn't need to allow them back.

"We have three shifts to cover during each twenty-four-hour period, with one unpaired shift in each cycle." Liam held a clipboard. "We don't want to keep any one person on the unpaired shift for too long, so I suggest we—"

"Hold on, don't we also have the option to split up into two shifts?" JJ asked. Liam pursed his lips in annoyance at the interruption.

The five of them had crowded into the control room. Three screens and a large panel took up most of the space. The middle screen scrolled through a visual representation of the hibernation capsules within the Greater Edmonton Beehives, each individual pod coloured a healthy blue indicating positive life signs. To the left, the screen monitored heating and cooling systems, as well as the calcium pumps that kept human hearts healthy during hibernation. The right-hand screen showed a serious of maintenance tasks in order of importance.

"The three-shift model is much more efficient," Liam stated flatly.

"But we can also implement a hybrid," JJ pointed out, September nodding in agreement, "and who knows hybridity better than the Métis?" Andrew furrowed his brow in confusion.

"Sorry," JJ laughed. "The perils of shift work with an Indigenous Studies major who focused on Métis kinscapes. We get described in a lot of the academic literature as 'cultural hybrids,' and it's either weird anti-miscegenation crap, or it's nationalist revisionist crap. I like mocking it."

"So, the option is twelve-hour shifts or eight-hour shifts, right?" Brianne asked, and Liam nodded curtly. "Which means, assuming an eight-hour sleep schedule, only four hours of leisure time per shift, versus eight hours of leisure time per shift." She hugged herself in thought, rocking back and forth on her heels a little. "They both have their pros and cons. What does everyone else think?"

Andrew shrugged. "I'm fine with either."

Brianne looked at September, who was biting a corner of her lip in thought. "Honestly, I'd usually go for eight hours of leisure time," September said, "but I sort of feel like that time is going to drag on a lot over eighteen months. Maybe let's start with the twelve-hour shifts and see how that goes?"

JJ nodded. "What if we did two rounds of twelve-hour shifts, and then two rounds of the eight-hour shifts to really get a sense of which works best for us?" Liam glanced down at the clipboard with a frown, and JJ realized he'd already sketched out a schedule. Petty as it was, wiya couldn't help feeling a little smug about ruining his plans. His authoritarian traditionalist approach to everything was already grating, and wiya wasn't about to let him get the upper hand in anything.

"That makes sense," Brianne agreed. Andrew and September nodded in assent. Liam, outvoted, stiffly removed the written schedule he'd created and slipped it to the back of the papers, then began sketching out another chart.

They still had a few hours before the system became fully manual again. Shift changes were notoriously rough on people, as not everyone emerged from hibernation easily. The command centre could remain in automatic mode for up to seventy-two hours, but beyond that, constant human supervision was necessary to ensure that the facilities linked to their monitoring station were operating safely.

Their five-person crew seemed to have bounced back relatively quickly, so despite Liam's thin-lipped disapproval, they decided to have a little celebration. They propped the control room door open so that any alarm would reach them in the rec room.

And what were they to one another? Five strangers, now co-workers, who were also roommates and among a tiny percentage of humans left awake on Earth. It was a strange thing to even consider, JJ decided. The bulk of humanity was unconscious, and as wiya could attest, existing in a state of dreamlessness. It was what wiya imagined death probably felt like. All those billions literally in the underworld, while a few scattered groups existed above, the only fail-safe that ensured their future return.

A great deal of their training had been centred on conflict management, and wiya recognized that it was going to be crucial for them to work on getting along. JJ was a little ashamed of how wiya had been responding to Liam so far; like it or not, they would be on shift together for a very long time, and learning how to cooperate was not really optional. wiya hoped this informal gathering would help smooth out some of the initial hiccups in their interpersonal relationships.

It turned out JJ had no idea just how impossible that would be.

September had discovered a way to change the images projected onto the artificial skylight, and they were all currently watching a delayed live feed of the Martian sky from the Mars rover Unrequited. The gentle butterscotch colour of the feed cast a light that was flattering, JJ admitted, and everyone gathered around the pool looked happy and relaxed, even Liam. It certainly helped that everyone except Liam and Brianne had smuggled in a bottle of alcohol in their personal storage. They wouldn't have many opportunities to be together as a full group, which had its pros and cons, really, but it also meant there was no reason to ration the little alcohol they had. They'd also picked out some of the most promising IMPs and had a little banquet going.

JJ settled into a nest of pillows and towels beside September, who had done the same. Brianne and Andrew had spread a blanket out as though they were having a picnic, and Liam sat cross-legged on a single cushion between the two pairs, his IMP deconstructed and laid out in a metal tray.

"Can I pour you a drink?" September asked JJ, hoisting a stainless-steel water pitcher. JJ raised a questioning eyebrow. "It's powdered pineapple juice, some of my rum, and a little of the blue curaçao you brought. I think originally it was called a Blue Hawaiian, but I'm pretty sure that's got some colonial baggage, so I'm calling it a Blue Imp. Like the playground equipment."

JJ grinned and handed a glass to September. "This little fête certainly seems to have a theme—drinking Blue Imps, eating IMPs, getting impish. I like it!" September smiled, but out of the corner of wiya's eye, JJ saw Liam roll his eyes. wiya took a calming breath and chose to ignore it. Instead, JJ shifted attention to Andrew and Brianne. "What are you two drinking?"

Andrew hoisted a glass full of yellow liquid. "I made Screwdrivers. Powdered juice, of course, but it's not half bad. How do you like it, Brianne?"

Brianne looked a little embarrassed and took a tentative sip of her own drink. "I don't really drink much," she admitted, "which is why I didn't even think to bring something. Sorry about that."

JJ shrugged and smiled. "It's really no problem. We aren't going to get many chances to do this, and we have plenty for tonight. Although"—JJ cocked wiya's head to the side and drew a thoughtful nail down one plump cheek—"it might be worth trying to see if it's possible to do some brewing of our own. I bet we could get a good batch of something together before our eighteen months is up, maybe even stash something for our next shift?"

Liam made a disapproving sound in his throat. JJ calmly turned to look at him. "And how about you, Liam? Would you like a Blue Imp or a Screwdriver? We could probably figure out how to make something a bit different, if you have a preference?"

He straightened his back even more, puffing his chest out ever so slightly. His ginger braids hung precisely at each shoulder over his buckskin vest. JJ was pretty sure he wasn't going to be taking it off other than to sleep. He lifted his glass. "I'm drinking water. Alcohol and sugar are poisons and have devastated our communities for generations. We lack the genes necessary to metabolize either."

"That's been pretty thoroughly debunked, Liam," September said, before JJ could react. "All human beings have genes that produce enzymes to metabolize alcohol, and refined sugar has been around for almost three thousand years. Like any other population that has issues associated with alcohol and sugar, systemic issues are much more likely to lead to addictions or health problems than genetic predisposition."

Liam shook his head. "Alcohol and sugar are colonizer poisons. Maybe refined sugar has been around in other parts of the world for a long time, but not here on Turtle Island."

September pursed her lips. "Turtle Island has been the largest producer of sugar cane since the transatlantic slave trade began in the fifteenth century, Liam. Pacific Islanders were planting it almost four thousand years ago. You can't say it isn't an Indigenous product. It just can't be consumed in excess, like most things."

His face flushed. "I'm a registered nurse, I've done the research. Indigenous people are racially more vulnerable to addictions."

JJ was impressed with September's calm. The only sign she was even slightly annoyed was the minute flaring of her nostrils and the vaguely forced smile she maintained. "Race is a construct. There is more genetic diversity *within* populations than between them. Not to mention, here we have a group of Indigenous people"—she swept an arm to encompass them all—"who are pretty racially diverse, and that isn't unusual. You yourself clearly have a lot of European background, so if it's genes you're worried about, your white genes likely have more of an impact."

JJ's eyes widened and wiya took a sip of the Blue Imp to cover the reaction. Liam had visibly taken offence to that comment. "I am Métis. I am not white." He stared at September with barely contained anger.

Andrew broke in, his tone soothing. "No one is saying you need to drink, Liam. We all respect your decision. I think September is just saying that how we relate to alcohol or sugar depends more on how healthy we are in general. In any case, cheers!" He lifted his cup and nodded at Liam to do the same. JJ and September shared a wry glance, then raised their cups as well.

Maybe it was all that time in hibernation resetting wiya's body, but JJ felt the first effects of the alcohol much more rapidly than usual, and sank gratefully into the warmth that filled wiya's belly. It helped smooth the jangly edges of their interactions, and for a while the conversation moved on to the hydroponic system that lined the rec room. It would be at least a few more days before they'd be able to tell what the last shift had planted, and they all had some pretty strong opinions about whether kale would be a welcome addition or not. They worked their way through their dinner meals while the Unrequited streamed a sky that had gone more pinkish red than before.

"So Liam," Brianne was asking, "where *are* your white ancestors from? My mom grew up in Lanaudière, but her family were originally

Huguenots from Vassy in France. One of her ancestors actually survived the Massacre of Vassy. She ended up Roman Catholic, though, which is pretty ironic."

"I have no idea." Liam waved the question away. "It isn't important to who I am."

Brianne took another sip of her drink. "Of course it's important to who you are. Your ancestors are the reason you exist. I love learning about France, and we used to travel to Paris once a year when I was a kid. It was really beautiful."

Liam narrowed his eyes at her. "My ancestors are Métis, that's why I exist. I'm not going to celebrate colonizers." Brianne wrinkled her brow in disbelief. "In fact, this world would be a lot better off without white people."

Brianne looked confused. "Your ancestors were Métis, but that means they were mixed, just like I am."

"Not every mixed person is Métis, Brianne," JJ interjected. "Sure, originally the Métis were the offspring of Indigenous women and white men, but not all of those kids became Métis. A lot of them grew up in their mother's communities. The ones who stayed together eventually developed their own language and culture and shared similar goals. Being mixed today doesn't suddenly imbue someone with all of that, or link them to our shared history."

"I'm Métis, though," Brianne asserted. "My dad is Cree from Moose Factory, and my mom is French Canadian—that makes me Métis."

Liam snorted rudely. "You're Métis if your parents are Métis, just like you're Cree if one or both of your parents is Cree. You're Cree, not Métis."

Brianne furrowed her brow in annoyance. "Métis are literally the children of Indigenous people and the French."

"That's how it started, though there were Scottish and Irish mixes in there, too, not just French," JJ agreed, a bit miffed that wiya was being forced to back Liam up, "but it's not as though there is something magic about being Indian and white that suddenly gives you Métis culture. You wouldn't tell someone with a German parent and a Japanese parent that they are culturally Nigerian."

"Those are different countries, though!" Brianne protested.

"Are you a member of the Moose Cree First Nation?" September asked.

"Well yeah, because of my dad."

"So are you Mohawk?"

"What? No, of course not!"

"How about Mi'kmaq?"

Brianne shook her head in annoyance. "Obviously not."

"Well, a lot of Mohawk and Mi'kmaq have some white ancestry because they've been dealing with colonizers for hundreds of years longer than we have out here on the Plains. Why aren't you Mohawk or Mi'kmaq?"

"I don't appreciate the gatekeeping," Brianne said, visibly trying to compose herself. "I'm not trying to tell you that you aren't Indigenous because you're Black."

September muttered under her breath, and only JJ was close enough to catch it. "You wouldn't be the first to tell me that, though." JJ hoped Brianne would give it a rest.

She didn't. Brianne leaned forward earnestly, and some of her drink sloshed out of her cup. JJ realized she was a bit tipsier than she appeared. "But Liam, you're obviously mixed. Is it your mom or your dad who is white?"

Liam didn't react well to the prodding. He flushed deep red above his bone choker, the colour change made even more dramatic because of the lighting. "That is none of your business, and it isn't relevant. You might identify as white, but I don't."

"You don't need to identify as white, though," JJ snapped. "You clearly present as a white person, so why is the question so offensive to you?

Me, I've got white people in my family, too. Like September said, most Indigenous people these days are mixed in one way or another."

Andrew stuck a hand up in the air and waved a finger. "Not me. Full-blood over here."

September snorted. "Blood quantum? Come on."

Andrew grinned disarmingly. "I'm just saying. We still exist."

"Zero white people in your family line?" September asked. "All of your last 1,022 ancestors were 100 percent having babies only with other Indigenous people? I mean, even my family has a couple of white people."

Andrew shrugged and refilled his cup. "That's Métis, though. Mixed. Real Indigenous people aren't mixed."

"I'm sorry, *real* Indigenous people?" JJ said. "You may have noticed that some Métis are plenty brown." JJ stripped back wiya's sleeve to prove it. "And even the ones who aren't"—here wiya jabbed a finger at Liam—"are still real Indigenous people."

Andrew lifted his hands in mock surrender. "I don't mean it that way JJ, sorry. Of course Métis are Native."

"Why 1,022?" Brianne was swaying slightly, her cup full again nearly to the brim; Andrew was keeping her topped up. JJ took another sip of wiya's own drink and let the alcohol calm wiya down. JJ hadn't expected Andrew to be into blood quantum, but it wasn't all that surprising, either. It was a concept that had been forced onto them for centuries; it was inevitable they'd take it up themselves sometimes.

"That's if you count back ten generations," September was explaining. "We all have two biological parents at the second generation. Each bio parent has two bio parents of their own, your grandparents, so that's four in the third generation. Add them with your bio parents and that's already six ancestors in total, right?" Brianne nodded. "Well the number keeps increasing really quickly as your family tree branches out. In the tenth generation you have 512 ancestors, but when you add them up with all the other ancestors that came before, that's 1,022. Plenty of opportunity there to have at least someone in your ancestral line who isn't a *full-blooded Indian*." Her tone was wry.

Liam wouldn't look at September, pretending instead to be interested in the fabric of the pillow he was seated on. JJ saw something pass across Andrew's face, but it was quickly replaced with another dimpled smile.

"Ha!" Brianne pointed a finger in triumph at Liam, who made a sour face and sipped his water. "And what do you mean this world would be better off without white people? We wouldn't even exist if that happened."

Liam set his cup down and crossed his arms. "Well, we can't go back in time and stop the colonizers from arriving, but what if there was a way to get rid of white people now? You really don't believe things would improve?"

"Things have improved, though," Brianne asserted, looking to Andrew for support. He shrugged, and she seemed to take that as the confirmation she needed. "White people aren't evil, it's just that there are some bad people in every society. And racism really goes both ways."

JJ heard September exhale slowly. She had been leaning back against a few pillows she'd propped together, but now she sat up. "Racism doesn't go 'both ways,' Brianne. Indigenous people don't have the structural power to be racist toward white people."

Andrew nodded in agreement. "That's definitely true. We can't be racist against white people."

Brianne smoothed back her long hair, looking frustrated. "I grew up visiting my dad's reserve. I got teased a lot for not being as dark as my cousins, and there are so many ignorant opinions about white people, it's awful. They used to call me môniyâw, like it was something to be ashamed of!"

JJ was probably the only one close enough to hear September scoff softly, though it didn't show on her face at all. She was keeping her face very relaxed, and she didn't raise her voice. "Sure, there's prejudice, and a lot of justifiable resentment. But there's no *White Act*. Indigenous people aren't putting white kids in residential schools, or forcing them to only speak Cree. It might not feel nice to be othered, but trust me, Black Natives get it far worse."

"And that's racist, too!" Brianne declared earnestly.

September sighed openly this time. "It's anti-Black, yeah, and it's a part of white supremacy, because it categorizes people's worth according to how far away from Black they are. That's still not racism 'going both ways,' though."

"I don't believe in white supremacy." Brianne finished her cup and set it down. Andrew filled it again. "I've met plenty of poor white people, and there are—well, there were—Indigenous celebrities, people with big houses and good jobs."

JJ wanted to smack wiya's head in frustration at the naivety of this conversation. "Brianne, you're talking about privilege. Some people have more than others, but that doesn't negate white supremacy as a real structure with real power."

"It's racist if our own people reject us for being too white," Brianne stated stubbornly. She glanced at September and quickly amended, "Or too Black."

"That prejudice came with the colonizers," Liam said flatly. "I'm actually really amazed that with how much they hold Indigenous peoples in contempt, the world turned to us to ensure their safety."

Andrew nodded. "It's weird, isn't it? They spent so much time imagining what would happen if oppressed groups got control, always assuming that it would mean they'd be killed off, only to turn around and make it tempting?" He laughed.

Brianne turned and looked at him in confusion. "What do you mean?"

He spread his hands. "Just think about all the alien invasion movies you've ever seen. They're usually one of two scenarios: one, the aliens come in peace, then humans get paranoid and try to kill them and war breaks out; two, aliens come to conquer, enslaving all humans or killing them off. Usually it's that second one, space Columbus. White people write this stuff, imagining what it's like to be one of the groups they've colonized, and they act like oppression is universal, natural, even."

"I hate that," JJ agreed. "It's so obvious, too. I always felt those movies were trying to say, 'Hey Black, Indigenous, and People of Colour, better us than the nasty aliens,' like we should be grateful. There's always the assumption that if any of us got to be powerful, the first thing we'd do is wipe them all out."

"It's worse than that," September added. "When the aliens come to kill off all humans, suddenly pre-existing Earth hierarchies and oppressions, white supremacy, slavery, ecocide, all of it ceases to be relevant. These narratives insist that humans have to overcome our differences and work together, but they never actually address racism, sexism, transphobia, ableism, classism, or anything else. In fact, because there is an existential threat posed by an alien species, whiteness is absolved, in a way. Something much more pressing than addressing the vast inequality within our global communities wipes the slate clean. It's the ultimate move to innocence."

"They must not really believe it, though," Liam said, "or they wouldn't have put themselves in our power."

Brianne shrugged. "They aren't really in our power. though. These facilities mostly run themselves, we just need to keep up the maintenance routines. Besides, it's not just white people in hibernation. If we somehow sabotaged a Beehive, we'd be killing all sorts of people!" She shook her head, clearly upset. "My mom is in hibernation with my dad in one of the facilities in Quebec. Why should she be murdered just for being white?"

"No one is really planning to murder anyone." Andrew reached out and rubbed Brianne's upper arm reassuringly. JJ raised an eyebrow and exchanged a glance with September. "It's just a thought experiment. They must have workshopped this before implementing the training program, and we all had the same psych evaluations."

"Haven't you ever thought about what it might be like if white people never came to Turtle Island?" Liam asked Brianne.

Brianne laughed. "They did, though. We can't change that."

"But what if we could?" Liam's face was flushed slightly.

"You mean like time travel?" Andrew asked, amused.

Liam glanced at him, then quickly looked away. "Sure. Let's imagine we could go back in time and kill Columbus."

"Columbus didn't colonize this area, though," JJ pointed out. "We'd probably want to take out John Cabot."

"Preventing the establishment of the West Indian colonies might have nipped the transatlantic slave trade in the bud, though," September countered. "I get annoyed with people up here talking about 1492 when colonization didn't kick off until far later, but if we're time travelling, I say yeah, let's kill Columbus."

"Everything would be different," Andrew mused. "Not just here, but globally."

"Europeans would have ended up here eventually, no matter what," Brianne argued.

"Sure"—Andrew smiled at her—"but they'd have to deal with us as equals, not subjects, or objects to be cleared from the land they want to claim. They wouldn't be able to hoard everything for themselves, bring the earth to the brink of disaster, and leave us begging for scraps for centuries."

He fell silent, and the rest of them mulled it over for a few moments. It was a scenario all of them had considered at some point, but it was a little different a few drinks in, sitting inside a structure full of technology that their ancestors couldn't have imagined. Who was to say time travel would always remain out of reach?

"Well, turns out we don't actually have time machines." Brianne laughed softly, breaking the silence. "And no Elder I know would condone trying to ship all white people back to Europe. People like my mom have been here for generations, they belong to this land as much as we do."

"Just because they've lived on occupied lands for generations doesn't mean they have some ironclad claim to stay," Liam said incredulously. "Why would a few generations somehow equal millennia of Indigenous presence here?"

"Time immemorial," Andrew intoned softly, nodding.

"Shipping them all back to Europe, murdering them in their sleep, it's all colonial anxiety"—JJ accepted another pour from September, smiling in thanks—"and we're just parroting it. Settler guilt, just like the alien invasion movies. It's not how we actually want to deal with colonialism."

"So how do we deal with it?" Andrew asked sincerely.

"We've got land back now," Brianne pointed out, and Liam jeered. She raised her eyebrows. "Well, we do!"

"You don't think they're going to change their minds when everyone wakes back up?" Liam demanded. "You really trust them to stick to their promises, after everything?"

Brianne shrugged. "I don't think they have a choice. Every nation on Earth made some sort of deal and promised in front of the international community. They can't just take it back."

September frowned. "I'm not sure about that. Let's say they don't keep their promises, what then?"

"We protest."

Andrew guffawed. "We've *been* protesting. For centuries. Mica Bay in the 1850s, the Chilcotin War in 1864, Frog Lake, the Occupation of Alcatraz, Clayoquot Sound, Oka, Ipperwash, Burnt Church, Elsipogtog, Standing Rock, Churchill—"

"The Riel Resistance," Liam added. Andrew grimaced so slightly JJ wasn't quite sure wiya'd seen it, but then he nodded.

"Plus Black Lives Matter, Arab Spring, the Hong Kong protests, and on and on. None of it got us free. If anything, they have more power now than before, and they've gotten better at putting down resistance."

"Agent provocateurs, snitch-jacketing, co-opting resistance into the nonprofit industrial complex," September added, nodding. "There have been so many assassinations of Indigenous activists around the globe, and has it changed anything? Was anyone ever held accountable?" She looked up at the false sky angrily. "Even when they do charge someone, the fallout doesn't suddenly make colonialism crumble."

Brianne shrugged helplessly. "We just have to wait and see."

The group fell silent again, each person lost in their thoughts. JJ didn't have much faith that the full agreements would be honoured in 150 years, when humanity emerged once more from the Beehives, but wiya did believe some of those returned lands would remain in Indigenous hands. Maybe it would be enough. By then, nature would have retaken a lot of the planet. It was entirely possible that the change would inspire humans to design better systems. After all, they'd sacrificed a lot, come together as a global community to make this work; surely it couldn't be business as usual after all this?

"We have their intersectional scores," Liam offered, disrupting wiya's reverie.

The five of them regarded one another uneasily. It was true. Every pod was coded with personal information, vital stats: birthdate, gender, sexual orientation, and intersectional score. Race had been removed from census counts a few years before the Human Hibernation Project was launched, but had been reestablished in an easily translatable way by its inclusion in the calculation used to generate intersectional scores. The higher the score, the less likely the person was a white, heterosexual, able-bodied cis man.

"Think about it. If it had come to the race war all those neo-Nazis claimed was inevitable, I'm not sure we could have won. Especially here in Canada, with the US itching to invade anyway to control our fresh water." Liam leaned forward earnestly. "We have an opportunity our ancestors probably prayed for. A real chance to even things out, so when humanity comes out of hibernation, it doesn't just go back to the same system."

JJ scoffed. "Our ancestors had the chance to kill them off before they ever got established here, but they didn't think that way. Even after white people created the reserves and the residential schools, our people weren't calling for violence, they were calling for education."

Liam looked pained. "Gabriel Dumont wanted to blow up the rail lines and use guerrilla warfare. It was Riel who stopped him."

"Big Bear took his people to Montana rather than sign Treaty 6," JJ retorted. "They jailed him after the Riel Resistance, but he hadn't participated. There were a lot of leaders who chose peace."

"Even he was a warrior at one point, though," Liam argued. "He was there fighting the Blackfoot at the Battle of Belly River. When he became more pacifist, his son, Little Bad Man, and the warrior Wandering Spirit split off. They killed an Indian Agent who had been letting people starve to death. Sometimes violence is necessary."

"Indigenous people have always defended the land," Andrew added. "It gets called violent even when it's children and Elders blocking a road. Doesn't matter what we do—drum, sing, go to ceremony, or just be brown in a store. They've always justified their atrocities by claiming we were the dangerous ones." September nodded in agreement.

"You aren't talking about defending the land, though," Brianne objected. "You're talking about killing people who are completely defenceless. People who weren't there during colonization, who aren't even necessarily bad people, they're just white."

Even JJ had to roll wiya's eyes at that. "I agree that discussing literal genocide is pretty damn messed up, but *ongoing* colonialism is real. It doesn't matter if they were the original colonizers or not. The only reason this country, any of these settler nations, has any wealth at all is because of the transatlantic slave trade and Indigenous genocide. It doesn't matter if their direct ancestors did it, they still benefit from that. It's the legacy they've inherited, and I didn't see anyone rushing to reject the benefits or give anything back until they absolutely had to. It will be interesting to see if all that land they promised to give back actually ends up in Indigenous hands."

Brianne was visibly upset. "This isn't funny. You said yourself that race is a social construct"—she gestured with her chin at September—"so if someone were evil enough to do something like this, how would they even tell the difference between a white person and someone who is mixed, like Liam and me?"

Liam stiffened and opened his mouth to object, but September cut him off. "I'm not in favour of this sort of idea at all. Even if you could selectively turn off the hibernation pods, which you can't, there would be no way you could judge from that person's phenotype or their inter-sectional score whether they were the descendant of a colonizer, or if they also had other ancestry." September swept her gaze across the rest of the group. "You could have an Elder, for example, who has spent their life in the culture, fluent in their language, with all the wisdom they've gathered over the years, and a plan like this would wipe them out if they had any white ancestors. To me, that's absolutely horrifying, and I agree with JJ. Our ancestors wouldn't have chosen to do something like that." She looked directly at Liam. "Would you be okay with the idea that when you go back into hibernation, someone could look at you, decide you were a white man, and just unplug you?"

Liam regarded her coldly. "I'm willing to die, if it means wiping out white supremacy." He held her gaze for a long moment before relaxing and shrugging slightly. "But that wouldn't happen. You keep harping on me being white, but I'm Indigenous. My intersectional score reflects that."

"Oh, good. Guess we're just going to kill off the rich white Indians, then," JJ drawled sarcastically.

Brianne stood and hurled her glass against the hydroponic wall. When, made of harder stuff than regular glass, it seemed, it failed to shatter, she glared at them all and stalked off.

Andrew stood and made an apologetic gesture before following after her.

JJ exhaled heavily and looked at September. "Not the best start to our shift." September nodded, a worried look on her face. Liam stood, saying nothing, and made a point of walking the long way around the pool before exiting the rec room.

In the morning, things seemed back to normal, and their first few weeks of shift work went smoothly. JJ started to enjoy the routine and expected they'd make it through the next eighteen months without much in the way of trouble.

wiya couldn't have been more wrong.

It had been easier than I'd ever imagined. We first met in training, and it was so clear that here was someone absolutely desperate to be validated as an Indigenous person. We spent so many moments in deep conversation, my trail of bread crumbs gobbled up as fast than I could lay them out.

Human Hibernation Project Land Beneficiaries were housed in a different section of the Beehives so as to avoid any possibility of accidentally awakening civilians during a shift change. Representing the majority of Indigenous people in so-called Canada, they ranged in age from eighteen to forty-five. That left Elders and children in the general hibernation facilities.

I'd weighed the possibilities for a long time. A wholesale sabotage of the Beehives would kill off our young and our old, and I couldn't risk that. Every pandemic, every disease, every disaster had robbed us of the young and old over and over and over again. Thankfully, there were those intersectional scores. All I had to do was set the threshold for failures over a certain score. There would be some losses anyway, and some white people would be spared due to disability or whatever circumstances had caused them to have a higher score than their peers. Neither of these outcomes was ideal, but thinning out the population of colonizers was the main goal.

I know people will think it monstrous, what I am planning. I also know I'm not the only one considering it; I'd stumbled across a message board when the plan to exchange land for service was first announced. I found common ground with Indigenous peoples from Nigeria, Indonesia, Aotearoa, Hawai'i, and so many other places. We considered everything: deadly gene therapy that would target specific populations while they hibernated, physical termination pod by pod, cross-referencing old census records with current vital statistics. The oppressors' tools turned against them, the colonizer's worst nightmare given form. Every suggestion had a dozen drawbacks, reasons why it couldn't be perfect, ways people were going to slip through. It was something we just had to accept. We were at war.

We'd expected mass protests by the usual white supremacists demanding their own people be put in charge. After all, they'd always insisted we'd murder them in their beds the first chance we got, but they never rang the alarm. They didn't want to be left behind, so eager to go into the Beehives, to be with their loved ones, to avoid aging while the rest of the population hit pause on mother nature, to erase their debt. Whatever the reason, these barely cohesive groups disintegrated without so much as a whimper in favour of individual self-interest. Or maybe, after so many years crying wolf, they didn't believe their own propaganda anymore.

We are patient. No one can say we didn't try everything else first. We made peace, honoured the treaties no matter how many times they broke them. They murdered and enslaved us on a global scale, regardless. Still we persevered, building bridges while they squeezed more blood from us, denied us safe drinking water, poisoned our children with mercury, assassinated our activists around the world. When our war chiefs stepped forward, they were obliterated, and terror rained down on women, children, and Elders to ensure the lesson was clear. Eventually, resistance was peaceful, and when it wasn't, our own people decried the actions of those who took it further. I'm not saying it wasn't for good reason; they knew the devastation that would follow failure. That is why I am not going to fail.

And I have the perfect patsy. Blood so diluted that every effort is spent signalling Indigeneity, begging to be accepted, always clownishly dressed like someone stepping out of the nineteenth century. Attending every ceremony, taking and then running language classes, shifting to the role of gatekeeper. Had no idea how much contempt I was hiding, how much I detest all of them, these mixed-blood mutts and the white frauds who hide among them. It became obvious immediately that this one would never follow through on our "theoretical" discussions, had never done anything dangerous or worthwhile, frontline presence just to collect photo-ops and interviews, only social media posts and belligerent attacks on strangers. Full of sound and fury, signalling nothing.

We've pretended not to know one another, kept our distance, but one of these nights I'm going to be on a solo shift, and that's when I'll orchestrate a meeting. Hopefully others out there will be doing the same. Now is the time to truly unsettle these lands.

"UNSETTLED" EXPLORATION

If you know me or my work at all (and by this point I assume you do, to some extent), you may have noticed that I tend to want to end on a positive note. Early on in my world-building work with Molly Swain on the podcast *Métis in Space*, we explicitly rejected apocalypse as a precondition for a better world.

For one thing, Indigenous Peoples are already postapocalyptic peoples, having experienced multiple world-ending events: total collapse of our economic bases, plagues and pandemics, massacres, and too much more. A clear example of how the apocalypse is not merely a future possibility, but a lived reality, can be found in the Inuktitut-language film *Before Tomorrow* (Cousineau and Ivalu 2008). The events take place in 1840 and, rather than being a piece of science fiction, it relays a history that has been dismissed and ignored.

For another, as Kyle Whyte puts it, mainstream dystopic portrayals "erase Indigenous peoples' perspectives on the connections between climate change and colonial violence" (2018, 225). He refers to "ancestral dystopias" and the Anishinaabemowin concept of aanikoobijigan (âniksôtapan in Cree), which means both ancestor and descendant at the same time (228). He describes this perspective as intergenerational time, one that is not necessarily linear, something I explore multiple times throughout the stories in this collection. It allows us to understand ourselves as "living alongside future and past relatives simultaneously" (229). We do not need some future apocalypse either as a reality or as a hovering threat to motivate us to work toward a better world. Nor has apocalypse stamped out our hope, our joy, or our relationality. In fact, relationality is what has allowed Indigenous peoples to survive centuries of colonial violence.

So why do I end with a story that contemplates the complicated and perhaps impossible genocide of "white people" in the name of decolonization? Am I fuelling settler colonial fears of Indigenous revenge by having my characters debate the merits of such a plan?

Consider this: Robert J. Sawyer wrote the Neanderthal Parallax trilogy, which has two very interesting premises. One, he imagines that in a parallel dimension, *Homo sapiens neanderthalensis* (Neanderthals) became the dominant hominids instead of us (*Homo sapiens sapiens*) and posits some interesting cultural differences. Two, he contemplates castration as a method of punishing and suppressing violent crimes in men and preventing them from passing those violent impulses on to any offspring (eugenics), as well as creating a fictitious virus that targets only *Homo sapiens sapiens* men when they try to pass over to this parallel dimension, effectively ensuring that half of our world will never visit the other.[91] Rather than being incredibly dystopian, however, this trilogy, like almost all of Sawyer's work, remains extremely optimistic.

It is possible there is much hue and cry about this second premise somewhere out there in the world and I've never seen it, but I strongly suggest that if Robert J. Sawyer were not a white man, we'd never have heard the end of it. Do I think the author secretly wants a society where all men are killed off to stop male violence? No. That's the thing about fiction: it allows us to imagine otherwise, and sometimes what we are imagining isn't pretty, or even something we'd ever want to see happen in real life. We can write things that seem really negative, but that contain so much hope, it cannot be contained.

. . . .

91 He also explores sterilizing the relatives of a violent criminal, including women. Honestly the eugenics aspect to this trilogy is pretty problematic, but I've never seen it brought up at all.

What I'm saying here is that I am not, indeed, ending with a threat, nor on a pessimistic note. In fact, am not ending anything at all, because once this book is out in the world, the way readers take up these stories and integrate their reactions to them into their everyday lives (or not, it's up to you!) is both out of my control and beyond endings. I think the characters in this story do a pretty decent job of explaining what is wrong with the plan, and to be honest, I just wanted to write something a little darker than my other work. I think the notion of an intersectional score is much more dystopian and much more plausible than human hibernation and a plan to kill off "the colonizers."

Perhaps, buried in the story, I am once again suggesting that giving land back to Indigenous peoples is absolutely doable. In fact, it's already happening! It is something governments can act on very quickly, if they so choose. In this story, they do so in order to find people to maintain the hibernation project. In our current reality, they could do it for other reasons. This is something that is real, not science fiction, and we have a number of examples of how Land Back works (Sawatzky 2021; Hayden, Pasternak, and Yesno 2019; Gray-Donald 2020; Yesno 2020). We also have amazing Indigenous thinkers explaining how Land Back must foreground the safety of Black and Indigenous trans women, and how we can engage in Land Back practices by "decolonizing decolonization" by refusing to carry over patriarchal power relations into our organizing (simpson 2020; Pictou 2020).

I also really hope that you've come out of reading this collection with a much more nuanced view of who the Métis are, who we have been, and who we might be far into the future.

CONCLUSION

Indigenous futurism is a movement that includes a variety of forms of cultural production by Indigenous peoples, shaped by Indigenous epistemologies, that in some way push back against and challenge colonial constraints and ontologies. In calling my work Métis-futurist, I signal the specificity of the perspective and otipêyimisow-itâpisiniwin (Métis worldview) within which I am working.

Through the stories in this collection, I was able to engage in an autoethnography of manitow-sâkihikan, rediscovering and sometimes uncovering a tapestry of kinscapes across space and time. Let me tell you one day, over a hot cup of Red Rose, the many fascinating hours I spent researching when cast iron stoves came to Lac Ste. Anne, and how I decided that pigs were going to be raised there in the 1850s despite the fact that Sharon Morin confirmed for me that they were not present at that time!

Not only was this an exciting way to learn more about my community at the micro and macro levels, it also provided the context necessary to imagine otherwise in the past, present, and future. In imagining otherwise, we can grapple with the impact that historic and ongoing settler colonial oppressions have on our communities without accepting the inevitability of replicating these structures. Though all these stories imagine otherwise, they are also an invitation to act otherwise, to build a present and a future based on where our most fantastic decolonial dreams could possibly take us.

Through these stories, I want to imagine in collaboration with you, the reader, setting scenes to ask questions which, I hope, could help us build a reality that rejects apocalypse. What might Métis governance look like now, were we to accept that the nêhiyaw-pwat is a still-living alliance that requires constant tending? What place could we each take within our Indigenous nations, or in alliance with those nations, if it were understood that our unique gifts, our "superpowers," flourish best in service to a community that unequivocally loves and respects us in return? What knowledges could we remember or learn anew if we were more open to the global epistemological diversities of Indigenous pedagogies? How will we continue to use technology in ways that facilitate our cultural and physical survival as Indigenous peoples, and as a human race?

Most importantly, in what ways can we be the best kihci-aniskotâpânak—ancestors/descendants—possible?

ACKNOWLEDGMENTS

As always, I would be unable to do any of this work without the incredible support of ninâpêm, José Tomás Díaz Valenzuela. A lot of this writing was carried out during the pandemic, and my children really kept me going. kisâkihitinâwâw, wâpanacâhkos, sâkowêw, Neve, Emily, Isidora êkwa Arlis. You are all such awesome, unique people, and you amaze me.

I also need to express my gratitude to my partner-in-wine, cohost of the podcast *otipêyimisiw-iskwêw kihci-kîsikohk / Métis in Space*, and cofounder of the Métis in Space Land Trust, Molly Swain, without whom sad summer would have stayed sad, and I probably wouldn't have done half of the cool things I've had the opportunity to do since we met. May our karaoke future be so bright, we have to wear shades.

Marilyn Dumont was my supervisor during the MA thesis that forms the basis of this collection, and because of her very gentle prodding, I have finally started to figure out a workflow for my writing. It's been transformational, and more than anything I so appreciate Marilyn's humour and candour—no one will tell it to you the way it is like she does! Nancy Van Styvendale supervised me through the theoretical work that makes this collection such an odd bunny and continually inspires me with her work on penal abolition. Daniel Heath Justice literally kept me nourished through my writing, sending care packages of salmon and cream of Earl Grey tea. kinanâskomitinâwâw to you all!

Huge thanks as well to my agent, Stephanie Sinclair, and to Brian Lam at Arsenal. Catharine Chen has been an amazing editor to work with—this has been one of the least painful processes I've ever gone through! Big thanks to Cynara Geissler, who helped demystify the behind-the-scenes aspects of publishing that had continued to escape me.

There are so many other people I am indebted to, who I draw upon for inspiration, and who teach me. I tried as best I could to cite as many of them as possible, but with a focus on academic sources, I have definitely left out many of the people in my everyday life who are just as amazing and impactful in this world. My focus, when the global situation allows, will be on more deeply engaging in kiyokêwin, the Métis ethic of visiting with others. I don't ever want to take for granted again the ability to be in the presence of others.

kîsta mîna, kinanâskomitin, I thank you as well for being willing to read something that is a little strange. I hope it inspires you to do some "thinking otherwise"!

REFERENCES

Adams, Christopher, Gregg Dahl, and Ian Peach. 2013. *Métis in Canada: History, Identity, Law & Politics.* Edmonton: University of Alberta Press.

Ahenakew, E. 1929. "Cree Trickster Tales." *Journal of American Folklore* 42, no. 166, 309–311. https://www.jstor.org/stable/535231.

Ahenakew, Freda. 1988. *How the Birch Tree Got Its Stripes: A Cree Story for Children.* Markham: Fifth House.

Ahenakew, Freda, and H.C. Wolfart, eds. and trans. 1998a. *ana kâ-pimwêwêhahk okakêskihkêmowina: The Counselling Speeches of Jim Kâ-Nîpitêhtêw.* Winnipeg: University of Manitoba Press.

—, eds. and trans. 1998b. *Kôhkominawak otâcimowiniwâwa: Our Grandmothers' Lives as Told in Their Own Words.* Regina: Canadian Plains Research Center.

Alberta Energy. n.d. "Alberta Energy History Up to 1999." Alberta Ministry of Energy. Accessed December 31, 2021. https://www.alberta.ca/alberta-energy-history-up-to -1999.aspx#toc-6.

Andersen, Chris. 2014. *"Metis": Race, Recognition, and the Struggle for Indigenous Peoplehood.* Vancouver: UBC Press.

Anderson, Kim. 2011. *Life Stages and Native Women: Memory, Teachings, and Story Medicine.* Winnipeg: University of Manitoba Press.

Anderson-McLean, Maire. 1999. "The Landscape of Identity: *Man'tow Sâkahikan* or Lac Ste-Anne." *Religious Studies and Theology* 18, no. 2, 5–32. https://www.proquest .com/openview/2e8e534cb300244d0e0a505360fa3b36/1?pq-origsite=gscholar&cbl= 36810.

Artemiw, David. n.d. "Parl (dot) GC (dot) 1867." Accessed March 18, 2019. https://parldot gcdot1867.com/blog/2017/12/7/december-7-1867.

Beeds, Tasha. 2014. "Remembering the Poetics of Ancient Sound kistêsinâw/wîsahkêcâhk's maskihkiy (Elder Brother's Medicine)." *In Indigenous Poetics in Canada*, ed. Neal McLeod, 61–72. Waterloo: Wilfrid Laurier University Press.

Belcourt, Herb. 2006. *Walking in the Woods: A Métis Journey.* Victoria: Brindle & Glass.

Bhattacharya, Sabyasachi. 1983. "History from Below." *Social Scientist* 11, no. 4, 3–20. https://doi.org/10.2307/3517020.

Black, Mary B. 1977. "Ojibwa Taxonomy and Percept Ambiguity." *Ethos* 5, no. 1, 90–118. http://doi.org/10.1525/eth.1977.5.1.02a00070.

Bloomfield, Leonard. 1993. *Sacred Stories of the Sweet Grass Cree 1930.* Markham: Fifth House Publishers.

Bokahker, Heidi, and Franca Iacovetta. 2009. "Making Aboriginal People 'Immigrants Too': A Comparison of Citizenship Programs for Newcomers and Indigenous Peoples in Postwar Canada, 1940s–1960s." *Canadian Historical Review* 90, no. 3, 407–434. https://doi.org/10.3138/chr.90.3.427.

Borrows, Lindsay Keegitah. 2018. *Otter's Journey through Indigenous Language and Law.* Vancouver: UBC Press.

Burley, David. 2000. "Creolization and Late Nineteenth Century Métis Vernacular Log Architecture on the South Saskatchewan River." *Historical Archaeology* 34, no. 3, 30–33. https://www.jstor.org/stable/25616829.

—, and Gayel Horsfall. 2009. "Vernacular Houses and Farmsteads of the Canadian Métis." *Journal of Cultural Geography* 10, no. 1, 23–30. https://doi.org/10.1080/08873638909478452.

Callihoo, Victoria. 1960. "Our Buffalo Hunts." *Alberta Historical Review* 8, no. 1, Winter, 24–25. http://peel.library.ualberta.ca/bibliography/9021.8.1.html.

Cardinal, Harold, and Walter Hildebrandt. 2000. *Treaty Elders of Saskatchewan: Our Dream Is That Our Peoples Will One Day Be Clearly Recognized as Nations.* University of Calgary Press.

Cariou, Warren. 2010. "Dances with Rigoureau." In *Troubling Tricksters: Revisioning Critical Conversations*, ed. Deanna Reder and Linda Morra, 157–168. Waterloo: Wilfrid Laurier University Press.

Casale, Alessandro. 2019. "Indigenous Dreams: Prophetic Nature, Spirituality, and Survivance." *Indigenous New Hampshire Collaborative Collective.* https://indigenousnh.com/2019/01/25/indigenous-dreams/.

Committee on Toxicology. 1997. *Toxicologic Assessment of the Army's Zinc Cadmium Sulfide Dispersion Tests: Answers to Commonly Asked Questions.* National Research Council. https://www.ncbi.nlm.nih.gov/books/NBK233549/.

Cornum, Lou. 2015. "The Outer Space of Blackness and Indigeneity in *Midnight Robber* and *The Moons of Palmares*." MA thesis, University of British Columbia. https://dx.doi.org/10.14288/1.0220546.

Cousineau, Marie-Hélène, and Madeline Piujuq Ivalu, dirs. 2008. *Before Tomorrow*. Film. Toronto: eOne Films.

Daniels, Harry. 1979. *The Forgotten People: Métis and Non-Status Indian Land Claims*. Ottawa: Native Council of Canada, 1979.

Daschuk, James. 2013. *Clearing the Plains: Disease, Politics of Starvation, and the Loss of Aboriginal Life*. University of Regina Press.

Davis, Jeffrey. 2015. "North American Indian Sign Language." In *Sign Languages of the World: A Comparative Handbook*, ed. Julie Bakken Jepsen, Goedele De Clerck, Sam Lutalo-Kiingi, and William B. McGregor, 911–932. Berlin: Mouton de Gruyter.

Department of Labour, Economics and Research Branch. 1955. *Wage Rates and Hours of Labour in Canada*. Annual Report no. 38. Ottawa, ON: Department of Labour.

Dery, Mark. 1994. "Black to the Future: Interviews with Samuel R. Delany, Greg Tate, and Tricia Rose." In *Flame Wars: The Discourse of Cyberculture*, ed. Mark Dery, 179–222. Durham: Duke University Press.

Devine, Heather. 2004. "The Emergence of Freemen in Rupert's Land." In *The People Who Own Themselves: Aboriginal Ethnogenesis in a Canadian Family, 1660–1900*, 75–110. University of Calgary Press.

Dictionary of Canadian Biography. 1972. Volume X (1871–1880) "Thibault, Jean-Baptiste." http://www.biographi.ca/en/bio/thibault_jean_baptiste_10E.html.

—. 1982a. Volume XI (1881–1890) "John Dougall." http://www.biographi.ca/en/bio/dougall_john_11E.html.

—. 1982b. Volume XI (1881–1890) "Mistahimaskwa (Big Bear)." http://www.biographi.ca/en/bio/mistahimaskwa_11E.html.

—. 1982c. Volume XI (1881–1890) "Pitikwahanapiwiyin (Poundmaker)." http://www.biographi.ca/en/bio/pitikwahanapiwiyin_11E.html.

—. 1990. Volume XII (1891–1900) "Jerry Potts (Ky-yo-kosi, Bear Child)." http://www.biographi.ca/en/bio/potts_jerry_12E.html.

—. 1998. Volume XIV (1911–1920) "Aatsista-Mahkan (Running Rabbit)." http://www.biographi.ca/en/bio.php?id_nbr=7165.

Dillon, Grace L. 2020. In personal correspondence to author, Facebook. January 11.

—, ed. 2012. *Walking the Clouds: An Anthology of Indigenous Science Fiction*. Tucson: University of Arizona Press.

—. 2019. "Imagining Indigenous Futurisms." Facebook, October 7. https://www.face book.com/groups/349927541693986/permalink/2653514731335244/.

Dobbin, Murray. 1981. *The One-and-a-Half Men: The Story of Jim Brady and Malcolm Norris, Metis Patriots of the Twentieth Century*. Regina: Gabriel Dumont Institute.

Drouin, Fr. 1975. *The Oblate Mission of Lac-Ste Anne, Alberta*. Canadian Catholic Historical Association. Resumé of a paper, Edmonton. June 4. http://www.cchahistory.ca/journal/CCHA1975/Drouin.html.

Duncan, Kate. 1991. "So Many Bags, So Little Known: Reconstructing the Patterns and Evolution and Distribution of Two Algonquian Bag Forms." *Arctic Anthropology* 28, no. 1, 56–66. https://www.jstor.org/stable/40316292.

Duval, Jacinthe. 2001. "The Catholic Church and the Formation of Metis Identity." *Past Imperfect* 9, 65–87. https://doi.org/10.21971/P70P4Q.

Eckert, Andreas, and Adam Jones. 2002. "Historical Writing about Everyday Life." *Journal of African Cultural Studies* 15, no. 1, 5–16. https://doi.org/10.1080/13696810220146100.

Ens, Gerhard J., and Joe Sawchuk. 2016. "Economic Ethnogenesis: The Fur Trade and Métissage in the Eighteenth and Nineteenth Centuries." In *From New Peoples to New Nations: Aspects of Métis History and Identity from the Eighteenth to the Twenty-First Centuries*, 42–70. University of Toronto Press.

Ergin, Tolga, Nicolas Stenger, Patrice Brenner, John B. Pendry, and Martin Wegener. 2010. "Three-Dimensional Invisibility Cloak at Optical Wavelengths." *Science* 328, no. 5976, 337–339. https://doi.org/10.1126/science.1186351.

Esteve, Ferran. 2016. "Afrofuturism, Science Fiction and African Identity." CCCBLAB, March 22. http://lab.cccb.org/en/afrofuturism-science-fiction-and-african-identity/.

Federation of Métis Settlements. 1979. *East Prairie Metis, 1939–1979: 40 Years of Determination*. Edmonton: Federation of Métis Settlements.

Foster, John E. 1985. "Manitoba History: Paulet Paul: Métis or 'House Indian' Folk-Hero?" *Manitoba History* no. 9. http://www.mhs.mb.ca/docs/mb_history/09/pauletpaul.shtml.

Fromhold, Joachim. 2013. *Alberta History: West Central Alberta, 13,000 Years of Indian History – Pt. 2, 1750–1840*. Self-published.

Gaertner, David. 2015. "'What's a Story Like You Doing in a Place Like This?': Cyberspace and Indigenous Futurism." *Novel Alliances*. March 23. https://novelalliances.com/2015/03/23/whats-a-story-like-you-doing-in-a-place-like-this-cyberspace-and-indigenous-futurism-in-neal-stephensons-snow-crash/#_ftn1.

Ghostkeeper, Elmer. 1995. *Spirit Gifting: The Concept of Spiritual Exchange.* Duncan: Writing on Stone Press.

Goldberg-Hiller, Jonathan, and Noenoe K. Silva. 2015. "The Botany of Emergency: Kanaka Ontology and Biocolonialism in Hawai'i." *Journal of the Native American and Indigenous Studies Association* 2, no. 2, 1–26. https://go.gale.com/ps/i.do?p=AONE&u=googlescholar&id=GALE%7CA434690990&v=2.1&it=r&sid=AONE&asid=81846e78.

Gray-Donald, David. 2020. "What Is Land Back? A Settler FAQ." *Briarpatch*, September 10. https://briarpatchmagazine.com/articles/view/what-is-land-back-a-settler-faq.

Greensmith, Cameron. 2012. "Pathologizing Indigeneity in the Caledonia 'Crisis.'" *Canadian Journal of Disability Studies* 1, no. 2, 19–42. https://doi.org/10.15353/cjds.v1i2.41.

Gregory, Brad. 1999. "Is Small Beautiful? Microhistory and the History of Everyday Life." *History & Theory* 38, no. 1, 102–103. https://doi.org/10.1111/0018-2656.791999079.

Griffen, Ryan. 2016. "We Need More Aboriginal Superheroes, So I Created Cleverman for My Son." *The Guardian.* May 27. https://www.theguardian.com/tv-and-radio/2016/may/27/i-created-cleverman-for-my-son-because-we-need-more-aboriginal-super heroes.

Goulet, Danis, dir. 2013. *Wakening.* Film. Toronto: Eggplant Picture & Sound. https://vimeo.com/309738235.

Haig-Brown, Helen, dir. 2009. *The Cave* (ʔE?anx). Vancouver: Rugged Media. YouTube, 11:09. https://www.youtube.com/watch?v=SHZsdgfo11w.

Herzog, Lawrence. 2016. "Remembering the Corner Store." City Museum of Edmonton. July 5. https://citymuseumedmonton.ca/2016/07/05/remembering-the-corner-store/.

Hogue, Michel. 2015. *Metis and the Medicine Line: Creating a Border and Dividing a People.* University of Regina Press.

Huyshe, Captain G.L. 1871. "The Red River Expedition." *Royal United Services Institution Journal* 15, no. 62, 70–85. https://doi.org/10.1080/03071847109416525.

Imarisha, Walidah. 2015. "Introduction." In *Octavia's Brood: Science Fiction Stories from Social Justice Movements*, ed. adrienne maree brown and Walidah Imarisha, 3–6. Oakland: AK Press.

Innes, Robert A. 2013. *Elder Brother and the Law of the People: Contemporary Kinship and Cowessess First Nation.* Winnipeg: University of Manitoba Press.

Ito, Hiromu, Satoshi Kakishima, Takashi Uehara, Satoru Morita, Takuya Koyama, Teiji Sota, John R. Cooley, and Jin Yoshimura. 2015. "Evolution of Periodicity in Periodical Cicadas." *Scientific Reports* 5, art. 14094. https://doi.org/10.1038/srep14094.

Johnson, E. Pauline. 1893. "A Red Girl's Reasoning." *Dominion Illustrated* (Montreal), February, 19–28.

Justice, Daniel Heath. 2018. *Why Indigenous Literatures Matter.* Waterloo: Wilfrid Laurier University Press.

Kermoal, Nathalie. n.d. "Lac Sainte-Anne: A Franco-Amerindian Place of Pilgrimage." In *Encyclopedia of French Culture Heritage in North America.* Accessed October 3, 2019. http://www.ameriquefrancaise.org/en/article-347/Lac_Sainte-Anne:_A_Franco -Amerindian_Place_of_Pilgrimage_.html.

King, Hayden, Shiri Pasternak, and Riley Yesno. 2019. "Land Back: A Yellowhead Institute Red Paper." Yellowhead Institute, October. https://redpaper.yellowheadinstitute.org/ wp-content/uploads/2019/10/red-paper-report-final.pdf.

Klock, Geoff. 2002. *How to Read Superhero Comics and Why.* London: Bloomsbury Academic.

Kovach, Margaret. 2009. *Indigenous Methodologies: Characteristics, Conversations, and Contexts.* University of Toronto Press.

LaPensée, Elizabeth. 2017. *Deer Woman: An Anthology.* Albuquerque: Native Realities Press.

Lewis, Jason Edward, Noelani Arista, Archer Pechawis, and Suzanne Kite. 2018. "Making Kin with the Machines." *Journal of Design and Science.* https://doi.org/10.21428/ bfafd97b.

Little Bear, Leroy. 2000. "Jagged Worldviews Colliding." In *Reclaiming Indigenous Voice and Vision*, ed. Marie Battiste, 77–85. Vancouver: UBC Press.

—. 2016. "Big Thinking—Leroy Little Bear: Blackfoot Metaphysics 'Waiting in the Wings.'" Produced by the Federation for the Humanities and Social Sciences, June 1. YouTube video, 8:44. https://www.youtube.com/watch?v=o_txPA8CiA4.

Lyons, Scott Richard. 2000. "Rhetorical Sovereignty: What Do American Indians Want from Writing?" *College Composition and Communication* 51, no. 3, 447–468. https:// doi.org/10.2307/358744.

Macdougall, Brenda. 2010. *One of the Family: Metis Culture in Nineteenth-Century North-western Saskatchewan.* Vancouver: UBC Press.

MacEwan Joint Committee. 1984. *Foundations for the Future of Alberta's Metis Settlements: Report of the MacEwan Joint Committee to Review the Metis Betterment Act and Regulations to the Honourable J.G.J. Koziak, Minister of Municipal Affairs.* Edmonton, 7. https://archive.org/details/foundationsforfu00mace.

MacKay, Gail. 2014. "'Learning to Listen to a Quiet Way of Telling': A Study of Cree Counselling Discourse Patterns in Maria Campbell's *Halfbreed*." In *Indigenous Poetics in Canada*, ed. Neil McLeod, 351–369. Waterloo: Wilfrid Laurier University Press.

Mann, Mark. 2019. Senior editor at Beside Press in email correspondence with the author. January 8, 2019.

Martino-Taylor, Lisa. 2017. *Behind the Fog: How the U.S. Cold War Radiological Weapons Program Exposed Innocent Americans.* New York: Routledge.

Mathieu, Sarah-Jane. 2010. *North of the Color Line: Migration and Black Resistance in Canada, 1870–1955.* Chapel Hill: University of North Carolina Press.

Maynard, Robyn. 2017. *Policing Black Lives: State Violence in Canada from Slavery to the Present.* Winnipeg: Fernwood Publishing.

McCallum, Margaret. 2008. "Sir Hugh Allan." *The Canadian Encyclopedia.* January 16. https://www.thecanadianencyclopedia.ca/en/article/sir-hugh-allan.

McGregor, Jason, and Geoff Houghton. 2018. "Special Double Review." *Tangent.* April 24. https://tangentonline.com/print-quarterly/on-spec/on-spec-107-vol-28-no-4-april-2018/.

Métis in Space. n.d. "About." Accessed August 2, 2019. http://www.metisinspace.com/about.

Morgensen, Scott. 2015. "Cutting to the Roots of Colonial Masculinity." In *Indigenous Men and Masculinities: Legacies, Identities, Regeneration,* ed. Robert Alexander Innes and Kim Anderson, 38–61. Winnipeg: University of Manitoba Press.

"Ohén:ton Karihwatéhkwen." n.d. Produced by the Kanien'kehá:ka Onkwawén:na Raotitióhkwa Language and Cultural Center. Vimeo video, 6:10. https://vimeo.com/508434111.

Oosthoek, Sharon. 2017. "What It Means to Be Métis: University of Ottawa Researcher Sharpens Our Understanding of the Term." *Research Matters.* Accessed October 4, 2019. https://web.archive.org/web/20190828133659/http://yourontarioresearch.ca/2017/06/what-it-means-to-be-metis/.

Palmer, Alexandra. 2001. *Couture & Commerce: The Transatlantic Fashion Trade in the 1950s.* Vancouver: UBC Press.

Paquin, Todd, and Patrick Young. 2003. "Traditional Métis Housing and Shelter." Gabriel Dumont Institute. May 30. http://www.metismuseum.ca/resource.php/00720.

Pictou, Sherry. 2020. "Decolonizing Decolonization: An Indigenous Feminist Perspective on the Recognition and Rights Framework." *South Atlantic Quarterly* 119, no. 2, 371–391. https://doi.org/10.1215/00382876-8177809.

Riddle, Emily. 2018. "(Indigenous) Governance Is Gay." GUTS *Magazine* no. 10, December 10. http://gutsmagazine.ca/indigenous-governance-is-gay/.

Rieder, John. 2008. *Colonialism and the Emergence of Science Fiction: Early Classics of Science Fiction*. Middletown, CT: Wesleyan University Press.

Roanhorse, Rebecca. 2018. "Postcards from the Apocalypse." *Uncanny Magazine*, no. 20, January/February. https://uncannymagazine.com/article/postcards-from-the-apocalypse/.

Robinson, Scott L., Stephen I. Rothstein, Margaret C. Brittingham, Lisa J. Pettit, and Joseph A. Gryzbowski. 1995. "Ecology and Behaviour of Cowbirds and Their Impact on Host Populations." In *Ecology and Management of Neotropical Migratory Birds: A Synthesis and Review of Critical Issues*, ed. Thomas E. Martin and Deborah M. Finch, 428–460. New York: Oxford University Press.

Sawatzky, Katie Doke. 2021. "Sharing Treaty Land." *Briarpatch*, July 5. https://briarpatchmagazine.com/articles/view/sharing-treaty-land.

Schiefelbein, Wyatt. 2021. "Disability, Colonialism, and Indigeneity." Guest lecture presented in NS 111: Contemporary Perspectives in Indigenous Studies, University of Alberta, November.

Sharpe, Christina. 2016. *In the Wake: On Blackness and Being*. Durham: Duke University Press.

Shewell, Hugh. 2004. *"Enough to Keep Them Alive": Indian Welfare in Canada, 1873–1965*. University of Toronto Press.

simpson, jaye. 2020. "Land Back Means Protecting Black and Indigenous Trans Women." *Briarpatch*, September 10. https://briarpatchmagazine.com/articles/view/land-back-means-protecting-black-and-indigenous-trans-women.

Simpson, Leanne. 2014a. "Fish Broth & Fasting." In *The Winter We Danced: Voices from the Past, the Future, and the Idle No More Movement*, ed. the Kino-nda-niimi Collective, 154–157. Winnipeg: ARP Books.

—. 2014b. "Land as Pedagogy: Nishnaabeg Intelligence and Rebellious Transformation." *Decolonization: Indigeneity, Education & Society* 3, no. 3, 1–25. https://jps.library.utoronto.ca/index.php/des/article/view/22170.

Sing, Pamela. 2009. "Le loup-garou vagabond: du Québec au XIXe siècle au Far-Ouest franco-métis au XXe siècle." *Canadian Review of Comparative Literature* 36, no. 1, 63–69. https://journals.library.ualberta.ca/crcl/index.php/crcl/issue/view/1502.

Skelly, Julia. 2015. "The Politics of Drunkenness: John Henry Walker, John A. Macdonald, and Graphic Satire." *RACAR: Revue d'art canadienne/Canadian Art Review* 40, no. 1, 71–84. https://doi.org/10.7202/1032757ar.

Smiley, Jack. 2012. *Hash House Lingo: The Slang of Soda Jerks, Short-Order Cooks, Bartenders, Waitresses, Carhops and Other Denizens of Yesterday's Roadside.* New York: Dover Publications.

Snipper, Chick, dir. 2001. *Secret War: The Odyssey of the Suffield Volunteers.* Film. Toronto: Insight Film Studios.

Statistics Canada. 2017. *Aboriginal Peoples in Canada: Key Results from the 2016 Census.* Statistics Canada. https://www150.statcan.gc.ca/n1/daily-quotidien/171025/dq171025a-eng.htm.

Stevenson, Winona. 2000. "Calling Badger and the Symbols of the Spirit Language: The Cree Origins of the Syllabic System." *Oral History/Forum d'histoire orale* 19, 19–24. https://creeliteracy.org/wp-content/uploads/2012/12/calling-badger.pdf.

Swain, Molly. 2019. Cohost of *Métis in Space*, in discussion with the author. October.

Swartwood, Robert, ed. 2011. *Hint Fiction: An Anthology of Stories in 25 Words or Fewer.* New York: W.W. Norton & Company.

Tailfeathers, Elle-Máijá, dir. 2012. *A Red Girl's Reasoning.* Film. Vancouver: NDN Girls Production. https://vimeo.com/ondemand/aredgirlsreasoning.

Tingley, Ken. 2009. *North of Boyle Street: Continuity and Change in Edmonton's First Urban Centre; A Report for the Boyle Renaissance Project.* https://www.edmonton.ca/documents/PDF/5.6_A_BOYLE_RENAISSANCE_Historical_Review_final_FEB10.pdf.

Tsosie, Rebecca. 2010. "Native Women and Leadership: An Ethics of Culture and Relationship." In *Indigenous Women and Feminism: Politics, Activism, Culture*, ed. Cheryl Suzack, Shari M. Huhndorf, Jeanne Perreault, and Jean Barman, 29–42. Vancouver: UBC Press.

Tuck, Eve, and K. Wayne Yang. 2012. "Decolonization Is Not a Metaphor." *Decolonization: Indigeneity, Education & Society* 1, no. 1, 1–40. https://jps.library.utoronto.ca/index.php/des/article/view/18630.

"Two Tales of Fort Edmonton: The Bones of One Pound One." n.d. *Fort Edmonton Park*. Accessed January 15, 2019. https://www.fortedmontonpark.ca/1846-fort/two-terrible -tales-fort-edmonton/.

Vincent, Fiona. 2013. *What Is the Moon Doing?* http://star-www.st-and.ac.uk/~fv/sky/ moon-general.html.

Voth, Daniel. 2018. "Order Up! The Decolonizing Politics of Howard Adams and Maria Campbell with a Side of Imagining Otherwise." *Native American and Indigenous Studies* 5, no. 2, Fall, 16–36. https://muse.jhu.edu/article/721564/summary.

Vowel, Chelsea. 2016. "Allowably Indigenous: To Ptarmigan or Not to Ptarmigan. When Indigeneity Is Transgressive." In *Indigenous Writes: A Guide to First Nations, Métis & Inuit Issues in Canada*, 67–72. Winnipeg: Highwater Press.

—. 2020. "Where No Michif Has Gone Before: The Form and Function of Métis Futur-isms." MA thesis, University of Alberta. https://doi.org/10.7939/r3-4x0v-hy03.

Vrooman, Nicholas C.P. 2013. *"The Whole Country Was ... 'One Robe'": The Little Shell Tribe's America*. Montana: Drumlummon Institute.

"Wakening." n.d. IMDb. Accessed November 12, 2019. https://www.imdb.com/title/ tt3225532/plotsummary?ref_=tt_ov_pl.

Walcott, Rinaldo. 1997. *Black Like Who? Writing Black Canada*. Toronto: Insomniac Press.

—. 2015. "The Problem of the Human: Black Ontologies and 'the Coloniality of Our Being.'" In *Postcoloniality-Decoloniality-Black Critique: Joints and Fissures*, ed. Sabine Broeck and Carsten Junker, 93–104. University of Chicago Press.

Walker, David F. 2015. "The Token Superhero." In *Octavia's Brood: Science Fiction Stories from Social Justice Movements*, ed. adrienne maree brown and Walidah Imarisha, 15–22. Oakland: AK Press.

Watts, Vanessa. 2016. "Smudge This: Assimilation, State-Favoured Communities and the Denial of Indigenous Spiritual Lives." *International Journal of Child, Youth and Family Studies* 7, no. 1, 148–170. https://doi.org/10.18357/ijcyfs.71201615676.

Waugh, Neil. 2018. "Neil Waugh Outdoors: A Pretty Sheet of Water." *Edmonton Sun*, July 13. https://edmontonsun.com/travel/local-travel/neil-waugh-outdoors-a-pretty -sheet-of-water.

Whisonant, Robert. 2015. "Bullets, Firearms, and Colonel Chiswell's Mines." In *Arming the Confederacy: How Virginia's Minerals Forged the Rebel War Machine*, 61–73. New York: Springer.

Wiesel-Kapah, Inbal, Gal A. Kaminka, Guy Hachmon, Noa Agmon, and Ido Bachelet. 2016. "Rule-Based Programming of Molecular Robot Swarms for Biomedical Applications." In *IJCAI'16: Proceedings of the Twenty-Fifth International Joint Conference on Artificial Intelligence*, ed. Gerhard Brewka, 3505–3512. Palo Alto: AAAI Press.

Wolfart, H.C. 1998. "Commentary." In *ana kâ-pimwêwêhahk okakêskihkêmowina: The Counselling Speeches of Jim Kâ-Nîpitêhtêw*, ed. Freda Ahenakew and W.C. Wolfart, 141–197. Winnipeg: University of Manitoba Press.

—, and Freda Ahenakew, eds. and trans. 2000. *âh-âyîtaw isi ê-kî-kiskêyihtahkik maskihkiy: They Knew Both Sides of Medicine: Cree Tales of Curing and Cursing Told by Alice Ahenakew*. Winnipeg: University of Manitoba Press.

Whyte, Kyle P. 2018. "Indigenous Science (Fiction) for the Anthropocene: Ancestral Dystopias and Fantasies of Climate Change Crises." *Environment and Planning E: Nature and Space* 1, nos. 1–2, March, 224–242. https://doi.org/10.1177/2514848618777621.

Yesno, Riley. 2020. "Four Case Studies of Land Back in Action." *Briarpatch*, September 10. https://briarpatchmagazine.com/articles/view/four-case-studies-land-back-in-action.

CHELSEA VOWEL is Métis from manitow-sâkahikan (Lac Ste. Anne), Alberta, currently residing in amiskwacîwâskihikan (Edmonton). Mother to six children, she has a BED, an LLB, and an MA and is a Cree language instructor.

Chelsea is a public intellectual, writer, and educator whose work intersects language, gender, Métis self-determination, and resurgence. Cohost of Indigenous feminist sci-fi podcast *Métis in Space*, cofounder of the Métis in Space Land Trust, and author of *Indigenous Writes: A Guide to First Nations, Métis & Inuit Issues in Canada*, Chelsea blogs at *apihtawikosisan.com* and makes legendary bannock.